In the Family Way

Also by Lynne Sharon Schwartz

Ruined by Reading: A Life in Books
The Fatigue Artist
A Lynne Sharon Schwartz Reader: Selected Prose and Poetry
Translation: *Smoke over Birkenau*, by Liana Millu
Leaving Brooklyn
The Four Questions (for children, illustrated by Ori Sherman)
The Melting Pot and Other Subversive Stories
We Are Talking About Homes: A Great University Against Its Neighbors
Acquainted with the Night and Other Stories
Disturbances in the Field
Balancing Acts
Rough Strife

In the Family Way

Family Way

AN URBAN COMEDY

•

LYNNE SHARON SCHWARTZ

Perennial

An Imprint of HarperCollinsPublishers

A hardcover edition of this book was published in 1999 by William Morrow and Company, Inc.

HarperCollins books may be purchased for educational, business, or sales promotional use. For information please write: Special Markets Department, HarperCollins Publishers Inc., 10 East 53rd Street, New York, NY 10022.

First Perennial edition published 2000.

Designed by Bernard Klein

The Library of Congress has catalogued the hardcover edition as follows:
Schwartz, Lynne Sharon.
    In the family way : an urban comedy / Lynne Sharon Schwartz.—1st ed.
    p. cm.
    ISBN 0-688-17071-4
    I. Title.
PS3569.C567I5   1999   99-22134
813'.54—dc21   CIP

ISBN 0-688-17790-5 (pbk.)

00 01 02 03 04 ❖/RRD 10 9 8 7 6 5 4 3 2 1

Contents

When the Way is lost, there is goodness.
When goodness is lost, there is morality.
When morality is lost, there is ritual.
Ritual is the husk of true faith,
the beginning of chaos.

—*Tao Te Ching*,
adapted from the Stephen Mitchell
translation

The true narrative form of our time is the sitcom.

—James Kaplan,
New York magazine, October 20, 1997

Family Tree

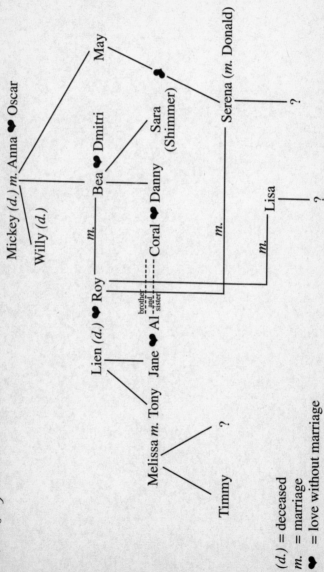

Mickey (d.) m. Anna 💗 Oscar

Willy (d.)

May

Bea 💗 Dmitri

Sara (Shimmer)

Serena (m. Donald)

?

Lien (d.) 💗 Roy — m. — Bea

Al — brother and sister — Coral 💗 Danny

Jane 💗 Al

m. — Lisa

?

Melissa m. Tony

Timmy

?

(d.) = deceased
m. = marriage
💗 = love without marriage

Part One

•

Introducing the Family: One Day and Night

I

"No! Never! It's totally out of the question!"

"Why so hasty, Roy?" Serena chided him with an intimate smile. "You weren't so stubborn when we were married. Can't you even entertain the notion?"

"Entertain? I've been entertaining it for two minutes and that's more than enough. You're not even talking about a quick, uh, a quickie. You're talking about a lifetime commitment."

At the word "commitment," her smile shifted to one of maddening indulgence. Roy's former and second wife sat at her ease in the reclining chair as she had often done during the five years of their marriage—long legs stretched out and crossed at the ankle, clogs dangling from flawless feet. It was hot, but Roy, along with his extended family, disliked air-conditioning: a tribal prejudice. A breeze blew in the open window, ruffling the slender, prongy leaves of the spider plant, making magazine pages turn as if they had invisible readers. Serena was wearing shorts and a man's white shirt tied at the midriff—maybe even his shirt. Was there a word, it would naturally be French, for the spoils of divorce, the counterpart of *trousseau*? Her skin suggested an ad for suntan lotion. A devotee of physical fitness, she worked out at the local health club; when she wasn't plying her trade as a massage therapist—a vocation that Roy, a true therapist, tacitly placed on the outer limits of the helping professions—or urging on the recalcitrant in her capacity of personal trainer, Serena engaged in various forms of locomotion: bicycling, running, Rollerblading. In her blades she was even taller than the mildly imposing Roy.

Studying her, he was threatened by an oncoming wave of anger at the wreck of what had been for him a happy marriage, as marriages go; he enjoyed being married, was not hard to please. But that was an old issue by now, an old tired anger even; he ducked under it as he would have in the ocean, and it passed him by, leaving him calm if a bit breathless. To confront this latest outrage.

"Okay. Let's entertain it for a minute. Why this sudden desire for motherhood? You never wanted any when we were married. You do remember—"

"We wouldn't have been good parents together, Roy. It never felt, I don't know, right."

"I don't know what you mean. I'm a very good parent."

"You definitely are. I didn't mean that. I meant us as a pair." She was out of the chair in one swift motion, loping over to the couch to loom above him, her pelvis at eye level. He could smell the familiar odor of her sweat and hair conditioner and something else, something new, like lilacs.

"I wasn't ready then. And it wouldn't have been fair to you either. But it's different now, with May. We've been together almost three years—I know we're going to last. It feels settled. We want to be a family. A little family within the bigger family, I mean."

"Well, that's just dandy." Roy sprang up and walked to the window; there were the patient joggers lapping their way around the reservoir like souls condemned. They were visible because the building next door had been torn down, providing a park view—temporary, but construction in New York was famously slow. The view was a boon, but the joggers were oppressive in their endless motion. With foolhardy exceptions, they retreated at night, but no matter how early in the morning he looked out, there they were, Serena possibly among them. She had that doggedness. "Can't you imagine how I feel, hearing you talk this way?"

"Oh, Roy." She came up behind him and placed a consoling hand on his shoulder. "Is it still so painful? After all, now you have . . . Lisa, is it?"

"That's not the point. A woman, Serena. A woman. After all those years together. It makes me feel like a fool."

"Well, you shouldn't. It's not your fault. You were very nice and you did your best. I've told you. Women like you, you shouldn't need reassuring on that score. I never wanted to deceive you. I just didn't know." She smiled with cunning. "Can I help it if I was a late bloomer?"

"Stop giving me your naive speech." He poked her shoulder gently. "It doesn't suit you."

"So, will you reconsider? Maybe we should discuss it sitting down. Come."

"I won't reconsider. I won't even consider. Why me, anyway? Can't you just register at a sperm bank or something?"

"You're much more fun than a sperm bank."

"I'm glad you think so."

"Of course I think so. And this way May and I know exactly what we're getting." She had led him back to the couch; now her hand was beneath his shirt collar.

"Well, no. You can't say May knows what she's getting, can you?" He had to grin despite himself. One thing they had shared was a sense of humor; that is, she had laughed at his jokes. He had a feeling that wry little jokes would not be a highlight of his future life with Lisa.

"Not in that sense, I guess not." She was unbuttoning his shirt and he submitted. Let her be the aggressor for once. He could toy with her just as she had done with him. "Wait!" He pushed her hand away. "What's that noise?"

"It's only the window washers in the hall."

"Bea is so efficient." He sighed. Bea, his first wife, lived upstairs; her mother owned the building, but with eighty-year-old Anna in decline, Bea had gradually assumed its management.

Serena was curled up close to him, sitting on her heels. She raised her arms and began making a braid of her straw-colored hair. That hank of hair must be awfully hot. Didn't lesbians usually have short hair? Serena hadn't cut hers when she converted. "Why you, anyway? I mean, you and I have had our day. I'm surprised you didn't send May down here. Trap me with novelty."

"We thought this would be easier. You understand. You and I know each other, and I don't mind—"

"Thanks so much."

"While for May, aside from the complications in the family, it's, well, she wouldn't want to. She'd find it . . . distasteful." She tossed her head and fastened the braid with a scrunchie she pulled from her pocket.

"Distasteful." Again he laughed. She was clever. Lisa, in contrast, was earnest. But earnestness had its appeal; you knew exactly where you stood. "And you don't? Find it distasteful?"

"I think I've made that clear, haven't I?" She put her hand on his belt, but he thrust it away.

"Cut it out. I haven't changed my mind. What do you plan to do about this child—assuming it would even work, just one time."

"I assumed, Roy, that we'd try until we succeeded."

"I see. And you'd be the mother, and May . . . ? And me? What would I be?"

"You'd be whatever you wanted to be. Have as much or as little involvement as you chose. If it's a boy it would be nice for him to have a role model, with all the women around here. But in either case May and I would have the day-to-day responsibility. That's what we want. Of course if you have some objection to fatherhood, we do have an alternate plan. We could have someone assist you, a sort of backup—"

"Look, Serena, I may not want to do this but if I did, let me assure you I could do it without assistance."

"That's not what I meant. I've never doubted you. I meant I could have another donor, so that we wouldn't be sure . . . You get it. There wouldn't be the same feeling of responsibility."

"I must say for a dyke you certainly get around. And who would this other donor, this assistant, be?"

"We were thinking, you know, just to keep it all close by, Dmitri. It's convenient, and he's healthy and a good person. What's the matter?"

"Dmitri!" Everywhere I go, thought Roy, that Russian follows.

Dmitri, once a professor of modern literature in his native land, was here reduced to being the superintendent of their building. He had moreover been Bea's lover for a considerable time during their marriage—ample compensation for his reduced social standing. And now Serena, Bea's successor, was proposing him as co-father in this absurd project. The trouble was, Roy could understand Dmitri's popularity—the guy was so likable, even he could hardly bear a grudge.

"Roy?" Serena bent over him again, the braid swishing against his neck. "This isn't the time for technical details. Don't you still like me just a little bit? Ah, yes." She fumbled with his zipper. "I see you do. Here's my answer." She gently pushed him back onto the couch and stretched out on top of him. Yielding, he dug his hand into her shorts. Warm and familiar down there. Oh, the memories . . .

"What about Lisa?" he breathed. "How will we—"

"Lisa doesn't have to know right away. By the time she finds out she'll be used to us."

"Oh no." Roy attempted to rise from her clutches. "Oh no. Don't think you and Bea are going to incorporate her—"

"Nothing of the kind." She bent down, her lips nearly on his. "We'll take good care of her. We'll make it all right."

It was no use. He rolled over on top of her and closed his eyes, his pleasure marred only slightly by the sound of jackhammers at the adjacent construction site.

"Roy, sweetheart, do you mind?" she murmured after a few moments. "They say with the woman on top it's more likely to be a girl. And we would prefer a girl. . . ."

It was a busy day for Bea. Every day was busy: had Aristotle posed for her the question of the contemplative versus the active life she would not have hesitated for an instant; she could not have spared an instant. Besides being heiress apparent to the twelve-story apartment building just off Central Park West, Bea ran a catering business from her accommodating kitchen, recently remodeled for the purpose, a hellish procedure. The versatile Dmitri had conceived the design and joined the hordes of workmen in breaking down the wall. "Like the Berlin Wall," he said, cradling a chunk of plaster with reverence. While her former husband Roy, three floors below, was attempting to impregnate his former wife Serena, Bea prepared canapés for a party over on Riverside Drive in honor of a visiting Korean violinist. She stopped stuffing mushrooms and shook a skillet in which bacon strips, destined to be wrapped around bits of veal, danced and crackled; a row of skewers lined with the marinated veal made stately rotations under a flame. The baby occupying the playpen in the center of the kitchen, frustrated in his attempts to hoist himself to his feet, began to whimper.

"Don't cry, sweetheart. I can't play right now," and she jiggled the Busy Box, producing a tintinnabular rendition of "Three Blind Mice," then fed him a strip of bacon drying on a paper towel. Her son Tony and his wife, Melissa, dauntingly ambitious young lawyers, would be horrified, Bea knew, at the baby's eating bacon. Their tacit support of the global economy and all its evils did not touch the principles of purity and freedom, in the sense of fat-free, that governed their son's diet. But they need never know. Timmy did not yet speak; the secret would rest forever in preverbal limbo.

Bea had never known Tony at the gurgling stage. He and Jane, his twin, had become flesh of her flesh by an act of will, or rather an absorption of the heart, the instant they stepped off a plane at seven years old, speaking half a dozen words of English. They were born of Roy's liaison with a Saigon prostitute twenty-nine years ago during his tour of duty. At the moment of their birth, Roy was in the hospital with a ripped-open thigh; he was shipped home before he could make inquiries about their welfare. All this he told Bea with some embarrassment, not long after their son was born. Yes, I knew, I knew, he confessed to her astonished questioning, Danny cradled in her arms, but what could I do? Under the circumstances . . . Okay, but they must find the babies, she insisted. And not a moment too soon. When at last they turned up after prolonged but indefatigable efforts on Bea's part, they had just been placed in an orphanage. Their mother was dying.

Thus it was that Tony and Jane, known then as Thao and Xuan, stumbled groggily off the Boeing 747 and into the waiting arms of their new family, their new country, which they quickly adopted as their own to a degree Bea found perplexing. They had no interest, at eight, or ten, or twelve, in her dutiful efforts to promote their cultural heritage. They preferred the Rolling Stones and *The Flintstones, The Brady Bunch* and Mary Tyler Moore and *Sesame Street*. Bea gave up in defeat. After college, it was SoHo for Jane, then Parabsurd, The Theater Beyond the Absurd, in a renovated warehouse, for her performance pieces. Tony, who turned out more worldly, was presently indentured at Crawford, Drew, Chang, and Bonaventure, the distinguished law firm.

With some satisfaction, Bea lined up four dozen stuffed mushrooms on a tray. A brief pause to make funny faces at the baby, eliciting a few chortles, and she removed a batch of chicken wings from the oven. She ate one with approval; the baby would surely like one too, but he might choke on the bone, and she had neither time nor inclination for the Heimlich maneuver. Could you perform it on a baby who didn't walk yet? You might break a rib. She would put a couple aside for his supper and take out the bones. As she checked the water heating for the spinach tortellini, the phone rang.

"Yes, Mom, I am. Very. I'm doing a party and I've also got Timmy. . . . Because the nanny quit and you can't hire just anyone these days. They could blow the house up or throw the child out a window or whatever, so I'll do it for a couple of weeks. I don't mind, really. . . . No, I can't come up to watch TV—especially in broad daylight, it feels practically immoral. Why don't you come down here? I'm sorry, then you'll have to be alone. Maybe when Shimmer comes home from camp I'll send her up. . . . Shimmer. Sara, of course. Don't you remember? She decided she hates Sara and wants to be called Shimmer, so why not make her happy? What's in a name? Well, don't then, call her anything you like." With the phone tucked between ear and shoulder, Bea arranged the glistening red-brown wings on a platter, then popped the tortellini into the boiling water, checking the clock—four minutes would do. She executed a little dance to amuse Timmy, waving a dish towel matador style, and gave him a raw carrot.

"You haven't received the rent checks because it's not the end of the month. . . . Yes, he'll clean the boiler before it's time to turn on the heat, but this is August. . . . They were here last month—we don't have to worry about the elevator for a while. . . . Yes, I remember that time you got stuck. It was awful, but I don't think it'll happen again. Are you sure you're okay? . . . No!" Bea paused in her work, suddenly attentive. Her eyes were very dark, and they flashed bright against her olive skin. "Roy is not here. I'm not married to Roy anymore. It's been nine years and you know it." Bea's hair, a mass of unruly waves, was graying. She was forty-nine, but the gray made her look younger, not older, since her face had the lively hopefulness of youth. She would look prematurely gray forever. "Mom, are you sure you didn't fall or something? . . . He's still in the building, where else would he be? I mean, he's still family, the father of my children. . . . No, he's not married to her anymore either—" Though he may well be fucking her as we speak, she thought. "He has a new one. Mom, I can't talk anymore. Come on down if you like. Otherwise I'll drop in tonight."

She had barely hung up when the doorbell rang, followed by the sound of a key. Several people had and freely used the key to Bea's apartment; just now it could hardly be Roy, and it was too early for her youngest child, Shimmer, a counselor in a summer day camp; Dmitri, after eighteen years in New York, was attending a workshop intended to help new arrivals find work in their original professions. Those footsteps in the hall—heavy, sullen steps—announced her younger sister, May, who occupied the penthouse, where there was ample light for her paintings.

"Baby-sitting again? I don't know how you stand it in here, Bea, with the oven going, and all that steam. It's a wonder you both don't pass out."

May was built on a grand scale, with strong wide shoulders and legs like pillars. She wore a long man's shirt streaked with paint. Her thick, coarse hair, still dark, was piled on top of her head with haphazard, drooping wisps and strands.

"Hi. I'm running late. As long as you're here would you slice those

10

peppers into rings? And jiggle his rattle—if I don't drain these tortellini they'll be ruined."

May jiggled the rattle and made succulent kissing noises for Timmy, who chuckled loudly. "Dadada." He pointed at May.

"He's a little mixed up, isn't he?"

"He doesn't differentiate yet. Use this knife. Unless you'd rather go and visit Mom for a while. She just called."

"I'll do the peppers."

"She didn't sound quite right again. Confused."

"Yes, last week she told me to have Fintan clean the incinerator."

"Oh no!" Bea lowered her eyelids in horror, then giggled along with her sister. Fintan was a super of yore—Bea and May had been mere girls during his tenure—who had long ago drunk and smoked himself to death, liver and lungs vying for first place in the rush to destruction. The incinerator, moreover, had been removed years ago when garbage-burning was banned in the interests of respiratory health. Nowadays garbage was stacked in plastic bags by Dmitri, who amused himself by arraying them like a latter-day Stonehenge.

"She also asked me again whether I ever thought about getting married and raising a family."

Bea handed her two heads of cauliflower. "Break these into little flowers. Bite size. That in itself doesn't prove anything—she's been saying it for years. But I do think she's going downhill. And once that starts it can go very quickly. A slippery slope, as Melissa says. We ought to start thinking . . . I'm afraid sometimes, when I think of her alone up there. She could fall, or set the place on fire."

"Could we take this up another time, Bea?" May laid down the knife and beseeched her sister. "What the hell do you think is going on down there? She's been with him over an hour."

"Oh, that." Bea tossed the tortellini into a bowl and added olive oil, then pulled another tray of wings from the oven. "It takes time. It's not like teenagers in the backseat of a car, after all." She put the baby's bottle on to warm and, raising a cleaver, approached a bunch of scallions.

"An hour seems more than enough for this business."

"It would've been worse if she came back right away, wouldn't it? You want her to succeed. Maybe she had to use some persuasion. I don't think Roy would agree just like that. He is a man of some integrity."

"Integrity!" May gave a hoot.

"Well, he is, in his way. You're always sneering. But you thought he was good enough to be the father of your child."

"It was his genes we wanted, not his ethics. Things like integrity or the lack of it are not inherited."

"No one knows that for sure. It's all still up in the air. I was just reading— Anyway, Roy tries to do what's right. And he also tries to make himself happy. He has a good instinct for happiness. If the two things sometimes come in conflict, well, what else is new? But I'm sure he gave in, in the end. I know him."

"Maybe it wasn't such a good idea. We could have gotten a stranger, without all the emotional involvement. Or Dmitri."

"Well, yes. Except . . ." Bea was torn between the urge to defend Dmitri, who she felt would have been more than adequate for the task, and her dread of his falling into the muscular embrace of Serena. "When it comes to helping out, say with school or college, Roy's a much better bet. Dmitri hasn't got a dime. And a stranger might be even worse. She's so unpredictable, she might like him. At least with Roy it's safe. She's already divorced him."

What a blow that had been to Roy. Even now, four years later, Bea recalled it vividly, with a measure of pity. He had come upstairs for solace, undone by the news that the pale-tressed Serena, for whom, despite pangs of conscience, he had left Bea, was abandoning him and his five-room apartment a mere two hundred yards from Central Park. "Just tell me, Bea," he had cried as he joined her on the sofa, "what could a woman like Serena see in . . . excuse me, but, well, a woman. A woman like May." These things happen, she told him. You can't explain love. How come he didn't notice? he moaned. How come Bea didn't tell him?

She soothed him in her bed, by far the most efficacious way, no trouble at all. Roy was a pleasure to have in bed: accommodating, generous, almost childlike in his avidity and good-natured curiosity, and, despite his being a psychotherapist or perhaps because of it, untouched by doubt or self-awareness. That afternoon Bea had expected he might be subdued and melancholy, but happily he was not. Afterward, he rolled away, lit a cigarette—he had stopped smoking, but the trauma of rejection weakened his resolve—and fondly called Bea a libertine. She laughed and sent out for Chinese food.

It took him a long time to get over Serena's defection. For months he brooded, was reclusive, vague with the children, passive in the family. By and by he recovered, and would attend Thanksgiving and birthday dinners as usual, the whole family gathered in Bea's spacious dining room, extra leaves in the table; soon he would carve the turkey or the roast as he had in the old days, and the sight of Serena and May across the table, their elbows touching and very likely their knees as well, did not smart with the same keenness.

"Safe," May echoed dourly. "That's one way of seeing it. On the other hand he could revive old feelings—"

The phone startled the baby and he began to cry. "Pick him up, would you? . . . Mom? . . . Well, why don't you sit in the lobby for a while? It's cool there, and you can talk to people."

"No," Anna said petulantly. "I don't like that new doorman you hired. I can't understand a word he says."

"Carlos is not so new. He's been here five years. He's from Santo Domingo, just like Oscar. You had no trouble understanding Oscar."

"Oscar." Anna sighed. "No one's like Oscar. If we can't have Oscar, why can't we have Russians? Even Poles. Didn't I tell you to hire only Russians?"

"That's against the law. You have to hire the ones who are qualified. You're not allowed to discriminate." Bea ran her hands over the mound of vegetables waiting to be assembled in an artistic design.

"Discriminate? Since when is it discrimination to hire who you like?"

"About twenty or thirty years now. I'll explain it to you later." She hung up and gazed at her sister.

13

" 'Crosspatch, draw the latch,' " May was crooning. Timmy, perched on her knee, kept trying to grab May's feathery earrings, and when she teasingly pulled away just in time, he lunged for the silver medallion around her neck, making his animal grunts. It was high time for him to break into speech. Sara and Danny spoke their first words at nine months. But you had to speak to them in order to elicit speech. It was only common sense, now corroborated by the latest research: the language apparatus was all there, ready and waiting, but needed to be activated. Certain faculties of language had a limited time span in which to be activated, a window of opportunity, as it were. Like fruit: if not used in time, it rotted. Did Tony and Melissa make sure the nannies spoke to him in English?

"Say Aunt May, Timmy," Bea halfheartedly addressed her grandson, "not ga-ga. We have to do something about her, May. She's not remembering what she said a half hour ago."

"That happens to me all the time. Can I put him down? I want to go upstairs to work. I can worry better on my own."

"Go on. By the way, could you find the window washers and tell them not to forget the mirrors in the lobby? They did the last time." She tested the bottle and held it out to Timmy, who was whimpering at being back in the playpen. He reached for it eagerly, but Bea took pity on him and lifted him into her arms.

She stood at the living-room window as he sucked with glee. The building, purchased by her parents almost fifty years ago after an unexpected inheritance, was on a cross street, gracious enough, but lacking the panache of Central Park West. The construction on the corner, or deconstruction—for the past two months an unsightly pile of rubble dotted by sinks and toilets—certainly opened things up: the park, the reservoir with its moving ring of joggers, the East Side and environs. The life of the city unfurled like an opera framed by her window: bicycle messengers darting in and out of traffic, their shouted obscenities audible even on the tenth floor; suicidal skaters, swifter than the buses into whose paths they careened; the hot dog stand across the street that seemed never without a customer—just now a clump of

14

soccer players gathered round, one by one lifting cans of soda and tilting back their heads to drink; the black nannies slowly wheeling the white babies in strollers, all of which recalled the infant in her arms, his moist lips parted in sleep, a few drops of milk rolling lazily down his chin.

She placed Timmy back in the playpen, filled the pastry shells with a ricotta and scallion mix, and ate one. Excellent! If only they didn't reheat them for too long. And suddenly, in the late-afternoon hush—the jackhammers next door retired for the day—she realized she was alone in a silent house. This happened so rarely, she'd almost forgotten what it was like. As if a background whirring like the hum of a refrigerator, something so constant that you came to ignore it, had abruptly clicked off: true silence. Bea breathed deeply and felt the air seep through her, as if she had been given permission to expand to her full breadth. Was this the flow of inner energy Danny spoke of whenever he returned from an occasional weekend with the Buddhists? But very soon her pleasure was tinged with a faint anxiety. The thought of her children was always accompanied by a faint anxiety. Indeed, on the rare occasions when the anxiety deserted her, she rushed to retrieve it, as if to save the children from unknown danger. It was almost a relief to hear Shimmer bounding down the hall. No doubt about those footsteps. Footprints. "I hear his footprints," Danny would say when he was barely three and Roy came stomping home. Danny was still the only child then—it was before the twins came. "I hear his footprints." How they had laughed. And look at him now, subsisting on a patchwork of odd jobs her immigrant grandparents would have scorned, had such jobs been available—copy shops, video stores, coffee bars.

"Oh, give me one before you wrap it up!" Shimmer popped a scallion tart into her mouth, then scooped up the baby and began tossing him into the air.

"Don't do that! He just had his bottle. He'll throw up all over you."

"Ugh." She hastily put him down.

"Aren't you early today?"

15

"Friday we get out an hour early. Today we made papier-mâché. Monday we'll paint it, and that's about it for my art skills. I still don't know why they didn't hire me for sports."

"Because they already had someone for sports."

"Magenta got to teach swimming and that's a sport."

"Who?"

"Maggie. She changed her name to Magenta."

A sturdy, athletic girl, on the high school basketball and track teams, Shimmer was wearing cutoffs, sneakers, and a T-shirt that read UNIVERSITÉ DE SORBONNE, acquired in a thrift shop. Her long wavy hair was indeed shimmery, tied back in a ponytail; it had been a sandy brown like her father's, but she recently treated it with a substance that produced a metallic mauve tinge. In winter her attire was frightful, Bea thought, *Grapes of Wrath* grunge or Gestapo leather, but summer, with leather, denim, and flannel renounced, brought improvement. Heat was a fashion leveler. Shimmer was a stable girl, Bea knew, and yet she worried; she'd been only six at the time of the divorce. She had witnessed too much, too young. But then they all saw and knew too much nowadays. There was no more innocence, except perhaps at Timmy's age.

Shimmer sat down as if she wished to talk but made no effort to do so, like those people who telephone then wait for the other to speak.

"Any plans for tonight?"

"Uh-uh." She scrutinized her mother at work as if recording her actions for future review.

"This is for a party for a Korean violinist," Bea volunteered. "The people who are giving it are friends of Salman Rushdie. They hinted they might be having a party for him soon. That might be interesting, don't you think, to cater Rushdie's party? I'd like to go to that one."

"Who is he again?" Shimmer took Timmy out of the playpen and held him on her lap, wiggling his fingers.

Bea sighed and told her. "If you're not busy, do you think you might go up and see Grandma? She sounds lonely, but I haven't been able to get away." To her surprise, Shimmer agreed with alacrity, as if offered some coveted entertainment, like a ticket to an R.E.M. concert.

16

"See if she seems a little off to you. I think she's forgetting things more than usual. She keeps complaining about Carlos. I mean, what's wrong with Carlos except that he's not Oscar?"

"I don't like him either. He has a smart-ass attitude. I told you we should've hired a woman. We could've had the first woman doorman in Manhattan. Wouldn't you like to be on the cutting edge?"

"Maybe next time. Meanwhile see what you think. Thanks, sweetie."

As the door slammed, Bea knelt at the playpen to talk to Timmy, once more whining at his imprisonment. As soon as he was toilet-trained, Melissa declared this morning when she dropped him off, he would be enrolled in school. "School?" Bea was startled. Well, it wasn't really school-school, Melissa said in her brisk manner. "More like a little play group. They learn little things; they interact; they have their music and gymnastics." Melissa brushed lint from her gray linen skirt, precisely the regulation one inch above her knees, which, like everything about her, were irreproachable. Now and then Bea yearned to glimpse her daughter-in-law brushing her teeth or throwing up or removing a tampon. Melissa could not be ignorant of personal and domestic disorder, not to say slovenliness, having been raised by an alcoholic mother with a succession of live-in companions, but you would never know it. She was a triumph of will over environment, and Bea, despite her distaste for perfection, had to admire her.

Toilet training reminded Bea to change the baby's diaper, after which she called Carlos, the unpopular doorman. "Carlos, do you think you could spare Ernesto to take an order over to Riverside Drive for me? Great. Thanks so much."

Help was a problem. Bea was reluctant to use Maxwell, one of the local panhandlers, again, though he was a clever man with an ingratiating manner. Long ago she had rescued him from the street corner with an offer of a delivery job and a bed in the basement. But her clients objected. Not openly, but business slackened, and when she made inquiries, it was clear that the party givers, compassionate as they might be in the voting booth, cringed at Maxwell's appearing on the doorstep bearing their gourmet dinners. He was all cleaned up, Bea pointed out, they could see for themselves: in her very own shower, and wearing Roy's discarded clothes, still in excellent condition. Besides, she had sent him to the clinic for a checkup, even financed an HIV test (negative). It was no use. In truth, while Maxwell's job performance had been exemplary, he had a tendency to revert to his former habits in between delivery stints. And could she presume to interfere with the way he spent his free time? No. It was too bad. She had tried; if she hadn't her own family to look after, she might have tried harder. Nowadays when she saw Maxwell on the street she gave him dollar bills. He didn't seem to bear a grudge.

At last she sat Timmy in his high chair and gave him his supper. He clearly preferred the barbecued chicken—carefully deboned—to the health food Melissa had left for him. Bea didn't have the energy to talk to him anymore, but she turned on the radio so he could hear spoken English. In a corner of the kitchen that had been Danny and Tony's old bedroom before the remodeling, Bea kept a reclining chair. While Timmy munched and modeled the food on his tray like Play-Doh, Bea tipped the recliner back and relaxed. Together they listened to a description of past atrocities in Bosnia, then to details of cutbacks in day care and meals-on-wheels for the aged and infirm. Before long she was asleep.

II

That night, Danny fell in love in a dim Lower East Side lounge where the nonsmoking rules were ignored in a spirit of hedonism. He was seated between his older sister, Jane, and her boyfriend, Al, at a table so small their shoulders were almost touching. Another love born in the bosom of the family. And why was that? Dr. Whiting would ask, were Danny still seeing him. Never mind. This was the real thing. Love at first sight. Or rather first sound. Its object was the girl they had come to hear, who stood in the spotlight holding the mike with a lover's tenderness, a girl with honey-colored skin and delicate bones, taut hair on a finely shaped head, a wide mouth, throbbing throat, and slinky dress cut away at the shoulders, a girl who sang "My Man" in a silky, smoky voice more heartbreaking than anyone since Billie Holiday, whom otherwise she did not resemble at all; no, Danny thought, she looked like a clean-living girl, the kind who worked out at the gym or even kept a NordicTrack in her bedroom—if not, she could use his anytime, purchased secondhand from a fellow usher in a downtown art cinema several jobs ago—the kind of girl who majored in music some-where like Brown and bought the dress not off the vintage clothing racks on lower Broadway where Jane shopped, but at some classy bou-tique on Madison Avenue, a girl who could dance as well as sing, and in bed, well— He cut short his fantasies before they became too great a distraction, for her song was ending on a low tapering note like a fading wick. She smiled an urbane, remote smile, accepting the burst of applause as if it were her due. The regal tilt of her head was dis-maying. She would never look at him. What had he been thinking?

She was Al's younger sister, Coral, just back from two years in

Paris. This was her first New York appearance, Al explained on the way over. Even Jane hadn't met her yet. They would love her, he said. And Danny did.

Al stamped his feet, whistled, and slapped his hand on the table. "Wasn't that incredible? What did I tell you?" People at nearby tables waved at him, for he was known there too—he was a jazz pianist.

Coral sang several more songs, two in French. The room was hushed, the listeners rapt. Even the waitresses stopped serving. Good. Danny hated the clink of glasses during a show, the arms reaching out, so disrespectful to the artists, to Art itself. The crowd was young, more blacks than whites, and better dressed than at your usual Lower East Side place. A snazzy crowd, as if they grasped their obligation to create a worthy setting. Danny was trained to notice things like that. Partly trained. He had dropped out of the film program at NYU after a year, convinced that he possessed neither the talent nor the audacity to succeed in the film industry, so rapacious. His father pronounced his decision depression, pure and simple. Well, he would. Danny didn't see it as depression—he went about his part-time work in the video store and the copy shop with customary good nature—merely as inadequacy. If he were still in school, though, he would use Coral in a film. Dress her in sequins and feathers . . . No, that was too Josephine Baker, whom she also did not resemble in the least. She wasn't openly seductive with the audience. Her manner was aloof, her voice intimate. The combination was dynamite.

When her act was over, she came to their table, and Al leaped to his feet to hug her. The lights were up, the bustle and chatter resumed. Coral ordered a diet Coke, waving away the smoke from the next table. So he'd been right. He felt almost dizzy with her sitting so near, her presence blurred by the afterimage of her standing onstage in the spotlight.

She turned to Danny. "Are you the brother who's in film?"

"Oh, no," he stammered. "No."

"Then what? You're not the lawyer brother, I can tell." She gazed straight at him with an ironic smile.

"This and that." He found himself unable to utter the words "video store" or "copy shop," even though he had just been made assistant manager of the evening shift at Ape Copiers. Instead, uncontrollably, he stood up, poised to flee.

"Hey, Danny, what's with you? Where're you going?" Jane asked.

He bumped into a waitress carrying a loaded tray—thank God it didn't spill, that would be the end—and called over his shoulder, "I'll be right back. I mean, I have to go. I have to get up early for work."

A half hour later, in bed, he buried his head in his hands in shame, seeing it all unreel before him. She must think he was a pig and she was right. One simple remark and he was struck dumb by his curse, his affliction: his shyness. He had thought the most virulent phase of the disease was past, that with time and discipline he had brought it under control; this relapse was crushing. The last time he had been able to speak freely in the presence of a beautiful woman was with Miss Pinkman, his fifth-grade teacher who had left midway through the year to fight illiteracy in Nicaragua. Worst of all was the crush he'd had on his father's second wife. Serena. At least that was over. The memory still made him shudder. How many sleepless nights she caused him, how many excruciating moments, unable to meet her eyes. Not even the patient ministrations of Dr. Whiting, the psychiatrist at school, had helped. What helped was that she left his father for his Aunt May. Those elaborate fantasies spent on a woman who turned out not to like men after all: a double mortification. And if he was mortified, imagine how his father must have felt. Danny had been the most sympathetic of Roy's four children.

An image of Coral poised on the NordicTrack just opposite his bed was coming into focus, while he ached with a familiar, comforting self-disgust—comforting because it was his emotional home. The image grew more vivid, irresistible. She was striding in shiny blue and purple Lycra, and then with nothing on at all, and then she was leaping across the room, not intimidating now but hungry for him, falling into his arms, not the least like Serena—no, dark and warm and lavish—and he was blessed with speech as fluent as his brother Tony's, Moses transformed into Aaron, and his hands, become enormous, giant hands, touched her everywhere at once, and her skin was like flower petals,

21

one vast petal. Oh God, he moaned, reaching for himself, you cowardly prick.

Melissa sat up in bed, her knees crossed in a half-lotus position and draped by *The Wall Street Journal*. Bea would not have been gratified to see her at this informal moment: even without her professional uniform Melissa looked perfect. She wore an article of pearl gray satin sleepwear that on a child would have been called a playsuit. With her makeup creamed away, the contours of her broad, pale face were more prominent. Her eyes were large, flecked with green, under squarish glasses with gold frames; her straight glossy hair was tied back.

"Tony? Your mother mentioned there's going to be an apartment vacant in the building in a few months. Some old couple on the fourth floor? They had a terrible time last winter with those storms and the flu? Bea said they didn't know it themselves yet, but she's sure they won't stick it out another winter."

He looked up from his book. "The Riordans. They've been there ever since I can remember. Nobody ever moves out of that place."

"Well? You know what I'm thinking."

"Don't tell me you want to be sucked into that . . . that tribe my mother's running. She'd like to fill the whole place with family. I'm surprised she doesn't have Dmitri bringing over his relatives. They could run it as a commune. She could relive her hippie youth."

"Coming from you, sweetie, those cracks about bringing people over are not in the best of taste."

"You don't have to remind me. I know how good she is. But sometimes I wish she hadn't bothered."

"God Almighty! No good deed goes unpunished, eh? Do you seriously mean you would have preferred to grow up there? In an orphanage? I can just see you in the rice paddies. Right."

"I know it sounds weird. I just think . . . if I'd managed to survive,

I might've been better off in the long run. I guess Jane isn't crazy enough to feel this way."

"Damn right she's not. I doubt if there're a whole lot of opportunities for performance art in Vietnam. What long run? Better off how?"

"I would've known better who I am." He wished he'd known better than to reveal these thoughts to her. She understood nothing, nothing. How could he tell her that he sometimes woke with a start from dreams of his mother, his first mother, dreams where they spoke in his native tongue, long forgotten in waking life, and he lay sleepless for hours wondering who he was and what he was doing here? Alongside her hard bones, her satin teddies.

"Who you are? I know who you are if you don't. You're a ninety-thousand-dollar-a-year junior associate at Crawford, Drew, Chang, and Bonaventure, and you're going to be one of the best bankruptcy lawyers in the city. That's who you are."

"Bankruptcy. Do I want to spend my life helping rich bastards go into bankruptcy so they can start screwing people all over again?"

"Did something happen at the office, Tony? I wish you'd tell me. Why are you talking this way?"

"Nothing happened. I just don't want to move back to the building. Across town is close enough."

"We wouldn't have to live right in their pockets. We could establish some boundaries. But it would be so great for Timmy. That kind of family environment. And if we had more . . ."

"Don't think you could leave Timmy with my mom every day, Melissa. She's got a life, you know. She's running a business."

"Not every day, no. But he's so happy hanging out in the kitchen while she putters—today he didn't want to leave. And with all those women, don't you see? If they'd each help a little bit . . . Besides May and Serena, even your grandmother, she's not that far gone—sometimes I think she's the sanest one of the bunch—and Sara or whatever, Shimmer, is a good age for baby-sitting. Even your father's fiancée, the teacher, what's her name, Lisa, she probably gets home around four o'clock—"

"All those women, as you put it, even my grandmother, who forgets her own address lately, never mind take care of a baby—all those women work—"

"Work. Give me a break." She waved a dismissive hand in the air, her lacquered nails catching the light. "Who says you can't watch a baby while you're cooking or painting or giving massages? I sure as hell could. It's not like being in an office with deadlines and the fax machine rattling away and all the rest of it. Day care isn't the best way to bring up a baby, with strangers, not getting a whole lot of attention. Believe me, I know. Your father could help too. God knows he's had enough experience."

"He might be minding his own babies for all we know."

"Wouldn't that be cute? They could be friends. Cousins, sort of." She took his hand and ran her thumb along the palm. "I've been thinking, if we do want to have more, it might be good to get it over with soon."

Alarm clutched Tony's heart like a fist. He barely knew Timmy very well and she was thinking of another. He didn't even know who she was anymore. He'd fallen in love with a wiry-haired college girl in torn jeans, the feisty product of a childhood of benign neglect; she wrote punchy editorials for the school paper on global warming and strip mining. He took her brusque manner as a shield for the warm heart beneath—at least he inferred warmth from their hours in bed. They went to law school together and she emerged transformed, varnished; even the hair had somehow been transfigured. Again, he assumed the patina was no more than a new kind of armor. Now he wasn't sure what was beneath the surface. Or was it surface all the way down? She hadn't mentioned global warming in ages.

"How could you, with work and all?"

"There's a six-week maternity leave policy now. We finally put enough pressure on them. Remember, with Timmy, how I only got three weeks and I had to fight for that? God, I dragged myself back when my cunt was still gushing and my tits were dripping, I must have been in the bathroom twenty times a day. But as of yesterday, success. It just goes to show, if you've got twenty women associates bitching

24

about something . . ." She raised a victorious fist, then leaned over to stroke his thigh. "A bunch of us went out to celebrate—that's why I was late getting Timmy from your mother's. So I thought I might put it to use."

"Is that how it feels to you, getting it over with?"

She had been guiding his hand up and down her leg, but stopped abruptly. "You sound so shocked. I just mean the messy part. Actually having it."

He had only himself to blame. It was even what appealed to him, way back: she was tough; global warming aside, she admitted she was ruled by self-interest and presumed the rest of the world was the same. Compared to his devoted parents, who had tried to perpetuate the spirit of the sixties—his mother still kept her old love beads and Woodstock memorabilia—then turned crazy and blew it all with the divorce, Melissa had been refreshing. But living day after day with a neo-Hobbesian made him feel scraped raw. Not that it wasn't exciting. In bed, from the very start, she would do anything, even if it did involve parts being scraped raw—not so much her taste as her concession to innate brutality. And Tony's inclinations in bed were, if not precisely nasty, certainly brutish and short.

"I'm not sure I'm ready," he said weakly.

"We could think about it." Again she reached over and stroked him. "What's the matter, don't you like me anymore? Am I too gross for your delicate tastes?" She flicked the book off his lap and pounced on top of him. "I remember when you were the one who could shock me. The tricks you showed me. Can you still surprise me?"

It was no use resisting. She always won. And he wanted her. "You bet I can surprise you." He flipped her over and ripped off the playsuit.

"Hey! You don't have to do that. It does have snaps. Ow. Oh. Oh God," she moaned.

"You don't have that thing in."

"I . . . I started taking the pill."

"You're sure?"

"I'm sure."

He sank in. She was not trustworthy, but it was too late to think.

25

Always, when he entered her, there was a slight tightening or tensing—he felt it as a narrowing of the gates. Not that he was not welcome, only that he would have to overcome resistance, the merest hint of it. He didn't know if it was a reflex or a ploy—he couldn't remember feeling it with other women—but he knew he liked it. He liked the sense of overcoming resistance, and she knew he liked it. He pushed hard and long. Maybe he could dig down to some softness in her. She cried out, calling his name. When it was over, he felt empty, faintly sickened. Her face was utterly still, flushed, her eyes closed. As he watched, the color faded from her cheeks. She might be asleep. Maybe dead. He could start all over. A new life.

Timmy's wail sounded from the next room. "I'll go," he said.

"Maybe he'll stop," Melissa whispered, tightening her arms around him. "Stay with me. This is so lovely. I love you. Oh, Tony, it felt like it used to. Didn't it? You see, we can be that way again."

But Timmy didn't stop. His wails got louder and more persistent, and continued even after Tony changed his diaper, gave him a bottle, and paced through the apartment holding him.

"Bring him in here." Melissa stretched her arms out lazily. "Give him to me. He can sleep here. It's the only thing that'll calm him down."

"Don't they say that's not good for them? They'll get used to it or something?"

"So what? Here, sweetheart, Mommy's here, it's all right. We all like sleeping with someone," she murmured, "don't we?" Snug between them, Timmy quieted, even purred with pleasure. Soon he was asleep in the crook of her arm.

Melissa slept too. She looked content at last, no longer restless and avid. Was it the sex or the baby in her arms? Tony remembered sleeping with his first mother, he and Jane on either side of her in a tiny bed, together and at peace. Not like now, when he felt apart. Maybe he'd feel more at peace now if they had let him sleep with Jane when they first arrived—they were barely seven—but his father and Bea had a room with twin beds all ready. Still, he would crawl in with Jane, out of habit. Sometime during the night his father would look in on them and carry him back to his own bed, so that after a while he gave up. A year later he was sharing a room with Danny, and Jane got the small bedroom all to herself.

Jane. He needed to talk to Jane. She was the only one who could restore him to himself, whoever that was. It was one-fifteen, but she stayed up late.

He tiptoed into his study and settled in the leather chair. "Jane? Janie, it's me. Pick up if you're there. I'm sorry it's so late but..." He went on talking to the machine, willing his voice to penetrate her sleep. And at last she came.

"Tony? Are you okay?"

"I had to talk to someone. To you. I'm sorry. You must've been sleeping."

"It's all right. What is it?"

"Nothing. Just talk to me. Anything. Tell me what's happening with you."

Al's sister had arrived from Paris, she told him. They went to hear her sing. With Danny. Danny acted weird and walked out, something about getting up early for work. Early? The video store? Her group, Parabsurd, was putting on a musical version of *Medea*. A feminist version, interactive—the audience would hear both sides of the story and vote on what Medea's fate should be. Jason's too, why let him off?

Her gentle voice lulled him. He nodded in response, as if she were in the room. She was so good. She understood just what he needed; this was hardly the first time. A little stability. Grounding. A human voice.

Medea's ending might be different every night, so they would have to improvise. Jane was working on electronic music and might play the moderator or judge, depending. Danny promised to help build the sets—he was good at that—and maybe she could talk him into being an usher.

"That's about all I can think of at this hour. Are you okay now?"

"Yes. Thanks." He was more than okay. He was becalmed. "Is Al awake?"

"Awake and waiting." She giggled.

27

"Oh. Sorry. I'll let you go."

"It's okay. Good night now. Sleep well."

Jane and Al lived in an artists' loft in a SoHo warehouse. It was Al's place to begin with—he required a building that was empty at night so he could play the piano at any hour. Jane and her equipment had moved in four months ago. Before that, she had camped with a series of roommates, some of them friends from Parabsurd, The Theater Beyond the Absurd, a few of them lovers; she was so amiable that someone was always willing to take her in. Al hoped she would change and settle down.

Their tenancy was precarious: at one time the loft had been perfectly legal, indeed intended, in its postindustrial incarnation, for young artists, but under the present administration, less amenable to the arts and their perpetrators, it was no longer so. Nonetheless they remained, in the hope that no building inspector would happen by, and so far they had been lucky.

Their bed was a mattress on the floor. They sat propped up on pillows, drinking herbal tea, the streets outside as hushed as a country road at this time of night.

"What was going on with Danny? He sure got out of there fast."

"He's painfully shy, especially meeting new people."

"Shy, in your family? That's quite a trick."

"I think it's because of me and Tony, you know, the way we turned up out of the blue when he was just three? Like, there he is, the only child, doting parents, and suddenly these two bigger kids appear—funny-looking, slanty eyes, can't speak a word of English. Your new brother and sister. Have fun. That could do something to you."

"Maybe. But he wasn't so tongue-tied when he first met me."

"It's mostly women. Anyway, you. You're such a pussycat. Who could be afraid of you?"

28

"White ladies who see me walking down a dark street."

"That's different. Danny's probably tormenting himself right now. He must've really liked Coral. You know, sometimes the more you like people the less you can talk to them? She was terrific. She should get more gigs."

"I'm talking her up to everyone. What she really needs, though, is a job, any kind of job. And a place of her own. She can't keep staying with my folks. My Uncle Gerard said she could be a receptionist in his office, but she says she can't stand the smell of doctors' offices. Anyway, Gerard's so proper and she's a free spirit."

"Like you." Jane touched his face. She liked the soft stubble that never got shaved away.

"Come on. No minister's son can be a free spirit. And a black man, here? Forget it. Come closer to me, babe. I have an idea."

"Funny, I was thinking the same thing. We must be in love."

"Uh, before we get too . . . Look, Janie, don't get mad like you did last time, but did you think about what I said about—"

"About what?"

"You know. Kids."

"Babies!" She leaped up. Pale pink tea spilled on the sheets. "Again? No! I told you I'm not ready. I may never be ready. We're not even married."

"We could be married. That's the easy part."

She paced quickly back and forth in the dim room, tugging at her short, spiky hair. She was very thin in her white baby doll nightie; in the lurid light from a streetlamp, she seemed a wraith. "You want to get married, you want kids, next you'll be wanting Tupperware. When you talk like this, it's like your evil twin or something."

"Okay," Al said quietly. "You can stop dancing around. I think I get the idea. Come on back."

She flopped down on the bed beside him, both of them in the path of a window fan blowing the hot air around. "I thought we were okay as we are. But you really mean it, don't you?"

"Yeah. But never mind." He pulled her on top of him. She was so light he could barely feel her weight.

"No funny stuff, all right?"

"What do you mean?" He let go, affronted. "Am I some stranger? What do you mean, funny stuff?"

"Calm down. I just mean, like, I had a friend once, a guy pulled out her diaphragm at the last minute? He didn't like barriers or something?"

Al looked away. "You've known me awhile. You think I'd do a thing like that?"

An interesting idea, he thought as he slowly took off her nightgown and stared at her in the half-light. Why didn't he ever think of things like that? He was too nice, that was why. The minister's son. Or the son every minister would want. He didn't even like to drink much—two beers, and he felt heavy and fuzzy; his fingers slipped on the keys. He must be the only jazz musician in history who got dizzy when he smoked a joint, and he had tried the stronger stuff only a few times, afraid he'd get hooked and ruin everything. His parents sent him to boarding school and summer camps to keep him off the street, his father's buildings supplying the money. "Real estate?" Janie joked when they met. "That's something we have in common." Except his dad was serious about it; Jane's family's one building was more of a hobby. Then a good men's college, far from the city where his parents feared for his safety, a college with a Quaker background where he didn't feel quite as out of place as he'd dreaded. He'd tried to act the bad city kid but it was a poor act. He was outgoing and trusting, or as trusting as any black kid could be in a white school, studious and even-tempered. What he wanted most was to play the piano. He'd done some stuff with a few of the outlaw boys, both black and white—taken trucks on joyrides then abandoned them, broken a few windows—but they never got caught, and Al took no pleasure in it. He soon gave up and accepted a fate of respectability. And unfailing luck. Back in New York, he played the piano as much as he could wish. He was big and muscular and wore tight dark clothes and a bandanna around his head and dark glasses, but no one could be intimidated for long. He was unregenerately decent and stuck with it.

"What are you dreaming about?" Jane whispered in his ear. "Remember me? Come back to me."

"Sorry, babe. I was just thinking about my luck." He clasped her to him. Dreamy skin, luscious hair, sweet lips. He took it slow. He always liked it slow, and he liked to watch her pleasure in him. They were good together, he thought; their bodies knew each other from the start, not that there weren't still things to find out. He was about to enter her when the phone rang.

"Shit," she muttered. Her body stiffened.

"Don't go."

"Jane? Janie, it's me. Pick up if . . ."

"That's Tony." She sat up.

The voice was relentless. It talked and talked.

"I know that, Jane. He can wait." He tried to kiss her but she moved her face away.

"I have to get it." She was up, darting to the phone.

"Jesus F. Christ." What could he do, tie her down? It was painful, totally painful. "Jane," he called softly.

She gave him a helpless shrug, holding out her palm for patience. Medea. She was sitting there naked talking about fucking Medea while his balls were aching. Talk about a tight family. Still, he liked them. Not the twin brother so much, but the others—her mother, even her grandmother, a ballsy old lady who knew his dad from a landlords' organization. She'd recognized the name immediately, Jane had reported. "Wait a minute," Anna said. "If your boyfriend is the Reverend Redwood's son then he's black, right?" "Right, Grandma." "Well, I don't care. You think I care? I was in the Young Socialist League long before you were in training pants." That was okay; it could be worse. He could deal with them if he had to. It would be easier if she were black, but he loved her. The other thing was more of a problem.

"Jane," he muttered. "Get over here!"

She told her brother good night as if he were a baby.

"I'm sorry," she said, flopping down on the mattress. "He needed me."

"*He* needed you? I need you too."

"Well here I am," she chirped. "Something for everyone."

Roy reclined on his fiancée's futon in her studio apartment. Her toy apartment, as he termed it. His own place, just a short walk away, was more comfortable as well as cooler, but Lisa preferred it here, at least for now. She needed to feel some autonomy in their relationship, she'd explained; in his place she felt enveloped, almost erased, by his things and his history, especially as he had lately revealed that his two previous wives, as well as his former sister-in-law and mother-in-law, lived on the floors above. "It's too much," she groaned. "How do you stand it?" "Real estate," he said. "Intimate relations in New York are governed by real estate."

In his case there was a good deal more than real estate involved, but he needn't burden her with questions of what she would call "lifestyle" until after they were married. Roy was prepared to yield on many issues—he was, as his wives could attest, an easygoing man, hardly controlling—but he wasn't giving up that apartment: the space, the low rent, the excellent location. Yes, the construction next door made it noisy, but it wouldn't last forever. And Anna was a trifle stingy about the heat—a minor annoyance when recalled in August. Otherwise, thanks to Bea and, yes, Dmitri, it was very well run. Lisa would appreciate it once they were married. She could bring along whatever she liked, though as he looked around the room—the kitchen being a few appliances in an alcove—he couldn't see much worth preserving. There was a small desk, like a child's, piled with folders from last term's ninth-grade class, a drab Salvation Army couch, an unpainted bookcase, a dining-room table converted from an abandoned spool for electrical cable she had picked up along the piers—someone must have helped her lug that home, perhaps her old boyfriend, Billy Moran, an unsettling notion—a worn hemp rug, movie posters on the wall, and the ubiquitous piles of bubble wrap she was addicted to popping in odd moments, a habit that, depending on his mood, Roy found alternately endearing or exasperating. A girl's room. Except for their different tastes in cultural icons, it could be Sara's room, Shimmer's rather; Shimmer's first apartment would no doubt be very like this, if she managed to move out of the building. Lisa was certainly girlish—he could hear her in the shower, singing the score from *The Wizard of Oz*. Maybe spending so much time with teenagers kept her girlish. At any rate, it would do him good. He had few delusions about why a man of his age would seek out a woman of thirty-one, and was as tolerant of his motives as he urged his patients to be of theirs. Awareness is everything, he liked to say. Awareness? he imagined Bea's retort. Awareness is just the first step. He smiled. Dear Bea.

Despite the stifling heat he was glad, this evening, to be in Lisa's apartment rather than his own, scene of his trespass with Serena. That was going a bit far. Stretching things, even for him. Although the actual experience, now that he had a quiet moment for recollection, had been, well, pretty fantastic, spiced as it was with old memory and new mischief. Even in her dyke phase, she remembered how to make a man feel good. He could still see her vividly, zipping up her shorts and slipping into the clogs. She had saved the shirt for last. "I don't know how to thank you, Roy," she said. Lying spent and confused on the floor, he managed to rally and offer a smile. "Just don't name it after me." She knotted the shirt—his old white shirt—as before, at the midriff. Wistfully, he had watched her go.

But all that was beside the point. He should have been thinking of Lisa. If Serena became pregnant—and while he hoped fervently that she did not, the notion of his immediate success tickled him just a bit—there would be no way to keep it from her: he knew the women, the harem, as he secretly called it, too well. She would find out. All he could do was see that she didn't find out before it was absolutely necessary, certainly not before they were married in December; the wedding and honeymoon were planned to coincide with her Christmas break. Meanwhile, never again. There were reputable agencies to satisfy Serena's goals.

Lisa came out of the shower delectably wrapped in a royal blue embroidered Chinese robe, her abundant hair slicked down. Damp and rosy, she looked about sixteen years old. She could be a friend of Shimmer's, one of those girls dressed like truck drivers who paraded around Bea's apartment, piercings and studs in odd parts of their faces, even, in one instance, the tongue, which sent a shudder through his groin.

Lisa sat beside him on the lumpy futon, her knees curled under her. "Roy?" She would often start a conversation with this tentative murmur of his name.

"Yes, what?"

"You know, considering that we're getting married, there's one subject that, it's funny, we've never even discussed."

He waited, but clearly he was supposed to encourage her. She was running her fingertips down his chest from the collarbone to the navel, which he found distracting. "What's that, Lisa sweetheart?"

"Children. I don't even know how you feel about children."

"You mean you want a baby?"

"Well, it's not that I'm totally . . . I mean, it seems like when people get married they should know how—"

"Lisa. Darling. Just tell me. I can take it."

"Okay. Well, the way I see it is, I'm young, this is my first marriage— Oh, sorry, I didn't mean it like that, I certainly plan on its being my last, believe me, I only meant compared to you. . . . Okay, I guess I do want a baby. One, anyway, to start."

"We can have a baby. Sure. There's not a whole lot to discuss. With Bea we never—"

"Maybe not for you, you've done it so many times"—now she was rummaging through his pubic hair—"but for me it's different. It's also a different era, I mean about child care, how we'll work it out. I mean dividing the child care—"

"Lisa, sweetie, you're not even pregnant, we're not even married. We don't have to discuss child care right this minute, do we? God, it's hot, isn't it?"

"It is." She got up and let her robe slip off, crossed the room, pausing to step smartly on a stray piece of bubble wrap, which emitted a resounding pop, and flicked on the air conditioner he had insisted on buying for her. "Why didn't you turn this on?"

"I hate it, that's why."

"But on a night like this, Roy. Otherwise we'll, you know, stick together, and that's so icky." She rejoined him on the futon. "I didn't mean we have to work everything out now. I'm not a total idiot, you know. You like to treat me that way, and when you do that to people, they start acting that way—it's been demonstrated with children in school: Expectations condition performance. All I meant was, however it was when your kids were born, child care is more of a joint thing now, at least in certain segments of the population—our segments— and I just need that to be kind of accepted between us before—"

"Lisa, if I treat you like a child, you make me sound like an octogenarian. Where do you think I've been all these years?" If she knew the hours he'd put in listening to women complain about their husbands' domestic shortcomings. If he had ten dollars for every hour . . . but in fact he had a hundred dollars for every such hour. And married to Bea, how could he possibly have eluded one iota of the experience, from the smell of Desitin to the dried curds on his collar, from *Mother Goose's One Hundred Favorite Nursery Rhymes* to Open School Week? But at the thought of Open School Week a tenderness came over him, and he remembered meeting Lisa, how he had been captivated by her clear, lilting voice—so different from the faintly querulous, yet assertive, voice in which she was now addressing him—and her small, expressive hands, which he suddenly grasped in his own. "Let's not talk, Lisa. Come here. Do what you were doing."

"You really do like me, don't you, Roy? I mean, seriously. It's not just for this or that I'm young?"

"Yes, sweetie, I really do like you. Seriously. Yes, like that. Yes, slow. Oh baby, I do like you, I sure do."

"May, it's after midnight." Serena, coming from bed, rubbed her eyes in the bright light of the studio. May sat on a folding chair in the center of the room, staring at a half-finished painting: a field of poppies with a bent black bicycle in the middle and several shadowy figures in one corner. She didn't turn around.

"I'll be there soon. Go to sleep without me."

"I want to go to sleep with you. Come on."

She finally looked over her shoulder. "Can't you see I'm working? I'll come when I'm ready."

Twenty minutes later she fell heavily into bed.

"Why are you huddling so far away? Come here." Serena reached to pull her closer but May resisted.

"I thought you were asleep."

"I was waiting for you."

"Since when do you have to wait up for me?"

"I felt like it. Now, how's this? Does that feel good? Does it do anything at all for you? How about a very special massage? The *spécialité de la maison*?"

"Not now. I'm not in the mood. I wouldn't want to wear you out after your exertions. I mean, you've already had a busy day elsewhere."

"I knew it. May, we agreed. We talked it all over. We decided together—"

"Especially if you've been successful, you need your rest."

"Oh, will you please not do this? You're being absurd. You think I did it because I wanted to? A baby was your idea in the first place, remember?"

"You certainly spent enough time on it. You could have conceived half a dozen with the time you put in."

"It's not just a mechanical— I had to act a little enthusi—interested, I mean. Roy's not a stud in a corral, for chrissakes. It took a while to persuade him. Did you think I'd just walk up and start sniffing or what? I had to use finesse. And then . . . Well, would you like to do it in fifteen minutes? Then have me leap up and be out the door?"

"Not quite like that, but I don't see why you couldn't treat the whole thing as a contractual matter."

"May. This is more than a contract. Feelings are involved. I was married to the guy. I know him. He's still hurt that I left. There was that to deal with too."

36

"I'm sure you did. Did you both recall all your old habits, for old times' sake? I can imagine."

"Oh, forget it." Serena moved to the edge of the bed. "I'm going to sleep. You can lie awake torturing yourself if you like. You won't get any more help from me. Good night."

"And then," said May after a long silence, "what if it didn't work? What if you have to do it again?"

"Are you nuts?" Serena sat up. "You think I'd go through this again? You hardly said a word all evening, and now this? Thanks, but no thanks. It's off to the fertility clinic. I don't need to deal with your crazy jealousy."

"Oh, so that's the reason you wouldn't do it again. My jealousy. That's what bothers you. Uh-huh. As far as him, you wouldn't mind. You could manage as often as necessary. I see I have my answer."

"You don't have any answer. I'm not stooping to an answer."

"And if it did work," said May, "whose child will it be anyway? Yours and his, right? The mommy and daddy. Where do I fit in?"

"May." Serena stroked her shoulder. Moonlight from the large window lit May's face and made her skin radiant. Her breasts were large and lush. Her hair was black against the white pillow, as stark a contrast as in one of her paintings. "We've been through this a million times. It'll be our baby. We're the parents. We don't have to assign male or female roles anymore. And believe me, Roy'll have his hands full soon enough. I'm willing to bet this Lisa will start hearing her biological clock ticking. No, he understands his part, and if he wants to be the nice uncle from downstairs, what's wrong with that? Especially if it's a boy. And Roy is not a bad representative, as men go. We could do a lot worse. Everything will be fine." She leaned over and kissed her.

At last May relented. "I hope you're right."

"I'm right, goddammit. You make me so mad sometimes." Serena ran her lips and tongue over May's nipple. "I should really punish you, not go near you for weeks."

"Ha. That'd be the day."

"Well, I'm mad. You really deserve to be kicked around a little. There." Serena punched May's jaw lightly a few times, then moved down to her shoulder and arm. Lightly, then becoming less light.

"Hey, hey." May grabbed her wrist. "I'm an old-fashioned girl, remember? I'm not into any of that postmodern dyke S&M stuff. Beat me gently."

Anna lay seething at the car alarm that had erupted with the opening bars of "Oh! Susannah" every ten minutes for the past two hours. If only Oscar, her much-lamented friend and former doorman, were still here, she could call down and have him do something. There was nothing Oscar could not handle. Though he had not worked nights, she recalled. Always went home to his sister, no matter how much she tried to cajole him. She must stop thinking of Oscar; it got her too worked up. It even made the alarm seem louder. If she were younger, or if Mickey were alive, one of them could go down and break the bastard's windows with a crowbar. Some people left notes on the windshield, but she and Mickey, with their Young Socialist League past, favored more direct measures.

Aside from the alarm and the intermittent sounds of traffic far below, the building was quiet. She had lived in it for fifty years and was a connoisseur of its sounds, attuned to every creak and crunch; she could identify running toilets and rattling windows and the occasional yelp of a faltering smoke alarm, elevator cables groaning, the distant rumble of the washing machine in the basement, mice pattering in the pipes. . . . But now, past midnight, all was still. A deceptive stillness. She knew what they were doing all through the building, even if she couldn't hear it. She could imagine the squeaking of bedsprings, the sighs, the moans. Every one of them, her own family included, even her daughter May and the girl athlete, bouncing and bumping, pumping and grinding through the night. And why not? It was the only thing that made life livable. Nature should have arranged it so that old people did it more, not less; they certainly needed cheering up more. What else did she have to look forward to?

Everyone thought old people like her had forgotten all about those things; they were even hesitant when they talked, skirting around sex or dirty words the way you did with children. Well, she could tell them a thing or two. How she would love to go on one of those afternoon TV programs where people told the shameless, outrageous things they did. Who said there was nothing new under the sun? But did you ever see a guest over forty? No! As if they never gave it a thought. Well, she thought about it plenty. Everyone assumed that since Mickey died she hadn't gone near a man, but she could surprise them about that too. Did they suppose a healthy woman widowed just over sixty would starve herself and become a dry old lady? Some, maybe, but not her. She had had her friends over the years. If balmy Florida had not lured Herb Brownstein, she would have him still. Never a postcard, even. In the old days they talked about the husbands providing for the wives. A good provider, the women called their men. Aren't I a good provider? Mickey would joke in bed. Without him she had had to provide for herself. Only not lately. Not since Herb. She often wondered, lying awake, if there was some man around who would still want her. It wasn't impossible. She was not bad-looking for her age. A bit on the thin side, but she preferred that to the flesh so many old women carried around. It jiggled and slowed you down, while she could still move fast if she had to. She was still convinced Oscar had had his eye on her, a fine-looking man, just around her age. Okay, eight or ten years younger, but at this point a few years didn't count. It probably wasn't a good idea with an employee, although Bea had been carrying on with the Russian super practically from the minute he arrived, and no harm done. Maybe she'd been too aloof with Oscar. She could no longer recall very clearly the circumstances of his leaving, but his English was not so good and there was a misunderstanding. Alas. Maybe she should forget her pride and take a serious look around the Senior Center one of these days, see if she could get something going. No one too old—the last thing she needed was someone dropping dead on top of her.

That had just missed happening with Mickey. They had had one of their best nights in a long time—that she could still remember though it was almost twenty years ago—and then she woke to find him flat on his back, more still than any sleeper had a right to be, his mouth open in such a dumb grin that she almost said, What are you grinning at? Then she felt the chill coming from his body and covered him up, and she knew. Really she'd known before, from the first instant, but wouldn't let herself believe it. The rest was a blur, her shrieks, the phone, his ghastly silence, the girls running up, and Roy with the children at his heels in their pajamas. "Take them away, take them away," she howled, but no matter how loud she yelled it didn't wake Mickey, usually such a light sleeper.

Sixty-four, three years older than she was. They met at a demonstration when she was still in her teens. Fortunately the other Young Socialists had told her enough about free love so she didn't waste much time. He was so strong, built like a truck, she thought for sure he'd last longer. When they first bought the building—no more Young Socialists then—he carried washing machines and sinks on his back, both of them working like horses for years, the super and the superette he called her, until they could afford to hire help.

At least he lived to see the girls grow up. Their first child, a boy, died at three years old of diphtheria, and it was months before she wanted to get up out of bed. Even then, she waited years before she got pregnant again, with Bea. And he had seen the grandchildren, all except Sara. He didn't care that the first two came from Bea's husband and some Vietnamese whore; when Bea finally got them here, Mickey loved them like his own. At least something good came out of that shitty war, he used to say.

Funny how as you get older, right in the middle you sometimes think this could be the last time, something could happen, a stroke, a heart attack, even to Mickey who was so strong. And it never was. Except the time that really was the last time, she didn't think it, she was so caught up in it. He got her all excited, she almost came from just his hand but she didn't want that, she wanted something better, and then he pulled her up over on top of him and she could feel him thick and hard as a young man. It wasn't always that way toward the end, after all he was no youngster though he always managed, she had to hand it to him. But that night, maybe his body knew something, like it was his swan song. He laughed about it too. Something must've got into me, he said, and, Well whatever got into you got into me too, she said, and there wasn't much more talking because he was pumping away, rocking her back and forth, she could practically feel it right now lying here in the heat if she tried hard, and she did, she concentrated, and then it was first her and then him half a second later but hers was always much longer or else it was two or three run together, she hardly knew, it could seem like it was over but the next minute it was starting again or going into another stage the way they say about missiles. She started before him and finished after him and they were making their noises, and a while later he tried to do it again with the mood still on them but he couldn't get it hard a second time even when she helped. It feels lovely, sweetheart, but it's not doing any good, it's all used up, he said. Come up here to my mouth, he said, and she did, though she was always self-conscious sitting there with all her parts right in his face. She knew she didn't have to be after so many years but still she was, and she gripped the headboard of the bed, and God, he licked and poked until she thought she'd die of it. . . .

By now she had her hands between her legs and was rubbing, not the way Mickey used to but her own special way, moving back and forth, and she could feel that nice flow, even now she still gave off the juices, she could even get a whiff if she leaned over, and the odd thing was with all this remembering Mickey and that last night, what really set her going even at her age was remembering that man who came to fix the boiler, she didn't even know his name, the time Mickey wasn't home and the only time, well, almost the only, she had done it with someone else. That man walked into the apartment—they lived in the super's apartment in the basement then—and no one else was home, the girls in school, and somehow they both knew. She'd always wondered how these things happened with total strangers. There were women in the building who confided in her—as a landlady and super, not to mention a gregarious person, she was in a position to receive confidences, and unlike most supers she was not a gossip—about how they'd done it with the refrigerator man or the delivery man or whoever, but the thing she never understood and never managed to ask was, How,

41

exactly? How did they get from the point of This is where the pipe is leaking, to the point of climbing into bed? These were not scarlet women as her mother would have called them, not even especially good-looking women, just ordinary women like herself with husbands and children, yet there must have been something about them, some word or look that let the fellow know it was okay to make a move. So finally she knew, though it wasn't anything you could pin down. A feeling in the air, a current passing from one to the other. With them it was some joke he made, a little banter, and she responded not as the super, smiling ladylike and polite, but as a real woman ready and willing, a tiny shrug of the shoulders, a movement of the eyes, and he looked back the same way, then a touch on her hip and he said, Oh, sorry, as if it were an accident. And if she did nothing that's what it would be taken as, an accident, but instead she said, That's all right, don't be too sorry, and touched him back, half accidentally, still leaving an out just in case, and then they were at it. This fellow was no Mickey, not sweet and gentle but a little rough, a little bit in a hurry—well, he was on his route, he had other calls to make. He didn't bother undressing her, just helped her yank her panties down and shoved up her dress and one two three, it was coming over her like a storm. It must have been the idea of it that got her excited so fast, grunting and gasping like the whore she felt herself at that moment to be—who would have known being a whore could feel so good?—and before you know it everything was back in place. Good-bye, and thanks, she said, grinning, for doing such a good job on the boiler, and he grinned and said, My pleasure, I hope it breaks down again but I'll tell you, I'm a good fixer, it should last a long time. I wish I wasn't in such a hurry.

It was over that quick, but luckily she had a good memory, for this kind of thing at any rate, so she could go over and over it, from the moment his hand was going up her leg and he was asking, Where's the bedroom? and she was leading him by the hand, almost running. Yes, she could run it in her head anytime she wanted, moving her hand faster, a little bit inside and a little bit outside, in and out together, and oh, she could still, she was still alive, yes, maybe it was those funny green pills she got in the health food store that promised renewed vigor, but whatever it was, she could still make it go on and on, starting it up again when it began to fade, and he and Mickey merged in her mind till she was past thinking, nothing at all in her mind, the feeling crowding everything out and filling her up. . . .

"Oh," moaned Bea. "Oh," as she pulled him closer, farther in, all the way. She wished she could swallow him whole from down there. But this would have to do.

Dmitri was muttering something in Russian.

"What?" she murmured, gripping her legs around him. She didn't want to miss a thing, but he didn't answer. A moment later he collapsed on her like a helium balloon and sprawled across her body. They lay quiet for a while, then he rolled over and pulled the sheet up around them both.

"Are you cold, Dmitri? It's stifling in here."

"It was excessively air-conditioned in the classroom. I still feel the chill."

"How's it going? Did they tell you anything useful?"

"It's fine. I'm an excellent student. Much better than back in Odessa. I pay attention, I don't whisper to the other kids. . . ."

He had a point, Bea thought. School for everyone. For babies under two, for bearded men of forty-five. She herself ran something of an informal school, a school for wives.

"They instructed us in how to prepare a résumé. And how to approach an interview. Don't say too much. But on the other hand, don't say too little. Don't be too aggressive," he said, gripping her breast, "but on the other hand don't be too low-key." He let his open palm barely graze her nipple.

"That's nice, the low-key way."

"You like? How would nine years as a building superintendent look on a résumé? Any teaching job I could procure would be out of the city, Bea, in some little hamlet. So would you come with me? Leave your little day care center here, your, what do they call it, extended family? You could still work. People need to eat everywhere. You could even go back to the viola. I've never heard you play. Bea! Don't fool around now. I want your undivided attention.''

"I thought that's what I was giving you.'' She moved her hand away. "I don't know. Leave the building, the family, the business, everything? Start all over?''

"With me.''

"Yes.''

"Not much compared to all the rest, eh?''

"Yes, much. You know I adore you. You're what makes all the rest possible. I couldn't do anything without you.''

"You could adopt a family wherever we go. Some people who can't manage their lives on their own.''

"You're mocking me. You think holding things together is easy? It's not. You think I'm comical. An absurd old woman.''

"Certainly not an old woman. Look at you, you're beautiful, look at those breasts, those legs''—he flung the sheet off them—''those shoulders, that hair.''

"Are you teasing me?''

"No. I'm loving you. What's the matter? You're preoccupied.''

"I am. But I don't want to talk. Only about love. Let's talk about love. Let's play a game.''

"Like what? The Czar and the Peasant?''

Bea laughed. "What's that?'' Had he played it with lovers back in Russia? she wondered. She would never know. The subject was taboo. There were so many things about him she would never know. How different from Roy, about whom she knew too much, without ever having to ask.

"What do you think? Now usually I would be the Czar and you would be the peasant, but with a woman like you, I'm not sure. You may have to be the Czarina.''

She frowned. "I don't like the way that sounds. Am I so despotic? Can't I be a princess? No one knows, but all I've ever wanted is to be a princess.''

"I've never made love to a princess. You'll have to show me how."

"It's not very hard." She turned to face him, inching her hand down his belly. "What does the ordinary populace feel about princesses?"

He gave his broad, benign smile. "They worship them."

"Very good. You're a bright young peasant. Okay, start worshiping."

Down the hall, Shimmer, aka Sara, was on the phone with her friend Magenta, formerly Maggie. For sleepwear Shimmer wore a long black T-shirt with the sleeves and neck cut out. She sat cross-legged on the bed with only the night table lamp lit. A stick of incense she had bought on the street from the Muslims scented the hot air, its smoke rising in a thin curl that caught in the draft of the window fan and wafted in her face.

"So, you were starting to tell me at the pool. Did you actually do it?"

"Well, I guess . . . well, yeah. I sort of did."

"What do you mean, sort of? Either you did or you didn't."

"Okay, so I did."

"Shit!" Shimmer shouted, then, recalling the lateness of the hour, lowered her voice to a whisper. "So how was it?"

"It was good. Fine. I mean it's, like, hard to describe."

"Try."

"Well, we were sort of fooling around on the bed—"

"Wait, was this at his house or yours?"

"His. I told you, his parents are away for the summer."

"Is he staying there all alone?"

"Yeah. He's eighteen, he's going to college in the fall, so, sure."

"God, what heaven. I don't think I ever spent a night alone in my life. So how did it happen?"

"We were doing the usual stuff and then it just sort of . . ."

"Did he say anything?"

"You mean like could he? No, he just, it was just happening."

"So did you say anything?"

"No. Maybe. I don't remember."

After a pause, Shimmer said, "You're not telling me anything. You used to tell me what you did with the others. Why are you all of a sudden withholding—"

"Because it's just . . . different, Shimmer. I don't know. It's hard to explain."

"Did it hurt?"

"At first it did. Yeah, it hurt, but then once he . . . it, like, stopped hurting."

"So it was good?"

"Yeah. It was not as great as I expected, like you see in the movies, you know, writhing and making lots of noise, but it was pretty good."

"It didn't enhance your communication skills, that's for sure."

"Shimmer, this is something private. You can't expect me to give you a blow-by-blow account." Magenta giggled.

"I don't know why not. You've done blow by blow before."

"You'll see when you do it."

"At this rate who knows when that'll ever be? That's the point. How long am I going to have to wait?"

"When the right guy comes along, you'll know."

"That's fucking terrific. What a line. Have you thought of setting it to music?"

"If you just want the technicalities you can read plenty of books about it."

"I've read books. What I want is a firsthand account from someone I trust."

"Well . . ." Magenta giggled again. "Have you ever seen one, you know, uh, standing up, like, pointing into the air?"

"You mean naked?"

"Yes."

"No, actually. No."

"It's, like, formidable." She pronounced it with a French accent.

"Really."

"Yes, really. It kind of has a life of its own."

"I think I'll go to sleep now," said Shimmer. "I'm tired. While you were being initiated into life's great mystery, I was baby-sitting my grandmother in front of the TV. I mean, my life is one barrel of laughs."

"Okay, so I'll see you at work tomorrow."

"But just tell me, are you going to do it again? I mean, is it a thing you would care to repeat in the near future?"

"Oh sure. I think so. It's, like, part of life, you know what I mean?"

Part Two

•

Ten Years Ago and Onward: The Virtual Family

III

I found our new super!''

Anna's ragged croak came out of nowhere. Bea dropped the banana she was slicing. Five-year-old Sara looked up from her finger painting on the kitchen floor, then, as her grandmother appeared in the doorway, smiled and waved, palm flat and tilting like a fan.

"Mom, you scared the hell out of me. Can't you ring the bell first? A little respect for privacy? Please?"

"What's so private about cutting up a banana, I'd like to know. Okay, I forgot. I was so excited, I couldn't wait to tell you." Anna, in a red sweat suit and gold house slippers, was aglow with satisfaction, the same glow she emitted after bargaining triumphantly with a contractor or wheedling a tenant out of some desired improvement. "I found him at the Ukrainian Social Club. We had coffee and such a nice conversation. Speaks a beautiful English. A beautiful Russian too." She sat down and nibbled from a mound of shelled walnuts on the table. "From there he was rushing off to a meeting of some society for oppressed ethnic groups. A man with a social conscience, even."

"Could you eat the ones from the bag, please? These are all chopped up for a curry. Why a new super? What's wrong with Umberto?"

"Umberto's going to Guatemala to be with his dying mother. Didn't I tell you?" She took a few nuts from the bag, examined them, and put them back. "A week, two weeks, I don't mind, but who knows how long it'll take? I can't wait indefinitely."

"Come on, that's cruel. It's his job. Can't you find someone temporary?"

"I told this fellow it might be temporary, but listen, Bea, I really like him. An educated man from Odessa. A man of good character. If he works out I'm going to keep him. Let's hope Umberto's mother drags on for a while. That's not cruel, is it?''

"Sara, sweetie, here's your banana. I sliced it up the way you like it." Bea set the plate down next to her daughter, absorbed in her art. "Pick them up with this toothpick, isn't that fun? Your fingers are filthy. I don't like doing this to Umberto. Anyhow, if this man is so educated why does he want to be a super?''

"He's so educated he can't find a job, you know the story with these refugees. He was some kind of college professor. Talks like he reads the dictionary. Right now he's a shipping clerk at Tower Records. A super is better, flexible hours, you get to deal with people. And maybe he likes me, Bea, did you ever think of that?''

Here we go again, thought Bea. Anna often fancied herself an object of desire for employees and repairmen. And who could tell? She might be right. Certainly the recently widowed Oscar, their doorman for twelve years, with manners as flawless as an English butler's, was attentive.

"Really?" she asked cautiously. "How old is he?"

"Not likes me that way!" Anna laughed, and Sara repeated her cackle to perfection. "A little mimic we've got here, eh? Making fun of your grandma already? He's around thirty-five, forty. I'm old enough to be his mother. I was thinking maybe for May. He needs some consolation too. He had some trouble back there—I couldn't worm it out of him but I could tell, this is a man who knows what it is to suffer. I don't mean from politics. I mean from love, maybe.''

"Okay, but still. May?''

"May. Your sister. What's wrong?''

"Mom, she's told you many times she's not interested in a man. May is a lesbian, Mom. She's gay.''

"May is gay," squeaked Sara. "It rhymes.''

"Look what you're teaching the child. Is that really necessary, to rub her face in it?''

"Wait a second." Bea poured them coffee and sat down. "I thought you understood. I thought you accepted it.''

"Gay, May, play, tay, fay," Sara sang.

"I accept, I accept. But that doesn't mean it can't change. Nothing in this life is forever. If the right man came along . . ."

"Some things are forever, Mom. This is one of them."

"We'll see. I want you to meet him, give me your opinion. Tomorrow morning, ten o'clock, we'll have a real interview. Maybe Roy wants to come too? We could get a man's opinion."

"Roy doesn't know anything about the building. He can barely change a lightbulb. The two of us will be enough."

"Maybe I can get May to come down."

"Forget it. You know she's not interested in the building. Plus she has her show coming up. She has to finish those heads."

"No! Don't tell me she's going to show those awful things in public?"

"They're very unusual. The gallery is excited about them."

"Why such a talented girl would want to make heads out of garbage she finds in the street is beyond me. She always had to be different. In every way."

"She can't help it. She *is* different. What's this Russian guy's name, anyway?"

"Dmitri. Dmitri Panov. He's been here eight years."

"Eight years? And he still needs consolation?"

"He's a Russian," Anna said. "A man with a heart, not like here they run from one to another in five minutes. But don't get the wrong idea. He's not gloomy at all. Charming. I tell you, it was a pleasure to converse with such a charming man."

"But I have a right to look for happiness." A pregnant pause. "Don't I?"

"I can't answer that for you, Deirdre. That's something you have to answer for yourself."

"Why? I think it's a pretty simple question."

She was a new patient. Relatively new—six weeks. A bit early for this kind of restlessness, but she was bright and quick, though naive. "I think most people would agree with me. I mean, off the record, can't you give me a personal opinion?"

"But that's all it would be," Roy said in his temperate way. "My personal opinion. Your opinion is the one that counts."

"You won't? Okay, I'll tell you my personal opinion then. My personal opinion is you don't have a personal opinion. Maybe you don't have any opinions at all, and what's more, you don't care. Well, why should you? You just do this for a living. You know, from the beginning I knew I should have gone to a woman. It's easier to talk to a woman. But I was so stressed out, and you were the first person they referred me to. And you were in the neighborhood."

Roy cast a surreptitious glance—eyes only—at the clock on the wall behind her. Six and a half minutes left. Better than if she had gotten to her resentment at the start; it might have used up the whole session. Still, it would be dicey to resolve this, even provisionally, in the short time remaining. He should have felt it coming. It went right to the heart of things, to the transference, and to this patient's wish to be cared for. It was crucial and required concentration, usually his strong point. But he had relaxed ever so slightly as the session neared its end.

Not have a personal opinion? He had children not much younger than the girl sitting opposite him in her long flowered dress—Jane had a dress just like it—and combat boots. He had a wife. They were all seeking happiness, naturally. Five minutes to navigate through this gummy web of language—opinions, rights, happiness, God Almighty. What did all that have to do with anything?

"Can't you say something? It's maddening, you know? You probably wouldn't care if I left and never came back. Would you? I mean, how can you talk to a person so intimately and not even care if they walk out?"

She was right, in a way, Roy realized. He had been staring into space. He forced himself to confront the challenging blue eyes. A pretty girl, soft ruddy face with tumbling masses of strawberry blond hair. Long fingers locked and tense. She did not present any exceptional problems.

He would have managed well enough if he hadn't allowed himself a bit of rest.

"If you feel you'd do better with someone else, I wouldn't persuade you to stay. But I certainly would care, though maybe not quite in the way you mean. I'd like to feel I was doing my work well, and if you were disappointed, I'd be disappointed in myself. Look, Deirdre, why don't we get back to what you were saying before? About your boyfriend. When he disappears for days at a time and then returns, how do you respond to that?"

"You still didn't answer me. How could you not have an opinion? What do you think I pay you for?"

"Not for my opin—"

"Call it counseling. So, counsel. I mean, it says that about the pursuit of happiness right in the Constitution. So you won't be incriminating yourself. You'd be in good company—"

"The Declaration of Independence," he corrected automatically, then could have kicked himself. Stupid! Couldn't he let it go? He was no more her civics teacher than her moral adviser. Too many years of giving help with homework.

"The point," Roy said in kindly, measured tones, watching the second hand of the clock, "is not whether you have a right to look for happiness. No one's disputing that except maybe you yourself. The point is, What would make you happy? What do you really want, what's best for you, and what's the best way of getting it? And are you setting up any obstacles for yourself?"

"Oh," she said, somewhat mollified. "Is that it? That simple?"

"It's a big part of it. And maybe not as simple as it sounds. There." He smiled. "You see, you got me to state an opinion." Let her have her small satisfaction; she had worked hard for it, and it didn't compromise the process. "And now I'm afraid we'll have to stop for today."

A close call, but he had recovered himself; his timing was perfect. He had a few minutes to prepare his mind for Donald, who presented quite a different set of problems. With Donald there was no relaxing—neither the opportunity nor the inclination arose.

55

As usual, Donald flung off his jacket, folded it carefully before laying it on the chair, then proceeded to unbutton his collar and yank at the tie as if he wished to destroy it. And he was off. At a predictable point in the hour he arrived at the customary burden of his oratory.

"She doesn't love me. How could she? You know, I was seeing a woman once, this was way before Serena, and one night we were having a fight and I said to her, You don't really love me, and you know what she said? That's right, Donald, because you're unlovable. And it's true. No one has ever loved me, not in my entire thirty-four years. I bet that's a new one for you, Roy. Have any of your pathetic patients ever said that to you before? Never, never, never!"

Donald banged his fist on the small end table for emphasis. The lamp flickered and its tear-shaped paper shade trembled. Even the box of tissues gave a small bounce. Roy made a note, for next time, to move the jade figurine of Buddha out of harm's way; it was all he had left of Lien, aside from the twins, of course. Lovely Lien! He still thought of her sometimes, even though it had been so brief. Her gentle ways, her saucy eyes. Jane was very like her. But Lien had never had a decent chance at life.

"Did you hear me, Roy? I said no one has ever loved me. Earth to Roy! Earth to Roy!" he bellowed.

"I heard you. How could I help it?" Roy said quietly. Donald might well be correct. It would take an unusual person to love him. At once accusing and defensive, sardonic and aggrieved, he sought love in the most unproductive manner. Months ago, early in the treatment, Roy had suggested that it might be unrealistic to expect others to greet his antagonism with affection or to welcome his barbed criticisms. But the suggestion had been ignored. A pity, given Donald's natural advantages. Donald had the sullen, insouciant good looks of a male model. His expensive clothes hung admirably on his lean body. Roy had often wanted to ask where he got the silk ties; maybe the allegedly unloving wife with the beguiling name bought them. His straight hair hung darkly over his forehead, shading his brooding gray eyes; his features were sharp and even; his thin mouth flashed a smile swiftly and arbitrarily, as if generated by a faulty switch. A faintly sinister smile. He might be attractive to women, Roy mused, if only he would remain silent. But Donald was loquacious.

"Why don't you answer then? What do you think of that?"

"You mean about no one loving you? How can I respond to that, Donald? I don't have that kind of information. I would hazard a guess that you're exaggerating. Almost everyone has been loved by someone."

"Do you think all parents love their children?" His mood abruptly changed. Boyish, plaintive, he leaned forward, brushing the mobile hair off his forehead.

"That's another question that's impossible to answer. I suppose the great majority do."

"You're so cagey, Roy. Do they teach you that in therapy school? Sometimes I wonder if you learned anything at all. I've heard these days people can just hang out a shingle and do therapy."

Certain patients induced an intolerable craving in Roy. Even though he had stopped smoking, he still kept a fresh pack of cigarettes in his desk drawer. "Would it bother you if I smoke?" he asked.

"It's your office. Go ahead." Donald was more jittery than usual. He crossed and uncrossed his legs, stroked his upper lip, picked at his fingernails. Roy felt uneasy thinking of him wielding the delicate instruments of his trade, which was periodontics. He pictured him in surgery, as Donald called it, his handsome head bent over a helpless open mouth, pink and damply vulnerable like some quivering newborn animal, his restless fingers holding some sort of minuscule sharp instrument.

"It's my office, but if it bothered you I wouldn't do it." He lit up and took a deep drag.

"It ruins your gums. People don't realize. Not to mention all the other effects. Believe me, ten years from now you won't be able to smoke in a public place. They're just beginning to realize how harmful it is."

"Well then," said Roy, attempting a grin, "I'd better do it now."

"People never think about their gums," said Donald, "until they start hurting. They take them for granted." He rearranged himself yet again. "Has it ever occurred to you that if you spread out your gums, both the hard and soft, end to end, they would form one of the largest organs in your body?"

"I can't say that it has." Roy glanced at the clock on the wall. Thirteen minutes more.

"If you go by square inch alone, your gums are larger than your stomach or pancreas."

Roy waited. It was common knowledge that patients with massive resistance, presenting itself in far-flung digression, could in the process supply intriguing or useful information. One colleague had gotten tips on the stock market, another was advised on the best time to sell his co-op apartment; still another had gotten his daughter into Juilliard on the recommendation of a patient who played the cello in the New York Philharmonic. Lawyers, nutritionists, journalists were generous with data. And he had Donald. The gums are larger than the pancreas. Well, Bea might enjoy that.

"But no one knows, or even cares. I don't get any respect. People give more respect to a podiatrist than to a periodontist. They also confuse the names, you know, podiatrist? Do you know how much calculus you're carrying around under your gums right this minute? I bet you don't even floss. Do you?"

"Now and then."

"Now and then won't do the trick. That stuff eats away at the bones and before you know it your teeth are dropping out. When was your last periodontal cleaning?"

"I honestly don't remember. I've never had any trouble with—"

"Ha! So you think. And you're a so-called educated person. Which reminds me, you never answered my question. Did you just hang out a shingle?"

"I didn't realize you wanted my qualifications. I have an M.S.W. and a Ph.D. in psychology."

"From where?"

"NYU."

"Couldn't get into med school?"

Roy inhaled deeply. "I never wanted to go to med school."

"So you say. That's what people always think about dentists and periodontists. Not that they even make any distinction. Dentists, periodontists, one and the same. No one has any idea of the years I spent . . . Have you heard how people talk about periodontists? It's a big joke, that's what it is."

"I've never heard people joking about periodontists." That was a lie. After Bea took Anna to a periodontist last year, she set off gales of laughter at the dinner table, imitating the periodontist's lecture on gum care and reading aloud from the pamphlets he had pressed on her.

"Well, they do. Just this morning I saw a woman who had never had a periodontal cleaning. You wouldn't believe what I found in there. A regular garbage dump. So, just as I'm going in with the probe, she says, Oh, please be careful, I have a loose filling. Can you believe? Listen, I told her, what do you think I am, your hairdresser? I'm a periodontist. That always shuts them up. Well, she wasn't in a position to say much anyway." Donald chuckled at the memory, then his face darkened. "No respect, no love, sometimes I don't see the point of living. I don't remember a whole lot of love as a kid. My father died when I was nineteen—just my luck. Even if he did love me once, who knows if he'd love me now, the way I turned out? He'd probably laugh at my being a periodontist too."

"Why, did he used to laugh at you?"

"I don't remember. I just assume people will laugh at me. You know that. Or you should by this time. You ought to take notes, you know? And my mother . . . You know how mothers always complain that their children don't call them enough? I call my mother religiously, every Monday night at eight, and she never sounds glad to hear from me. She doesn't nag me to visit. She always hangs up first. I can hear the TV in the background. I think she doesn't want to miss her quiz show."

"You might try calling at a different time, when she's not watching the show."

"Gee thanks, Roy. That's really great advice. Why do I think you never give advice?"

"What about your wife, Donald? That seems the more immediate issue."

"She doesn't have any respect for me either. She won't even come in for a cleaning. I did it once and she says it was too painful."

"Donald. That doesn't mean she has no respect for you. It means she doesn't like having her teeth cleaned."

"She's bored with me. I know it."

"How do you know? Has she said so?"

"I just know! She doesn't have to come out and say it. A person can feel these things. I was just thinking, Roy, you with your M.S.W. and your Ph.D., you get close to a hundred an hour, on average, say—I know you're a good soul, bleeding heart liberal, so you probably have a sliding scale. I average three hundred an hour, if you include surgery. Of course my overhead is a lot higher—what do you have here?" He gazed around the room scornfully. "Nothing. A few sticks of furniture. Books. So why am I here crying to you?"

"Donald, when did you last get the feeling that your wife was bored?"

Donald burst into tears. "One day I'm going to come home and find her gone, I know it. She doesn't say anything, so you can't tell what she's thinking. But any day now she'll decide that's it, she can't stand me anymore. Just like everyone else." He reached for a tissue.

"Okay, Donald, breathe deeply and try to relax. Okay. Do you tell her about your fears?"

"Are you kidding! I don't want to put ideas in her head. Roy, I love this woman so much I don't know what I'd do if she left me. I think I'd have to kill myself."

"Do you let her know how much you love her?"

Donald shook his head.

Roy glanced at the clock again. "I'm afraid we'll have to stop now."

Donald was always docile about ending the hour, unlike otherwise more tractable patients. Bravado and insults aside, he respected authority. Well, naturally, the bravado was an indirect sign of his respect for authority. He wiped his eyes, blew his nose, and reached for his jacket.

"Roy, you know I don't really mean all those things I say. I don't know why I say them. You're my only friend. Really. My only friend in the world.''

They stood up simultaneously. Roy smiled, checking the impulse to pat Donald on the back. "See you next Thursday. And Donald, you might think about what you just said—why you say these things if you don't really mean them."

Even though Bea had a set of keys, she was scrupulous about ringing her mother's bell, to set an example. But Anna called out, "Come on in, it's open." She found them at the kitchen table, speaking Russian and drinking tea out of jelly glasses.

"Dmitri Panov," Anna announced, and the prospective super rose to shake her hand. He was tall and lanky, with a courtly, pensive air, a type one might expect to find in a university library rather than crouched over aging pipes. His hair and beard were streaked with gray; he wore new blue jeans pressed to a sharp crease, a denim shirt, and a tweed jacket.

"How do you do? I'm delighted to make your acquaintance."

Her mother was right. His English was excellent, more than adequate for tenants' complaints and repairmen's double-talk, as well as Anna's demands. Very shortly Bea would grow addicted to the broad Russian *l*'s and drawn-out vowels, the rough gutturals, curiously seductive. He did not resume his seat until she had sat down.

She was not prepared for this. She had expected someone murky and brooding, disheveled, Dostoyevskian, someone pitiful, for whom they would, at Umberto's expense, be doing a favor. Her mother's generous impulses were so rare that Bea encouraged them on principle. But despite appearances, surely there was something terribly and invisibly wrong with Dmitri Panov; a man of his bearing, with that competent alertness, those limpid green eyes, that wry, bemused smile, could find work anywhere. Perhaps he was a criminal on the lam? She had just read a magazine article about Russian serial killers. Was *that* the mysterious grief?

She was strangely flustered, like a young girl who has her hand kissed for the first time. Dmitri did not of course kiss her hand; she only had the sense that he might, under other circumstances. Though she had interviewed numberless superintendents and doormen, Bea could not recall what questions to ask. Anna on such occasions asked few questions, as though any information she did not already possess was worthless; she preferred to lecture future employees about expectations and routines. But today she reminisced about Russia, places and families she hadn't seen since she left as a tiny child. Could she really remember?

Finally Bea roused herself. "Have you had any experience doing building repairs?"

He could handle any problem that arose, he said with a smile: plumbing, electricity, carpentry. What he did not know he would learn from books; he had learned English from books. Besides the literature, *Roget's Thesaurus* was invaluable, his constant companion. Again the wry smile.

"But of course I will provide references." He handed Bea a neatly typed page. "Dmitri Panov," it was headed, "Professor of Modern European Literature." "I like the neighborhood," he added inconsequentially. "I would like to live near trees."

Hardly a qualification, Bea nearly said, but asperity wilted in his presence. Not caution, however. "Do you have a green card?"

"I am a citizen," he said proudly, producing the navy-blue passport. Bea stared at the photograph, then up at Dmitri. It hardly did him justice; he looked wan and strained. His tragic past, no doubt. He had improved since the photo.

"So you want to take a look at the apartment?" asked Anna. "It's in the basement. Not a palace, but not bad either."

Was it settled, then? Was it sufficient for her mother that he was sexy and liked to live near trees? "I'm not sure," said Bea, "we've made it clear that this is probably only a temporary job. Our regular super may be back in a few weeks." Her words gave her a pang of dismay. "If we do take you on, you couldn't move right in. His things are still there, you see. It wouldn't be right. Until we know his plans."

"I understand," he said calmly, weightily, as if accepting the terms of a secret mission.

"You should also know you'd be on call all hours of the day or night. You never know when people may develop problems, and they can be very demanding. It's not an easy job," she said as the three descended to the basement.

Conscientious, she persisted, but it seemed nothing could deter him. "You realize, too, this is the snow season. It's a lot of work, keeping the sidewalks cleared, the steps to the basement. You'd have help, but still . . . Tell me," she said at last, "why on earth would a man like you want this sort of job? Perhaps you might find something in your own field."

"Someday maybe. When, as you say, I pull my act together. Meanwhile . . ." He stepped back, allowing Anna and Bea to precede him out of the elevator. "This appears quite congenial."

As she brushed against him accidentally, moving down the hall— tidy and freshly painted, thanks to the punctilious, if surly, Umberto— Bea felt a slight electric shock travel through her.

"I had a woman today, she was complaining before I even began. Everyone exaggerates. They think they're feeling something even if I pump them so full of novocaine I could do brain surgery."

Donald had a tiny brownish spot on his lapel. A business lunch? Did dentists have business lunches? Roy pondered. Surely they had to eat, although if Donald's terror of plaque was the prevailing professional view, they might well refrain. Would they discuss calculus buildup while they ate? Probably not. A busman's holiday, something of the sort. Did they clean each other's teeth, and were they sadistic about it? Or maybe they sought out strangers, to avoid the uneasy mix of personal and professional. Distant strangers. Don't wait up, dear, I'm going for a cleaning. They would board a train or a plane for a nearby city. . . . With effort, Roy squelched his fantasies and regarded Donald. His trousers were ever so slightly creased. His shoes had a few scuff marks. Not good signs.

"The idea of surgery made her uncomfortable, she said. You think you're uncomfortable now, I told her, just wait and see how uncomfortable you'll be if they start falling out."

"I'm sure you're right about all matters concerning teeth, Donald, but there are ways and ways of telling people. Sometimes a more diplomatic approach—"

"I can't. It's not my nature."

"What exactly do you mean by your nature?"

"You know, I'm a nasty person. I don't mean anything more profound than that."

"Have you thought about what I suggested last time?"

"You mean about why I act so hostile to you? I don't know, Roy, it's just kind of irresistible. I mean, you just sit there and take it. Maybe I'm trying to get a rise out of you."

"What would you feel you'd accomplished if you got a rise out of me?"

"I don't know." Donald brought two fingers to his lower lip and moved them in small arcs, as if to aid thought. "Probably nothing. Maybe I'm wasting my efforts. You're so . . . harmless, you know? Other people, when I insult them, there's a risk. They could answer back, or if they're patients they might complain or leave. But you? What could you do? Besides, you're getting paid."

"So you pay for the privilege of insulting me, is that it? But that's puzzling. You do it to others for free. Is it only the absence of risk?"

"You're right, Roy, it is a puzzle. Very clever. I guess you did learn something in therapy school after all."

Roy smiled. He thought of the pack of cigarettes but resisted. Piece of cake so far.

"What about your wife? Are you sarcastic with her?"

"Never, I swear. I'm so nice to her, you wouldn't believe it's me.

Maybe that's why she's bored. Maybe I should try treating her the way I treat everyone else.''

"I don't think that's the solution. You might ask yourself, though, why you're not tempted to treat her badly.''

"Because I love her. It's no big mystery. I don't love anyone else. But it's no use, because she doesn't love me.''

"How does she show that?''

"Come on, Roy. You can be such a bore. Always the same old questions. You're supposed to help me, not interrogate me.''

"The reason I ask those questions,'' Roy replied, ''is to see whether your feelings are a response to an actual situation or to a situation you're creating in your mind.''

"What's the difference? I mean, isn't every situation created in the mind?''

"In a way, I guess so.''

"I took two philosophy courses in college,'' Donald said proudly, even a bit shyly. ''I still remember a lot.''

"Donald, I have a suggestion. You came here, you said, to talk about problems in your marriage. I think we might do much better if you came with your wife.''

Donald sat upright. "You mean bring Serena in here? To talk like—like this?''

"Yes. What would you feel about that?''

"Pretty weird. I can't imagine it. First of all, she'd know that I'm—that I'm afraid, that I think she doesn't love me. And then, well, I just can't picture her sitting here having this kind of conversation. She's not the type.''

"What type do you have to be?''

"Not like Serena. She doesn't really talk. She's not analytical. I don't know what she thinks or feels.''

"This could be a way to find out.''

"I'm not sure I want to find out. You mean we'd all three talk together? Is that what you have in mind? Like, couples therapy?''

"We could do that, or I could see each of you separately. We'd meet together once and see how it worked.''

Donald was silent for a moment. "What's the trouble, Roy, is business that slow? Got to send the kids to camp or something?"

Roy took a deep breath and clasped his hands. "I can only tell you that's not my motive. I really think I could help you better if I saw both of you. If it makes you too uncomfortable, never mind, but why not think it over? Meanwhile I'm afraid we have to stop now."

"You're afraid? What are you afraid of?"

Roy stood up, smiling. "It's just an expression."

"A line you memorized from the book, right?"

"See you Thursday. If you decide to come in with your wife, just give me a call, okay?"

Donald paused at the door, shoulders slumped, then turned to face Roy. "You really think, I mean, just between us, it would be a good idea?"

The unguarded tone took Roy by surprise. "Yes, I do. I wouldn't suggest it otherwise." He gazed a moment at Donald. "But tell me, when you say just between us, what exactly do you mean? Who else do you think is talking?"

"I don't know. I always feel, when I'm sitting there"—he waved his arm—"and you're there, it's like we're in a play or something. Like we're both saying our lines."

"No. It's always just between us, Donald."

"Sometimes I think maybe we could get somewhere if we just talked. . . . Listen, Roy. Would you come out for a drink with me sometime?"

"I, uh . . . Thank you. Maybe sometime. But just now that's not what this is all about."

"Forget it. Happy New Year, Roy."

From the start Dmitri proved efficient and capable. Also gracious, even to the most irascible and repair-prone tenants, a quality one hardly expected in a superintendent. From her years of experience in building management, Bea had come to assume that supers must, possibly for self-protection, be bad-tempered and, above all, elusive. Umberto, the most elusive, did not return, nor did they hear from him. After three weeks a friend came by to collect his things. His mother was doing better, the friend said, and he had decided to remain in his country.

When she went downstairs, frequently, to consult with Dmitri on building trivia, Bea found him reading bulletins from the National Coalition Against Censorship and the Committee to End Oppression of Ethnic Groups, or doing crossword puzzles from a book. He brewed her tea. She hovered near him at the stove as if she were held by a strong thread. One day he turned from the stove and they fell into each other's arms.

Donald and his wife were the last patients of the day. When they were gone, Roy released the lever of the reclining chair and sank back. What a relief to give up all efforts at self-control, even the small effort of sitting upright. He closed his eyes and lay quite still; his insides felt oddly mobile, as if organs had come loose from their moorings. He tried to empty his mind; one of his colleagues from the institute was keen on meditating after arduous sessions, but it usually made Roy drowse off. When he opened his eyes, the light was fading. Shadows filmed the building across the street, and the sounds of cars moving through the slush had thickened. For once he was glad, despite the bleak weather, of the ten-block walk home. It would clear his head.

On the avenue he exchanged pleasantries with Maxwell, Bea's sometime helper, and gave him a dollar. He greeted Oscar at the door and exerted himself to make small talk with the neighbors in the elevator— Mrs. Rodriguez had lavish praise for Jane's baby-sitting skills. Home at last, Roy stamped the snow off his boots and hung up his coat. More than anything else, he wished for solitude, a futile wish. He could hear them from the hall, and when he reached the dining room he found his family already gathered for dinner. Chattering, passing around the food, they resembled the lively TV sitcom families that had so entranced

Tony and Jane when they first arrived; they could stare for hours even before they knew much English. Bea had told him not to worry, it would expedite their learning, and so it had. The mother in those shows was always cheery and competent, if a bit frayed; the children bickered affectionately, with no real malice; never did the father return home profoundly distraught, consumed with lust.

He tousled Sara's hair, greeted the others, and leaned down to kiss Bea's mouth. She hated cheek kisses, said they made her feel like a wife. On the mouth or forget it.

"Hi. I was starting to wonder about you. Everything okay?"

"Fine. I had a long phone call." He fetched a bottle of wine and the corkscrew from the kitchen. "How about you? I didn't get a minute to call."

"Very hectic day." She was cutting up Sara's chicken leg while Sara arranged her peapods in the shape of capital letters. "I have to find some help for deliveries. I can't use that new doorman, Javier, Oscar's nephew. He's got enough to do getting used to the routine." Now that Sara was in school Bea could devote herself to the long-planned catering business; a major difficulty was pacing the work—feast or famine, she said.

Roy regarded them all without really seeing them. He was seeing *her*. He could not think of her by name, for fear it would bring her closer. He hadn't expected Donald's wife to be of any special interest. He no longer recalled what he'd expected—hostile? mousy? as nutty as Donald?—so potent had been the reality. Donald had said she was beautiful, but Roy had not taken that literally. She was large, wide-boned, athletic-looking. Yes, Donald mentioned that she was a personal trainer. She had forthright features, the most enchantingly smooth skin, fair hair casually caught back in a barrette. No jewelry. Bea's long silver earrings, jiggling as she bent over Sara's plate, suddenly seemed tiresome. Serena lived up to her name.

He became aware of the jabbering voices that had barely paused to mark his arrival. The children, he noticed, wore heavy sweaters. Roy began to feel chilly himself.

"If they knew we weren't plain old white bread we'd have a better chance of getting in," said Jane. "This way it's just two more East Coast urban kids. Don't they usually ask for photos on college applications?"

"Not for a long time," said Bea. "They don't want to be racist, or be suspected of being racist. This way it's color-blind."

"Why is it so cold in here?" Roy asked. "Isn't the heat on? Or is your mother embarked on an austerity program?" Anna had been known to go down to the basement at odd hours and reset the thermostat of the boiler; soon enough the super would hear of the problem and restore the setting to legal requirements; meanwhile she reaped an infinitesimal savings and some measure of satisfaction.

"No, she called to say she was cold too. I called Dmitri. I hope to God the boiler isn't broken again. At this rate it won't get through another winter."

"We should have kept our Vietnamese names," Tony muttered, his mouth full.

"It wasn't so cold this morning, was it?"

"It started cooling down around five," said Jane. "Our fingers got stiff when we were making the salad."

"You could put the Vietnamese names on the applications, like middle names," Danny suggested.

"Brilliant as usual," said Tony with a sneer. "That would just confuse them."

"Why? That's not a bad idea," said Jane.

"We should have kept the names anyway. Why didn't you let us keep our names?" Tony asked Bea accusingly.

"Don't you remember? When you went to school you wanted names like the others. You picked names you heard on television. We wanted you to feel comfortable so we let you. Sara, are you warm enough?"

"Well, sure, we were only seven years old. How could we understand? You didn't teach us to understand. You didn't let us keep our heritage."

"Your heritage? What kind of heritage? Your heritage is *The Brady Bunch*. The Rolling Stones. Big Macs. Barbie," said Danny. "Do you even remember anything from before?"

"How do you know what I remember? I remember a lot. And I never played with Barbie or Ken. That was Jane."

"I'm not cold." Sara peeled off her sweater.

"I don't remember much, frankly," said Jane.

"Sara, put that back on. Tony, really, dear, you were so young. I did try to teach you—I went to the library and got books—but you weren't interested. You wanted to play baseball."

"That was long ago. You never tried again."

"Maybe they'll call you for an interview," Danny said. "It won't matter that your math scores are low. One look and you're in."

One look, Roy thought. Could it happen that way? It had never happened before; he was trained; he thought he was immune. He could barely concentrate on his food, even though the tension of the past hour and a half had left him famished. The session itself had not gone well, but he'd been prepared for that. Donald was evasive and bristly, Serena reticent and apparently puzzled by the procedure. "I hate this," she finally murmured. Not with any anger, just matter-of-factly. "I hate trying to discuss such intimate things with a total stranger." Roy had had to resort to platitudes: Think of him as a professional, like a doctor. He wasn't making judgments, merely trying to help sort things out.

"I hate school," said Sara. "And I hate Miss Jackson."

"In the private schools they call the teachers by their first names," remarked Jane. "Miss Jackson sounds so formal. What's her first name?"

"I don't know. I just know I hate her."

Roy turned to Sara with what he hoped was concern, but all he could see was Serena's face, remote, inscrutable. Donald was right about that too. He should give more credit to Donald's perceptions. Very likely he was correct about her being bored. "Why do you hate Miss Jackson?" he asked Sara. "What has she done that you don't like?"

Sara thought for a while. "She's always making us have quiet time. It's not because we're tired, it's because she's tired."

Everyone laughed except Tony. "I can see her point," he said. "Sometimes people don't have to do anything. You just look at them and hate them."

"That's very unfair," said Bea. "She's a perfectly nice young woman. You're all fussing about these applications and Sara just wants to be in the conversation."

"No. I really hate her."

"You could have written something about your background in the essay," Roy contributed. "Did you? I can't remember."

"I did," said Jane. "I showed you."

"I didn't. They'd just wonder why we don't know more about it. That would be worse."

Roy pierced his braised chicken with more force than needed. "So major in Asian Studies," he snapped.

"If the boiler is seriously broken, it could take a while," Bea said. "People will be calling day and night."

"That's assuming we get in," said Jane. "What if we don't get in anywhere?"

"You'll get in," Bea reassured her. "I never heard of anyone who didn't get in somewhere. I hope you're not going to spend the next two months worrying."

"The point is," Tony said disdainfully, "we shouldn't have to major in Asian Studies. We should know that. It's who we are."

"If you feel that way why don't you go back? Then I could have my own room. Cold as it is."

"Danny! What an awful thing to say." Bea set down her glass with a pained expression.

Roy imagined an intimate dinner with Serena. A warm, cozy room. The scent of her close by. Candlelight gleaming on her long neck. Elegant food—though really, there was no faulting Bea's cooking. The chicken was superb, as was the green savory rice. Few restaurants could do better. An intimate dinner with Serena, food supplied by Bea?

"I'm planning to, as soon as I can," Tony retorted. "Anyway, you'll have the room all to yourself when I go to college. I know you can hardly wait."

Bea put her hands to her head. "Stop! Will you both just stop it? This is awful."

"I remember the essays now. I thought they were very good," said Roy, but his attempt to help was ignored.

"It's just ordinary sibling rivalry, Mom," said Jane. "Except in our case it's more complicated."

"I don't want to go to school anymore." Sara poked her finger in the mound of rice on her plate. "We always have to line up."

"That reminds me, Roy. Next Wednesday is Open School Night. Can you go? I have to do a big corporate party. It would really be hard. You can meet the hateful Miss Jackson."

Serena's silence might have meant many things—wariness, self-possession, boredom. Or she had simply closed the books on the marriage. Roy couldn't tell. Why had she agreed to come to the session? Only to please Donald? If she was finished with him, then why bother to please him?

"Roy?"

"What? I'm sorry, I didn't hear you."

"Open School Night." As Bea repeated her request, the doorbell rang and she leaped up to answer. The children lapsed into silence, as if their contentiousness were no more than a performance for her benefit. Despite his relief Roy was slightly injured: Was he not worth performing for? She returned with Dmitri in her wake, who didn't seem at all cold in his usual blue denim shirt and jeans. Small wonder—it was enviably warm in the basement. Dmitri also had the dazed look of someone newly awakened; well, a single man could nap whenever he felt like it. Roy would enjoy lying down himself, but he must make some time for Danny, too often overlooked amid the others' clamor.

"Forgive me for disturbing your dinner. I checked a few of the radiators but there was nothing amiss. It must be the boiler. I'll have a gander at yours to be sure." Dmitri tipped the radiator but there was no gurgle of water, nor any hiss of steam.

"Have a seat while you're here. Have you had dinner?" Bea asked.

He wasn't hungry, he said, but sociably pulled up a chair. "This does not look good, Bea. The boiler, I mean, not the dinner. The dinner looks very good." Everyone smiled, even Tony. The man had a way about him. Strange that he would want to bury himself in that basement. He had once queried Roy intently about social work school, but apparently his interest had subsided. "It'll have to be turned off, I suspect. I hope not for any significant duration."

"We can't turn off the boiler in this weather. That means no hot water too. The tenants will be up in arms. And after a day or so it'll be frigid."

"Nothing compared to a Russian winter."

"People here are not used to Russian winters. That is not our standard of measurement. Anyone for some lemon chiffon pie? Sara, it's your favorite."

"Do I have to go to school tomorrow?"

"Yes, school is every day. You're a big girl now. But Daddy will talk to Miss Jackson. Roy, you never said. Can you go next Wednesday?"

"Yes, all right. Remind me the night before, will you?"

"Wednesday is my track meet," said Danny. "I told you last week."

"So you did. I remember. Okay, look, we'll work something out." He stood up, exhausted. "I must lie down for a while."

Before he was out of the room the doorbell rang again, followed by the sound of the key.

"Did you call him, Bea?" As usual, Anna's voice preceded her entrance. "Oh, here you are," she addressed Dmitri. "This is very nice, all of you sitting here like one happy family—hello, hello, all you lovely children—and meanwhile the building is becoming an igloo. My phone is ringing off the hook with complaints. They say you're not home."

Dmitri rose with slow grace. "I was checking the radiators before I summoned help. All will be well, my dear Anna. Bea, may I use the phone in the kitchen?"

"Don't you my dear Anna me," Anna called after him. "Save your sweet talk for the boiler men." But Roy could see she was flattered. Earlier supers had never dared to address her so informally, and even Oscar, her personal favorite among the staff, was unfailingly correct, if not cowed.

Anna took the chair Dmitri had vacated. "That man is not working out the way I expected," she muttered, and reached over to Sara's plate for a morsel of chicken.

"Would you like some dinner, Mom? There's plenty more. That's Sara's dinner."

"I'm not hungry, I just like to pick."

"It's okay," said Sara. "I'm finished anyway."

"Don't fire Dmitri, Grandma," said Jane. "He promised to teach me Russian."

"What do you want to learn Russian for? You're in America."

"She's right," said Tony. "If anything, you should learn Vietnamese."

"You're like a broken record, you know?" said Danny. "What good is Vietnamese going to do? We don't even have diplomatic relations with them."

"Oh, since when did you become the expert on international affairs?" said Tony.

"You think I don't know anything. You'd be surprised."

"I would, you're right."

"Stop it," said Roy, from the hall door. "All of you. I don't want to hear another word from any of you."

"It doesn't make any difference whether I talk or not. No one ever listens," said Danny.

Sara was in tears. "I didn't even say anything. Why can't I talk?"

"Oh, never mind. Talk all you want. I'm going to lie down."

"What's with you?" asked Anna. "Came home with a chip on your shoulder? At least you were in your nice warm office. Bea, let me know what happens with the boiler. I'm going back upstairs to have some peace." She stalked out.

Roy left the room and Danny followed him a moment later. Tony announced that he was going to a friend's house. With the large male bodies and deep voices gone, the room suddenly felt spacious and serene. Bea took Sara on her lap. "He wasn't angry at you, darling. He was angry at the boys. Go play in the living room for a while, and then I'll come and read to you. There, that's a good girl."

She sat gazing at the remains of the dinner while Jane cleared the table. "Thanks, Janie. I don't know what I'd do without you."

"Don't sweat it, Mom. In a few years they'll be the best of friends." She stacked plates expertly, having worked as a waitress in camp the summer before. After she disappeared into the kitchen, Bea heard the sound of running water, the syncopated clink of plates being lined up in the dishwasher, against the basso continuo of Dmitri's cajoling voice on the phone. She poured herself a glass of wine. Very soon Dmitri came to sit beside her and took her hand.

"All alone?"

"If you call this alone." She withdrew her hand.

"So careful," he murmured, shaking his head.

"I have to be. It's my family. I can't afford not to."

"You're chilly. I wish I could take you in my arms. Imagine it. I have my arms around you, and you're getting warmer and warmer. All over. Can you feel it?"

Bea smiled. "I'm trying. The spirit is warmed, but the flesh is cold. Are they coming?"

"In an hour or so."

"You're wonderful. Umberto could never do that. Neither could I."

"I have years of experience. Back home we are apprised of how to do these things or we come to grief. Tomorrow, Bea? I faint from lack of love."

"Let's see. . . . If Sara goes to play at a friend's, yes."

"I want a whole evening with you. Come next week, the Opened School Night."

"No, I told Roy I was too busy, and it's true. I won't start doing that. Outright lying, I mean."

He leaned over to kiss her. "Such scruples. Such integrity. How long are we going to skulk around like children, Bea?"

"I don't feel childish. I feel adulterous."

"I feel like the slave girl in the musical. 'We kiss in a shadow, we hide from the moon,' " he crooned. " 'Our meetings are few and over too soon.' "

"You're full of surprises. How on earth do you know that?"

"I am an aficionado of old musical comedy. Did I never tell you? In the shipping room at Tower Records we listened to tapes throughout the night. We kiss in the shadows, Bea."

"What's so bad about that? It's so snug and warm in your apartment, right next to the boiler. Even if it is a little dark."

"I want to 'kiss in the sunlight and say to the sky, Behold and believe—' "

"Shh!" She fended him off just in time, as Jane returned to collect the serving bowls.

"Isn't she a fantastic daughter?" said Bea. "She could run the house on her own, better than I could."

Jane's mild face hardened. "I will never run a household. Never!" At Bea's look of dismay, she added, "It's not that I mind helping out, Mom. But for myself, never. It's not in my game plan."

"What is your plan? I mean, how do you plan on living?"

"I'm not sure. But not like this."

"I shall take my leave of you both."

"I don't blame you," said Jane. "It's warm down there, isn't it?"

"For now, yes, but the cold will seep down to me too. Then by tomorrow morning we'll all be warm again. Bea, seriously, you must convince Anna about the new boiler, or else this will transpire again and again."

"Again and again," sang Jane as she returned to the kitchen. "Tomorrow and tomorrow and tomorrow."

"Maybe she's the one I should worry about," said Bea. "Meanwhile—"

"Meanwhile, Bea, tomorrow. My love. My wild orchid. My landscape with the secret bog."

"Bog?"

"Maybe I made a mistake. Fen, mire? I keep studying the thesaurus."

"What are you talking about?"

He stood musing, then smiled in triumph. "The secret grotto!"

"Oh. That's a bit better. You should be careful. Other women might take offense."

"There will be no other women."

"You'd better go, Dmitri. I love you too," she whispered.

"Oscar!"

He looked up from his small desk in the lobby, where he was sorting FedEx parcels in their bright blue and orange boxes. Anna peered over his shoulder, wondering whom they were for and what they contained, but without her glasses it was no use.

"Yes, Mrs. Anna?"

"Oscar, have the plants been watered today?"

"Not yet. I will do later. After the mail."

"They look a little dry."

"Okay, Mrs. Anna. Right away."

At the front door, Javier, Oscar's nephew recently arrived from Santo Domingo, cast him a look of compassion. Oscar called out something to him in Spanish. She caught the word *agua*.

"When was the last time the hall windows were washed?" She stared long and hard, giving him ample opportunity to notice.

"The windows, they are the job of the super."

"I know. I just wondered."

"I will find out."

Frustrated, she wandered off, circling the lobby, running her fingers over the mahogany tables, bending down to study the Turkish rugs, and scrutinizing the new gay couple over by the mailboxes. The good-looking one must be an actor, she decided; he carried a copy of *Backstage*. Finally she returned to Oscar's post.

"You need anything, Mrs. Anna? The gasman, he goes through the building. The floors, they are wax yesterday."

"Oscar," she said slyly, "don't you notice anything different?"

He looked around in puzzlement. "What? The rugs, they are vacuum the other day, the brass is polish. No bugs. Everything in order."

"I don't mean the lobby," she said with impatience. "I mean me."

"You?" He stood up and removed his glasses. Javier, busy with the watering can, turned to stare. The elevator creaked and came to a halt, releasing the gasman, who waved his hasty farewell and disappeared through the revolving door. "You are feeling okay?"

"I'm feeling fine! I mean my hair. Don't you see anything new?" She patted the side of her head.

"Your hair. Oh. Very nice, Mrs. Anna. New hairstyle?"

"It's the color. How do you like it?" It was called Copper Sunset, and the hair of the girl on the box had a soft, burnished glow. Anna feared hers might have come out a trifle brassy.

"Very pretty. Before was brown, right?"

"More like auburn." The previous color was Autumn Russet, but it had faded to a drab burnt sienna. "You're not a very observant man," she teased. "Were you the kind of husband who never noticed when his wife changed her hair?"

"My wife," he said soberly, "had always the black hair. It never change."

"Ah. Not everyone is so lucky. I felt it was time for a change. I haven't even shown my daughters yet. You're the first one. I wanted to get a man's reaction. Women are so critical."

"Very lovely. Javier," he called for assistance. "*Mira*. You like Mrs. Anna's new hair?"

The young man obediently approached, carrying his watering can, but Anna ignored him.

"Any packages for me?" She nodded at the stack on the floor.

"I don't know yet. Is not all sorted."

"If you find anything, bring it up when you have a break. I'll give you a cup of tea. A sandwich, if it's lunchtime."

"Thank you. For lunch I like to walk in the park. Get out in the air."

"Oh, you like to walk? Even in winter? Me too. Let me know sometime when you're taking a walk and I'll go with you."

"Okay, Mrs. Anna. Sure."

"Don't forget." As she could think of no further reason to remain, she ambled toward the elevator, which two boys with skateboards graciously held open.

After so many years Oscar was still shy with her. She had tried to put him at ease, especially since his wife's death two years ago, shortly before Herb Brownstein from around the corner deserted her for Florida. But Oscar seemed diffident. Still, he was a fine-looking man, with dignity, even if he was on the short side. She preferred tall, although Mike Russo, Herb's predecessor, who had succumbed to a cerebral hemorrhage, had been short also. You had to take what you could get. Oscar was sturdy for his age, still vigorous. No doubt he missed the attentions of a woman. From what she'd heard, Spanish men liked a woman to fuss over them. Well, she could fuss as well as the next one, if he'd give her a chance. There was a lot to be said for a mature woman. With the single men of her age moving away or going downhill fast, she had no choice but to look to a younger man. She didn't mind in the least his immigrant status and his flawed English. Hadn't she been an immigrant once herself? And a member of the Young Socialist League? She could tell him all about it, if only she could break down that Latin reserve. Her sigh mingled with the groan of the elevator cables. Never say die, that was her motto.

Not since his neophyte days had Roy felt so anxious while awaiting a new patient. Nor was it an anxiety that might be alleviated by any of the usual techniques. It was beyond the scope of professional discipline. He straightened books on shelves. He smoked a cigarette, then opened the window to clear the air. A cold blast streaked through him. He even turned on the radio and heard the news headlines—yet another terrorist hijacking, more government scandal—and the weather report. He flipped it off. A blizzard was predicted but he was indifferent, unable to see any future beyond this hour; the coming snow, it seemed, would never be swirling around his head. Or if it were, he would be a different man by then, in a different life.

She was close to ten minutes late. As a rule patients were not late, unwilling to miss a moment of their allotted time. To her, though, the hour was not precious; she sought nothing, came under duress. It humbled, even angered him: to be so stripped of his value, to have his skills, if not scorned, certainly not prized. Maybe there had been a mistake last time—his body chemistry unaccountably awry—and when he saw her today, he would be unmoved. It would be more of a relief than a disappointment. But when she walked in, he knew there would be no relief. He felt the same. More so.

She sat down opposite him, legs crossed, and waited. He noticed her boots, oxblood with a thick medium heel, laced to the knee. Beautiful boots. He felt tenderness even for the boots.

The silence was lasting too long. He invited her, in his customary way, to speak.

"There's nothing I have to say. I told you last time. I mean, this whole . . . seeing you . . . is Donald's thing. I don't see how I figure."

"You're his wife. Of course you figure."

"Look, I don't have anything against you, I know you're just doing your job, but really . . . Donald said you said it would be a good idea if I came, so here I am."

"You've never seen a therapist before?"

"No. Why? You look surprised." She smiled for the first time, and the air immediately lightened. How could Donald find fault with her teeth? They were beyond reproach. "Do you think everyone should do this? Sort of the way Donald feels about flossing?"

"No. It's just that these days . . . Well, maybe so. A lot of people your age have had some therapy."

"Well, you have virgin material. Go ahead. Do your thing."

Was she by any chance flirting? His heart leaped. But he mustn't presume. Above all, never breach professional decorum.

"Suppose you tell me how you came to marry Donald."

"How I came to marry Donald?" She shifted her position. Good.

His instincts were working on automatic pilot. He had unsettled her composure.

"How I came to marry Donald." She repeated the words with the merest hint of irony, a schoolchild preparing to deliver a report. "Let's see. He lived in my building, right across the hall. I ran into him a lot. He was good-looking—he still is. He had nice clothes. I'd just broken up with someone, you know how it is. He asked me to go places and I went. We liked to do the same kinds of things—skating, hiking, we rode bikes in the park. Physical things, you know. He seemed nice. He can be, when he tries. I don't know how he is with you. But he does have his appealing side."

They would make a handsome couple, Roy thought, the sort he saw strolling down Columbus Avenue of a Sunday morning: perfectly groomed, perfectly matched—the contrast of dark and light—with perfect lives. Maybe he had even seen them. But no, they lived down in the East Thirties. Perhaps dentists congregated there, the way therapists did uptown.

"That sounds like a lot of reasons," he noted.

"You're right. I get your point. I don't have a real answer."

"Well, maybe think a little more about it. There's no hurry."

"I don't really like thinking about things all that much."

"Is that why you were reluctant to come here, because you might have to think?"

"What's the difference why I was reluctant?" This time she laughed. "That's just the kind of thing I don't like to think about. I mean, this isn't like school, is it? I never liked school much either."

Roy smiled with her. "No, it's not like school. It might help, though, if you could risk it. You think thinking is dangerous?"

"Yes, frankly."

"What's dangerous is not thinking."

"I've heard that before. But I'm not convinced. I've managed fine so far."

"Are you managing fine? What I mean is, Donald sees some problems in your marriage. So there's a good chance you might see some too. Is that right?"

"Look, the truth is, I don't know why I married him. Just to—to get out of the whole business, you know what I mean? Have it over with and not have to think about it. I don't know. Maybe that's it. Maybe it's not. Anyway, I did it and it's done."

"How do you feel about the way the marriage is going?"

"How it's going? Look, it may sound strange to you, but I was brought up in a very old-fashioned way. Small town. Midwest. My parents were pretty old when they had me. We went to church. You do what you're supposed to and you don't complain. Yes, some people are still like that, believe it or not. You make your bed and you lie in it. I said I'd stay with Donald till death us do part, and that's what I'm doing."

Roy lost his bearings for an instant. He had never heard a patient utter such views. She reminded him . . . yes, of Bea. Would Bea say the same were she asked why she stayed with him? A crushing thought. No, Bea had better reasons. And here he had thought she was the antithesis of Bea.

"Look, Serena." He had to draw a breath after using her name. "I'm not trying to undermine your—your values. But sometimes, if there are obvious problems in a marriage, it helps to reexamine the premises, to ask yourself if you're—"

"Aren't there problems in all marriages?" she burst out.

At last. Her face was flushed. She ran her fingers through her hair, then folded her arms protectively at her chest. "Well? Aren't there?"

"Yes," he said gently, "there are. And we're here to try to deal with the problems in yours." Thank goodness he was getting a grip. Okay now. Way to go. He had a useful dynamic going here. He was even growing accustomed to her presence, could look at her without gaping like a boy face-to-face with a football hero.

Serena got up and walked to the window, where she stood with her back to him, her arms hugging herself, though the room was not cold. Anna was right—his office was comfortably warm and he was grateful. Especially grateful that he hadn't set up his practice in one of the ground-floor apartments in the building, as Bea suggested long ago. He studied the smooth lines of Serena's back as he waited patiently for what would come next. It was often this way; the more distressed they became, the calmer he became.

"Okay, look!" Almost a shout. She spun around. "I am so bored I could die, okay? Do you know a person could die of boredom? Well, they could. Is that what you were waiting to hear? Well, you got it. No one could tolerate Donald, and believe me, I am a very tolerant person. Very. I don't know what he says to you, but in general he has two subjects: teeth and how badly the world treats him. Neither of these is exactly thrilling, especially after a couple of years. You get the picture? So what am I supposed to do? You tell me. He says he'd kill himself if I ever left, and I believe him. He could. I always believe Donald. He's not a liar, and even though he sees the world in a pretty bizarre way, when he talks about himself he's very accurate. I don't want that on my conscience." She turned back to face the window. Roy could see a few flakes beginning to drift down. It was amazing how fast they thickened. Within minutes it could be a real storm. Dmitri would be in his element, wielding the shovel. He waited.

"And he doesn't say it any less since he's been seeing you, I might add. Oh, I know what you're thinking. I should leave anyway, or at least talk to him about it. But I don't know how. And leave him for what? I don't know what I want. I don't know if there's anything better out there. I'll tell you one thing, though. He means what he says."

Instinct told Roy to keep waiting. And instinct, yet again, proved reliable. As Serena burst into tears and covered her face, he could not help thinking, despite his totally unsuitable longing to take her in his arms and console her, how good he was at his work.

He let her weep. He sensed she did not weep often; she did it awkwardly, turned away from him, trying to stop prematurely and then succumbing to a new rush of tears. "Oh, this is so embarrassing," she managed to say, and Roy's stomach constricted with the fear that she might run away. Donald was right. She made you feel she could bolt at any moment. Indeed everything Donald had told him was borne out by this meeting.

"Serena," he said, "how would you like a cup of coffee?"

She looked at him, her face red and blotchy, a disadvantage of the fair-skinned. "Really? I thought that wasn't done."

Roy stood up and grinned. "What's one cup of coffee? I think we can bend the rules that far."

"Donald said you wouldn't have a drink with him."

"That was different. Come on, get your coat. It'll make you feel better."

"It's snowing," she said, plucking a tissue from the box on the windowsill.

"There's a place just down the block." There was also a coffeepot in the closet—supplied by Bea—which he had used for patients in similar distress, but he needed a change of scene. An ordinary setting. She didn't wish to be his patient, after all; that was clear enough. She pulled on her coat, a very smart, long camel's hair coat with a fur collar. Roy resisted the urge to help her. The moment they were out the door she brightened.

He knew something about her now, a number of things. She had shown him the path, so to speak. But he would not abuse his position, urge her into treatment simply to learn the best way to win her. That would be truly reprehensible. He would play by the rules, in a neutral setting, and take his chances. He felt as though he had embarked on an adventure in uncharted territory, and could barely contain his excitement. He wanted to dance through the falling snow, but instead he took her arm—she was still sniffling—and guided her toward the cozy, discreet warmth of the Café Botticelli.

"Are you busy?" Bea whispered into the phone. "Everyone's out. No orders. I thought I might come down."

"Come," Dmitri whispered back dramatically. "Already my heart pounds with anticipation."

She stepped out of the elevator onto a plastic drop cloth. Ah, yes, the painters; she'd forgotten. Dmitri was almost too efficient; all the energy he might have expended on seeking work in academia was devoted instead to the upkeep of the building. A pity. Was it her duty to encourage him more? And risk losing him? The basement was an obstacle course, buckets and pans everywhere, one painter on a ladder, another using a broomstick roller on the ceiling, a third hauling the recycling bins out of the way. Dmitri sauntered from one to the other, pausing to oversee their progress like a landowner at his dacha.

"Ah, you have come. The door is open, please go in. I'll be there in a moment."

Bea sat down on the bed, on which he had spread a red satin quilt. On the night table was a book called *Arctic Dreams,* the place marked by a solicitation from the ACLU, along with a vase of hothouse roses, quite as if he had been expecting her.

She was under the quilt when he entered, unbuttoning his shirt. "A tryst," he said. "What an unexpected pleasure."

"What about the painters?"

"They won't interrupt. Now, my lovely one . . ." He approached. The phone rang.

"Can't you let it go?"

"No. They'll come down. They always do. Yes? . . . Yes, Mr. Gruber, I will be glad to come and attach it, but not for an hour. . . . Why, do you need a shower right away? . . . Good. In one hour." He hung up. "He has acquired a new shower head. With a rotating massage."

"Could you unplug the phone?"

He obliged. "And now . . . But first I must gaze at you." He flung the quilt off her. Luckily the bedroom was snug and warm; the neighboring boiler made a reassuring hum. "Beatrice, I want to drink the sweat from inside your thighs."

"Is that an old Russian expression," she asked, "or did you just make it up?"

He was too occupied to answer. "Bea," he said later, as she lay blissfully on top of him, "Bea, I have been thinking. There are many opportunities for work in Alaska. I have investigated in the library.

They need teachers. We could be pioneers. Erect a cabin. Romp in the snow."

"Maybe harpoon our food?"

"You jest while I am serious."

"You know I can't. We've been through all this. Sara's just started school. And Danny. What can I do but what I'm doing?"

"You know what you can do. You can behave like an honest person and tell him. What do you say—call it quit."

"Quits. I've told you, I could never leave Roy. I don't believe in it. We have . . . something. Anyway, he needs me. He'll have to leave me."

"Who would leave you? That will never happen."

"No, you're mistaken. I have a feeling. . . . Maybe not too long now."

"Don't I need you too?"

"Not really. You just like me."

"Put your hand here." He guided her. "Do you call this like or love?"

Never laugh at a man in bed. Bea knew that much. In any event there was no need to respond, for the doorbell rang and Dmitri sprang out of bed to the intercom. "The elevator inspectors," he announced somberly on his return. "Their visit, too, is unexpected, but not so welcome as yours. Our tryst is over."

It was just as well. Domestic details awaited her like a mound of stones to be rolled up a hill, Sisyphus's boulder cracked into numberless pebbles of trivia. Running the family was like running the building; they were both too responsible to be carefree lovers. Her long-ago idle dreams of a lover—dreams she had never expected or even wished to come true—had featured languorous afternoons, long walks on sun-dappled forest paths. How different this was. And yet, and yet, she thought as she pulled on her sweater and smoothed down the quilt, she had never come close to imagining the erotic delights of Dmitri. If she lost him to Alaska, he would be an indelible memory.

He was at the elevator, chatting with the inspector—baseball, of all things. "Please allow the lady her ride before you begin," he said, nodding gravely as the door slid shut.

"So!" Ruddy and exuberant, his hair dotted with droplets of melted snow, Donald began speaking the moment he entered. "How's it going with her? She won't tell me a thing but you can, Roy, can't you?"

Since he had come in with Serena three weeks ago, Donald had taken on a new bounce, a hopefulness Roy couldn't help but find touching. And saddening.

"You know I can't, Donald. You wouldn't want your privacy violated, would you?" A poor opening. He must do the deed swiftly and cleanly, as honorably as he could, given the circumstances.

"Can't you just— Well, are you sure it's better to see us this way, separately? You said you'd try talking to us together."

"That didn't work too well the first time. Look, Donald, there's something difficult I must say to you."

Donald paled. "She's leaving. I knew it, I knew it! You fucked up, didn't you? At least before you got your brilliant idea she was there, even if she was unhappy. Now look . . ." He punched the tabletop again and again. The jade figurine, souvenir of Lien, had been removed to a distant shelf. "Fucked me over, eh? And I trusted you!"

"No, no, that's not it. She's not leaving, as far as I know. But I haven't made much progress either. I mean, I haven't been able to change the situation. And frankly, I don't think I can. It's not, uh, easy to admit this, and I can fully understand your—your displeasure. Your anger. But I—I find that your problems are beyond my expertise."

"What the fuck does that mean, beyond your expertise?"

"It means I can't work with you anymore. I don't feel qualified to help, and it wouldn't be right to continue when I—"

"You must be kidding. I know what it means to be professional. I deal with patients too. When I don't like someone, I don't tell them I didn't learn how to handle their case. Roy! Roy, I could sue you. I never heard of a therapist firing a patient. I'm the one paying, remember? I'm the one who can get rid of you.''

"This is not periodontics, Donald. It wouldn't be fair to you. Don't you ever get a case you just can't handle? Don't you ever refer a patient to someone else, to a—a specialist?''

"I *am* a specialist! People are referred to me!''

"Of course. I know that. I didn't mean—''

"You mean there're specialists in therapy? That's what you're saying? Each kind of neurotic gets his own shrink? Why didn't you tell me that six months ago? You didn't read the chapter on nuts like me? You were absent that day, is that it?''

"I can understand that you're angry. You have every right to—''

Donald stood up, shaking his fist. "Don't you tell me what my rights are. I know what my rights are.''

"Okay, Donald. Okay.'' There were a few known cases of therapists who had been shot by their patients, several more who had been slugged. But Roy remained calm. Donald was almost certainly harmless. This was simply an unpleasant scene that must be gotten through. In thirty-eight minutes it would be over. "Do you want to sit down and discuss this more—''

"No!'' he shouted. "Don't patronize me! Don't you think I know when I'm being patronized?''

"I'm sorry. I didn't mean to patronize you.''

"You just don't know any other way to talk, right?''

"That may be,'' said Roy. "But—''

"What did she tell you? Did she say terrible things about me, is that it?'' He began pacing around the room; Roy was grateful for the distance. "I swear to God, it's not true. I never laid a hand on her. I don't fuck around, I don't drink too much, I even pick up my socks, for chrissakes. There's nothing worse than what you know from me. If she told you—''

"She hasn't told me anything.'' It was true; they had hardly spoken of Donald. To the revelation that he had threatened to kill himself if she left, Serena had added only that Donald might well kill her, or Roy, or even a patient, if he knew they had had dinner together. Twice. "Let's hope it's a patient, then," Roy had replied. "It's not funny. And it's not right for you to joke about him either." *Touché.* Roy had resolved to terminate Donald's treatment forthwith: he would not risk losing her respect and whatever else she might come to feel. The two evenings with her, plus the protracted cup of coffee, had been as rejuvenating, as invigorating as—as what? All he could come up with were sports and nature clichés: a swim in a cool mountain stream or a walk through freshly fallen snow. But he couldn't recall swimming in any mountain stream lately, and he hated snow; it was all he could do, these wintry months, to trudge home each evening. The feeling, he concluded, required no metaphor. It was the renewal of love, pure and simple. The reclaiming of himself, the self he had imperceptibly lost, what with the entropy of family life. No matter what happened—and the uncertainty itself was bracing—he could not let that slip away again.

"Then why, all of a sudden?" Donald resumed his seat, his tone familiarly plaintive. "How can you do this to me? I don't get it."

"I'm sorry. I really am. But I do think you'll be better off with someone else. It may not seem that way right now, but believe me, there are plenty of excellent therapists who—"

"You know me," Donald wailed. "You're used to me. Who else would put up with me?"

Roy controlled the urge to smile. "Lots of people. I can give you some names if you like."

"At a hundred bucks a shot, sure, lots of people. Okay, I see you really mean it. Okay then, motherfucker. I don't need any names from you. I've had it. And I don't see that it's done a damn bit of good." He rose and grabbed his jacket from the chair. "Thanks for nothing, Roy."

"We still have some time left, Donald. We can talk more about it if you like, so we don't end with this kind of feeling—"

"Go to hell."

Roy did not see him out or shake his hand as he customarily did with patients whose treatment was completed. Once he heard the outside door close, he stretched out on the couch. Because of the aborted session he had more than half an hour before his next patient, a compulsive shopper, now technically known as an overspender. She preferred to discuss her legal problems with creditors rather than her psychological ones, and today he might just indulge her. He was limp with weariness.

"The light is keeping me up," Roy complained.

"I'll be done in a minute." Bea was scribbling on a notepad, planning the menu for a dinner on the East Side to benefit a battered women's shelter; since the guests would be dining to the tune of five hundred dollars a plate, the food had to be impressive, yet not so fancy as to induce guilt. Expensive ingredients in an aura of simplicity. A tangy marinade for the roast and an imported pasta with artichoke sauce might do. A lemon tart? Or a lemon mousse? Yes, lighter, after the meat. She could work out the details in the morning. Perhaps Maxwell might be dispatched to the greenmarket, if he was sober. She switched off the lamp and slid down beside Roy.

"Bea," he said, "can you give me some advice?"

"What?"

"I have this patient. . . ."

How many bedtime conversations had begun with those words? With all his experience and his excellent reputation, why could he not manage his caseload without her assistance? Especially as she often found her solutions simplistic, or intrusive, or in one way or another impracticable. Yet he kept asking.

"Only if I get a consultant's fee."

As recently as six months ago Roy would have given a sexy riposte: "There'll be a special treat," or "The reward will be worth the trouble." Tonight, however, he judged that unsuitable. "You know you're good at this. Give it a whirl. It's a couple. I've seen them both. The woman is thirty or so and she's stuck. She's been stuck in place for months like an animal with a foot in a trap, and I can't seem to make her budge. She's been married four years and she's bored to death with her husband, I mean bored to the point of having fantasies of murdering him in his bed—"

"That's nothing. All women think that now and then."

"Come on, Bea, I'm not kidding."

"Neither am I. What does he do?"

"He's a periodontist."

"No wonder. Remember that wretched little periodontist who told my mother she'd lose all her teeth unless he cut up her gums? I thought she'd faint in the chair. Gum disease, he kept calling it. Like it was cancer or something. I guess that makes them feel important. As if they'd gotten into medical school."

"Bea . . ."

"I mean, the colossal arrogance . . . And she's still got all her teeth. This one, your patient's husband, probably talks about plaque day and night."

"Calculus, he calls it. The first time he said it I got mixed up and thought maybe he was a mathematician. Anyhow, she, uh, needs to get out, but she can't bring herself to leave him. He's such a pathetic case she thinks he'd fall apart. Of course there are complex issues here— I'm not giving you the whole history—"

"Don't bother, it's not necessary."

"But the point is, she's wasting away emotionally. We keep going round and round, but I can't find a useful way for her to look at it. Her rationalization is she feels too sorry for him."

"That's it?"

"Mmm."

"This is a very easy case you're presenting, one of the all-time easiest."

"Really?" Despite his guilt, Roy felt a rush of joy. He had agonized for more than a month before resolving to consult her; could a solution have been so near at hand all the while?

"Yes. It's useless to try to get her to leave. If she's been stuck so long, she's not going to get unstuck, and her instincts about him may be right. Chances are he *would* fall apart. He's got to leave her, not the other way around."

A thud of disappointment. "But how? If he's so dependent and attached?"

"He's got to fall in love. Believe me, he won't have the same scruples. He'll confess, she'll let him off easy, he'll feel guilty—a little guilt and pain will be good for a periodontist—and she ends up the virtuous one, brave and forbearing."

"Hold on. If he's so boring, who's going to want him?"

"Oh, Roy, since when has that stopped any man? There's always a market for a man with a steady income. She married him, didn't she? Sometimes it takes a few months for a bore to show his true colors. She must have some deserving friend. Or enemy." She pulled the blanket to her chin. "Can I go to sleep now? They're coming early in the morning to check the doorbells. The B line is out."

"It's clever, I grant you that. Very clever."

"But? I know. You can't make such a direct suggestion. Especially not such a frivolous suggestion."

"That would be a problem, yes."

"Well, process is your department, Roy. Isn't that what your training was all about? Good night."

Was this something he could take seriously? Like everything Bea said, it did have a bizarre logic. She cut to the quick. He would consider it tomorrow in the clear light of day. But a troubled mind kept him awake. This was a rotten thing he'd done. Perhaps one of the most rotten. As bad as leaving the twins in Vietnam, or maybe worse, because in that case there were mitigating circumstances: he was young and frightened, wounded; there was a war going on. Moreover, since Bea had set things right it really didn't count anymore. The children were grown and thriving, no lasting harm done. . . . He was a good father. This, then, was perhaps the worst.

But he would find a way to live with it. In time, he knew, he would even forgive himself. As he often told his patients: Not all guilt is something you want to get rid of. Some guilt is justified—if, that is, you choose to inhabit a moral universe. Think about it. The problem is not the guilt. The problem is finding a way to live with it. You forgive others, don't you? Find a way to forgive yourself.

Was she sleeping? He couldn't tell. He edged nearer and pulled her close; they still slept entwined though they had not made love in many months. Odd that she never mentioned the absence of sex; she could hardly not have noticed, nor was she reticent. On the contrary.

Bea, despite appearances, was not asleep. As she settled comfortably into his embrace, she tried to estimate the limits of Roy's shrewdness. Safe limits. And so far as she knew, he rarely connected the situations he encountered in his practice with his own life. For the time being, at least, the delicate balance she strove so hard to maintain could continue.

IV

$\mathcal{J}$ane walked briskly across the campus. The air was warm, still summery soft. Everything she saw made her happy—the newly cut lawn where three boys in shorts tossed a blue Frisbee, the Gothic-style buildings whose sunstruck windows gave off brilliant flashes of color, the students moving purposefully in groups of two or three, backpacks bobbing along. Away! On her own! No one earnestly concerned for her welfare. It wasn't that she didn't love them all, or didn't appreciate having a close-knit, stable family; so many girls here bemoaned their parents' ugly divorces, the horrors of joint custody, the obnoxious stepparents. No, for sure she was lucky. Except it was so hectic at home. So much going on, so many people trooping in and out. Painters. Repairmen. Her mother's constantly changing delivery help. Grandma! She grinned, recalling Anna's stinginess, her absurd flirtations, her memory lapses. A few of the girls, used to big empty suburban houses, found dorm life noisy and stressful; for Jane its privacy was a relief. Bliss to have a roommate who went quietly about her business. Bliss to do what she pleased without anyone's being *interested*. At home they were so interested it was enough to make her lose interest.

She was rushing to look up a play by someone she'd never heard of, Clifford Odets, so that tomorrow she could audition for the first production of the Drama Society. Even if she didn't get a part, that was okay. She could work on the sets, sell tickets, whatever. Of course it would be great to get a major role. She envisioned herself onstage, taking her bows to wild applause, a talent scout seeking her afterward in the crowd, calling her name. . . . Someone *was* calling her name. She turned to find Tony racing toward her.

"Where are you going?" he panted.

"The library. Where are you going?"

"I'm coming. From English. It's high school all over again. Write an argument paper. Abortion: pro or con. Capital punishment: pro or con. Vietnam War: pro or con. Ha! I haven't seen you in days."

"I know. I've been busy." She slung her knapsack to the other shoulder. "So, how are the guys on your floor?"

"They're okay, I guess. I haven't really gotten to know anyone. Why couldn't they put us in the same dorm?"

"You know. They like to separate twins." She had to look away. She hadn't told him she'd requested a different dorm, the envelope quickly sealed and mailed before he could see it. He told her everything, while she found she was telling him less and less.

"It doesn't matter. I'm thinking of dropping out."

"Dropping out? That's crazy, Tony. You just got here. Look, let's sit down a minute. Here, under the tree. Now, what's going on?"

"I keep thinking, what am I doing here? What am I doing anywhere? I lie in bed sometimes and . . . I can't figure out what it's all for."

"You thought that way at home too, so you might as well get a degree while you're thinking. You think too much, you know? What about the Asian-American Student Organization? I thought you wanted to join."

"AASO," he said glumly. "Sounds like asshole."

"Only you would come up with that."

"It's just a minority ghetto."

"It's not a ghetto," she protested. "It's a group. They do things. You said you were interested."

"Why don't you join if it's so terrific?"

"Because I don't feel the same as you. I have other things I want to do. We don't have to feel exactly alike."

"How come you're having such a great time?"

"I love being away. I loved camp too, remember? I can't stand watching Mom run around taking care of everyone. I always feel I need to help her. Number one daughter. She does for everyone else, never for herself. Here I can put it all out of my mind."

"She likes managing everything. What else would she do?"

"Plenty. I don't know, have a life. She wanted to be a musician once. Do you know she still has the viola in the back of the closet? Anyway, listen, you've got to get your shit together. Stop being so negative. This is your life, you know?"

"I feel I don't belong here. I keep remembering what it was like before. You know. The air. The smells. Even the food."

"Which there wasn't a lot of. I remember what it was like being hungry. I cried sometimes, I was so hungry."

"Don't you ever think, if it wasn't for that war, and Dad . . . You know he picked her up. I mean, we wouldn't even be here. It's like we're not meant to be here, you know what I mean?"

"Who's meant to be anywhere? The point is, we *are* here."

"But by accident. She was just a—a prostitute. A whore. A tart. A hooker."

"You make it sound like a crime or something. She had to be. A lot of girls were. I probably would be too, if I were there. And you'd do the same thing as Dad. I bet you would. What does it matter now? It happened. You can't make it unhappen."

"But if that's what made us, then, like, who are we really?"

"Anyone you want. No one's stopping you."

"We're here because he paid her. You see what I'm saying? You know, I never told you . . ." He hung his head and pulled up clumps of grass. "Last year I picked up someone on Eighth Avenue and paid her. I wanted to see how it felt. With someone you don't even know or care about."

She looked at him curiously. "I never knew. So what was it like?"

"Awful. We hardly talked. I just, you know, did it. It was like she wasn't a real person. I felt terrible. I walked around half the night, after. I could never tell anyone else these things. You're the only one."

"Maybe you should talk to other people. You stay alone and brood, and it makes you feel worse. I think you like feeling miserable. Anyway, it wasn't like that with them. He loved her. Maybe not the first time, but he kept seeing her, didn't he?"

"You believe that? That he loved her?"

"He always tells us he did. He loved her and he loves us."

"I know he loves *us*," he said dismissively. "But her? He left and got married pretty quick. How could he do that if he loved her?"

"It's not so simple. You think things should be simple and clear, but they're not." She chuckled. "God, imagine their faces if they knew." She bumped his knee with the heel of her hand. "What'd she look like? Old or young? White, black, yellow, or brown? Or half-and-half?"

"I don't want to talk about it. I don't even remember her face. I hardly looked at her. I remember other things."

"Well, whatever she was, she wasn't as lucky as you are. Think of that."

He tossed a clod of earth through the air. "I hate feeling lucky. Look at them all." It was the hour when classes were changing; the paths were crowded. "*They* don't have to feel lucky or grateful."

"How do you know what they feel? I don't mean grateful like groveling. I mean, just accept what you have. It's yours."

"You sound like Mom. It must have rubbed off on you. I don't feel like anything's mine. Except . . . ."

"Me, right?"

"Right."

"Well, I am. But that's not enough. Look, I really have to go. I'll call you later, okay? We can get a pizza or something."

"Okay." He stared, as if he needed something more.

"What?"

"The Thompson Twins are coming next Friday night. Do you want to go? I could get tickets."

"I'm going." Again, that nasty twist of guilt. "A guy in my dorm asked me."

"You have a date?"

"Yeah. You don't have to look so surprised. It does happen."

"That's quick. Do you like him?"

"Maybe. I don't know yet. Why don't you ask someone? You don't have any trouble getting girls."

"I'll see."

She looked back before she opened the grand door of the library. He was still sitting cross-legged under the tree, ripping up clumps of grass.

Danny lay in the dark pondering Cindy Shaefer's ass. He had a clear mental image of it: small and compact and mobile. Because of the coincidence of their schedules—her math class opposite his Spanish class, both of them proceeding to chemistry on the floor above—he could, with the proper timing, often manage to be right behind her on the stairs. The two halves nestling in her jeans were like two perfect . . . what? Honeydews. He was familiar with her breasts as well, from the orchestra, in which he played the trumpet. She played the flute, and when she raised the instrument to her lips the fabric of her T-shirt shifted in a certain way that outlined her tits. But because of the greater opportunity for close study, it was her ass that haunted him.

With his eyes now used to the dark, he glanced over at the opposite bed, flat and smooth, without the usual hulk under the blanket. He would never have imagined he could miss Tony, but the room felt abandoned, as night after night he lay forlorn. All by self, as Sara liked to say. He wondered how it was going for him at college. Even if Tony was busy, he could pick up the phone, it wouldn't kill him. Absence, in its forgiving way, enhanced his brother. He wasn't so bad, really. They got along better alone than with the others around, as if their wrangling were a performance, though it felt authentic enough while it happened. Alone, Tony sometimes told him things. About girls, for one. He'd told him what it was like to screw Lidia Velasquez, and Anita Brown too. How incredibly damp and soft it was down there, how they squirmed and made noise. Other boys told Danny that Tony had done it with Barbara Nowicki. Apparently his brother had had something of a reputation in the senior class; he did it, then dropped them, and the girls turned against him. Well, so what? At least he did it. They let him, even wanted him to. How do you get them to want to? Tony hadn't told him that. He'd probably say it was something you knew by instinct. But that was the point—what if you didn't have the right instincts?

He had hardly ever slept alone in this room since he was around four years old, and it was weird without the sound of his brother's breathing. It wasn't that he was scared of monsters the way Sara sometimes was, only that the air felt strangely thin and cold. Alien. It reminded him of all the secret emptiness in a world that appeared crowded, like the loneliness of packed subways or elevators. Or the opposite—outer space. The dark chill of faraway starry reaches. How lonely astronauts must feel. He would never in a million years want to do that. Imagine if something went wrong and you ended up floating around for the rest of your life. The food would run out, you'd waste away, or if you ran out of fuel you could go zooming down and crash. . . . Unless the centrifugal motion—or centripetal, he could never get them straight—kept you going eternally. But even right here on solid ground, it was amazing how alone a person could feel. Everyone spoke and laughed and argued, but there was always that hollow space inside, a whole invisible world, dark and cramped and inexpressible. He turned on the bedside lamp and reached for the pad and paper he kept on the night table. "My self is as solitary as a star," he wrote, then on a new line: "Shining for no one in space." After some thought he changed the first line: "My self is as sole as a star," which had a better rhythm, and also "sole" was a pun on "soul." That was good. So was the alliteration of the *s*'s. "Shining for no one in space" was wrong somehow; it sounded like it might be shining for someone elsewhere, not in space. Which was true in a way, but still not exactly right. Well, let it go for now. What next? What was the point? "Is there a soul, near or far, To comprehend my hidden face?" He regarded this for a while, then crumpled the page and threw it to the floor in disgust. What rot! On a clean sheet he wrote, "two perfect honeydews." Those words seemed more true, even in their brevity and incompleteness, than the verse he had thrown away. But "two perfect honeydews" was not even a statement, just a little idea. An image. He could never finish this poem anyhow. You couldn't write a poem about a girl's ass, especially a girl you had never spoken to. "Ode to an Ass," he thought, grinning despite his misery. Or should it be "Ode on an Ass"? Neither one would go over very well in Creative Writing. Nor could he picture it in an anthology alongside all those odes to birds or trees or whatever.

At least with Tony gone he could turn on the light whenever he liked. Though Tony might laugh at him for his fumbling at sports and general clumsiness, he never laughed at his late-night writing habit, only asked him to wait till he was asleep so the light wouldn't keep him up. If anyone in school, or even his family, could see him writing this crap they would think he was a fag. Fags were sensitive, weren't they? Most likely the kind of guys who sat up alone at night writing poetry. Maybe he was. He didn't think so, and he certainly didn't look faggy—if anything, he resembled a bear or an ape—but you could never tell. It might sneak up on you.

His father might not care if he was a fag; he was tolerant that way. Still, he didn't think his father really liked him. Oh, he loved him in a vague way, but love and like were not the same. The way he supposed he loved his grandmother, more or less, because she'd been around all his life, but he couldn't actually say he liked her. The only consolation was that his father didn't seem to like Tony any better. Sure, he did all the things a father was supposed to do, but he seemed impatient with their endless boyhood, waiting it out until they became men like himself. It was obvious he liked the girls better, but then who wouldn't? Even Danny liked his sisters better than he liked Tony and himself. Who wouldn't like Jane? She was so damned nice, if he didn't know her so well he would think it was an act. She was hardly ever moody or nasty, and never seemed to have serious problems, though she must. Everyone had problems, or so Danny hoped; the notion of an inner peace that eluded only him was too hard to bear. But whatever Jane's were, she kept them to herself. She'd probably have lots of kids, all happy and normal. And Sara was just a baby, cute and smart, so naturally everyone loved her. But he and Tony . . . And this sense of kinship with Tony—a kinship of the surly and malcontent—became a comfort in the dark of night. The dark night of the soul—that was exactly it. Where had he heard that? He might give Tony a call one of these days.

He crossed out "two perfect honeydews" and crumpled that sheet as well. He wasn't likely to forget it in any case. Maybe now he could sleep. But first he reached into the bottom drawer of the night table for one of the *Playboys* stored there. Did his parents still do it? Most likely; they were barely in their forties and not in bad shape. At times he thought them ideally matched, living in perfect mutual understanding, and at other times, when he glimpsed certain looks cross their faces, he sensed that their cramped inner worlds might be as impenetrable and solitary as his own. He opened to a favorite photo, kicked off the quilt, and adjusted his boxer shorts for optimum convenience. The picture was nothing at all like Cindy Shaefer, but it didn't matter. He couldn't do this so blatantly were Tony asleep in the other bed. The solitary life had its advantages.

Waking in the dark, Bea felt Roy close by. His back, not his front, she quickly ascertained. She pressed close, lacing her arms around his bare chest, slipping her leg between his. Not a provocation to love— not suddenly after so many months; she knew the precise date. Purely affection. Habit. Warmth, above all: Anna maintained that heat was neither legally required nor necessary between 10:30 P.M. and 6:00 A.M.

Roy, wide awake, turned, threw an arm over Bea, and arranged her body in a convenient position. A moment later he shifted again.

"Mmm," she grunted. "Stop moving around so much."

"I have to tell you something."

"What?"

"Wake up first. Bea? Don't fall back asleep."

"I'm up."

"I don't know how to tell you."

"Do you remember the last time you said that?"

"No, when?"

She lay flat on her back, putting space between them. "When you told me about the twins. It can't be anything like that. Those kinds of things don't happen twice.''

"Bea, this isn't a joke.''

"Okay, I'm listening.''

"Don't try to make it easy for me. I don't deserve it.''

She was obediently silent, making him regret his words. Why, after all, shouldn't she make it easy for him if that was her impulse?

"Wait, I need a drink of water.''

"Would you bring me some too?''

He climbed over her body. Her hair was strewn across the pillow as it used to be after they made love. For an instant, nostalgia paralyzed him; then he fetched the water. "Here.''

"Thanks. Is this going to take a lot of time, because I'm really tired and it's almost four o'clock. People kept calling all day about the new cable charges, and then the washer broke down.''

"Bea, there's this woman. . . .'' He waited, but she did not stir. "This woman who has . . .''

She was so still he thought she might have fallen asleep. At last she said, "I can't do it for you, Roy. I don't know the rest of the story.''

He thought of what he advised his patients when they told their stories. Take responsibility. Avoid the passive voice—that of course only to the ones who had enough grammar to comprehend. Begin sentences with "I.'' "It feels incredible even to me but I . . .'' He took a breath. "I've fallen in love with—'' He couldn't bring himself to utter the words "another woman." "With someone.''

"Another woman, you mean.''

He winced. "Yes.''

"Well?''

"Well, what? Aren't you going to react? What do you have to say?''

"I think you need to tell me a little more first. Do you want the light on?''

"No,'' he said hastily. "It's better in the dark.''

Bea half sat up, leaning on one elbow, looking down at him. "Who is she? Not a patient, I hope.''

"Why, would that bother you more? No, not a patient. Almost a patient. She started out as— She's the wife of a patient."

He had never known her so unresponsive. Help me, he urged silently. You tell me the story. But how could she? He needed to tell it to her first, so she could give it back as she'd done with the twins. He had supplied the bare facts, and she returned his story in acceptable form, the form it had kept ever since: You were lonely, Roy, she said. Frightened. You were hardly more than a boy, thousands of miles from home and scared for your life. And you loved her, you really did love her, in a way. The kind of love that happens in those desperate situations. And she loved you too, even if—even if . . . Here Bea would falter, gather momentum, and forge onward. You wanted to do the right thing. Of course you did. You would have brought them all here if you'd been able to. But you didn't know how. You felt lucky to get out alive. And later, well, you didn't exactly forget, but you were so glad to be back safe that you just pushed it out of your mind, sort of.

And in time Bea's version of the story supplanted his own, which was murky and troubling, both more complex and more crude. She simplified. And in simplifying, she soothed. He had told her once, after she analyzed one of his difficult cases in a few pithy sentences, that she could put any situation through the purifier of her mind and have it emerge lucid and tractable. A mental Cuisinart. "Put this through the Cuisinart," he would say with a laugh, offering her some unwieldy tangle. And she always obliged.

But her clarities were never free. They came with obligations. The story of the twins, for instance, didn't end with the telling. Now that you've told me, Roy, we've got to find them. Find them? he echoed faintly. Well, sure. Just talking isn't enough. We've got to do what's right. She penetrated the warrens of the Defense Department, with her fearful tenacity keeping up a barrage of letters, phone calls, even visits, until the children, abstract reminders of his carelessness, materialized. At the beginning, each time Roy looked at them his heart swelled with gratitude to the saintly Bea. Then in time he took them for granted; they became "the kids," along with Danny and, later, Sara. The kids, wrestling in front of the TV. The kids, who needed braces and bicycles. Who's picking up the kids? Those kids make so much noise. Which of you kids finished all the brownies?

"The wife of a patient?" she repeated. He had tried to prepare for any of the variant responses of an injured wife, but Bea was not complying. She was behaving the way he did in session, patiently gathering information before risking a comment. But that mode of behavior was never intended for real life. Didn't she know?

"I was so goddamn conscientious. That was what did it. I wasn't getting anywhere with him alone, so I suggested he bring—"

"Wait a second. Wait just a second. You're not talking about the periodontist, by any chance?"

"Uh, yes."

"Oh, Roy. Oh, shit."

He braced himself for condemnation, but none came. Nor did encouragement, those sweet, motherly prods. "So he came in with his wife." Still nothing. A helpmeet she was not, at this juncture. "Believe me, Bea, it was what any responsible therapist would have done."

"I'm not having trouble believing you."

"No. Okay. So he brought her in and . . . I don't know how to explain it. Something happened."

"Love at first sight?"

Thank God, a trace of acidity. Emotions—his raw material—were easier to deal with than self-possession, which could be irksome.

"I only saw them together twice."

"What do you want? A medal from the Psychoanalytic Institute?"

"I just meant I didn't continue once I realized I couldn't be objective."

"And did she, uh, feel the same?"

Under cover of darkness, he let his face relax into pleasure, if not quite a smile. "I think there was something. . . ."

"You're telling me this guy pays you to fix his marriage and you take his wife? The wife who was so good-natured she hadn't the heart to leave?"

"I think that's a little reductive. I told him I couldn't work with him

104

anymore. Look, Bea, this is not what we need to talk about. I'm just telling you out of—out of . . . because it's only fair. But that's history. It's now, what's happening now.''

"So what's happening now?''

"You're refusing to react, is what's happening.''

"Roy, it's almost four-thirty. In a couple of hours I've got to get Sara ready for school, and the exterminator is coming first thing. I have to take him through the building. Dmitri has an early class. Is this simply a confession or— What is the point? Do I really need to know?''

"Bea, will you forget the exterminator? I want to live with her.'' He thought he heard her gasp but couldn't be sure. It might have been a gust of wind. "I'm in love.''

"I see. All right, I just have to think.''

"Think what?''

"About how we might work this out.''

"Bea, this is not a matter of strategy, of writing to the Defense Department. It's our lives. Our family. Seventeen years of marriage.''

"That's what I'm thinking. You're planning to leave, move out, is that it?''

"That's what I'm trying to tell you. I'm sorry. I'm so sorry. I never thought this could happen to us. But you know things haven't been . . . right for a long time. We haven't—''

"I know all that. But we have to be practical.''

"Before we get practical, aren't you angry? Hurt, resentful, bitter, any of that?''

"You sound disappointed.''

"Maybe I am. I expected . . . something. It's almost—'' "Insulting'' was the word he omitted. "Don't you even care?''

She sat up straighter, plumping the pillows behind her. "Of course I care. How long has this been going on, by the way?''

"A few months.'' Six months, in truth. Four, if he wished to be technical. When did infidelity begin? With the thought or with the act? A thought is an act, in its way. Donald, with his two courses in philosophy, would have an opinion about that.

"You could have told me before.''

105

"I couldn't face the end, is the truth."

"Who says it has to be the end? I don't see it that way. There's too much between us to ever end, Roy."

"But how else . . . ? Divorce is very ugly. There's no two ways about it."

"It doesn't have to be ugly. And it's not the end."

"Are you saying you won't agree to a divorce?"

"A divorce is a piece of paper. I'm not going to fuss over that. A family is something else. There's no need to destroy a family. Where were you planning to go? I mean, do you have plans?"

"I hadn't thought that far. I just thought we'd start talking, and—"

"You know the Blackburns are moving out at the end of the month?"

"What does that have to do with—"

Oh. She was astounding, he had to admit. Either far simpler or far more clever than he knew. It seemed he had spent years trying to figure out which. Indeed, it might have been pure exhaustion, intellectual exhaustion, that had impelled him to Serena. Serena, so sleek and new and glamorous. Ready to be discovered, and in time he would easily discover all. But Bea, his dark, ample Bea, was deeply, perennially mysterious. With his eyes adjusted to the dark, he could see her clearly, one strap of her white nightgown fallen to leave her shoulder bare, her large breasts rising gently with her breathing, the gardenia smell of her skin, her coarse hair wild from sleep. He had an erection. Could they possibly . . . ? No, not after so long, and especially just now; it would not do at all. Still, she was his wife. She had brought his children back to him. They had had two more together. In the delivery room he had watched them push their way out of her, framed by her sturdy legs. He remembered her raising her whole body, arms outstretched, reaching for Danny—the grace of the gesture. He remembered also burying his face between those legs, and the sounds she made when she came, low moans that went on so long—it feels like it'll never end, she would say. It feels like it could go on forever, always newly amazed, gasping. Serena was quick and sharp and somehow remote, her cry almost like a shriek. No, these thoughts were not helping.

"Roy, are you awake? Did you hear me?"

"Yes. The Blackburns."

"You know the apartment. It would be perfect. It's on the seventh floor. You'd still have a view."

"Are you sure you understand, Bea? I want to live with her."

"I understand. It's big enough for two. Unless she's a welder or something of that nature. What does she do?"

"She's a massage therapist. Also a personal trainer."

"Fine, there's that extra bedroom if she wants to have her clients come."

"Bea, please! I'm trying to leave and you're planning my life. You don't even know her."

"Well, I'll meet her, won't I? Don't you think I'm interested in—"

"Bea, this . . . the way you're talking . . . This isn't normal. I'm telling you our marriage is over. This is a kind of denial."

"What you're talking about is sex, Roy, and that's been over for a while. No one's denying that. A marriage is never over. The way I see it."

He tried to recall the Blackburns' apartment. He had been in it once or twice long ago to collect Jane, who was friends with the daughter. Would it be any less drafty, three floors below? "How many rooms is it again?"

They discussed the Blackburns' apartment, its two large bedrooms, its recent renovation—new plumbing and new paint job—its small but adequate kitchen; Serena, unlike Bea, was not much of a cook.

"Think it over. You know what it's like finding a reasonable place around here. The children don't have to lose a father and go through all that disruption just because we don't feel like sleeping together anymore, do they?"

Roy was startled. He had thought it was he who had lost interest. He had even suffered guilt over it. Did she mean she too . . . ?

"Wait a minute, Bea. Is there something going on here? Someone, I mean?"

She gave the low laugh he remembered from happier nights. "It never occurred to you? I thought you were being discreet and civilized."

"Bea! Tell me!"

"That's not the issue now, is it? Right now we need to plan how to manage this. We're not going to be angry, or fight over money, or the kids, or all the things people do. We're going to behave like a family, as we always have. I'll talk to this woman—what's her name anyway?"

"Serena."

"This Serena, and we'll work it out. We'll explain to her that this isn't a connection we can break off just like that. It wasn't only sex between us. We have a life together. She'll understand, if she's a reasonable person. She didn't want to end her own marriage, did she? You had to persuade her. It'll be better for her too, not having to deal with a furious ex-wife. Believe me, this is the way to go. Look, Roy, it's starting to get light. I really must get some sleep." She slid down under the quilt.

"I can't believe you're rolling over and going to sleep after this. This is your marriage breaking up."

"Yes," she murmured, "but life goes on. Or so they say."

He lay down beside her. "Bea. Come on. You can't be sleeping yet."

"What?"

"Who is it?"

"Who is who?"

"The man."

"I'm too tired. It doesn't really matter, does it? I'm not the one who needed a change."

Soon the room took on the gray-rose tinge of early dawn. Roy couldn't tell if he'd slept or for how long. "Bea." He shifted around. "It's cold."

"The heat will come up very soon."

"I'm cold now."

She moved closer so that their bodies were touching.

"I'm still cold." Tentatively, he put an arm around her. No resistance. He pressed closer and enfolded her. Warmth seeped into him. "I'll miss you." No answer. "Does it help to know that?"

A long time passed before she spoke. "I'll be right here."

He heard the bedroom door being pushed open, followed by light footsteps.

"Can I come in?"

Six-year-old Sara, who from time to time would crawl into their bed, had chosen this morning for one of her visitations.

"Sure, sweetie, climb right in," said Bea.

Roy moved over, and an instant later felt his daughter's slight body, encased in her flannel Dr. Denton's, between him and Bea. "Hi, hon," he whispered. "All comfy now?" She was facing her mother and seemed to have fallen asleep instantly, sprawled out so he was pushed to the wall.

"Okay, Mrs. Anna. A fast cup of tea. Then I have my work."

At last! She bustled around the kitchen, triumphant. "Don't worry about the work. If I myself am telling you it's all right..."

"Is too much happening down there for Javier alone. Deliveries, taxis, cable TV man."

"You're a very conscientious person. I can see that. Now, there's chocolate chip or peanut butter. Which do you like? Or take some of both."

"Thank you. You make a good cup of tea."

"This is nothing. You should try my split pea soup." She sat down opposite him. "So tell me, are you living alone since your wife passed away?"

"I live with my sister and her family. The husband, the daughter and son-in-law, and the grandchild. And my niece is expecting again. A little crowded, but I have my own room."

"So you gave up your apartment?"

"My children, one return to Santo Domingo and one move to San Diego. My sister say is not good to stay alone, I must stay with her. It has the goods and the bads."

"She's right. It's not good to live alone. I should know. My husband's been gone nine years now. Although I can't say I've been exactly alone all that time." She produced an ambiguous smile, expressing respect for the dead along with a persisting lust for life. "Some women, being alone doesn't agree with them. It's not their nature, you know what I mean?"

He inclined his head gravely, whether in appreciation or deference she could not tell.

"Some women are not ready to be finished with certain things. I'm sure you understand, you're a man of the world. I've had some companionship, and I don't mind saying I enjoy male company. But as far as alone, I'm alone in the house."

"You have your family here. Is nice for a widowed older lady."

"It is nice, but it's not the same as what I'm talking about. But maybe you have a lady friend. A nice-looking man like you . . ."

He set down his cup and fingered the brass buttons on his uniform. "I go now, Mrs. Anna. I work the extra hours to help out the children and grandchildren. And Mrs. Melnikoff, she wait for me to bring the baby crib from the basement. Her son and the family come for the weekend."

"Mrs. Melnikoff can wait. We're just starting to have a real conversation."

"Thank you for the tea." He rose with finality, standing very erect. "A pleasure, and good day."

"If that's how you feel. I'm sorry you won't stay longer. Maybe another time? I could cook something."

"My sister, she cooks too good." He patted his stomach and laughed feebly. "Got to watch the pounds."

"Oh, no, you're a fine figure of a man. Wait, I'll let you out."

He was at the door before she could say another word.

"You wouldn't believe what the bitch is up to now. Her goal must be to drive me nuts, I swear." Sam paused expectantly and Roy obliged.

"What is she up to?"

"It's not enough that she keeps the apartment and everything in it.

Now it's the kids. Kids are not property, I tell her. They're people. No one owns them. Isn't that right?''

"Sure."

"She says I never paid attention to them so why should I have them summers and holidays? She'll tell it to the judge too. There's not a word of truth in it—you know that—but does that stop her? No. Next she'll be on to child abuse—she's on top of every new trend. You know, before this, Roy, I was just your ordinary neurotic, but now I have real problems.''

Patients like Sam Browder, a heavyset, garrulous, and amiable man around his own age, made Roy feel grateful for his luck. For his sensible wife, about to be ex-wife. Bea might be righteous, but she was never irrational or vindictive. He almost wished she would show a bit of the resentment and anger that were only natural; her decency was hard to take. It was no mere show of good behavior either, designed to make him feel guilty. No, she was the same as always; you would never know their lives were in a state of upheaval. Keeping him from his children was the farthest thing from her mind. Indeed she insisted that the children's welfare must take precedence over their own feelings. What were her feelings anyway? He wished he knew. Sam certainly had the advantage over him in that regard.

"Do you have any idea of what I'm talking about?" Sam asked.

"I do, I do," said Roy. It was safe to take liberties. He had known Sam for years. He would turn up at intervals and come for several months, more out of a yearning for camaraderie, it appeared, than for introspection. Then he would drop out of sight. What Sam wanted, Roy suggested early on, might more easily and cheaply be found over a poker game or at the gym. True, many men had difficulty giving voice to their feelings, but not Sam. What held him back, then, from confiding in friends? Roy had asked. Pride, perhaps? What was it that threatened his pride? But Sam had not responded to this line of inquiry. Although Roy was not the sort of lazy therapist who permitted infinite strategies of avoidance, he had concluded that with Sam the path of least resistance would be the wisest.

"Why, are you divorced?"

"I'm, uh, in the process of a divorce right now, as a matter of fact." To his surprise, the bald statement triggered a rush of shame, as if he were confessing to some less than heinous, yet distasteful offense, like drunken brawling or siphoning money from a trust fund.

"How do you like that? So tell me, are you going through this shit too?"

"Not exactly. Look, I'm afraid we have to stop now. Let me just say, Sam, frankly, it sounds like you need a good lawyer more than a therapist. Make sure you've got someone who's being very firm with her lawyer." Thank heaven that wasn't his problem. Bea was having no truck with alimony. Her business was doing nicely, and rent, naturally, was not an issue. If I run into trouble, she said, I know you're right downstairs. As far as the children, there was no question but that he would do his part. When he assured her of this, she had shrugged as if it were beneath their dignity to discuss it. No, they were not petty people by any means.

Sam rose and rested a hand on his paunch. "I told the lawyer, you can compromise on the money, the assets, whatever. But not the kids. I have to see my kids. They're everything to me. I've knocked myself out for them. And her. And she goes and finds this nutritionist—I still can't believe it. If it wasn't happening to me I'd laugh. Maybe he gave her a love potion. She's always been into the latest food fads and whatnot, so I never gave a thought to the nutritionist. It's not my business what she eats, right? Then I find out what he's feeding her, the motherfucker. It's mortifying, is what it is." He gazed down at Roy. "That's not by any chance what happened with you, is it? I mean, some bastard comes along and pulls the rug out from under?"

"Uh, no. No, it isn't."

"Oh, I get it. It was you, then. Found a bit of fresh flesh, eh? How do you like that, mild-mannered Roy. Well, well."

"I'm afraid we really do have to stop now, Sam."

"Okay. But it sucks, Roy. I'll tell you, it really sucks. Okay, see you next week."

"Good luck, Sam."

V

*R*oy had never described her and Bea had never inquired, so she was surprised when she opened the door. She had imagined a weak, nervous creature, but the rangy young woman who had acceded to her position appeared composed and, had Bea been given to alarm, alarmingly self-possessed.

"You're Bea?" she said.

"Yes. And you're Serena."

A coolness emanated from her, as though she and her creamy clothing had just emerged from a steely underground vault and still kept the chill. She was a medley of pale—milky skin, straight wheaty hair falling nearly to her shoulders, camel-colored slacks and sweater—yet dramatic, with red lipstick and big dark eyes which seemed not to blink to the customary degree, giving her gaze the aspect of challenge. East Side, thought Bea as she led her to the living room, private schools, classy women's college, all of which assumptions were mistaken. Serena—rural Minnesota, state university—relaxed into a soft chair; only her hands were restless, clasping and unclasping. Forty years earlier she might have extracted a cigarette from a gold case, inserted it in a holder, and blown smoke rings. Passing her on the street, Bea might have taken her for a fashion model, but she was not quite gaunt enough, and her face did not show the required vapidity. It was expressive: wariness, even latent anger, lit her eyes and tensed her muscles; curiosity played over the wide mouth. There was the vulnerable point, Bea decided; she must speak to the curiosity. Above all, be discreet. Measure her words. Take the long view.

"Can I get you a drink? A cup of coffee?"

"Maybe a glass of water," said Serena, in a voice unexpectedly thin. "Do you have San Pellegrino by any chance?"

For an instant Bea considered elevating the club soda to San Pellegrino, but refrained. Unless absolutely necessary, dishonesty was wrong and unpolitic. She served it undisguised, along with a tray of crackers and some caviar she'd saved from yesterday's order, should the occasion warrant it. It did. Serena greeted the caviar with approval, almost relief, as if coming upon a friend in alien surroundings.

"I've been looking forward to meeting you," Bea began.

"I'm not sure why."

"It's only natural to be curious about the sort of woman Roy would fall in love with. Don't you think? Weren't you curious about me too?"

"Sure. But I wouldn't have gone so far as to ask you over. I would have lived with my curiosity."

"And now you don't have to. Here I am."

"Here you are." She took a cautious sip of club soda.

"Try the caviar. It's very good."

"Thanks. I'm not hungry."

"I won't poison you, you know."

"Oh, all right." She dabbed a cracker with caviar and bit in gingerly. "So you were curious. So you've seen me. So now what?"

"I get it." Bea was drinking a rather stiff scotch. "You think I must be angry. You think I've asked you up here to make you feel guilty or torment you. Quite the contrary. I thought we could be friends."

Serena gave a meager laugh. "I feel like I'm in a movie or something. But I don't have a script. I have to improvise. Why would you want to be friends with me?"

"A lot of reasons. We'll be living in the same building, we'll run into each other—"

"Speaking of the building, I guess I should thank you for the apartment." Again she dug into the caviar. "This stuff is very good, by the way. It's a nice apartment, and it saved us the trouble of looking."

"My pleasure. This way Roy isn't so far from his children. I'm concerned that they're not too disrupted. You know how it is."

"And not so far from you either."

"Roy and I will always be good friends. How could we not? We're family, after all. But as far as what you're thinking, I'm not interested. There won't be that kind of tension. I'd just like to think of you as part of the family. A new member."

"Part of the family?" This time she laughed out loud, and a few grains of caviar fell onto her slacks. She dipped a cocktail napkin in the club soda and patted the stain. "What is this, orientation? Like joining a secret society? I'm not interested in any tips, if that's what you mean. Anyway, you're still young. You'll probably remarry yourself."

"For the moment I'm content as I am. As far as instruction, I wouldn't dream of it. I never tell people what to do. I mean, what's the point? They never do it. Besides, I can see you'll manage fine."

"I think so too. So what is the point of this?"

"Just what I said. Friends."

"Look, Bea, it's not that I want to be enemies. I like to get along with people. And then the kids—I don't want to make things any harder for them. But friends . . . It's not exactly an ideal setup for friendship."

"You don't trust the situation. Well, I can hardly blame you. It's not the usual thing. But who says we have to do the usual thing? Look what divorce does to families. And it doesn't have to be that way. We can be a different kind of family, if we all behave sensibly. No one needs to get hurt. Just look what happened with your husband. I mean your former husband, the periodontist."

"What do you mean, what happened with my former husband?"

"You mean Roy didn't explain?"

"Explain what?"

Bea leaned forward confidentially. "Roy told me a little about your situation, oh, months ago. Before . . ."

Serena's face grew a shade paler as she sat up, gripping the arms of the chair. "He told you about me and Donald?"

"Not exactly. That is, I didn't know who you were at the time. He presented it as an anonymous case. He's in the habit of asking my advice, sometimes, about his work. You know how husbands do that. I bet yours did too."

"Well, no, he didn't. What could I possibly know about periodontics? Frankly, it seems like a racket to me. Someday people are going to catch on, and . . . Never mind. You mean to say Roy, uh, consulted you?"

"He explained the problem, as I said, hypothetically, and I suggested . . . It seemed only logical to me. You see?"

"I don't know what to say. I'm really stunned. He never told me. . . . I assumed that was his idea. Look, I'm sorry, I'm really kind of . . ." Serena stared at the rug for a while. "Would you have any white wine around, maybe?"

"Sure." Bea returned with the wine and lit a cigarette. "You don't mind, do you? I don't do it very often, but—"

"I stopped two years ago. Go ahead, blow it my way. So you really told him that Donald should be the one to . . . ?"

Bea nodded.

"It's funny, first I thought it was off the wall, and then I thought it might be worth a try. I guess he couldn't very well tell me it was your idea. Or—who knows?—maybe he could. You must have been furious when you realized . . . How did he ever—"

"I wouldn't say furious. I suppose I felt a bit outsmarted. Because, to tell the truth, I'd thought of it earlier myself." She paused. "I mean, I'd thought of it *for* myself."

Serena choked on the wine and coughed briefly. "Are you saying what I think you're saying?"

"I didn't have the will. Or it wasn't quite my style. But it worked for you, I gather. How's he doing, by the way? I never did get the rest of the story. Once I figured out Roy's . . . involvement, it wasn't something I wanted to pursue. But I always felt I deserved to know how it worked out."

"God, you're a sly one, aren't you? He's all right, I guess. We're not in what you'd call close touch. I don't have the same feelings as you do about family. Although Roy sometimes worries that he'll find out and come after him with a hatchet in revenge. Or maybe a periodontal probe." She paused to smirk. "Anyhow, the last I heard he was still with her."

116

"Who was she?"

"Well, you wouldn't believe, but a former girlfriend. Someone he ditched before me. She's the manager of the Gap, not far from where we lived. Donald liked clothes. During the week it was more Brooks Brothers, but for weekends, the Gap—you get the picture. He couldn't go in there, though, because he was afraid of meeting her. He had to go to one further uptown. Anyhow, a word to the wise . . ."

"You tipped her off?"

"How else could I get it started? I didn't tell her everything, but she's not so dumb. I made her promise not to tell. But if she does, well, it'll be water under the bridge by then."

Bea regarded her admiringly, almost as a kindred spirit. "I never really thought about the details."

"No, you left that to me."

"And you managed very well."

"I guess. It didn't even take very long. That kind of shook me up. I thought he was a little abrupt. Oh, sure, he felt terrible. But he said first instincts are sometimes right. I was hurt—I mean, I had to be— but understanding."

"And does he know—"

"About Roy? Not from me he doesn't. A clean break. So I guess I owe my good fortune to you, assuming it remains good fortune."

"I can't take much credit. I'm sure you would have figured something out in time. I've just been around longer."

They studied each other in silent acknowledgment, the way a master and an aspiring disciple might, on first meeting, recognize a mutual affinity, the promise of a fruitful association.

"It's always a gamble, isn't it? Marriage, I mean," observed Serena.

"You'll find Roy is quite dependable."

"That's very good, coming from you. I didn't mean him personally. I meant more the condition itself. Even when it's good, it's never quite what you expected. There always seems to be something missing. I don't know what I could have been thinking when I married Donald. I was on the rebound. Maybe I was temporarily insane. But it didn't take long. Can you imagine having to hear about gum disease all the time? Hi, honey, have a nice day at work? That was all he needed. By plaque possessed. He would have hacked my mouth to shreds if I'd let him. Do you think that could be grounds for divorce? Imminent danger?''

''I've always assumed dentists wanted to be doctors, so the mouth becomes the body in miniature. A sort of microcosm. Did Donald want to be a surgeon?''

''No, as a matter of fact he wanted to be a basketball player. He played in school. But he was too short for the big time. I was a half inch taller than him. He hated when I wore heels. I think he took up periodontics to get back at the fans he never had. I suppose when people are in that chair, the dentist looms tall enough.''

''My mother had a terrible experience with a periodontist.'' Bea told her about the dentist who had pressed a series of surgical procedures on Anna, foretelling her teeth's desertion unless she complied. ''A noxious little man.''

''I probably know him. I must've met every periodontist in New York. They have parties, you know. They have their little jokes. What was his name?''

''Oh, I can't remember. Allman, Yelman, Hellman?''

''Hayman. That's my Donald.'' She seemed unsurprised, while Bea, for the first time during this colloquy, was caught off guard.

''You're kidding. I don't believe it.''

''Maybe I'll smoke one of your cigarettes. Do you mind?''

''Here. Don't you think that's the oddest coincidence?''

''No. It happens all the time.'' Serena inhaled with the profound pleasure of a prisoner released after serving years with good behavior. ''Life is all coincidence.''

As if the gods were rebuking her presumption, there came a prolonged and extremely loud noise like the clanging of a temple gong. ''What's that?'' Serena leaped up. ''Is it a fire?''

''No,'' Bea assured her. ''Either the elevator is stuck or someone's breaking in through the roof door. It's okay, really. The tenants keep going up there and triggering the alarm. Dmitri'll take care of it, or Oscar. Usually I go, but this is too interesting. I must say, I feel a little better about it all now. I always felt a trifle guilty over Donald. It seemed so manipulative. But that son of a bitch deserves anything he gets. My mother asked him some question, and he practically told her to shut up, he wasn't her hairdresser. Come to think of it, he looked a bit like a hairdresser. A pretty boy, you know? Believe me, I feel for you. How nice that once in a while life gives you a chance to wreak revenge."

"Well, it's over now. God, that noise! Listen, I owe you one, Bea. Maybe you'd like a massage sometime? Just let me know."

"Thanks. One day when I'm not so busy. Oh, I have an idea. Maybe you could help my sister. She lives right upstairs. She's an artist and she has a bad back—she's always lifting heavy casts and things."

"No problem. I'm very good with backs. Oh, thank God it stopped."

"It always does," said Bea complacently.

"So you're Roy's new wife?" May leaned her cheek against the edge of the door, scrutinizing. Her smile was more amused than welcoming: Serena wondered if she might have a smudge on her nose or a leaf caught in her hair; she had been repotting Roy's plants.

"Come on in." May stepped aside, revealing a huge room, cluttered yet calm. A purposeful clutter. The walls were covered with very large, square canvases to which the paint clung in dense, glossy glops. They looked wet. They would always look wet, Serena realized. That was the point. Two long metal tables in the center of the room held tubes of paint, rags, pencils, scissors, masking tape, photographs, magazine clippings and scraps of paper, bits of wire, cheesecloth, wadded newspaper, and mugs filled with brushes. On a narrow shelf along one wall was a row of heads, smaller than life size and evidently made of found objects, with hollow eyes, jagged noses and mouths, and spots of color in arbitrary places, eerie and funny at once.

"It's the same apartment as Bea's, isn't it, but you've taken down some walls."

"I also had the ceiling raised a couple of feet. I need the right dimensions and the right light. My mother didn't like the idea but I pressured her until she gave in. Now it's perfect."

"Do you mind if I look at the paintings?"

May shrugged. Serena walked around slowly, taking them in. Anything to escape from the intensity of that look. From her knowledge of Bea, she had—unreasonably, she saw right away—expected May to be a comfortable sort of person. She was anything but. Large and barefoot, dressed in a black smock and leggings, with a broad olive-skinned face and thick, sculpted features, May reminded her of portraits of noble Indians, fervent and austere. The fervor in May's face was not moral dignity, however. The paintings were also intense—violent abstractions with scattered patches of calm. Serena had once dreamed of being a painter herself, but quickly grasped how slight her efforts were. Every time she looked at work that was genuinely good, she remembered her own failings. These were the kind of pictures she would have liked to paint, but hadn't had the nerve or, probably, the talent.

"They have tremendous energy. They're terrific. I'm totally impressed."

"Yeah, people are," said May without much interest.

"And those heads. I've never seen anything like them."

At this, she perked up. "Oh, you like the heads? Good. They're my touchstone. I can tell a lot about people depending on whether they like the heads."

"You mean I pass?"

"Right."

"Are you very successful?"

"Sort of."

"I used to follow the art world but I haven't lately. I guess I should have heard of you."

"It doesn't matter. You want to sit down?" May pointed out a metal folding chair spattered with paint. "It's okay, it's dry."

"So, what about your back problem?"

"It's interesting that you should be a massage therapist. I mean, you and Roy together. He does the mind and you do the body."

120

"But we're not planning to go into partnership."

"Men usually marry the same woman over and over, but you're nothing like Bea. Then again, he still has Bea around, so why not diversify?"

"You're a little like Bea. In looks, anyway. Not, uh . . ."

"You're right. Bea got all the good nature in the family. I'm more like my mother." May padded over to the refrigerator and took out two cans of beer. "I don't bother with glasses, do you mind? Cleaning up is too much trouble."

"Thanks." Serena popped the top and drank. She never drank beer, but her will was numbed; she felt compelled to accept whatever was offered. "I suppose if Roy had wanted someone like Bea, all he needed to do was come upstairs. To you."

"To me?" May let out a guffaw. "Roy can't stand me. And he didn't want anyone. He was perfectly content, or so we all thought. Until he met you."

"Are you angry on her behalf? Bea doesn't seem angry."

"Oh, Bea. She doesn't know what anger is. She's always living in the best of all possible worlds, no matter how it changes. No, I'm not angry. It's true I was shocked. But looking at you, I sort of get it. You're very beautiful. And cold. Bea is too warm for him. You know what I mean?"

"No, actually. Why do you say I'm cold?"

"Because you are. It's not an insult, just a statement of fact. Cold is enticing. I'm very drawn to cold women myself."

Serena cleared her throat. To her horror, she was feeling a warmth in her thighs. "Why is that?"

"Come on, you can't be that innocent. Because of the challenge. Of seeing them thaw. My last lover was an ice maiden. And for the pain. Some of us are in it for the pain."

"The pain? You mean . . ."

"No!" May laughed. "Not whips and chains. Jesus! I mean emotional pain. Don't you know about the pleasures of pain?"

"My previous marriage was pretty painful, and I never enjoyed it. I was happy when it was over."

121

"It wasn't the right kind of pain, then. There has to be a powerful sexual connection to generate the right kind of emotional pain. Maybe you'll have it with Roy."

"I hope not. So, about your back, what exactly is the problem?"

"Oh, let's not talk about my back. It isn't hurting right now. This is more interesting. Isn't it? You're interesting. You look subtle, but in fact you're probably very straightforward."

"Isn't it a little early to start making judgments about me?"

"Not judgments. Speculation. If we get to know each other better I can find out how I was mistaken. Or not mistaken. What do you think? Am I right?"

Serena wished with all her might that she were giving a massage instead of being interrogated. She hadn't anticipated being required to think. She enjoyed her work because it didn't require thinking, or not this kind of thinking. Roy, thank goodness, did not demand this of her; with Roy she could relax. They got along well, sharing a love of comfort both mental and physical. Only her very first love affair had required her to think in this manner; it had been with her high school social studies teacher, a woman also drawn by her beauty and her perceived coldness, and when that affair was over, Serena had renounced introspection as far too risky and likely to lead her off the safe path. May's light taunting reminded her of that teacher, Andrea Albright. Serena had never told a living soul of their affair. By force of will and by accepting the attentions of men, she had managed to relegate Andrea to a sealed cabinet of memory. On the rare occasions when Andrea came to mind, she tried to remember her as Miss Albright, poised at the blackboard listing the evils of colonialism. May was calling forth different memories.

"I think I'm straightforward, yes. I'm not sure what looking subtle means. Frankly, I don't think a lot about those kinds of things. I like to do physical things. Running. Rollerblading. Do you do any exercise? If you don't mind my saying so, you look like you could use some."

"Stretching canvases is enough exercise for me." She seemed impervious to insult. "And sex."

"Sex can't keep you in shape," Serena replied blandly, and drank her beer. The sky outside was easing from blue to gray, and as the light changed, the paintings darkened as well. The air in the room felt heavy. Serena walked to the window and looked down at the park. "The view is better from up here."

May came and stood beside her. Serena didn't turn, only felt her there. "I love this view," she said, "especially the lake and the trees. Sometimes I see people on horseback. When I can't sleep I stand here and watch the park at night."

"It's very warm," said Serena, and lifted the hair off her neck.

"That must be the first time anyone's complained about this building being too warm. I'll open a window."

"No, don't bother, I've got to go anyway. I mean, if you really don't want a massage."

"I don't feel like a massage just now. Maybe another time."

"I set aside the hour. I could have scheduled another appointment. It is work, you know."

"We could take a walk. Then you'd be getting exercise. I know you fitness types—you can't waste time. Okay? I'll just put on some shoes."

"Mommy, is Dmitri your boyfriend?" Sara asked one warm Saturday afternoon in April. She had been lying on the floor with her aunt, both drawing pictures with new pastels. May's gifts of art supplies were always of the highest quality, even though Bea had told her the expense was not necessary for a seven-year-old. Last year Bea had had to confiscate a gift of palette knives, which would surely have drawn blood in time. Now Sara stood up, as if her question merited a more sober posture.

May laughed, and Dmitri, reading a newspaper in the reclining chair, joined in. "Come here, sweetheart. Are you jealous? I'll be your boyfriend too." Sara did not move.

Bea straightened up from watering the plants. "Why do you ask that, dear?"

"Because you go into the bedroom."

"We're not in the bedroom now."

"You are sometimes."

"Dmitri and I are very good friends, Sara. But you're my best little girl and always will be." She went to embrace her, but Sara stepped back, her hands clasped behind her.

"And Jane," she said.

"Of course, and Jane. Jane is my best big girl and you're my best little one."

"Your mother has many close friends," Dmitri noted.

Sara seemed abruptly to lose interest in the subject. She plopped down on the floor again and picked up a pastel.

"I met Serena the other day," May announced.

"Oh. And how was the massage? Did it help?"

"There wasn't any massage, as it turned out. We got to talking and ended up taking a walk in the park. She's an interesting creature. A lot more interesting than I expected. Of Roy, that is."

Bea gave her a warning glance, nodding toward Sara.

"I think I may befriend her. She seems like she could use a friend."

"Are you thinking of making trouble? I detect your troublemaking tone. I wish you wouldn't, May. For my sake, if nothing else."

"Friendship is always good," Dmitri observed from behind his paper. "Friendship is the spice of life."

"Variety is the spice of life," Bea corrected. "And you don't know what she's contemplating."

"I don't even know myself. I'm a creature of impulse."

"That's the trouble. I thought you were still brooding over Valerie."

"Poor Valerie is fast becoming a memory. I miss her help, though. She was a good assistant."

"Serena is my friend," said Bea. "That's quite enough."

"Bea, you've never been the possessive type. And I have so few interests. She liked those heads too."

Sara looked up from her drawing. "If people are divorced they can have a boyfriend. I don't care. I just want to know. Is he?" She nodded toward Dmitri.

"Yes." Bea sank into an armchair, her head flung back. "Yes, he is. All right. Dmitri is my boyfriend." Dmitri reached over to take her hand.

Sara studied them, two fingers in her mouth. "I want to go down and see Daddy."

"Don't you want to finish your picture? It looks really beautiful."

"He said I could see him whenever I wanted, that's why he didn't move away, so I want to see him now."

"All right. Let me call first to see if it's a good time. He might not be home."

"I can call." Sara pressed the buttons, announced herself, then frowned.

"What's the matter?"

"It wasn't Daddy," she said, hanging up. "A man said fuck off, kid."

"People are so awful! You got a wrong number. Give me the phone."

"I'm going." And she dashed into the hall.

"Take the stairs," Bea called as the door slammed. "I don't like her going in the elevator alone."

"The building is as safe as the Pentagon," said Dmitri. "Oscar is vigilant."

"She reminds me a little of Valerie," May mused. "Serena, I mean. But she's more intelligent. *She* would never suddenly remember she was an abused child."

"May, Roy is content. I'm content. Can't we leave things as they are? May? Are you listening?"

All at once came the clang of an alarm. "The elevator! Sara must be stuck." Bea raced to the door, the others following. In the hall they found Sara, flushed and excited.

"Grandma's stuck!" she shouted over the clamor.

"Can't she turn that thing off?" yelled May, her hands over her ears. "We get the idea."

"I'll fix it from the basement. Tell her she'll be liberated in a moment." Dmitri ran for the stairs.

Doors opened and neighbors gathered in the corridor, their hands cupped over their ears.

"Sara, go down to Daddy's. Take the stairs. This is bad for your ears."

"I like it. I want to see what happens to Grandma."

"Where is she, anyway? Mom, where are you? What floor?"

"Between nine and ten, goddammit," came Anna's voice over the alarm. "Hurry up before I suffocate."

At last the clanging stopped, but the silence held its piercing echo for several seconds. The neighbors began chattering as people do in a mild emergency. Sara jumped up and down in delight. "Will she get out? Should we call the fire department?"

Oscar, uniformed and panting, appeared from the stairwell. "Where is Mrs. Anna?"

"Just below us," May said.

The elevator cables creaked. The lighted number, which had stopped at nine, moved to ten.

"You are here, Mrs. Anna," Oscar called, as loudly as if the alarm were still ringing. "Press 'Open.'"

"I pressed! You think I'm an idiot?"

"Press again. Is working now."

Slowly the door slid open, revealing Anna, snarling and red-faced. But the car was almost a foot above the floor.

"I help you out, Mrs. Anna. Careful now." Gallantly, Oscar held out his arm, and Anna stepped down as if from a horse-drawn coach.

"Why can't he keep this thing in working order? It always happens, the first warm day. Where is he?" she shouted, scanning the crowd. "Do you think I pay you to shtup my daughter?"

"He was only reading the paper," said Sara.

"He went down to the basement, Mom," said May. "That's why the elevator started up."

"You are outrageous," Bea hissed. "We should've left you in there." She turned to the curious neighbors. "Everything's okay now.

We'll call the service and have them check it out. Oscar, thank you. Will you put up a notice, please, and see that no one uses it?'' She led Anna into the apartment. "Where were you going, anyway?"

"What does it matter? It's a free country. I wanted to see if Oscar had Javier polish the mailboxes. You know they don't do a thing unless you keep checking."

May chuckled and murmured to Sara, "You should ask *her* about boyfriends."

"I thought you were going down to Daddy's."

"I wanted to see what happened. Is anything else going to happen?"

"No. It's all over now. Go on." Sara headed reluctantly for the stairs. "Now"—Bea addressed her mother—"if you ever say anything like that again, either alone or in front of a dozen people like you just did, I'll move out and you can run this place yourself."

Anna put her face in her hands and collapsed onto the couch. "I'm an old woman, I'm your mother. Look how you talk to me. I just had a terrible experience—what do you call it?—a traumatic experience."

"Traumatic. Not bad," said May. "Where'd you learn that?"

"I keep up with things. Phil Donahue. Geraldo. I learn plenty, believe me."

"You knew you'd get out," said Bea. "You weren't scared, just angry. And in front of Sara, too."

"All right, I'm sorry, I forgot myself. But who ever thought? When I first found him, I was thinking of May."

"Me? I don't want a man. I had all the men I'll ever need before I was twenty."

"You never know. You're just bitter. If the right one came along . . ."

"Mom," said Bea, "I have things to do. Can I get you some tea or anything first?"

Anna rose with hauteur. "No, I can tell when I'm not wanted. Tell your lover boy that the basement dryer is making funny noises, and Mrs. Cavalcante has a broken faucet, and to call the exterminator. I found a huge dead roach in the hall this morning."

"You're running the place. Tell him yourself. You also might thank him for getting downstairs so fast, so your traumatic experience would be brief. And remember to walk up. The elevator isn't working.''

"I'm not senile yet.''

"Just think," said May when Anna was gone. "Someday all this will be yours. The exterminator, the electricians, the property taxes . . .''

"Ours.''

"Yours. I don't want any part of it. I'll sell out. Don't worry, I'll give you easy terms. I'm not greedy. Just send up enough heat, is all I ask.''

"Well, it's a long way off. She's right. She's not senile yet.''

"Do you think Serena is bi?" May asked. "I have a feeling she might be bi.''

"It never occurred to me. I don't think along those lines.''

"I do all the time.''

"I know. But May, really, it's asking for trouble. Can't you look elsewhere?''

"I have to follow my bliss.''

There was a shuffling sound in the hall and Danny entered, in his school baseball uniform and out of breath. "The elevator isn't working. I walked up nine flights.''

"We know. Grandma was stuck in it. I'm sorry you had to walk. Have something to drink.''

"I struck out three times today. They put me out in right field. That's where they put people who are useless. I'll probably be on the bench all semester. It's the story of my life. Last year it was track, and I couldn't do that either.''

"Yes you could. You may not have been the best, but you certainly could do it.''

"Someone was the best. Why wasn't it me?''

"I never excelled at sports either," said May, "but look, I succeeded in another walk of life.''

Danny regarded his aunt as he would some occult specimen. "I don't see how that relates to me.''

"Forget it. I was trying to show some interest.''

"Isn't baseball about teamwork?" asked Bea. "You're part of a team. Everyone has a bad day sometimes."

"It's about hitting the ball when they pitch it to you. That's what it's about. I'm going to take a shower."

"Drink something first. You're so hard on yourself, Danny. Maybe if you were more tolerant, you'd feel better. You might even play better."

"Don't try to sound like Dad, Mom. You can't really pull it off." He left the room and slammed the bathroom door shut.

"The divorce is getting to them," May said.

"Danny was always this way."

"Bea, you keep pretending everything is all right."

"What's wrong with that? Is it better to act as if everything is not all right? How would that help? Anyway, it *is* all right. I mean, however it is, is the way it has to be. Except for that damn elevator. That's not all right." The telephone rang, and Bea picked up instantly. "Yes, Mrs. Chin, it's being taken care of. . . . Yes, as soon as possible . . . We all want it—I'm on the tenth floor myself. I'm sorry for the inconvenience." She hung up. "She called Mom, but she said she wasn't feeling well and I'd handle this. They'll be calling all afternoon."

"Put a message on the machine."

"How brilliant. I never would have thought of that."

"I'll do it. If you're calling about the elevator," May said firmly into the machine, "the news is that the repair service will be here later this afternoon. We're sorry for the inconvenience and will do our best to have it running by the end of the day."

"How do you know they'll be here later this afternoon?"

"I don't, but that's what you've got to say. Haven't you learned anything all these years?"

The phone rang again. Bea and May stared at the machine like scientists awaiting the results of a novel experiment.

"It's not about the elevator, Mom. Pick up if you're there."

"Janie!" Bea grabbed the phone. "I'm so glad it's not a disgruntled tenant. How are you, love?"

May waved good-bye. With relief, Bea sank into the chair by the window to talk to her daughter. The easy child. Every family must have one. How she missed her.

Jane was fine, and school—near the close of her sophomore year—was fine too. She was auditioning for a modern-dress version of *Electra*. Tony was fine too. A little depressed.

"About what?"

"He doesn't need a reason. Life in general. He still wants us to be in the same dorm. He'd share a room if we could, honestly. He's so codependent. The other day, can you believe, he said we should both go to Vietnam after we graduate. But don't worry, I'll keep an eye on him. Meanwhile, how are you, Mom?"

"It's sweet of you to ask. I'm fine."

"And Dad?"

"He's fine too. So is Serena."

"I didn't ask about her."

"Well, you should. She's part of the family now."

"Oh, Mom, come off it. You don't have to act noble with me."

"I'm neither acting nor noble. I'm okay with things as they are."

"Uh-huh. Tell me about it. What about Dmitri? Is he giving you what you need, at least?"

Bea smiled into the phone. "Dmitri is fine. He's talking about enrolling in a computer course."

"Yeah, right. Last time it was acting classes so he could do voice-overs for TV."

"It's not easy, starting life again in a new place. Hold on, I think that's him at the door now." Indeed Dmitri appeared, grinning and breathing hard. He stroked Bea's hair.

"Okay, take care, Mom. Give everyone my love. Even Serena, if you must. Is Danny around?"

"He's in the shower."

"I'll call him later, then."

Bea hung up and took Dmitri's hand. "My boyfriend. What a life."

"The elevator service will be arriving in about an hour. They'll buzz me here."

So May's phone message had been the truth after all. Why, then, did

130

May chide her for assuming everything would be all right? Didn't she do the same with inanimate objects?

"Let's go lie down, Bea. Enough commotion for one day."

"Sara might—"

"We'll close the bedroom door."

*

Anna climbed the two flights slowly, pausing to rest at the landing. She hoped she hadn't looked too awful when she was rescued. Luckily it wasn't the kind of mishap that ruined your hair. At worst her face would have been flushed. She wasn't the type to go pale when she had a scare—pale made you look ancient, half dead. And she hadn't tripped and fallen but, thanks to Oscar, managed to step out gracefully enough. She might have broken a hip like the woman around the corner who slid on a loose rug. You never knew when your turn was coming.

She checked the damage in the full-length mirror. Not too bad. A little powder, fresh lipstick, and all would be well. She ran a comb through her hair, still thick, by the grace of God. Bea and May thought she should give up the arduous monthly sessions with Miss Clairol and let it go gray. Well, they could think all they wanted. Mother Nature could use a little help sometimes. Even Bea should have touched up that gray long ago; maybe she'd still have her husband around. Though, to tell the truth, he was around so much it hardly made any difference.

She turned to peer over her shoulder. From the back, in her jeans and pullover, she looked decades younger; it was always a pleasure to note that she was slimmer than either of her daughters. Finally she phoned down to the lobby.

"Oscar, is that you?"

"Yes, Mrs. Anna. You okay now? Any trouble?"

"No trouble. Every time I call you it doesn't mean there's trouble."

"Good. Then what I can do for you?"

"Would you come up here for a minute? I need to talk to you."

"Mrs., is very busy here. Saturday afternoon, everyone come in and out. And now the elevator, I keep explaining to the people. How about you tell me on the phone?"

"I'd rather tell you in person. Get Javier to take over for you."

"With no elevator, is many stairs to walk."

"Dmitri can turn it on for one trip. Have him set it manually."

"Okay, right away." Was that the tiniest note of irritation? He would soon change his mind.

It was a good fifteen minutes before he rang her bell. "What took so long?"

"Dmitri is out and the elevator is not working, even by manual. So I walk," he panted.

"Oh, that's too bad. Come sit down in the kitchen. I'll give you a glass of water. There, make yourself comfortable. Maybe you'd like a cup of tea instead? Or a little drink?"

"You know I no drink on duty, Mrs. Anna. Water is fine." He drank the entire glass and set it down with a manly thud. She liked his hands, well shaped and hairy, even at the knuckles. "So. What I can do for you?"

"What's your hurry?" She sat down opposite him. "I want to thank you for helping me out of the elevator just now. It was very kind of you and I appreciate it."

"No trouble at all." He smiled graciously. "I am always happy to help out a lady."

She smiled back. "That's really all. I just wanted to show my appreciation." She reached her hand across the table and laid it on his.

"To thank me, you call me to walk eleven flights?" He wiped his brow with a crisp white handkerchief.

"Ten. You started at one."

"You can thank on the telephone. I'm a man of sixty-three years. Soon to retire. Ten flights!" He still had not quite caught his breath.

She removed her hand. "I'm sorry about the walk, but I was only trying to be friendly. I'm surprised at your attitude."

"You are surprise? I also am surprise. I think I go back to work now." He started to get up.

"Wait a minute. Don't go yet. Aren't we friends? I really thought the elevator would work. Last time it worked manually, remember? Oscar, tell me, you're a widower how long now?"

"Three years."

"And you're not lonely? You know you can come up and talk to me anytime you feel like company or a little break. I know how it is. I've been widowed longer than you."

"I know, Mrs. Anna. I'm sorry your husband die so soon. I live with my sister and her family, like I tell you. The daughter and the husband and two children. Is not lonely."

"Of course. I meant lonely in a different way. Are you sure you won't have some tea? Maybe sit in the living room?"

"Mrs. Anna, you are very nice lady, but I have my work. If I no do my work, you no like, right? You no pay."

"Oscar, you don't understand. I'm inviting you." Again she stretched out her hand, but he rose and stepped out of reach.

"I am truly sorry, Mrs., but I cannot be your friend like you want. Is not for me to do."

She stood up to face him. "I thought you were a gentleman."

"This *is* to be gentleman. I can no explain better. You should go to the Senior Center, you find a nice gentleman your own type."

"The Senior Center!" She gasped. "How dare you tell me what to do!"

"Okay, sorry, forget, I go now."

"You go is right. You go and don't come back."

Oscar turned ashen. "I think you make joke."

"I no make joke." She could have bitten her tongue. It must be catching. "You're finished."

"This is no right. I work for you very careful, always do how you like, always on time. Thirteen years, Mrs.!"

"And not one more day. Go!"

*

"That was Jane on the phone just now. She asked if you gave me what I needed."

"And what did you tell her?"

"I didn't tell her anything." Bea smiled and stretched languidly as Dmitri circled his palm over her breast. "Everyone thinks I'm devastated over the divorce. Eaten up with jealousy. My life in a shambles. At this stage, especially, to be left for a younger woman. I don't think I feel devastated, but they make me wonder. Is it denial? What do you think? Am I just putting up a brave front?"

"If I thought that, what would I think of myself? Only you know the truth."

"If we'd gotten together afterwards," Bea said as she helped him peel off his shirt, "yes, then you might be my consolation prize. But that's not how it was." She paused. "Maybe I'm your consolation. Am I? Is that what this is all about?"

"No. Maybe. Is that a bad thing, to be a consolation—what did you call it, consolation prize?"

"It depends. How can I know if you won't ever talk about what pains you?"

"Why speak of sad things? Here everyone believes in talk talk talk. No one has a good word to say for silence. You call it repression. I call it dignity."

"Repression is what you forget. You haven't forgotten anything. It's not dignity when something—I don't even know what—weighs on you all the time and interferes with—"

"Do you feel anything interfering at this minute?"

"No," and she laughed. "Not right this minute. But with people you love, it's a relief to talk. To have things clear. So we're close."

"How much closer could we be? And you don't speak either. When I asked if you would leave him for me, you made quips." He was on top of her, speaking slowly, with long pauses. "Remember?"

"I told you I didn't believe in breaking up families."

"Enough. Talking does not help. You see how it makes me lose my urgency."

The knock at the door, in contrast, was very urgent. It was Oscar. He was sorry to interrupt, but he was so troubled by what had just happened that he had to tell Mrs. Bea.

*

Aha! thought Anna when the phone rang. She had a feeling he would change his mind. She flicked off the TV; she didn't know what she was watching anyway, but the sound of voices always calmed her.

"Mom, what happened? Oscar was just down here. He said you fired him."

"Oh, it's you. I had to. He was rude."

"Oscar, rude? That's impossible. Oscar is the soul of courtesy. You know that. Maybe you provoked him."

"You believe him over your own mother? What nonsense did he tell you?"

"He didn't tell me anything. He said it was for no reason at all, out of the blue. He was very upset."

"Well, of course he wouldn't tell you what he did."

"Then you tell me."

"I can't."

"Well, give him a chance to apologize, then. You can't let him go like that after so long. He's the best doorman we ever had. We'll never find anyone as good."

"This is final. Don't tell me how to run my business. I'm still in charge."

"Fine. You can find a new doorman yourself. I don't want any part of this. It was awful, having to see him so wretched. I was embarrassed."

"*You* were embarrassed. No one ever takes *my* part!"

"Maybe there's a reason for that," said her heartless daughter.

VI

Serena finished lacing her boots and looked up, her face still rosy. "This must never happen again," she declared.

May laughed.

"I'm serious." She pinned her hair back and adjusted her sweater.

"Okay. Next time you knock on the door I won't let you in."

"Aren't you cold that way? It's always drafty in this place. You should put something on. Or at least cover up."

"I will," said May, stretching on the bed. "After you've gone."

"I just came up to visit, you know."

"Fine. Have it your way."

"I thought we were becoming friends. Can't we just be friends?"

"Apparently not." May lazily scratched her right breast. On the rumpled bed, with her hair loose, she reminded Serena of a painting. Something by Rubens, but not quite so soft and pink. Matisse, maybe? Those Moroccan nudes?

"I'm married to Roy. You don't seem to understand. I want to stay happily married to Roy."

"Darling, I'm not arguing with you. You're arguing with yourself. Hit the light on your way out, will you? I'm going to take a nap."

They were playing gin rummy on Danny's bed before the dinner guests arrived, when Sara suddenly said, "*She's* coming."

"She? Who? Who she?" Danny teased.

"You know. *Her*. Serena." She made a face, as if the name tasted sour on her tongue.

"Oh. Well, she has to. They're married."

The occasion of the family gathering was to welcome Danny home for spring break of his freshman year in college. He understood his mother's motives perfectly: she produced these events to keep alive the sense of an intact family. And he had to admit that she succeeded, more or less. As far as tonight in particular, she felt that he had never been sufficiently fussed over; so often, major events had diverted everyone's attention—the arrival of the twins, Sara's birth, the divorce. She wanted to make up for past lapses. Fine. Let her try, if it made her feel good. He would accept the attention.

He also understood Bea's relief that he had outgrown his adolescent gawkiness and melancholy, his fits of self-flagellation. Only there, he thought, she was deceived. It was true he no longer looked or moved like a bear, and had learned the strategies of conversation. Learned how to hide, as he put it. But the space inside was no less cramped and murky, the air no less suffocating. He was still insufficiently loved and no doubt would be forever.

If there was anyone who did love him enough, it was Sara. A sprightly nine years old, she had sat on his bed that afternoon while he unpacked, regaling him with the fourth-grade news. She was the class math whiz; they had seen the dinosaur at the Museum of Natural History; she was sometimes allowed to stay up for *Star Trek;* she had a boyfriend in her class with whom she traded T-shirts. She seemed to have gotten over the worst soreness of the divorce; her complaints about Serena were more ritualized, lighter in weight. Or had she too, at so tender an age, learned to hide?

"I wish he didn't have to take her everywhere."

"Why? Is she mean to you?"

"She tries to act nice. She gives me presents, like when they went on that safari she brought me an African thing for my hair. Once she gave me a massage. Mommy wants me to like her, and Aunt May likes her and she hardly ever likes anyone. But I don't. Do you like her?"

A painful question. What would he feel when he saw Serena this time? At Christmas there had been the same engulfing longing, searing his heart. Ever since he was sixteen and his father invited him down to the new apartment to meet her, the sight of her—so sleek and smooth, so cool, he imagined, to the touch—had lacerated him straight through, erasing in one stroke Cindy Shaefer of the honeydew ass and all the girls he had coveted in secret. Only then it had been worse: he could hardly be near her without getting a hard-on. Now at least his body behaved better, it too having learned some decorum, but the longing had ripened along with him. That his father had this magnificent, aloof yet kindly woman all to himself was intolerable, and Danny's fantasies, no longer shaped by *Playboy,* took the form of wooing her away by feats of charm and virility he could never in a million years achieve. He was mortified by despair. Dr. Whiting, the shrink at school, kept assuring him it would pass. Danny could hasten it along by turning his attention to the available girls on campus. "Someone more appropriate. Yours, not your father's." What Whiting couldn't seem to grasp was that his desire for Serena, however agonizing, was less risky. A safe haven of pain.

"I have gin." Sara threw the last card face down on the pile and displayed her hand in triumph. Gin indeed. Four threes, jack, queen, king of clubs, and seven, eight, and nine of hearts.

"Whoo! You really got me this time. I have, let's see . . . ten, twelve, eighteen points. You're killing me."

"Write it down. And don't cheat."

"What do you mean? I never cheat."

"Well, do you? Like her?"

"She's okay. I don't think much about her."

"You don't need to. You don't live here anymore."

"Do you miss me, champ?" He rumpled her hair.

"Yeah."

As he shuffled the cards, making the waterfall that she admired, they heard the doorbell. "You ready?" He looked her over. "Go fix your hair and wash. We should have helped Mom in the kitchen."

"She doesn't like help."

"We should do it anyway. We'll help clean up, okay?"

"Will you sit next to me?"

"Sure," he said. "Just like before. Remember you used to say you would marry me when we grew up?"

"Come on." She blushed. "I was just a baby."

"Okay, sorry." She was too old to be teased about it. It was a comforting thought, though. He would probably never inspire that wish in anyone else.

"Did anyone ever do that? Marry their brother?"

"In Egypt, long ago. Cleopatra and her brother. She was the queen. And I think in Hawaii—that wasn't even so long ago. In the Russian royal family they married cousins and passed down hemophilia. That's a blood disease. Through the genes. Okay, let's go, kiddo."

Although the food would have served a dozen, the gathering was far from complete. Tony was spending the week bicycling through New England with his girlfriend, Melissa, and Jane was at a performance art workshop. May was in Boston for the opening of a new show. Dmitri might drop by later for dessert; he had enrolled in a class on memoir writing, in the hope of doing a book about his childhood in the Soviet Union, if he could manage to colloquialize his thesaurus-based English.

After the exclamations over Bea's coq au vin had subsided, Danny resolved to be nice to Anna, sitting on his right. Anything to avoid the gaze of Serena, across from him. "So, Grandma, how've you been? Still taking your long walks?"

"It keeps me in shape. At my age it's no good to sit still for too long. But I forget things. Next time you come home, I might not even remember your name."

"But you do now?"

"Don't get smart with me, Danny boy."

"What's my name?" asked Sara.

"You were named after my poor sister. That I could never forget. At least I hope not."

"Grandma, we'll test you. Go around the table and tell everyone's name."

Anna shook her head and frowned. "So this is my future. An object of ridicule."

"Please?"

"Sara," Bea said. "Stop."

"How are things going at school, Danny?" Serena said helpfully.

"Fine." He looked down at his plate. Ten to one the next question would be what was he majoring in.

"Do you know what you'll be majoring in?"

"I'm not sure. Maybe computer science."

"Computer science?" said Roy. "That's a switch. What happened to your music? Your poetry?"

God, if he would only not bring up the poetry! "I still play when I can. But computers, you know, that's the biggest thing. I don't know. Maybe film."

"Any girlfriends?" Serena asked coyly.

He felt his face go red. How dare she take that tone? It was bad enough when his grandmother did it.

"Not right now," he said through a mouthful of rice. "I'm too busy."

"Too busy? That's a new one," said Anna. "Since when is a boy too busy for that?"

He feigned a coughing fit and headed for the kitchen. When he returned, Serena was describing how Chinese martial arts kept the body in proper balance. She had recently taken up tae kwon do. Danny ate methodically, eyes down, her light voice enveloping him like a cloud. This was worse than before. Now he hated her. How could you hate what you loved?

Shortly after the pecan pie, Anna announced that she was leaving. "I'm worn out. You can all carry on without me. That's how it'll be someday anyway." She gripped the table and pushed back her chair.

"We should go too," said Roy. "We'll walk you up, Anna, make sure you get in okay."

"Oh, she told you? So my daughter can't even let me keep my little bit of dignity that's left."

"It's no disgrace, Mom. We're all glad to help. Would you rather stand there fumbling with the lock and have to come back down?"

"I'd rather not need help."

Roy kissed his children and ex-wife, praised the dinner yet again, and took Anna's arm.

"I'll stay and help clean up," Serena said.

"No, that's okay. The kids'll help me."

Serena bent to kiss Sara, who stood stiffly, her head tilted as if for the pirate's blade. When she leaned over Danny, she whispered, "Did I embarrass you before? I'm sorry." She kissed him lightly on the cheek. He half expected her to pat his head, as she might a large and stupid pet. He wished he could die right then and there.

The departing guests were met at the door by Dmitri. "Am I too tardy for the festivities? I'm so sorry. I wanted to get the recycling bins outside for the morning pickup."

"Come on in," Bea urged. "There's plenty left."

Would she let him stay, Danny wondered, or was she still playing at discretion? Bits of poetry sprang up in him, about empty beds and empty arms, but he shoved them back down. Now that he had read some real poetry in a freshman seminar called The Self, the Soul and the World, he was more convinced than ever that his own was garbage.

*

In bed, Roy read the paper while Serena flipped through a fashion magazine. He had a sense of incompleteness, the evening unresolved. Beyond missing Tony and Jane, he missed, and not for the first time, the detailed discussions he would have with Bea after an evening out: they would exchange items of gossip they had picked up, analyze everyone's moods and responses, demeanor and clothing—what did the visible signs reveal about the unseen depths?—puzzle out the import of minute social contretemps, evaluate who had been interesting and who a bore. Of course one would not be quite so critical with one's loved ones, but still, these talks had often been the best part of a night out, the evening's dross spun into gold. Serena, however, was content to come home, smile vaguely, and read a magazine.

"That was nice, wasn't it?" he ventured.

"It was okay."

"Why, didn't you have a good time?"

x

141

"Sure, it was fine." She pulled the quilt higher around her chest.

"Danny looked good, I thought. College agrees with him. Or maybe it's just being on his own. What did you think?"

"He did seem more grown up, I guess. I don't think he likes me. I make him uncomfortable. Sara doesn't either."

"Oh, I wouldn't go that far. It may be a little awkward for them, but with time . . ." This was not what he had had in mind.

"It's been nearly three years. But what does it matter? Could you give me the section with the crossword puzzle?"

"Of course it matters. We could work at it. Maybe have them up more often so they'd know you better."

She put the magazine down and turned to him. "Actually I offered to make this dinner. I thought it would be nice if we had the kids up here for a change, but Bea said no, it was easier for her. Which is probably true. So I let her. When someone is so good at everything, why struggle?" She resumed her reading.

"Serena, darling, is everything all right? With us, I mean. Is it working for you?"

"Sure. It's working out fine."

"I sometimes think . . . We don't talk enough. I don't know what you're thinking."

"I'm probably not thinking anything. You're used to very verbal people, Roy. Big talkers. I'm just not."

"But I wonder . . ." Roy moved closer to her. "Maybe you used to say the same thing to Donald. Didn't you tell him things were fine too? How do I know you're not feeling just as miserable?"

"Please!" She threw her head back and laughed. "Don't remind me! You're nothing like Donald. This is very different. Believe me, you'd know. You especially—don't you know everything? No, things are fine. I'm very comfortable. Really."

"Comfortable," he echoed. Yes, she seemed neither happy nor unhappy, simply exuded an uncomplaining mildness. He found it a mystery, but perhaps she was right and it was only blankness. How could that be, though? No one was a blank. "Don't you ever want to tell me things? Like how you feel about, I don't know, everything? Anything?"

"Roy, is something bothering you?"

"It's very odd. In almost three years we've never discussed children. Don't you find that strange?"

"No. You have a lot of children. You're very involved with them. We sometimes talk about them. We just did."

"Serena, you know what I mean. Do you ever think about having children?"

"No," she said, stretching and yawning. "I don't want to take care of anyone. And I don't think I'd like what it would do to my body."

"Oh, women's bodies go right back into shape. Especially someone like you, in such good shape already."

She was staring at him, finally alert and curious. Ah, perhaps now they would have a real conversation. He ached to hear her speak. About anything at all. He loved her so much that he wanted more of her. More! It felt like a howl in his chest. Impossible that there was nothing beyond this. But already he knew his longing would end in making love, which she would do agreeably, maybe even enthusiastically. There were times—not always, but often enough—when he could rouse her to a keen excitement. But immediately after, she would lapse back into her good-humored blankness, so that he was always left wanting more. It reminded him of the way certain male patients described their sex life. The moment it was over, they disconnected, they said. Some were bothered by their own detachment, while others took it as the natural order of things. Needless to say, their partners were often distressed. It had never been Roy's mode, and certainly not Bea's—good God, no—but now, on the receiving end, he was as frustrated as his patients' unknown lovers. Maybe it was Serena's way of keeping him hungry, a gnawing, uneasy, almost bitter hunger.

"Roy, do you want a baby? Is that what this is all about?"

"No, to be quite honest, I can't say that I do. I've been there. But if you did, I'd gladly do it. Sometimes I feel . . . maybe you need something."

"If I need anything, it's not a baby, I can tell you that much."

"Oh." So that was that. There would be no more children. If he had been quite honest, as he claimed, then why this small ache of regret?

It was for her, he realized. He wanted them for her. Such feelings were possible. Not all his training had ever persuaded him that generosity and altruism did not exist, or that self-interest was the sole human motive. He wanted them for her. To possess something together with her. To possess something. To possess her.

"So what do you need?"

"I don't know, Roy. I never think I need anything in particular until you start talking this way. Then you get me thinking and get me all confused. If you wouldn't talk this way, I'd be fine."

"All right," he said wearily. "I'll stop. I can't seem to make myself clear. About what *I* need, I mean."

At this point, surely she should encourage him? Probe, ask questions: What *did* he need? What *did* he want? But Serena rarely asked questions beyond the ritualistic. How was work? Did you like the movie? How did the conference go? Her questions had ready answers, easy answers. A good wife, she wished to be properly informed about his doings, in the same spirit as he diligently read the newspapers. Roy yearned to be asked questions whose answers he didn't know, questions that would draw out mysteries. Bea, despite her no-nonsense ways, always went straight for the mysteries.

He dimmed the light and reached out for her. "Come to me," he said. "Come, Serena. Do you want to?"

"Sure." She gave him a sexy smile. "Why not?" He understood it was a relief for her. She wanted to be let alone, and this was the way. She wrapped her long legs around him and moved in a way she knew he liked. If ever he said he liked something, she was sure to remember and do it again, and had she ever expressed a preference he would happily have pleased her as well. But she did not. When it was finished she smiled benignly. Roy felt like weeping. He wanted to do it over and over, but even if he did it all night he would not have what he wanted of her.

"I don't want to do this anymore."

"I remember. Are you all torn up with conflict? Poor sweetie. Let me soothe you." May took her in her arms again.

"No, really, I mean it. Come on, stop. It isn't funny." Serena giggled nonetheless as she slipped out of May's grasp. "I've really got to go. We're having people for dinner." She pulled on her lace panties, then the matching bra.

"Why don't you ever have me for dinner?"

"I'd be happy to have you for dinner. But you don't like Roy. And you don't like dinner parties."

"It's okay. I've had my dinner. Yum."

Serena blushed. "Really, May. You're so juvenile sometimes."

"I am. I admit it. Don't forget your scarf. And your belt. You're so well accessorized, you could be in *Vogue*."

"I was a model for a while. It only lasted a few weeks. I couldn't stand all those people pawing at me." She put on her earrings and looped a gold chain around her neck.

"I can imagine."

"Good-bye, May." Serena bent over the bed to kiss her. "I'm sorry, I just can't keep doing this. It's too hard."

"Roy wouldn't mind. I'm a woman, remember? It doesn't really count."

"You don't know Roy at all. He's not that narrow-minded."

"Fine, sweetie. I'll see you in the elevator or something."

"Jane? Janie, are you there? Open up!"

Tony's pounding on the door woke her from sleep. As usual after a closing performance (a Christopher Durang play, just the sort of zany thing she liked), the cast had partied most of the night. Jane had attended her morning classes, then sacked out for the afternoon. Ever since her sophomore year she had requested a single room. More and more, she loved solitude.

"All right!" She threw on a robe and stumbled to the door. "Stop yelling."

He burst in, waving an envelope in her face. "Look at this! I got into Chicago! First choice! Melissa too."

Tony was transformed from the self-pitying, lanky boy of yore. Taut and muscular from working out and playing basketball, he had even grown an inch. His face was alive. He was not loath to smile now and then, though he still did so parsimoniously. And it was all due to Melissa, Jane thought ruefully. Wonder Woman. Jane was wary of her; anyone who managed to be both Waspy and grungy was suspect. It was true she had urged him to make friends. But she never thought he'd become besotted. With a calculating, ambitious, overachieving . . . Still, Melissa obviously adored Tony, and in the glow of her adoration he flourished. For that Jane was grateful. No more wild talk of hitching a freighter to Vietnam to look for his roots.

"Congratulations!" Sleepy as she was, she managed a broad smile, a big hug and kiss. "That's fantastic. My brother the lawyer."

"We both got them this afternoon, in the same mail."

"It's great, Tony. I'm really happy for you. Can I just go to the bathroom? I'm barely out of bed."

"Get dressed and let's go have a beer. My treat."

"Make it coffee. But I should really treat you."

"Nope. In three years I'll be making eighty thousand a year. My treat."

In the café just off campus he told her his plans. He and Melissa would get an apartment together; she grew up in the Chicago suburbs and knew the city. When they graduated, they would get hotshot corporate jobs to pay back the student loans. Melissa hated depending on her father, whose checks arrived from far-flung resorts with barely a greeting. Then once they were out of debt, he would do what he really cared about: immigration law. Melissa wasn't sure yet, maybe entertainment law. Or environmental. There was plenty of time to decide. They might even get married.

"Married? While you're still in school?"

146

"We might. After the first year, if we get good summer jobs, we could manage. Why wait?"

"Aren't you thinking kind of far ahead? I mean, marriage and all? It sounds so, like, final. The end of the line."

"It is final. It's finally the beginning. I'll finally have a life." He ate another croissant. "You don't like her, do you?"

"What do you mean? Sure I like her."

"Janie, this is your brother here. You can't hide anything from me."

You'd be surprised, she thought. "I do like her. She's just different. I'm getting used to her."

"Different from what?"

"Us. Our family."

"That's for sure. Why do you think I fell in love with her?"

"I thought for what she is, not for what she's not. Anyway, her family sounds even messier than ours."

"Yeah, but hers is, like, clean messy. I don't know how to explain it. They don't pretend to be anything but messy."

Jane brooded over her coffee.

"Don't worry." He flashed the smile and tugged playfully at one of the royal blue braids framing her face. "I know what I'm doing."

"Okay!" She squeezed his hand. "I'll be your best man. Or bridesmaid. Whatever. And later you can slip me some of that eighty thou a year to support the arts. Have you told Mom and Dad yet?"

"No."

"Well, call. Make them happy."

"I can't get used to calling them separately."

"It's over three years. How long is it going to take?"

"Maybe forever. It's too weird, all of them living together in the building. Mom says she and Serena are friends. Friends? I mean, he fucks her over like that and she's never even mad or jealous? I don't get it."

"With Dmitri around she doesn't need to be jealous. I don't think it's weird. I think it's cool. Imagine if they didn't speak to each other, and we could never see them together. Anyway, tell them you got in. They'll feel bad if you wait."

VII

$\mathcal{S}$erena had learned happily to accommodate her guilt at relishing Roy's Tuesday and Thursday morning departures. On Tuesday and Thursday mornings he left at eight-thirty for his stint at the clinic. Generally Roy was good-tempered and easy to live with (saintly, compared to Donald), but on those mornings he grumbled and fretted until she couldn't wait for him to leave. He didn't like getting up early; he didn't like the clinic. The patients, he told her, were in graver straits than his private patients, although strictly speaking one ought not to distinguish among degrees of pain. Pain was pain; every patient, whether rich or poor, jobless or employed, healthy or moribund, had a right to take it seriously. But off the record—and seven-thirty on Tuesday and Thursday was off the record—the patients at the clinic were so messed up and fucked over that his kind of help was less than a Band-Aid. Poverty, drugs, alcohol, violence, abuse, AIDS, prison, parole, the whole enchilada. Not to mention no health insurance. In the face of all this he felt useless. Could understanding and refining their own emotional processes really mean much? What good was heightened awareness while they still had all the rest to contend with? It might make things worse. Maybe Maxwell, Bea's enterprising homeless friend, was astute to eke out a living on the streets and flee social services like the plague.

Roy expounded, with anecdotal illustrations, as he dressed and drank his coffee, and Serena listened, sympathetically, she hoped, murmuring assents at suitable moments.

"And to top it off there's that goddamn garbage truck every Tuesday and Thursday. A preview of the jaws of hell. We don't even need an alarm clock anymore.''

"You're right. It is very annoying. More coffee?''

It was not hard to be sympathetic; she agreed with him, and she knew her task was finite. But oh, the relief when he was out the door and off to his futile labors.

Fortunately the goals of her work were more modest. She had no pretensions to changing her clients' destinies or consciousness, merely alleviated their aches and enhanced their energy; how they employed their new-found well-being was their own business. She rarely scheduled sessions before eleven. It was her habit, on Tuesdays and Thursdays, to linger at the kitchen table with a second cup of black coffee and *The New York Times,* conveniently delivered to the door by Carlos, now that Oscar was gone. She read the paper like a magazine, perusing the table of contents for anything of interest, which she usually found toward the back, in the pages reserved for the arts, fashion, human interest, gossip, health and nutrition. Her favorite was the column by the paper's longtime health writer, whether it dealt with matters far from her immediate concerns—incontinence or sunstroke or dysthymia (a stubborn inclination to melancholy)—or of specific professional interest, such as lower back pain and fallen arches, and it was in a mood of utter relaxation, reading about the effects of caffeine, that her eye fell upon a brief nearby item for which she was quite unprepared. Not that one could ever be prepared for such a shock: EAST SIDE DENTIST SHOT BY PATIENT.

She had a funny feeling even before she saw the photo. Her first thought was how much Donald would have disliked being called a dentist. How often she had heard him bemoan the widespread and shameful ignorance, tantamount to contempt, of how crucial gum care was to general as well as oral health—the very foundation of dentistry—and of how painstaking had been his course of study. And now, in glaring capitals, to be labeled "dentist," no doubt owing to the narrow space allotted for headlines. At least the flattering photo would have pleased him. She knew it well; taken on the occasion of his graduation from periodontal training, it had sat moodily on his bureau.

But these were swift flashes. Donald! Her hand shook, and the coffee nearly spilled. She set down the mug and read carefully. Apparently an irate patient, someone Donald would have called a loose cannon—his term for patients less than grateful for his treatment or distressed by his bedside manner—had risen peremptorily from the chair, taken a gun from his pocket, and fired twice at the chest, killing Donald instantly. The dental assistant who was always in the room—not only to assist but also to guard against possible charges of sexual harassment—had had her back turned, preparing some instruments at a table. By the time she heard the shots and screamed, it was too late. The patient, who had fled, was apprehended running down the stairs. The elevator, Serena recalled, was maddeningly slow, and the stairs were a wise choice, albeit to no avail. Less space was devoted to Donald's aborted career than to the assassin, who had a history of mental, as well as dental, problems and claimed Donald had received his just deserts: he was ''an incompetent butcher'' as well as ''a rude (expletive).''

She had often thought Donald's manner might bring him grief one day, had even warned him about it when he gleefully reported his office repartee. But who could have imagined something like this? Loose cannons. So Donald had been right. He would have enjoyed knowing exactly how right. Divorced, the article said. No children. So his second marriage had not gone well either. His first was not mentioned. At least Roy's intermittent fears of being chased with a hatchet or a spoon excavator could be laid to rest.

To her surprise, Serena burst into tears. Poor Donald! To come to such an end. And so unloved, as he always claimed. So sad. Dysthymic, possibly? She alone knew the scope of his woes, his sufferings over paltry body hair and knobby feet, and what had she done but add to it? She had sworn, until death us do part, but she had parted long before death. Hers, anyway. Had she known this would happen, she might have waited.

This was totally crazy. What she needed was a dose of common sense. Someone to tell her it was one thing to be shocked, but really, this had nothing to do with her. It was in no way her fault. Someone to exorcise this absurd, overwhelming guilt. Guilt for leaving him, guilt for having married him in the first place.

She dressed hurriedly, checked the article in case it had been a hallucination, then dialed Bea's number. Not home. Bea was always home. She was supposed to be home. Moreover, there was one of those businesslike messages Bea had gotten in the habit of leaving: "If you are calling about the cable TV, the news is . . ."

Grabbing her keys and the paper, she dashed out, and moments later was ringing May's bell, long and loud. Mr. Banerjee from across the hall stepped out and gave her a curious glance as he locked his door.

May opened at last, pulling her red silk robe around her. "What's the matter?" It was the first time Serena had seen her wholly serious. Alarmed.

"Look at you. I could have been the exterminator. Don't you ask who it is?"

"What is it? Is Bea all right? The kids?"

"Yes, yes."

"Well"—and May resumed her ironic manner—"I'm not supposed to let you in, remember? Go away. Anyway, it's too early. It's not even nine o'clock."

"May, please, I've got to talk to you."

"Okay, but you pleaded. Keep that in mind."

Serena fell onto a hard folding chair, the only kind there was. "Look at this." She held out the paper.

"What? 'T-shirts Back in Vogue Under Long Print Summer Dresses'? 'Drinking Rising on College Campuses.' You came up to tell me that?"

"No! This!" She grabbed the paper and pointed.

" 'East Side Dentist . . .' " It took a moment, then light dawned. "That's him? Your ex? Not bad-looking." She read a few lines and began to chuckle. "Bea brought my mother to him once, did you know? In fact she said she'd like to wring— Serena. You're crying."

"Of course I'm crying, dammit. Do you think I came up here to laugh? I lived with the guy for four years. I left him."

"It's a good thing you did. How'd you like to be dealing with this?"

"May! He said no one loved him, and he was right."

"You're serious."

"Do you think it was my fault?" she whispered.

"Oh, sweetie, come now." May knelt and put her arms around Serena. "Get hold of yourself. It's a shock, I know. It's awful, but you had nothing to do with it. You haven't seen him in years. It was some nut. Don't do this to yourself. Come have some coffee. You'll feel better."

Serena was limp. May had to drag her into the kitchen. "It says on the opposite page that caffeine is very bad for you," she said weakly, wiping her tears with a fist.

"So are a lot of things. Have you told Roy?"

"Roy? No. It didn't occur to me."

*

"Roy? I just got your message. Is everything okay? You never call me from the clinic."

"Oh, Bea. Where were you?"

"Out. As my message said. What is it? Are the kids all right?"

"The kids are fine. I'm sorry, I didn't mean to scare you. Do you have this morning's paper? . . . Good. Look on page six, Section C."

"This is very mysterious. Okay, hold on a minute. Let's see, 'Drinking Rising on College Campuses.' But they graduated. It doesn't say anything about law schools. And Danny never even touched—"

"Not that. To the left."

" 'East Side Dentist . . .' Oh, my God. Wait, let me read . . . Incredible. You know, I thought of doing it myself. If there was ever anyone who had it coming . . . You know, he really does look like a hairdresser."

"I can't reach Serena. She's not home. Do you know where she is?"

"Roy, I'm not her keeper. How would I know?"

"She's never out this early. She's expecting a client at eleven. I'm worried. She could be upset."

"Her? About him?"

"It may be irrational, but people do get upset, Bea. They get guilty. I know her. Serena is not as cool as she seems."

"Really? That's good news. But guilty? I would think this should put any lingering guilt to rest. I mean, if he was still suffering over her, now his suffering is over. But I'll see if I can find her. I'm sure she's fine."

"Get back to me, will you? I can't leave. I'll tell them to put you through even if I'm in session. Thanks, Bea."

*

"May," said Bea, "will you please pick up? I know you're in. God, these machines are uncivilized. Suppose I was—"

"Take it easy, I'm here."

"Is Serena there?"

"How did you know?"

"I'm a witch, okay? The same way Pop knew when the boiler was about to break down. Roy called. He's a little frantic. I guess you heard about the periodontist from hell."

"Yes. She was very upset."

"She was? You mean she's recovered?"

"Somewhat. It was a shock. She's lying down."

"Will you please have her call Roy? And don't make any trouble."

"Me? She came up here looking for solace. She called you first, actually."

"And I deserted my post, is that it?"

"Where were you?"

"I had to go down to the rent board, if you must know. Someone's got to do these things."

"Well, should I have turned her away in her hour of need?"

"Just send her back, all right?"

"Why is all your solicitude for him?"

"Only indirectly. It's really for me, May, don't you understand?"

"What's wrong, Mom? You look terrible." May stepped in and set down her packages. "Why are you crying?"

153

"Oh, it's nothing. What could an old woman have to cry about?" Turning her back, Anna shuffled away from the door.

"Mom! Cut that out. Come on, I'll make you a cup of tea."

May hadn't been in her mother's apartment in some time. She had to open several cabinets before she found the teacups, the very same cups she had disliked in childhood, thin bone china with a floral pattern, curving out to scalloped edges. Their fragility was irritating and they held very little. Her mother should have some sturdy mugs, especially as she was given to dropping things lately. After she set the water to boil, May pulled up a chair beside Anna, who sat with her head in her hands, silently weeping.

"Mom." May put an arm around her shoulder. "What happened? You can tell me."

"Nothing happened." Her voice had none of the usual brashness. Bea often told May she was just like Anna, the same bravado shielding a sensitive soul. May didn't buy the sensitive soul part, for herself or her mother, yet here was Anna quite unguarded and helpless.

"It must be something. You don't just sit at the kitchen table and cry for no reason."

"How would you know? You're hardly ever here." She raised her head. Her eyes were red, her cheeks blotchy. A sorry sight, May thought. "What made you come up, anyway?"

"You had a package, I think it's your prescription from the AARP, so I told Carlos I'd save him a trip. Also, the market had that Lithuanian rye you like, so I got you a loaf."

"Oscar used to bring up the packages right away. This new one waits."

"Well, you have no one but yourself to blame for that. You shouldn't have let him go." What a mask that face would make: a picture of abject misery. She would love to do her, but Anna would probably not submit. Anyhow, it would mean spending hours in her company. "You're not crying over Oscar, are you?"

"No! What do you think I am, crazy? A hired man?"

"So what's wrong?" She stroked her shoulder.

154

"It's the baby. My baby who died. I can't remember his name."

"You mean Willy? His name was Willy, Mom."

"Willy!" She sobbed harder, in great heaves. May rocked her in her arms.

"It's his birthday tomorrow and I couldn't even remember his name. Willy!"

Willy was the boy Anna and Mickey had lost to diphtheria at three years old, long before Bea and May were born. Throughout their childhood they had listened to endless Willy stories—his beauty and amiability, his precocious turns of phrase. Every September 11 Anna would say, "If your big brother was alive today, girls, we'd be having a birthday party," and on holidays she would sigh, "If only Willy was here!" Willy would be what, fifty-five or -six now? And she still noted his birthday? Maybe she reminisced about him to Bea. May felt a warmth behind her eyes.

"His birthday. I'm sorry, Mom. Shh, it's all right."

"It's not that," Anna said impatiently as May stroked her. "That's an old pain. It's me. You know what it means that I can't remember my baby's name? It means I'm losing everything. Soon I won't even remember your names."

"Me and Bea? Don't worry. If that happens, we'll wear signs."

"It's no joke. All these years and it suddenly flies out of my mind. Where is it all going? My life," she groaned. "My life."

The kettle whistled and May went to turn it off. Anna was right; this lapse was not insignificant. It could only get worse.

"Thank you," said Anna as May set down the tea. "This is very nice of you."

"You don't have to thank me. Here, you like sugar, don't you?"

"You're a good girl, deep down. I know you love me. You just don't know how to show it."

"I showed it, didn't I?"

"Yes, you did. I think mothers and daughters should be close. I'm close with Bea. I'd like to be close with you too, but you seem like you don't want to."

"You're not the easiest person to be close to."

"I know. But you're just like me. In some ways, anyway. We're two of a kind. We should understand each other."

"Okay, well, from now on we'll try. Only sometimes I feel you don't want me any more than . . ." May caught herself before she could ruin the moment. As it was, the strain of ambivalence was making her back ache. She was thinking, as she had not done in years, of how wonderful it might be to have a sympathetic mother. Could this be the start of a great change? Of course not. People did not transform at seventy-seven. It was folly even to hope for it. Yet the very thought brought her perilously close to hope.

"I do want to be close. But sometimes things get in the way." Anna paused and sipped. "You know, May, things can change. You wouldn't believe, the things I hear people tell on television. On *Geraldo,* for instance, the crazy things they did. But even they change."

"What do you mean, things can change? What things?"

"You know what I think? About you, I mean?" Anna looked better, revitalized by the tea. "Let me tell you. As a mother."

"I'm not sure I want to know."

She regarded May shrewdly, as if about to explain to a tenant why the rent had to be raised. "What I think is, you got bitter as a girl and that's why you're the way you are. But it doesn't have to be that way."

"I can't believe you're doing this. No, it must be a bad dream."

"Doing what? Can't a mother give her opinion? Look, lots of times a girl has a bad experience and doesn't want to try again. In my day she'd just sit home, but nowadays there are, what do you call it, options. Believe me, I understand. I was in the Young Socialist League, we knew about free love, we knew about all kinds of love. You think you invented it? But May, listen to me, you don't have to be one of them. Think about it. You're still a good-looking—"

May had already risen. She slammed her cup into the sink, where it made a satisfying crack. "The package is on the table in the living room. I should have known. God, when I think I let myself be taken in . . . For the birthday tomorrow, the name is Willy. Write it down so you don't forget." She stormed out of the kitchen.

"May, I didn't mean anything. May? Wait a minute."

"What?" she called from the door.

"You won't talk to me?"

"I have to go. I stayed too long already."

"May?" Anna caught up with her and and gazed up piteously.

"What?"

"Wait five minutes and I'll go out with you. I was just going for a walk."

"A walk? Where are you walking to?"

"Just a walk. Aren't I allowed?"

Yes, and get lost while you're at it, thought May as she opened the door. "I'm not going out. I just came in, remember?"

"Oh, that's right. May, wait a second."

"What now?"

"What do I owe you for the bread?"

The door slammed.

When May called Bea that evening to report this encounter, she was disappointed in her sister's response. Bea was less bothered by Anna's memory lapse and what it might portend, or by her craven manipulation of May, than she was by the walks. Why these frequent walks, Bea wondered, often in bad weather and after dark? Where was she going? What was she seeking? "Who the hell cares?" said May, and hung up unsatisfied and lonely. Maybe she would call Serena. On second thought, no. Roy might answer.

"Bea? It's me. I absolutely must talk to you. Something's come up. . . ."

"One second, Roy." She turned the chicken breasts on the grill and stirred the boiling potatoes. "Sure, but not right this minute. I've got a big book party at five and I've got to—"

"Not now. I'm in between patients. I thought I might stop by at lunchtime. Believe me, I wouldn't bother you unless—"

"I can't. They're sending someone to pick up the stuff at four—I can't send Maxwell to the East Side—and I won't have a spare minute until then." She tossed the cooked beets in the blender and pressed the button.

"Make it six, then, I'll be— Bea, are you there? I hear this terrible noise."

"Sorry." She turned off the blender.

After she hung up, she checked the chicken breasts, pressed the blender's button for another moment, then reached for the phone again. "Serena? You told him, right?"

"Oh, Bea. I was sleeping."

"It's almost eleven."

"Really? It's a good thing you called. I've got to run someone around the reservoir at noon. Yes, I told him. How did you know? You must be psychic or something."

"Not yet, but I'm working on it. He called." With the phone tucked between her shoulder and neck, she drained the potatoes and began peeling a carrot.

"That was quick. What did he say?"

"Nothing. He was in between patients. He's coming over later, though. How'd he take it?"

"Not well. Not well at all. Shocked. Offended. Humiliated. Tears, even."

"Oh, dear. Didn't he have any idea?"

"No. That surprised me, I must say. I thought he might at least have suspected something. It was awful, Bea. I could never repeat to May the things he said."

"Well, that's certainly not necessary."

"I mean, I understand he's hurt and all, but you'd think a therapist would be more clued in."

158

"I don't see why. Maybe you should have provided for him the way you did for what's his name. Donald."

"It never occurred to me. Don't you think he might have caught on to that?"

"We'll never know. Look, I've got to go, I'm working. Did you say when you were planning to move upstairs?"

"We didn't get that far. He was too, uh, agitated. It'll be soon, I suppose. I don't think he wants me around. He said he can't bear the sight of me anymore."

"That bad?" The doorbell rang. "I've got to go, Serena. Talk to you later."

Let it be a stranger, she prayed as she opened the door. Cedric, the exterminator, was not technically a stranger, but he did not share his intimate concerns.

"Isn't there anyone else to take you around?"

"Ernesto's sorting the mail, Carlos is watching the door, and Dmitri is out."

Ah, yes, his Human Resources workshop. "Okay, off to the kill."

Hours later, Bea lay on the living-room couch enjoying the fading sunlight. Despite her exhaustion, she had the aesthetic satisfaction that work well done always yields: the chicken seasoned to perfection and skewered with chunks of portobello mushrooms, the beet and carrot terrine vibrant in color, the miniature quiches crisp and golden. If she ignored the bell, Roy would let himself in.

"I'm in the living room," she called, and reluctantly opened her eyes. "My God, you look like Jack Nicholson on a bad day."

Roy sank into a chair, then rose immediately. "Do you mind if I make myself a drink? You wouldn't have anything to eat, by any chance?"

"I sent it all away. There're some hard-boiled eggs in the fridge. Or grapes."

"Why don't you make some extra to keep around?"

"I don't like that fancy stuff, you know that. I thought I'd send out for Chinese food for Sara and me. You can stay if you like."

"Where's Sara?"

"In her room."

He returned from the kitchen with a bottle of beer and a banana. "Who's the beer drinker? Not Sara, I trust?"

"Dmitri."

"I thought he stuck to vodka. Well, Bea, you're not going to believe this."

"I will. In fact I already know."

"You know?" Deprived of his climactic moment, he looked stricken. "How come you know everything?"

"Because people trust me and tell me things, and I observe keenly."

"Is this something I should have observed?"

"I don't know how she behaved with you. I suppose you couldn't have observed how often she went upstairs because you're away all day."

"Are you suggesting I should have stayed home and watched her? I don't keep tabs on people."

"I haven't suggested a thing. I'm answering your questions."

"You look sleepy. You're not going to fall asleep, are you?"

"No. If only I could."

"Why? Do you have trouble sleeping? You never used to."

"This isn't a consultation, Roy. You wanted to see *me*."

"But you sound so brusque. You're making me feel worse. I know it's absurd, coming to complain to you, but still—"

"I'm sorry. I'm just tired. Besides the exterminator, the floor waxers came to do the lobby, and the elevator is making those noises again. . . ."

"Can't Dmitri handle all that?"

"He does as much as he can. He's got too much to do as it is."

"I'll bet."

"It's a little late for jealousy, Roy."

"I didn't know that time either."

"That was different. I was very discreet."

"Meaning Serena hasn't been? But how could I have suspected this? Your own sister, Bea. A woman."

"It happens. Haven't you ever had gay patients who were married? Or bisexual? Or just plain confused?"

"That's irrelevant. Serena's my wife."

"Doesn't anything you learn carry over to your own life?"

"The whole idea is to be detached. I'm very good at that. If you'd ever had any therapy, as I suggested, you'd know what I mean. You also wouldn't find yourself managing everyone else's life and winding up exhausted like this."

"I've told you a million times, I'm not trying to manage anyone's life. I'm only trying to keep my family together while everything else is falling apart, and that's not easy. People come to me. Should I refuse to listen? I'm not getting paid to be detached, like you are. I'm not getting paid at all."

"All right, never mind. Do you know if she's planning to live with your sister, right upstairs?"

"Yes." She watched him drain the rest of his beer. "The place is big enough. She likes it here. She's gotten used to the neighborhood."

Somberly, Roy peeled the banana, pulling away the strings with care, as he had done for the children when they were small. Bea recalled many such details at which he was equally deft. Teaching them to tie shoelaces. Repairing miniature cars. Clipping the mittens to the edges of coat sleeves.

"I think you might have told me this was going on."

"Your marriage is not my business. You'd have been the first to tell me so if I had interfered."

"If everything was all right, yes. But with something like this ... You know we have a special relationship. I count on you. I hope you feel you can count on me."

"For certain things, yes."

"Bea." He got up, carrying the banana with the peel dangling over his fingers, and came to the couch. "Move over. That's better. The worst of it is, what I went through to marry her. I had to leave the person I loved. You. You know it wasn't easy. I disrupted things, not without plenty of thought. And guilt. For love, I thought. For a fresh start. For ... Well, you know what for."

161

"So?"

"So now she humiliates me by falling in love with a woman. You remember, Bea. I don't mean to boast, but I thought I did certain things pretty well. And your sister. Speaking objectively, what could she possibly see in her? In that way, I mean. With some women I might have an inkling, but May?"

"You can't explain love, Roy."

"You're mocking me."

"Sorry. But you did put yourself in harm's way. People leave people. And once they get going, it's easier the second time. Like going off a diving board."

"You're saying I would've been better off . . . ? Is this some kind of I-told-you-so? That's the last thing I need right now." He finished the banana and placed the peel, neatly folded, on the coffee table.

"It isn't any kind of I-told-you-so because I didn't tell you so. I didn't tell you anything, remember? It's simply the way things are."

"She doesn't love me anymore. That's it, pure and simple. That's what I can't accept."

"She may still love you. After all, you love me."

"But I don't want that kind of love. I want, you know . . ."

"Oh, that," murmured Bea. "Everyone wants that."

"I didn't mean— I do love you, Bea. You know I do, don't you?"

"Yes. I just said so myself."

"Do you really think . . . ?"

"Oh, don't say it, Roy. Please. I don't think I could bear it."

"What about you? I know you're happy with Dmitri but even so, don't you ever think—"

"No," she said firmly. "I won't let myself. This is a new, uh, configuration, that's all. I can't control the shape of things. I can only control what I do with it."

"Stop sounding like the corner guru and let's hold hands."

She moved her hand a few inches closer and he grasped it. They stared at the hands, locked together on the couch.

"It's a comfort," he said. He adjusted their hands so that the palms were face to face. "You have such large hands, Bea. Look, they're as big as mine."

"I know. You've told me many times."

Again he locked his fingers into hers. "Let's kiss."

"A comfort?"

"Well." He smiled. "A bit more than that."

"All right."

They slid closer together. Roy held her face in his hands and kissed her lips, gently at first, then harder. "I almost forgot how you feel. Oh, Bea." He reached under her shirt—actually an old shirt of his, he realized—and stroked her breast. "This feels so wonderful. There's no one like you. No one so—so . . . Bea? You're not sleeping, are you?"

"Of course I'm not sleeping. Do you think I'm made of stone?"

"You're so quiet."

"I was never a big talker at these moments, remember?"

"Ah. Is this one of those moments, then?" He groped between her legs. She was wearing tight leggings like the young girls, but he did what he could. "I guess it is. Let's go to the bedroom. What about Sara?"

"She's probably plugged into her Walkman. Anyway, we're her parents. How traumatic could it be?" She rose and let him lead her to the bedroom. "Take off your shirt," she said.

Obediently, he began unbuttoning, but she laughed and said, "No, take your shirt off me."

"How gauche of me. Of course." He undressed her slowly, caressingly, while she stood silent, smiling gravely. "My own Bea. How beautiful you are, still. I've always loved you. How could I . . . ?"

"Not that. Let's not be romantic. Let's just be . . ." She flopped down on the bed and pulled him on top of her. "You're a stranger," she whispered. "We've just met. Somewhere. Anywhere. And we'll never meet again. But we're dying for each other. We must have each other."

She was making him more excited than he'd felt in years. He wanted to plunge right into her, but didn't. He went slowly, as if she were an unknown woman, and under his hands she did feel new. He didn't know how she managed the transformation—it seemed as crafty and awesome as her turning common vegetables into fantastic concoctions. This unknown woman quivered under his touch, urged him on, moaning, and the more he delayed, tantalizing, the more she moaned until, avidly, she thrust him inside her and he was home.

And then, too soon, it was over. She sighed, she stirred, and he rolled off her. "Now let's be us," he said. "That was almost frightening."

"Really? I liked those people."

"Don't you like us?"

"Oh." And she laughed. "We're all right. But we're finished. So, do you feel a little better?"

"Bea, that's not why . . ."

"No? I thought—"

"Don't spoil it." After a while he said, "Do you feel guilty?"

"God, Roy, only you would talk about guilt at a time like this."

"All right, disloyal then."

"No. I do what I want. Anyway, he doesn't love me."

"Bea, of course he loves you. Anyone can see that."

"He worships me. It's not the same."

"Oh. Does that bother you?"

"Well, Doctor." She danced her fingers lightly along his chest. "I take what I can get. Being worshiped has its points."

"You've become a total . . ."

"What?"

"I can't think of the word. You're amoral. A libertine, that's it."

"*Moi?*" Again she laughed. "I'm very moral. I haven't changed. I'm in there fighting for family values. Roy, are you getting hungry? I am. Why don't I call the Chinese place? I'll get Sara to unplug and we'll all have supper. That would be nice, wouldn't it?"

164

Roy hadn't heard from Sam Browder in years, ever since he'd seen him through the acrimonious divorce. The lawyer must have performed equally well, for in the end Sam had won the joint custody he wanted, and his wife had agreed to acceptable terms. Sam had worked through his feelings to the extent that he could or would, and drifted away. Now he was back, slimmer, trimmer, ruddier. After his hearty greeting, Sam spent the first half of the session telling Roy how well things were going. Business was good—he owned a large sporting goods store; the child support payments weren't killing him as he'd expected; the kids were managing reasonably well, the older two in college. "But it's still hard on them, you know. It gets them all mixed up and sort of ages them too soon. That was almost the worst of it, seeing them suffer. Like when she married the nutritionist, that was real bad. But, well, what can you do? I guess the worst is over." After a spell of "fucking around," as Sam termed it, he had met a woman he was very attached to, someone his age, someone he could be serious about. But he wasn't about to jump into anything right away. "I'll go slow and see how it develops." All the while Roy listened patiently, showing pleasure in Sam's good fortune, one eye on the clock as he awaited the reason for his visit. If his instincts were correct, it would emerge during the last fifteen minutes.

"There's just one thing." Sam gave an embarrassed chuckle. "One fly in the ointment, so to speak."

"Yes? What is that?"

"It's so nuts, I . . ."

"Come on, Sam, we've known each other a long time. You came here to say it, so say it."

"Right. Okay, it's Laura. You know, my wife? Ex-wife. At the beginning I used to meet the kids downstairs—we were so mad we couldn't even look at each other. Then after a while I'd go up and say hello like a normal person. We'd even have a little chat. Plus we'd run into each other, you know, graduations, swim meets, stuff like that."

"Yes?"

"Don't play dumb, Roy. You know what's coming, don't you?"

165

Indeed he did. "Sam." He smiled. "I'm not a mind reader. If you want me to know, you'll have to tell me."

"All right. What it is . . . well, every now and then, we, uh, you know. Get together. We fuck."

"Uh-huh."

"That's it? Uh-huh?"

"Well, you've just stated a fact. What is it about that fact that bothers you?"

"That's not enough? To be screwing her while I'm seeing Terry? And while she's married to that half-wit food nut she dumped me for? You think that's not crazy? You think it's just business as usual?"

"It may not be business as usual, but it's not as unusual as you think. You're not the first, believe me. But anyhow, what aspect of it bothers you the most?"

"What aspect? I don't get where you're coming from, Roy. Every aspect. The whole fucking aspect. It's just not right. It's like, I don't want to be doing it, but I'm doing it. I'm used to her, you know? She always turned me on. It's like going back home. But it doesn't make any sense. I tell myself it's not going to happen, then it happens. I don't want to be doing it, but there I am, doing it."

"What does that mean, there you are? Who's putting you there? Is she?"

"No, it's kind of fifty-fifty, I'd say. It's like smoking, you know? You tell yourself it's the last time, and then all of a sudden you notice you're lighting up again."

"Yes." Roy thought of the cigarettes in his drawer, but tolerant as Sam was, this was hardly the moment.

"What do you mean, yes?"

"I was agreeing with your analogy. It's true, it's the same kind of conflict as in breaking any habit. But think about your words, Sam. You say, 'It's happening,' as if you're not a free agent, as if the impulse comes from outside. Maybe it would be good to examine how it happens. What you're doing to make it happen."

"Do you do it too, Roy?"

"Sam, I'm afraid we have to stop now."

"Stop! I just started. What is this?"

"Our time has run out."

Sam turned to look at the clock on the wall. "Whaddaya know. You're right. Why'd you let me run on so long? I barely got to the point."

"That's part of the point, that you didn't want to get to the point. Think about it."

"Ah, come on, Roy. Are you really going to send me away when we only talked for ten minutes?"

"I'm afraid so. But we can set up an appointment for next week if you want."

"I guess I'll have to, right? But meanwhile I'll be seeing Laura Saturday. We're going up to Bard for a parents' weekend. So what should I do?"

Sam was grinning, so Roy grinned back. He envied his simplicity. Quite right; it just happened. Floundering for a response, he recalled the many times he'd consulted Bea about his patients and she'd delivered her terse, commonsense advice. Dear Bea. He could hear her voice in his ear, coming to his aid. "What should you do? Control yourself, Sam."

VIII

*I*t had been so fortuitous: that was what Roy couldn't stop marveling at. It might just as easily not have happened. In fact, had he prevailed it would not have happened. Yet again he had Bea to thank for his good fortune. Accommodating, responsible Bea for once had stubbornly refused to go. She'd gone every year since she could remember, but tonight she was too exhausted to move; she had had to redo a platter of saltimbocca because Anna ate half of it while her back was turned, whether out of greed or malice she didn't even want to contemplate; she had argued with building inspectors who threatened a violation over bicycles cluttering the basement; she had had it; she was going to bed. Roy, for his part, had had a trying day too—that wretched clinic!— and was hurrying to a meeting at the institute. Besides, he'd gone plenty of times—remember the hateful Miss Jackson of first grade? She need not cast him as an absentee father. Bea stood her ground. He simply must forgo the institute and attend the semiannual meeting with Sara's teachers. Especially the math teacher, since Sara was having problems doing the homework. What was more important, Sara's math or the institute meeting? Roy dared not offer an answer. "All right! Just give me their names and so on."

It was a private school that shepherded its students from kindergarten through high school, chosen partly for proximity and partly for its benign atmosphere. Roy ambled through halls decorated with colorful projects: a unit on the circus, with student sculptures of animals and acrobats, another on the genesis of computers, another on folk music and exotic musical instruments. The drifting parents of the integrated student body, all clutching slips of paper, seemed mildly apprehensive.

Roy dutifully visited each teacher named on his slip, listening to reports of his daughter's virtues and flaws; as befitted the school's positive outlook, the alleged flaws—an occasional airy distraction, a touch of sassiness—were presented as cognates of the virtues. He would have preferred a more thorough account of Sara's academic progress, but the teachers dwelt on what they called socialization skills and motivation until he felt a trifle distracted himself, his mind wandering to the sacrificed institute meeting, which he would have enjoyed as always, not only for the camaraderie but for the excellent pastrami sandwiches sent in from the gourmet deli next door.

He saved the math teacher for the end: "Lisa, Room C32," last names being apparently superfluous here. The walls of C32 were a peach color and adorned with playful collages of geometric shapes, featuring Styrofoam packing materials and bubble wrap in various colors and sizes. An array of flowering plants in superb condition lined the windowsill, and on the floor below were enormous cushions in gaily tinted fabrics. Quite a few parents were seated and waiting their turn. At least he did not have to take a number as in a bakery, a practice he recalled from Sara's public elementary school. All he could see of the teacher was a mass of dark hair; she was obscured by a young black couple, very nattily dressed, sitting opposite her at the desk. Perhaps he should have made more of an effort—he was in jeans and a pullover. After a bit of trouble with the chair's movable armrest, he opened his newspaper. He must have lost track of time, for when he next looked up he was alone.

"Excuse me?" a young woman was saying. "Would you like to come up?" She rose to greet him. Or rather unfolded—she was tall. "Hi. I'm Lisa."

Had he seen her in the halls he would have mistaken her for a student. Her hair was long and fluffy, spilling down her back. She too wore jeans, on the tight side, and a gray silk shirt with clunky beads. She reminded him of someone. Of course. Bea. A younger Bea: ample breasts, olive skin, lush yet solid. He could imagine resting his head on those breasts; in fact he felt he already had, many times. Her face was not as strong as Bea's; it had an odd undefined quality, as if it hadn't kept pace with the body's maturity. Her gray eyes were feline and curious, as if they hadn't yet seen much and were still in a state of wonder, on the verge of asking a question.

"Sara's a terrific girl," she said when Roy introduced himself. What a rich, pure voice! Like music. "Really terrific. I had her last term too."

If only he had come then.

Sara had done fine at first, Lisa said, but now that they were getting into logarithms she seemed a bit lost. "Just this morning I started to arrange for some tutoring from one of the older students. I don't think it's a serious problem. A few sessions should get her back on track."

"Maybe I could help her." He had squeaked through high school math centuries ago with barely passing grades. But now he would be better motivated. He would have to give Lisa progress reports.

"If you think you could, then, great."

"I almost thought you were one of the students," Roy ventured. "You look too young to be a teacher."

She smiled brightly, showing perfect teeth. "I'm older than I look." But too young, Roy thought ruefully, for her to see he might be flirting, at his age.

There came a rap at the open door. Roy turned to find a boy in a leather jacket, faded jeans with tattered slits at the knees, and a helmet in his hand. He didn't speak, only questioned with raised eyebrows.

"Just a couple of minutes," Lisa called, and he waved and disappeared. Roy's heart sank.

"I'll start going over her homework with her right away, and maybe we can talk again soon, see how she's doing." He had nearly forgotten how to go about this. And if she regarded him as a man at all, she must assume he was married. "Let me give you my number, in case there's any problem."

"That's okay, I must have it in Sara's records."

"It's a different number. Her mother and I are divorced," he said apologetically, as if presenting a poor character reference.

"Oh, I didn't know."

"A friendly divorce. We didn't want to upset the children."

*

"I didn't know you knew anything about logarithms," said Sara when he offered to help.

"I was pretty good at them, as a matter of fact." Motivated as he was, Roy had mastered the review book in two nights. "Why didn't you tell me you were having trouble?"

"When do we ever talk?"

"Do you feel that way? I'm sorry. You can talk to me whenever you need to."

"Dad, I'm not a patient. It's not like I want to come to you with problems. I mean talk naturally."

"You're right, I didn't say that very well. We should do more things together. We can start with your math homework."

Sara was an apt pupil, with more mathematical intelligence than he had ever had. Once he explained exactly what logarithms really were, her difficulties vanished. Perhaps Lisa had not made it clear.

A week later he left a message at school; the office refused to give out Lisa's home number. She returned the call that evening.

"I thought I might stop in one day to talk about how Sara's doing. I've been working with her since our talk."

"Oh, right. Sara. Let's see. . . . Let me check my book. We haven't had any exams lately, but, hold on a minute. . . ." Roy heard the rustle of pages and pictured her at home—with her salary, it would be a small apartment—her hair tied back, maybe wearing just a long T-shirt, maybe with tinted glasses like the ones Serena used to wear at night after she took out her contacts. Glasses made women more sexy, he always thought, when they were half undressed. "Yes, her assignments have been better. Almost perfect. You must've done a good job."

"I'm glad. But there are a few points . . . I'd like to be sure I understand everything right. It's been a while, you know. Also to see that her grade isn't pulled down because of the early tests."

"Oh, we don't really give grades at Dewey. Just evaluations. It's nothing to worry about."

"Still, do you have any hours when you meet with parents?"

"Well, okay, I guess you could come in after school, say, Thursday or Friday?"

"Thursday. Around five or so?" By then Sara would surely be out of the building. "I have patients until then."

"Are you a doctor?"

"A psychotherapist."

"Oh. That's interesting."

"What do you find interesting about it?" he asked coyly.

"I don't know. Maybe 'interesting' isn't the right word. You know, therapists always make people a little edgy."

"You'll find me quite harmless, I promise. See you then."

Once again Carlos, the doorman, looked at her funny as she was setting out on her walk. What now? Last time he gave her that look, she realized after walking two blocks that a dish towel hung over her shoulder, a residue of cleaning the kitchen. No towel today, she'd checked. People at the Senior Center sometimes forgot their teeth, a gruesome sight, but that wasn't her problem despite the creep of a dentist Bea took her to years ago. Look at him now, six feet under, while she was still walking around with a full set. Her dress was okay, one of the long print twenty-dollar numbers Sara brought her from the outdoor racks she frequented, just like the old days when they bought clothes off a truck. "Here, I got you two more, Grandma. With a T-shirt you're all set. Way to go." The kid was right—no girdle, no stockings, totally *au naturel*. They flattered her too. Not a day over seventy. Maybe Carlos, never very friendly at best, was having a bad day. Javier, a polite young man, might have told her if anything was amiss, but Javier had left years ago along with his uncle Oscar. If only she hadn't fired him in a fit of temper over some little nothing, a peccadillo, after his long and devoted service. All right, so he had his eye on her—was that a crime? He was a man, flesh and blood. Whatever it was—and she could not recall precisely—she had made a serious mistake and regretted it ever since.

It was a warm, bright April day, a perfect day for the search. In front of the building the Rodriguez girls and the new Iranian girl on the ground floor drew hopscotch boxes in pink chalk and searched the gutter for a stone to use as a potsy. Amazing, how the old games kept coming back. As she paused to savor, as always, the sweet sense of ownership, like the contented feeling in the stomach after a nice meal, Dmitri emerged from the basement door. He resembled a homeless man, lugging two huge plastic bags of cans and bottles for the recycling bins.

"Isn't it a magnificent day?" he greeted her. "I'm about to polish the brass on the front door, just to be outside. Solar energy! And how are you, Anna?"

"You're certainly in good form today. Carlos looked at me funny. Do you know why?"

"Funny? Funny as to laugh? Are you sure?"

"Funny strange. I'm sure. Take a look. Is something wrong?"

Dmitri stepped back to scan her from head to foot. "Perhaps," he said mildly, "it was because you are sporting house slippers instead of shoes."

She went crimson as she looked down at her feet, then over at the little girls, who seemed oblivious.

"Charming house slippers," he gallantly offered. "Chinese?"

"I'll have to go back up. Make sure the hall windows get cleaned soon. I can see the dust from here. And did the man come about the dryer? I had complaints all day yesterday."

"All problems corrected. All systems on go."

She passed Carlos with a haughty stride, head high and eyes averted. When she returned moments later, properly shod, he was away from his post—a pity, for she could have dropped some remark about being

173

in such a hurry that she'd forgotten her shoes. Already she was feeling tired and she hadn't even begun. But she must persist. It was too fine a day to waste. She headed toward the park and turned south. The better buildings were down there, and unless Oscar had already retired, he was likely, given his skills and reputation, to be found in one of the better buildings. Bea had written an excellent reference; she remembered that much.

Her strategy was to enter each lobby and scrutinize the doormen. What a stroke of luck, should they come face-to-face! She would apologize as earnestly as she could; her speech was ready and had been so for some time. Let bygones be bygones. She'd been hasty, but she was willing to pay significantly more than before, even if he chose to work only part-time now that he was older. Meanwhile she asked each doorman if Oscar worked there or if anyone knew his whereabouts. Her inquiries of the union had yielded nothing, and Oscar's sister did not appear to understand English, at least on the phone. Twice Anna had received a stern answer—*no está*—and found herself unable to leave her name or call again. Nor could she bring herself to ask Bea's help. Aside from the question of pride, she felt a kind of moral rigor: she alone had caused this trouble and she alone would rectify it.

She tried to be methodical, but after so long it was hard to remember which lobbies she had already covered. The sly grins and narrowed eyes she encountered must mean she had asked before. Well, no matter. The personnel turned over frequently, as she well knew. With the neighborhood so much like a small town, though, she hoped her inquiries would not get back to Bea. She would never live it down.

She had walked for about fifteen minutes with no luck, then headed west to Columbus Avenue, when a strange thing occurred. She was no longer sure of where she was. The neighborhood was still familiar; the cleaner's, the deli, and the drugstore were the same places she had known for years, but they stood out from their surroundings as discrete sites rather than parts of a context. She turned round and round on the broad sidewalk, trying to orient herself as if she were in a strange city, as lost as she and Mickey had felt on their trip to Miami Beach. But it was common to get lost in a new place; Mickey had simply pulled out his street map. You didn't carry a map for your own neighborhood. Or if there was some sort of map in her head, the precise place where that map was kept seemed to be covered by a dense shade.

There was no place to sit down. Didn't there used to be benches on the streets? She recalled an ice-cream shop with two nice wooden benches in front, but it was nowhere in sight. If she could sit down she might get her bearings. The street signs—of course. If she knew which corner she was on, she could find her way home. But the signs turned out to be useless because she couldn't remember her address. Now she was really in trouble. Go into a store? But what could she ask? How could a stranger tell her where she lived?

She gazed into a shop window so as not to appear conspicuous, a loony old lady standing haplessly on the street. But she kept glancing around as if the rushing traffic might give her a clue. Why were those three girls, skimming down the avenue on skates, waving at her? Insane to be skating in the middle of traffic. They could get themselves killed. As they passed, she realized they were her daughters with that other one, the blond athlete. She might have waved and stopped them. But maybe it was better this way. Next thing you know Bea and May would put her away somewhere and she'd be strapped to a chair, drugged and singing folk songs.

The main thing was not to panic. If she kept walking, something would jolt her back. The terrible veil in her head would lift as suddenly as it had descended. But it was getting warmer, and she was tired; she might be wandering farther from home. Was there a police station nearby, maybe?

She reached in her purse for a tissue to wipe her face. Aha! How foolish she was! Look what happens when you almost give in to panic. She sifted through the cards in her wallet; the voter registration card must have her address. And indeed there were two printed lines below her name, but the type was so small she couldn't read them. She rummaged for her glasses, but she must have left them home, and at the thought of home, of her living room, where the glasses probably lay on top of the newspaper on the coffee table—all this clear and accessible so she knew she hadn't lost her mind—she felt a lurch in her chest. Oh, to be safe at home, where she knew where everything was!

Wasn't that Bea's friend Maxwell on the opposite corner with his Styrofoam cup? She couldn't be far from the building, then. She almost started toward him, but pride restrained her: she wasn't yet so desperate as to ask a beggar for help.

All right now. People forget their glasses all the time. That wasn't serious. But even if she could read the address, would she know how to find it? The street names had lost their meaning; they might have been in a foreign tongue. Then she noticed the taxis cruising down the avenue. Salvation! She hailed one with an imperious wave.

"Here." She handed the driver the card. "This is the address. I don't have my glasses."

She wished she'd gotten a Russian, who might have been sympathetic, but this man looked Indian. He studied the card. "This is right around the corner. You sure that's what you want?"

"What's it your business what I want? Your business is to drive where I tell you."

"Okay, madam. No problem."

A turn, another turn, and before she was even settled in, he pulled to a stop. Yes! Her very own building, utterly familiar and lovable. Another few minutes and she would have found it herself. It was all coming clear now. It had just been a temporary loss of nerve. A little spell. The fare was two-fifty—an outrage for so short a trip—and he really didn't deserve a tip after his impertinence. She found only two dollars in her wallet, though; she must have forgotten to take cash on her way out.

"Wait." It was embarrassing to borrow a dollar from Carlos, who came to help her out of the cab. But at least he saw that she had shoes on.

"Shopping trip?" Carlos asked. Three nannies with babies in strollers sat chatting on the ledge; they smiled up at her.

"Do I look like I was shopping? Do I have bags?"

"Maybe no luck." He shrugged and escorted her into the building.

"No luck is right," she muttered. She pressed the elevator button. Eleven. No trouble remembering that. The spell had passed.

After the brief conference Roy insisted on buying Lisa a cup of coffee to thank her for her time.

"It was no trouble at all, but okay, if you really want to, there's a machine in the basement."

"You deserve better than Styrofoam. Please. You must be leaving anyway, aren't you?"

He steered her to his favorite, the Café Botticelli, the old Italian coffee bar that was the scene of his earlier tryst with Serena. It gave him courage. *Coraggio,* as the proprietor, who greeted him warmly, was wont to say.

"So," he began, "how come a lovely young woman like you is drawn to mathematics?"

He knew it was a dreadful mistake the minute the words were out. She drew back. At least he hadn't said "girl."

"I don't think I understand that question."

"I'm sorry, forgive me. With all my experience, I should know better. It was a foolish attempt to start a conversation." She was silent, playing with the packets of sugar. "Can we start again?"

"Start what? I mean, what are we talking about, really?"

He must try another tack, a bold one. "What I'm talking about is that you're the most intriguing young woman I've met in years and I'd like to know you better."

"Intriguing" was a good choice. Better, these days, than "beautiful."

"Intriguing? Me? Maybe you don't get around much. Is this why you got so concerned about your daughter's math homework?"

"No, I've always been a concerned father." Did she sense irony? Roy thought not. "But I can't help noticing other things along the way."

"If you're saying what I think you're saying, I should tell you right off, I'm involved with someone."

"The guy with the helmet?"

"How did you know? My God, you're not stalking me, are you?"

"Oh, really now. He came to pick you up the night of the conferences, remember?"

"Oh, right. Well, we've been going out for a few months."

"But you can have a coffee occasionally?"

"I can have whatever I want. But I haven't wanted to."

"But you might consider it?"

"Look, uh, Mr., I mean Dr.—"

"Roy. I'm not a doctor."

"Roy. I'm not really up for this. I mean, I just came from a day's work and I have a yoga class in less than an hour. I really don't think this is right. I'm your daughter's teacher."

"There's nothing wrong with a cup of coffee. And in a few months you won't be her teacher. Look, Lisa, I don't want you to feel uncomfortable. Let's have our coffee, and I'll walk you to your yoga class, and if that's it, okay. Although I hope that's not it. Forget this ever came up. I honestly would like to know how you got interested in math. I've always admired people who can think abstractly."

She relaxed enough to describe, with the self-deprecation of the innocent, her mathematical bent—numbers games since she was a child, president of the Math Club in high school. Before long Roy found a way to work the conversation around to his tour of duty in Vietnam. Wartime experiences always impressed women, especially young ones, even if they deplored war. No matter that Lisa, had she been old enough, might have taken to the streets in protest.

"But did you know that it was a bad thing? I mean, was there a lot of inner conflict, or were you just, like, trying to stay alive?"

"I knew, but I didn't know how to get out of it. For me, it would have taken more guts to be a draft resister than simply to go when I was called. It was an awful time." He wouldn't mention Tony and Jane just yet. Without the war they wouldn't exist: there was his inner conflict. It was no doubt socially irresponsible to see the war in such purely personal terms, but he couldn't help it; he couldn't picture life without them. "There was plenty of conflict, sure. But hey, this is so grim. Tell me about yoga."

By the time they parted he had extracted her last name and phone number, and though she wouldn't make another date for coffee, her refusal had not been absolute. He sensed a flicker of curiosity. And why not? There must be a great deal he could offer that exceeded the resources of a postadolescent biker.

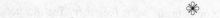

"Bea?"

"Roy!"

She must know. Her voice was rich with excitement. "Have you heard?" he asked.

"Yes, a little while ago. He was about to call you, so I waited. Isn't it fantastic?"

"Yes!" So Tony had called her first. Well, Bea was the mother. "It feels incredible. We're grandparents. Listen, Bea, are you busy?"

"I was making some calls. I want to tell everyone I know. Then I'll go to the hospital and see them."

"We can go together. Why don't you come down here first? I have a bottle of champagne. We'll celebrate. Where's Sara?"

"She's over at a friend's. I called her. Danny too. We can all meet there."

"Great. But meanwhile, come down. If we don't celebrate when we're happy, then when . . . ?"

"Maybe I will. I've hardly ever been in your apartment."

"Hurry up. I can't wait."

It was a half hour before she appeared, dressed for the occasion in one of the silk pants and shirt outfits that Roy liked. Maroon with gold trim. "You look gorgeous."

"I thought so too. I tried."

"Why did I ever leave you?" It was possible, by now, to say it jovially.

"I don't know. But you never did, really. So, bring out the champagne."

They raised their glasses in a toast. "I wonder what kind of parents they'll be," said Roy.

"Slick magazine parents. They'll trot off to work in their little suits and hire a nanny and have the kid in school before he's out of diapers. Or I'll wind up taking care of it. I don't even mind, at least for the moment. Isn't it amazing, how life is so awful and yet we can feel so happy when a baby is born? You'd think we'd feel sorry for the poor thing."

"Do you think life is so awful? I didn't know."

"Of course it is." She sighed. "But let's not dwell on it now. Maybe everything will all work out."

"What do you mean, work out?"

"Oh, everyone will be happy and content, no changes, no crises."

"How is that possible? There are always changes and crises. Without change we'd be dead."

"I know that's the common wisdom." Again she sighed. "But maybe just for a little while . . . Roy, do you really like Melissa? I mean, do you love her like a daughter?"

"Not exactly. Come, sit here by me." He pushed aside the pillows on the couch. "Not like I love Jane or Sara. But maybe I'll get to like her better. As long as Tony loves her. That's what matters."

"I don't like her much either. But I love her. When I realized this was the girl he loved, I made up my mind to love her, and I do. It's different from liking her. I could love anyone I made up my mind to. Except maybe murderers and terrorists. Maybe even them if I tried hard."

"I'm just the opposite. I can tolerate almost anyone, but love, no. I'm very choosy about who I love. But I love you."

"That goes without saying."

"It should never go without saying. Oh, it's so good to talk to you. Serena never talked. Here, let me pour some more. Hold my hand, Bea."

"Hold your hand." She obeyed, grinning up at him. "I know what that means. Why don't you just come right out and say, Hold my dick?"

"Because it's so indelicate. So hasty."

"I was never delicate. Was I ever delicate when . . . you know?" He was groping inside her shirt, and she responded by putting her hand on his zipper.

"No. That was something I liked. Your lack of delicacy."

"I thought it was something you didn't like."

"There was actually nothing I didn't like."

"Shall we move to another room? Do you have a bedroom on the premises? A bed? I've never been in your bedroom. This is going to be exciting. A new venue. Old wine in new bottles, so to speak. Oh, what a nice bedroom, Roy. You fixed it up so nicely. But you have to use a condom."

"Bea, I'm the father of your children!"

"I don't care if you're the pope."

"All right, all right. In a minute."

"Roy, let's—let's get on the bed. Not standing up."

"Oh, God, you're so beautiful, I can't bear it. Let me . . . I have to taste you first. No rubbers for that."

"Yes, yes. Oh, Roy. Oh, God. You bastard, why did you have to leave?"

"Wait. Stay that way. Again. I want to see you come again and again. Remember how you used to?"

"I still do, you motherfucker. Roy, put it on. Please. Oh, God. Oh, never mind. Just do it. Do it, do it."

He lay collapsed on her for a long time. No need to speak. Strange, the myth of sadness after sex. He'd never felt sad after Bea. After Serena, a little. After Bea, glorious. Loving Bea was like nothing else in the world. He could never give it up. Just once in a while was

181

enough. She was right about no turning back or starting over, the single condition she had imposed on their divorce. She was right about so many things, it was galling at times. But just now he felt so close to her that he wished he could tell her about Lisa. Talking might ease his obsession. Yes, it was absurd to be obsessed with a girl he hardly knew, a girl who could be his own daughter (though not as wise as the wry and incomparable Jane). Nonetheless he could not stop thinking about her. And really, why even try? What else was there to think about, in that department? If Bea chastised him, in her friendly, merciless way, he could reply that his pursuing a woman nearly twenty years younger and Sara's teacher to boot was no more reprehensible than Serena's defection to May. But any such discussion was out of the question, for the moment at any rate. Definitely not a propitious moment. Even Bea had her limits.

He rolled off her. "Do you think other grandparents behave like this?"

"I bet they'd like to. I'm sure my mother would be at it if she could."

"Your mother," said Roy, pulling her closer, "is not representative."

"Well, anyway, that was pretty nice, Roy." They laughed companionably. They had always been amused by understatement. "Pretty nice. You haven't lost your touch."

"Maybe I've improved with age."

"Or distance. This kind of thing has advantages over a marriage."

"I suppose so. Does it feel like a marriage with Dmitri?"

"No."

"Does it feel better than this?"

"I'm not going to talk about it. You know that."

"Not even a little bit? Just tell me, are there cultural differences? Does he murmur sweet nothings in Russian? Or do things I might not know about?"

"Roy!" She punched his shoulder lightly. "Stop it. If you want to be titillated, I can find a better way."

"Give me a few minutes. I'm getting old."

"Men don't like the idea," she said, climbing on top of him, "but

182

the truth is, men are not all that different. I mean more or less nice men who like women. Leaving out pigs and sadists.''

"Women," he said, helping her slide down his body, "are very different." How would Lisa be, if and when he ever got to the point? He would. He must. But the real Bea, with her tongue on his cock, moving with the slyness but happily not the swiftness of an adder, obliterated the imaginary Lisa.

She lifted her head for a moment. "Don't tell me about it, okay?"

"I really don't know why I'm doing this," Lisa said, once the waiter left them alone. "I promised myself I wouldn't, after we had lunch, then when you called, I don't know, I just heard myself saying okay." She giggled but quickly stifled it. How girlish she must seem. But wasn't that what older men liked, girlishness? Why should she care what he thought anyhow? She wasn't even interested. He was the one who kept calling. Her mother always said she worried too much about what people thought of her. What would her mother think if she could see her now? She'd certainly be pleased to see her dressed like a grown-up, as she would put it. But not pleased about Roy's age. Billy, on the other hand, would have a fit if he saw her in this restaurant with Tiffany lamps and draperies, fresh flowers and candles on each table, and waiters in little forest green jackets, real waiters, not actors or dancers. The kind of place Billy wouldn't be caught dead in, assuming he could even get together the money or the clothes to enter.

"I'm so glad you did. You look fantastic in that dress, by the way. Ready for adventure. Do you have a sense of adventure?"

"Not really. You'd be amazed at how unadventurous I am."

"Adventurous enough to ride a motorcycle. Do you have your own, or do you just sit on the back of your friend's?"

"Me, own a motorcycle! No, I've only been on Billy's a few times. Frankly, it scares me."

"As well it should. I hope you wear a helmet."

Lisa laughed—better than her prior giggle, she thought—and picked up the menu. "Now you sound like my father."

"Forget it, then. That's the last thing I want to sound like. So, what looks good to you?"

From habit, her eyes ran down the right side of the menu first: almost nothing under twenty dollars. A little arugula and goat cheese salad was eleven ninety-five. Buffalo steaks—they couldn't be serious. They must be like Buffalo wings. Incredible, but there must be people who ate in restaurants like this one all the time. Every week, maybe more. Probably not Roy, though. Psychotherapists didn't make all that much. She ordered soft-shelled crabs, a choice the waiter seemed to approve. Roy ordered the rack of lamb.

"Tell me something about your friend Billy."

"Why? To give you ammunition against him?"

"Not at all. I'm just curious."

"He's from St. Louis. He's in a band. A rock band," she added when Roy looked blank. "He's very talented. It doesn't feel right talking about him."

"Well, you definitely shouldn't do anything you don't feel right about," he said with a wry smile. He was teasing her, she could tell. Very clever. Trying to make her see, though she didn't want to, all of Billy's shortcomings. No money. No plans. Unreliable. He could blow out of town as easily as he had blown in, just one night before they met at a downtown club. She was there for her friend Adrienne's thirty-first birthday; a bunch of them offered to take her out, anywhere she liked, and Adrienne picked that wild place she read about in the *Voice*. They were among the oldest people there. Still, it was fun, especially after she met Billy, the wildest dancer on the floor. But no, Billy Moran could not be relied on. He didn't quite grasp that she had a regular job and couldn't drop everything to be with him when he had the urge. She'd always known Billy was a passing thing, but in Roy's presence it became starkly clear. What are you wasting your time for? her mother would say. You're not getting any younger.

"Are you in love with him?" Roy asked.

As if he were reading her mind. Fortunately the waiter arrived with their appetizers and took time arranging the table.

"Was that too intimate a question?"

"Yes. No. Yes, it was too intimate a question. No, I'm not in love with him, if you must know." Why had she said that? Why must he know?

"Okay, I'll drop the subject. Want to try an escargot?"

He was really very nice, she decided by the time they reached the espresso. And it was really wonderful espresso; she was a coffee lover, ground her own at home. The guy provided a terrific cup of coffee, she had to say that for him. She had drunk two glasses of wine—fast, to ward off her growing confusion—and could feel their effect. And again, as if seeing herself through Roy's eyes, which gazed at her steadily over their tiny coffee cups, she wondered why she was going out with a biker four years younger who lived hand to mouth, hadn't ever finished college, and couldn't live with her because he couldn't raise half the rent. He was camping out on the floor of a friend's loft in SoHo.

She asked a few questions too. Granted, being twice divorced was not the most terrific recommendation, but he seemed to be on good terms with his former wives, and he doted on his children. Four! Two part Vietnamese—that was interesting. And how brave of him to keep searching until he found them. He couldn't accept the idea of losing them. It showed character, as her mother would say. Substance. When he told her about his son's new baby, his eyes glowed. That was so sweet. He was even attractive, once she got over expecting him to be attractive in the way a guy her age would be. That of course was impossible. But he was sexy in an older-guy way, like someone in one of those *Masterpiece Theatre* programs, without the British accent. Maybe she did have an adventurous side after all. A couple of her friends had gone out with older men. How different could it be? It was the same equipment, only aged. Like cured meat. They lasted longer; that was what everyone said. But they couldn't do it as many times—that was the downside. Well, she might give it a try. See for herself. Not tonight, but sometime, maybe. How did she know what Billy did when he wasn't with her? He had lots of free time, when he wasn't messengering or doing odd carpentry jobs. He might be seeing other people—eighteen-year-old girls, whatever. It wouldn't surprise her one bit.

Roy took her home in a cab and got out with her. After such a lavish dinner she couldn't just leave him at the door.

"Do you want to come up for a drink or something? But I've got to be straight with you. I'm not up for—"

He waved her words away. "Lisa, it's fine. I'm not a kid. There's no hurry."

In the smallness and stillness of her apartment, things felt weightier, somehow. More serious. She'd never been alone this way with a man his age, she thought as she fetched him a glass of ginger ale. Only on job interviews, or with doctors. She must stop thinking of him as so much older—he wasn't doddering, for God's sake. And there was no need to impress him. He was already impressed, though she wasn't clear why. If he just wanted somebody young, there were plenty of . . . But no, he wasn't any kind of weirdo. He liked her. Why should she find that so hard to accept? He was wandering around, looking at her old movie posters and bookshelves and CDs as if he really cared who she was. Luckily she'd straightened the place up, except for a small pile of bubble wrap, partly popped, over on the couch where she sat when she watched TV. She had nervously popped a few bubbles before going to meet him.

He didn't stay long, just long enough. A guy who knew how to do things. She would kiss him good night, she decided. Test the goods.

He kissed her good night and a bit more. "You're so sweet," he murmured. "Just as I imagined." He was a good kisser, the slow, lingering kind, and not a nibbler, thank goodness. Maybe even the best, in fact. She'd have to go back through the list later, lying in bed. The rich food and wine had made her very tired and she couldn't wait to fall into bed alone. He stroked her hair as he was leaving and kissed her again, lightly. She swayed a bit as she shut the door, then idly popped a few more bubbles, enjoying their sharp crackle. This was all very surprising, and she'd better take two Advil to ward off the headache that the wine would surely bring.

"Did I hear you right? You must be kidding, May."

"I'm not kidding. Well, say something. You're making me nervous."

"I'm so stunned I can't speak."

"But you can eat."

"Yes," Serena said, biting into another croissant. "Maybe I have cravings already. Okay, well just for starters, where would we put it?"

On Sunday mornings May and Serena indulged in breakfast in bed. Since May had no patience for domestic labor, it was usually Serena who brewed the coffee and poured the juice and heated up the croissants. She'd become quite the little housekeeper, May liked to tease. She had managed to transform a small part of the studio into a living space—Ms. Minimal, May called her, or Ms. Danish Modern—but even May, who abhorred change, admitted it was nice to have a couch, even a table and chairs. The kitchen now fulfilled its intended function, and May had given up her old habits of ordering pizza in the wee hours and leaving the crusts on the windowsill, or absently dining on Mallomars while she worked. What she would not give up was any more studio space. To Serena's suggestion that they wall off an area where she could receive her massage clients, May had given a categorical no. She needed the whole space: the size of the space affected the size of the work; she needed to work at any hour of the day or night without strangers passing through; she needed the radio on, blasting rock music or opera—her tastes were catholic. Love is all very well, she said grimly, but work is work. And she needed to be alone, she said pointedly. Serena had joined up with a salon a few blocks away, an accommodation at first grudging, then happy. Love flourished better with brief separations, she found. To be near May all the time would have been exhausting; in the throes of creation, May sang, mumbled, swore, stamped. Still, despite May's moods and eccentricities, Serena had a sense of rightness for the first time in her life. If living with Donald had been a nightmare, then living with Roy had been sleepwalking. If not for May, she might have drifted on for years.

So it came as a shock when, awkwardly, unable to meet Serena's eyes, May muttered that she would like a baby.

"Where we'd put it? That's what's bothering you? There's plenty of room. We could wall off the far end of the studio, make a little room—"

"Wall off . . . ? But when I wanted to—"

"You had other options. You can't rent a room in a spa for a baby."

Serena finished her croissant before she spoke again. Finally, "You mean adopt one?"

"As a matter of fact I was thinking . . . You know?"

"I see. Well, who? You?"

"You."

"Me?"

"Uh-huh."

"Have them shoot it up me and then blow up like a balloon? May, really!"

"I'm too old."

"You're forty-four. You could still do it."

"But you're younger. And you're in much better shape." May glanced admiringly at Serena's taut legs, stretched out before her.

"I've never liked babies that much," Serena said dryly, after a long silence. "You have to do so much for them."

"They grow up, though. Then we'd have a person."

"I don't know. There's an awful lot to consider here. Isn't this a little drastic? I mean, adoption is perfectly . . . I can't even believe I'm taking this idea seriously."

"Adoption takes forever. Don't you ever just act on impulse?"

"Yes. But on my impulse, not yours. I thought we were fine as we are. Why?"

"Don't make me explain. It's too embarrassing. The usual reasons."

"Roy asked me a couple of times if I wanted a baby. But I didn't. I never saw myself as a mother. I'm, you know, a narcissist."

"Well, who do we know who isn't? This is different, though. We're different."

"Let me think about it for a while."

"Not too long, okay?"

"Maybe there's some other—"

The phone rang. "To answer or not to answer?" said May.

"Answer," said Serena, hoping it would distract her.

"Oh, hi . . . Not again! . . . What about Carlos? Oh, right, it's Sunday. Maxwell? No, I guess not. Okay, what's the emergency number?" She sighed and reached for a pencil. "Yeah, I'll stick around. . . . The elevator's out again," she told Serena. "Bea's doing a big party and Dmitri's at some seminar about careers in arts management, whatever the hell that is. That leaves me. Sorry, sweetie, I'd better get dressed."

Serena sank down under the sheets. If only May would forget the whole idea. But she wouldn't. Once she latched on to something she held on obsessively, the way she worked. May would urge and cajole and pester and eventually win her over, because she was the more tenacious one. To resist would only prolong the conflict. Serena had been brought up to believe in positive thinking. To greet the inevitable with a ready mind. Which did not preclude handling it her own way. She would find a way to like the idea. She knew how to get her passive clients to change their habits and attitudes; surely she could do the same for herself. But she would think through each step carefully and do it most advantageously, if do it she must. She would even find a way to enjoy it, to give the whole business an original spin. Above all, now, she must enjoy things. She had cut loose, and she must go forward. She had spent enough time dazed and drifting, hanging back from life.

"Hey, Roy! Long time no see." Sam Browder greeted him like an old friend, shaking hands warmly. What a decent fellow, Roy thought. What on earth could be troubling him now?

Sam had aged, naturally. He had lines around his eyes and his hair

189

was grayer, though no less thick and wavy. He had kept his weight down, but still moved with the heaviness of a larger man, as if his bones and muscles remembered the load they had once hauled.

"Nice to see you too, Sam. What brings you here?" Roy inquired with a tinge of apprehension. Recalling the vicissitudes of Sam's life, he felt an ominous link. He wished mightily not to hear what was coming.

"Before I get to that, I never thanked you last time. I had to cancel because things got crazy at the store, and what with one thing and another I never came back. I should've called."

"It's okay, don't worry about it."

"Remember I told you I was sleeping with Laura?"

"Sure."

"What you said at the end really helped. When I said I was seeing her that weekend and what should I do?"

"That I don't recall. It was, what, two, three years ago?"

"You said, 'Control yourself.' "

Roy laughed. "It worked? Good." He remembered now; it was Bea's tacit advice, by proxy. He should really turn over the hundred dollars to Bea. "So what's up now?"

His tingling impatience was close to dread—let's get it over with—as Sam went through the usual litany of delay. Everything was fine: the same genial girlfriend, the hectic store (in-line skating was doubling his income), the good medical checkup, the children . . . Roy glanced at the clock, the minute hand making its invincible and invisible circle.

He could wait no longer. "Sam, I'm glad things are going so well. But you must have come here for a reason."

"You're right. There's always a reason, isn't there?" He gave a nervous chuckle and began rolling up his sleeves. "Maybe I don't even need to talk about it. Maybe we should shoot the breeze awhile and it'll all go away, eh?"

"I don't think it works that way."

"Okay, okay. It's my daughter this time. Jennifer, my oldest. She's a set designer. Majored in theater arts and now she's working on a big show, even a union member. Twenty-five years old. A great girl, Roy, even if I am her father."

"And?" He breathed more easily: Jane was fine. He had seen her just last night in a rock version of *Phèdre* in a church basement. Although Tony, who also attended, had seemed rather grim, come to think of it.

Sam leaned forward, hands on his knees. "The trouble is . . . This lovely girl, who should be out dancing and having a good time, or else thinking of getting married and starting a family, this girl is seeing some putz she met in the theater, a good twenty years older than she is, if not more. I've met him. Looks are deceiving. He could be fifty. He could be older than me, even. It's . . . I don't like to look at the two of them together. I get ugly thoughts. . . ." He brushed away a tear. "This isn't what I had in mind for her. Funny, we all know guys who do that, and I never thought much of it. If anything, I envied them a little. But when the tables are turned and it's your own daughter, it looks a damn sight different, I'll tell you."

Roy cleared his throat. "Have you talked to her about it?"

"Why? You think I should?"

"Not necessarily. I'm just asking to get more information."

"After I first met him I did say, sort of casually, wasn't he a little old for her and she said no. You know that way they have, when they're very polite but they really mean mind your own business? Ever since the divorce, I, uh, I don't like to rock the boat. I figure they went through enough trouble. Why get them riled up?"

"You mean you're afraid of alienating her?"

"Afraid?" Sam got up and walked around the room, pausing to touch the jade figurine Roy had long ago placed on a shelf, far away from Donald's outbursts. Donald was long gone, poor guy; he might as well move it back to the table, where he could enjoy it. "How could I be afraid of my own kids? They're my kids."

"If you hesitate to tell her what you really think . . ."

"I just don't want to, okay?"

"Okay, Sam."

"It wouldn't do any good anyway. She's a grown woman. She's got to decide things for herself."

"That's true. I'm not suggesting that you tell her what to do. Only

191

that it might help to understand why you don't choose to be open with her.'' Cold silence from Sam. The next path of inquiry—actually it should have been the first, Roy knew—was, What is it about this relationship that bothers you? But he was loath to ask. There were twenty-five minutes left, time for a long and explicit answer. But he was a professional. He must.

''What is it about their relationship that bothers you?''

''That's what you said last time, when I told you about me and Laura. I mean, I come here and tell you these situations that, well, any normal person would understand what bothers me. Why do you have to ask?''

''Sam, it's not that I can't figure it out. I'm asking you to state it so you can hear all your feelings out in the open. Then you can judge which ones make sense and which may be coming from your own distortions or projections. You'll have a clearer sense of where you're at.''

''You sound like a shrink, Roy.''

''Well, I am.''

''Yeah, I sometimes forget. Okay, let's see. It'll be okay for a while, and then they'll start to feel the age difference. She'll want to go out and he'll be tired. They won't be interested in the same things. He's another generation. He's like us. He'll, you know, in bed, I don't have to spell that out for you, do I? I don't even like to think about it. Maybe she'll start looking elsewhere. Meanwhile they'll have kids. He'll be too tired to help out. Or else he takes them out to play, people think he's their grandpa. Then maybe he'll get sick and die. She's a young widow without enough money to take care of them. Sure, I'll help her out if I'm still around, but that's not the point. How'll she find someone else to start all over with, with kids and all?''

Roy had palpitations in his chest.

''And then I sometimes think, What did I do wrong? Maybe I wasn't there for her enough. Maybe she's looking for a father because I wasn't a good enough father. Is that enough for you? Clear enough?''

''Yes, I'd say that's a pretty thorough list, Sam. Okay, let's look at those items one by one. But bear in mind that she probably sees it all very differently. Not quite so negatively. That's why if you talked to her, you might come to see her point of view. There are other ways of seeing it, you know.''

"I don't want to see it any differently! The way I see it is my way. Why should I see it from her point of view if I'm not her?''

"I don't mean you'd change your mind completely. But you might feel less upset over it. You might find it easier to accept." He glanced at the clock again. Fifteen minutes to go. I'm afraid we can't stop yet, Roy, he told himself, irony like a penance.

Sam studied him with critical eyes, as if Roy were failing to grasp something essential. When he spoke, it was in a calm, knowledgeable voice, the voice he must use with his customers. "But I don't want to accept it. Why accept something you find unacceptable?''

"Wait, let me get this straight." Lisa bounced nimbly off Roy and settled beside him on her futon, propping her head on her hand. "You all live in the same building? You and both your ex-wives? Isn't it a little, I don't know, awkward?"

"No, it works out fine. I'm near my family, I mean near Sara at least, and you know what finding an apartment is like. It didn't make any sense to move. It's a good location, it's rent-controlled—''

"So that's why you never ask me over." She went to turn up the window fan. Roy watched her move across the room. He wished she would stop questioning and simply let him look at her. After three years of deprivation and injured pride, the miracle of having this splendid, lithe creature at his disposal made her small apartment, even with its stuffed animals and mounds of bubble wrap, seem a paradise. "It would be cooler in your place. You have air-conditioning, don't you? But you don't want to run into anyone you know." With a leap she was back on the bed.

"Not at all," he lied. He stroked her hip. "I'd like you to come over. I even asked you to move in with me." It would almost be like a harem, he thought. Shame on you, Roy, came the inner voice of the censor, though more amused than censorious. "But you didn't give me an answer. Would you?"

"Let's not rush things." She toyed with the hair on his chest. "All I meant was a visit, so we could do this in air-conditioning. I hate the heat. You get all sticky. And it's only June."

"I'll get you an air conditioner. I should've thought of that before."

"Really? It's not a very romantic gift, though, is it? I'd feel like you were, you know, keeping me or something. Imagine, me a kept woman."

"Nonsense. It would be a mutual convenience. Please. Go pick one out tomorrow."

"I'll think about it. But let's say I came over and we met one of your ex-wives in the elevator. Would you introduce me?"

"Of course. We're very civilized. And they're both, uh, involved with other people. There are no hard feelings."

"How convenient. Does Sara know we're seeing each other? Shimmer, I mean?"

"No, I don't feel that's her concern. Sweetheart, this is no fun. How would you like it if I kept asking you about Billy Moran? Have you told him yet?"

"Oh, God. Billy. Did you have to bring him up?" She buried her face in the pillow and groaned.

"Lisa. You promised you would."

"I don't see him much anymore. I certainly don't sleep with him," she protested. "Not the last two times anyway. I don't know how to tell him. I dread it. You don't know. . . . It's so hard."

Hard? She was complaining about hard after what he had been through? Bea's crushing patience and forbearance? Being abandoned by Serena? Hard! And with a boy who was surely not serious. On the other hand, he could still recall, with a ripple of guilt, Donald's fury when he ended their connection. A different sort of dismissal, to be sure, but facing the ire of the scorned was never easy. It was pretty low to have felt relief at Donald's death, and yet . . . If Billy Moran was anything like Donald, Lisa's task would indeed be hard.

"We all have to do hard things sometimes."

"Well, you're older. And you're a man. It's easier." There was a slight whine in her voice. "It's worse for a woman to reject a man. They take it very badly." She reached for the sheet of bubble wrap on the night table—green, from some cosmetics she'd ordered—and popped a few bubbles. "Billy's very insecure, underneath. He'll storm around, and I hate that."

Didn't she understand it was easier to deal with angry people? They were so transparent. To this day he was not sure what Bea had truly felt. And he would never know.

"Lisa, I'm in love with you. I can't bear your seeing— Do you have to keep doing that?" She stopped popping but ran her fingers over the bubbles. "There isn't anyone else, is there?"

"No! How can you even ask? We were having such a nice time and now you made me think about him."

"We'll have a nice time again. Come here. Put that stuff away. Can't you see how I feel? I need you. I want you all to myself."

"I know how you feel, Roy, but I need some time. It's such a big commitment. I never expected— I mean, this is like a really big life decision you're asking me to make. And there's this whole ready-made family, all your children . . . It's not what I ever pictured."

"What did you picture? Something like Billy Moran?"

"You just like to use him as a symbol. Like he's some kind of degenerate, dragging me down. He's just a young guy finding his way. You forgot what that's like. There's nothing wrong with Billy. We had some good times."

"All right. But he's not for you. You know I'm better for you." He drew her close and whispered in her ear. "We'll be happy. You'll see. You'll have air-conditioning on demand." He put two fingers inside her and moved them in and out expertly, using the thumb for the outer parts. Both his wives had remarked on how well he did that; was it conceivable that they had compared notes? "And anything else you want."

"Oh!" But after a moment she stopped moving and lay very still on her side, impaled. "This is one thing"—she was slightly breathless— "and making a real decision is something—"

"Shh. Isn't this nice?" He eased his tongue deep in her mouth. It was amazing, she was so ready. It took hardly anything to make her come. She was delectable. He removed his fingers and rolled away.

"What's the matter?"

"Will you tell him?"

"Oh, Roy, come on." She climbed on top of him and tried to nudge him inside but he eluded her.

"Roy!" She made his name into two descending syllables.

"Will you?" He pulled her forward so that she was almost above his face. "Will you?"

"Okay. Yes, yes!"

Part Three

•

The Virtual Family— Revisited

IX

*B*leakness seeped through Danny as he watched the taxis speed off. It was the wrong way for this peculiar day to end, though he couldn't envision a right way. Lisa's parents, flown in from Oregon, were being whisked to their hotel, looking vaguely forlorn. Jane and Al, panda-like in their down coats, headed downtown hand in hand through the light snow; Al had a late-night gig in Tribeca. The newlyweds waved gaily from their cab, in apparent relief; tomorrow they would set off for their honeymoon in Barbados. Shimmer rode uptown with them. She was going to a party with Magenta later, she said, when Danny suggested a movie. So another empty Saturday night loomed. Often Danny opted for the unpopular weekend shift at Ape Copiers to avoid just this predicament, but it was too late now.

Melissa must have felt the same sense of anticlimax. Shivering in her fur coat, she linked arms with him and Tony. "Are you doing anything, Danny? No? Come home with us. We can watch a movie, maybe get a pizza later."

"You sure you two don't want an evening alone?"

"No, that's a good idea," said Tony. "This is the first weekend in God knows how long when I don't have to work."

They had done their best to make merry at the small wedding ceremony and the protracted lunch afterward, but as he and Tony agreed in the taxi, it was pretty weird to watch your own father get married. Especially to someone barely older than you. Danny couldn't help being reminded, with a rush of chagrin, of his long-dead feelings for Serena. Those ghastly therapy sessions with Dr. Whiting! Idiotic, all of it. Well, there was no danger of his getting hung up on Lisa. She was pretty, but she didn't turn him on in the slightest.

"Coffee? Wine? Egg creams?" offered Melissa. Egg creams all around. They gathered in the narrow, streamlined kitchen while Melissa poured and stirred.

"Where's Timmy? I wanted to see him."

"Up at your mother's. She volunteered. He's staying over. It meant missing his gymnastics class, but he loves staying there. Cheers! Come on in the living room. Sorry about the mess. This is pretty much how it always is."

Timmy's rocking horse was in the middle of the room, along with his set of wooden blocks, his plastic interlocking beads, his toy bus and fire engine. Picture books were strewn everywhere.

"It's cool," said Danny. "I like all the kid stuff."

"It's a mess," said Tony. "Why doesn't she ever straighten up?"

"She does. It only gets messy all over again."

Danny sat on the floor trying to make the fire engine ladder go up and down. "Do you think Mom minded not being asked to the wedding?"

"No," Tony replied. "Why would she want to watch him marry someone else?"

"You know how she feels about family. She might have liked to make it a major tribal rite."

"Sure, maybe even do the cooking. Bring along Serena and May too."

"Bea understood," Melissa put in. "I asked her about it. She realized it could be a little hard on Lisa to have a former wife there. Not to mention her parents. Bea might be a bit much for the parents of the young bride. It's just as well they kept it small."

"She's so understanding that it's sick, if you ask me."

"But she's right, Tony."

Little by little Danny was being cheered, almost as if the egg cream were strong drink. This was much better than moping alone in his apartment, watching old movies or marching listlessly on the Nordic-Track. Melissa could be really nice when she chose to. She had a sharp tongue, but maybe she needed it, living with Tony. Lately Tony had been grumbling about her: she was ambitious, she liked her own way, she liked things far too much. Things, things, things! he would mutter with contempt. But Tony grumbled about everything and always had. While it troubled Danny to listen, he enjoyed being in his brother's confidence. He would never have dreamed, ten years ago, even five, that there would come a time when he and Tony would be on good terms, even close. Well, close might be overstating it—the only person Tony was really close to was Jane—but at least the anger was gone. Or transferred. Whatever. At last, Danny felt, he had a real brother. Such as he was.

"Her parents looked a little out of it," he said. "I mean, not exactly thrilled over this marriage."

"How could they be?" said Tony. "Their only daughter marrying someone twice her age? They must wonder what got into her."

"Well, we all know what got into her, don't we?" Melissa said. "That's pretty obvious. Anyhow, he's not twice her age. She's thirty-one. I asked her. My father's new wife is nineteen years younger also, and they're okay so far. It's not so bad. It only seems bizarre because he's your father. So what did you guys think of her?"

"She seemed okay," ventured Danny.

"She seemed inane."

"Tony!" Melissa wailed. "You're so negative! Can't we give her a chance? I mean, maybe she wasn't at her best today, surrounded by the grown children. That can't be easy."

"She seemed more like Shimmer's age than ours," said Tony, scowling. "Describing her collection of stuffed animals. I mean, shit. Can you see Dad snuggling up to stuffed animals?"

"She did seem a little immature," Danny said, "but she can't be all that dumb. She teaches math. They must talk to each other—you know how he likes to talk. I think Melissa's right. It was awkward. She seemed happy, though, like she loved him."

"He must have something," said Tony. "They all love him. For a while at least. I suppose they'll be having kids soon. Are you ready for more brothers and sisters, Danny? I don't think I am."

"You're not even ready for your own," Melissa said. "Danny, we have some news. I'm having another baby."

"Hey, that's great! Really great!" His eyes strayed reflexively to her middle. "I had a feeling when I saw you in that loose . . . because you usually wear, you know?" He wondered if he should get up and hug them, but Melissa was curled in the armchair—it would be too clumsy—and Tony appeared glum, studying the Persian rug. "So, uh, when?"

"Around the middle of May."

"We should have a toast." He raised his egg cream glass. "To the new member of the family. A brother or sister for Timmy. Come on, Tony."

Tony lifted his glass halfheartedly.

"What's the matter, aren't you glad?"

"Yeah, I'm glad. It's . . . I don't know, it's all sort of closing in on me."

"The way I see it," said Danny, "it's opening out. But you always think the glass is half empty."

"My glass is totally empty, actually." Tony smiled for the first time. "I'll get a refill. Anyone else?" He loped off to the kitchen.

"What's his problem?"

"He's so moody lately." Melissa sighed. "Whenever I ask, he has a different reason. He wants to quit law and move to a farm, or he wants to work with Jane on her performance pieces, or go back to graduate school in Asian Studies. . . ."

"Oh, Asian Studies. He's been talking about Asian Studies ever since I can remember." His brother's ingratitude at fate's bounty irked Danny more than ever. Here he was with a good job, tons of money, a great apartment, great-looking wife, a healthy kid and another on the way. In contrast, what did Danny have? A promotion to assistant manager of Ape Copiers? Terrific. He could take an ESL course and teach in Japan or Korea. Sure, if he was lonely in New York, imagine Tokyo or Seoul. Nearer to hand, he had heard about quick money to be made counting cars at a new shopping mall in Queens. And Tony was bitching! Danny would gladly have complained, but it wouldn't change things. He longed to know what would change things. Maybe the Buddhist retreat next week would put him in a more accepting mood. "I'm sure he'll be happier about it once it's born," he said lamely.

Tony reappeared with a full glass. "I am happy about it. But sometimes I wonder if life'll just keep going on this way. You work and have kids and on and on, and . . . That's it? There must be some way to break out of it."

"*Higglety Pigglety Pop! or, There Must Be More to Life,*" said Danny. "Remember that book, Tony? We read it when we were kids."

"Yeah, that about says it. Do you still write?"

"Not much anymore. It was all garbage anyway."

"Do you ever think of going back to school?" Melissa asked in the sisterly tone he disliked. "Not just film school. I mean, like, any school?"

"Not really."

"Well, are you seeing anyone?"

"Not right now. But I have someone in mind."

"Oh, good. So, who is she? Tell us about her."

"There's nothing to tell. I haven't even gone out with her. I just have her in mind."

"In mind's not going to get you anywhere. Why don't you call?"

Easy enough for him to say. Danny had been thinking about Coral since August without making a move, not even to ask Al for her number. By now she was surely seeing someone and wouldn't remember who he was, or would think he was a creep for waiting so long. Fear made him cringe with self-loathing. Hadn't Tony ever known the dread of calling a woman, or wondered why on earth she would want to hear from him? How come Tony got all the discontent and he got all the fear? You'd think the lousy traits might be distributed more equably.

"Did Tony ever tell you," he asked Melissa, "how he was a high school Casanova? With all his ugly moods, he always knew how to get girls."

"Like his dad," Melissa said with a smile.

No, for their dad didn't have ugly moods, thought Danny. Forever good-natured, he simply did exactly as he pleased, and things never

203

failed to work out for him. He had rough times, yes, but always landed on his feet. Or someone caught him. Often it was their mother.

"Like my dad?" said Tony. "No, I didn't marry everyone I had the hots for, or have kids with all of them. Do you realize if he and Lisa have a kid, he'll have children by three different women? Except for Serena. Funny that he never had any with Serena."

"She wasn't the type. She wasn't into family life."

"No?" Tony challenged him. "What do you think she's into now? Just because she's with May, it's family life all the same. Serena loves being in the midst of that . . . that commune they've got going there."

"I think you're awfully hard on your dad," said Melissa. "So what if he has kids with different women? He takes care of them, doesn't he? He didn't desert them, he supported them, he cares about them. He just wants to live his life. He's entitled to that."

"Oh, entitled," groaned Tony. "I'm sick of that word."

"You! You're sick of it! You're the one who feels most entitled to everything."

"Maybe I should go," Danny said. "If you're going to fight . . ."

"No. We're not going to fight." She reached over to squeeze Tony's arm. "We're going to act grown up even if we aren't. Let's call and have a movie delivered. What do you feel like? Horror, drama, action, romance? We can have anything we want delivered to our door."

"I was reading a book about Hawaii," Dmitri said, running his hand along Bea's thigh. "Have you ever been there?"

"No."

"The tourist business is booming, and why not? Splendid weather, beautiful beaches. We could open a guesthouse. Little Odessa by the sea. I could conduct the business and you could administer the cuisine. Fish. I love fish. A luau every week with fresh mahimahi. Maybe some smoked sturgeon for variety. No more cold winters. You and Shimmer would get golden brown and wear sarongs. What do you think, Beatrice darling?''

"I think we should make love while Timmy's still asleep. He could get up any second.''

"Certainly. We can make fantasies and love at the same time. Close your eyes. Forget the snow and think of a beach. You're on a surfboard. Give me your hand.'' He ran her hand up and down his chest. "Does this feel like a surfboard?''

"Not at all. It's too hairy.'' Not bad, she was thinking. Not a bad way to be spending Roy's wedding day.

"You are even less like a surfboard. You have far too many bumps.''

"Bumps? Is that what you call them?''

The phone rang.

"Don't, Bea.''

"I have to. No, stop. Hello? . . . What? . . . Mom, stop screaming, I can't . . . Oh, my God. Get the fire extinguisher! Next to the refrigerator! It's a grease fire,'' she told Dmitri. "Mom, get the fire ex—''

Dmitri was already at the door, luckily in his boxer shorts. The mind is a curious thing, she thought as she grabbed her robe; even in a crisis one could think of propriety. Months ago she had warned her mother to be careful, after a forgotten hot plate produced a small blaze that Anna managed to extinguish by herself.

Wait! The sleeping baby. Should she leave him alone? Yes, he wouldn't climb out of the crib. At the door she stopped short. Leave Timmy alone in a fire? What was she thinking? She raced to the spare room. No! Bring a baby to a fire? He was safer here. This was terrible, standing here debating like Hamlet. It was a small grease fire. Dmitri would put it out. No need to disturb the child. She raced up the stairs. But what if Dmitri's mysterious grief paralyzed him, like post-traumatic stress syndrome? Should she put out the fire herself or flee with Timmy?

Anna's door was wide open. In the kitchen Dmitri was coughing but otherwise composed, squirting the fire extinguisher at the oven while Anna watched, her mouth open and her hands at her cheeks as in

Munch's famous drawing. The room was thick with smoke. Small flames still leaped from the broiler, in whose tray rested a shrunken black steak. A scorched towel, bathed in white foam, lay on the floor. The bottom of the window curtain was similarly blackened and dripping. Choking, Bea opened the window.

"Oh, God. Mom, how did this happen?"

"Because I need a new stove! Why do you let me keep this old one? I could have burned to a crisp like the steak."

"Okay, Mom, it's okay. You're all right." She put her arm around her mother, who was shaking.

Dmitri sprayed the last of the flames to their death, then wiped his brow with a fresh kitchen towel.

"Look at this mess," Anna wailed.

"It doesn't matter. I'll help you clean up."

"And look at him! Practically naked. Is that any way to go around the building in broad daylight? You could give a person a heart attack, rushing in like that. I thought you were out shoveling snow."

"Mom, I don't believe this. You should be glad he got here in time."

"I'm sorry." Dmitri took a glass of water and sat down, his face gray, his eyes tearing from the smoke. "You're right, Anna, my attire is not proper. But I was reluctant to take the time to get dressed."

"What are you apologizing for?" Bea knelt beside him and took his hands, which were ice cold. "Don't pay attention to her, she's outrageous. Go get dressed or you'll catch pneumonia."

"Mom? Are you in here?" It was Shimmer's voice, punctuated by coughing. "Ohmygod! Not again!"

"Another party heard from," muttered Anna. "They run in and out like it's Grand Central Station. What are you all dolled up for?"

"I was at the wedding."

"What wedding?"

"My father's wedding. Remember?"

"How could I remember with all the nonsense that goes on here?"

"Our door was wide open and no one was home, so ... This is awful. We could have been killed."

"Only a little grease fire," said Bea. "It's all over. Dmitri put it out."

Shimmer glanced at him and looked away, blushing. "Uh-huh. I get the picture. Well, you're lucky, Grandma. You should get takeout from now on. It's safer." She dropped the burned towel in the sink, then, using a potholder, removed the tray from the broiler and tossed the steak in the garbage. "Couldn't you even put your clothes on, Mom?"

"No! I couldn't! It was a fire. Why is everybody worried about clothes at a time like this? What is more important?"

"I think I shall take my leave now," said Dmitri, rising rather grandly for a scantily clad man, "since the crisis is over. I'll stop in the apartment for my things, if I may."

"Wait just a minute." Bea fetched an old coat of Anna's. "Here. It's cold in the hall. Would you look in on Timmy while you're there? I'll be down right away. And if my mother can't thank you, I can. You were wonderful. And I'm so sorry. I know this wasn't—"

"It's nothing at all. Please, don't mention it." And he sauntered out.

"Couldn't you at least show some gratitude? He has feelings too, you know?"

"All right, I'll thank him later. Should I give him a tip, maybe?"

"No!" Bea shrieked. "Just be civil. Shimmer, careful with those high heels. The window's open." Shimmer was climbing onto the windowsill to remove the ruined curtain. "I can do that."

"No, you could trip on your robe and fall out. There, it's done. So, isn't anyone going to ask me how the wedding was?"

"How was it?"

"Boring. I think she may be pregnant. She looked a little fat."

"No!" Bea fell into a chair beside her mother. "It couldn't be."

"Why not, Mom? Wait and see for yourself."

"Well, he's not a bad specimen, Bea," said Anna.

"Who, Roy?"

"Not Roy," she said impatiently. "This one. Dmitri. Not bad at all, I have to say."

"Oh, you do? You really *have* to?"

Shimmer tried to muffle her giggles with a cough.

Even if Roy hadn't kept a meticulous appointment book, he would have known his patients by the way they entered. He left the outer door unlocked, being as indolent as he was intrepid, and he wanted an atmosphere of easy access. But Rhonda opened the door timorously, as if it were an act of presumption, and shut it without a sound. Now she must be walking through the carpeted waiting room, now removing her coat. He always had to summon her; she would never knock, far less venture in, even if his office door was open to show he was ready.

"Come on in, Rhonda."

She peeked around the edge of the door with the air of an unexpected, possibly unwelcome guest, a bony, copper-haired woman dressed as usual in a sweat suit that blurred whatever shape she might possess.

She might have sensed something, for she was, if not precisely unwelcome, hardly one of Roy's more interesting patients. A young widow—her husband had died of a heart attack a year ago—she did not, as he anticipated when she turned up six weeks ago, speak of loneliness or sexual longings or the common anxieties of the widowed; she worried constantly over her teenaged daughter, who, as far as Roy could judge, had been acting out since her father's death. The girl was incommunicative, sullen, and boy crazy. If only Shimmer were boy crazy. If only Shimmer would show signs of independence instead of hanging around the house, closeted in her room or clinging to her mother and grandmother.

"Hi, Dr. Power," Rhonda half whispered. She had been a dancer and now taught aerobics in a local exercise salon. Her voice was so wispy, her manner so passive that Roy couldn't envision her jumping about in so unremitting a manner; the one time he had tried an aerobics class, at Serena's urging, he had come home appalled at the shouted demands made upon him—reminiscent of basic training—and been sore for a week.

"Have a seat. You know, I'm not really a doctor," he said amiably. "It's okay for you to call me Roy."

"I know. You told me the first day. But I like to call you doctor even if you're not. I've always had confidence in doctors. It makes me feel you'll solve my problems."

In that case why not go to a real doctor? he thought. An inadmissible remark, of course, but he had to amuse himself somehow. It was his first day back at work after three glorious weeks in Barbados; beach and bed memories made it hard to settle down.

"Whatever you're comfortable with." He smiled. "But I also told you, I'm not a detective either. I don't solve anything. You do that. Or at least understand things better."

"I know, I know." The edge of irritation was a sign of progress. "Did you have a good vacation? You look suntanned."

"Very nice, thank you." He generally steered clear of his private life, especially with new patients. Besides, Rhonda lived and worked right in the neighborhood—best to avoid gossip. He was glad Sam Browder hadn't turned up since last spring; he might feel some discomfort telling him of his marriage. "And how've you been?"

"Me? I've been very upset about Maggie. She doesn't look well at all. She hardly eats, she won't talk to me, just whispers on the phone late at night. She used to tell me things. It's hard, when I'm working full-time. I'm out two nights a week, but I always call. A couple of times she wasn't there, and when I got home and asked where she was, I had the feeling she wasn't telling the truth. She could be anywhere—"

The telephone interrupted. Too bad, but the machine could take it.

"Have you set any rules about what she's—"

"Roy? Welcome back. I have some interesting news for you." He and Rhonda both started at the voice, as if an intruder had popped out of the closet. Serena, sounding sexy and amused. Fuck it! He darted to the phone. "*Very* inter—"

"Serena?" he said, louder than he meant to. "I'm with a patient," he murmured. "Can I call you in forty-five minutes?"

"Just one second. Guess what?"

It was years since she had phoned him at work. It brought back another life—he had to remind himself that he was newly married. "I can't guess. I can't talk now. I'll call you later."

"Wait. Can you meet us, let's say the Botticelli?"

"Us?"

"May'll come too. We should all be there. You must know what I'm talking about. Success! Take a bow."

He had almost forgotten. The memory made him light-headed. "Okay. About an hour. I'm very sorry," he told Rhonda. "I must've forgotten to turn it down after I checked my messages this morning." He spread his hands as if to say, Nobody's perfect.

"Was that your wife?"

"No."

"It sounded like it might be your wife."

"Let's get back to your daughter. Where were we? Yes, her going out at night."

He was not at his best for the remainder of the session. The issues Rhonda posed—the conflation of her widowhood with her daughter's exploding adolescence—should not have been unduly taxing, but his concentration, the quality he most prided himself on, was shattered. And since failures at work always left him dismayed, it was with a heavy heart that he trudged to the Café Botticelli. Heavy and fearful: he might meet someone he knew along the way. He often did. It was four o'clock; school was out. The Botticelli was not on Lisa's direct route home, but she might have errands.

He walked with his head down, and luck favored him; out of the corner of his eye he thought he spied Maxwell but he ignored him for once. Serena and May occupied a table in the rear, conversing with the alluring ease of happy couples. Seated and wearing a heavy sweater, Serena looked unchanged. But he knew. She greeted him warmly. "Ooh, so tan!" Even May was cordial. He kissed both of them on the cheek.

"I'm pregnant," his ex-wife announced with more animation than she usually mustered. "You did it, Roy."

"You did it too."

"Okay, we both did it. Isn't that great?"

"I still don't get it. You always said you didn't want children."

"She changed her mind," said May. "People change with circumstances."

"So I see. Well, I'm not sure what to say. Congratulations." He watched May fold and tear her napkin into petals.

"How do you feel about being a father again?"

"I don't think of myself as the father. I really haven't thought about it much since . . . Listen." He leaned forward and lowered his voice, though the nearby tables were empty. "I'm sure you both understand—no one must know about this."

"Bea knows," said Serena.

"Well, Bea knows everything. But no one else. Particularly Lisa." He paused. "Lisa is pregnant."

May crumpled the napkin and slapped her hand on the table. "You're good, Roy. Really good. Maybe you should go professional."

Serena placed her hand on May's arm. "May, he's done us a favor. Be nice."

"I meant it as a compliment. But okay. Though it may be a little hard to keep it a secret."

"Let's do our best, all right?"

"Are you sure, Roy?" Serena said. "Think about it. You'll be depriving her of knowing who her sisters and brothers are. All your other children. Especially now with Lisa—"

He raised a hand to silence her as the waiter appeared at last and they ordered their cappuccinos.

"It doesn't seem right," Serena continued, "for her not to know who her father is, even."

"How are you so sure it's a she?"

"I have a feeling. I didn't have the amnio. I'd rather be surprised. But I just know it's a girl."

"At forty years old," he said dully, "you should have it."

"I told her the same thing," said May.

"I'm sure it'll be fine. Is Lisa having it?"

211

"We haven't discussed it yet. But she's only thirty-one."

"Well, whatever. But we need to think about what your relationship to this child will be. She'll be part of the family, after all."

Could this be his opaque ex-wife who had rarely been inclined to talk about anything, least of all relationships? "Do I have to have one? A relationship? Beyond being friendly, that is?"

"We thought you might want to," said May. "That we should at least give you the chance. If you don't want to, fine, forget it."

"Wait a second, May. That's not really giving him a chance. He might feel differently after she's born. He might have some feelings about how she should be brought up."

"Sure, I'd have feelings about how she—or he—should be brought up, if these were ordinary circumstances. But they're not. I wouldn't choose to have a child of mine brought up by two, uh, women. But I don't see that I have any choice. Anyway, I don't feel like it's my child. I didn't want it. You know how it happened."

"What about Tony and Jane?" said May. "You might have said the same thing about them once, but look how things changed."

Why was it that every word May uttered grated on him so? "How can you compare Tony and Jane to this? The situation is entirely different. Tony and Jane are my children. They always were, ever since—"

"Look, Roy," Serena said, "I don't have your experience with kids, but I'm sure there're always questions coming up. Like schools and stuff. Or special problems, I don't know, medical expenses. Times when she needs a father."

"Isn't this a little premature? It's not even born yet."

"She."

"All right, she."

"It's good to plan ahead. What if something happens to May or me?"

"Are you by any chance talking about money?" Roy asked.

"Well, that might be part of it."

"Hold it." May frowned. "I'm a little surprised at this too. We don't need his help. We're both working. We can manage."

"But it's nice to have a little . . . cushion. I won't be working as much. What if you have a dry spell or the market changes and you don't sell as well? Anything could happen. I mean, I'm the one carrying this child. I have to make sure she has all she needs. And Roy wants something from us too. He wants us to keep it a secret."

Roy's coffee turned bitter on his tongue. Blackmail? Inconceivable. He couldn't even blame May, whose face had set in aversion, like a mask. Unless the two of them had arranged a good cop–bad cop scenario. Serena was shocking. You could live with a woman for years and never dream of what lurked within. Donald flashed to mind, and he felt a tug of camaraderie. No! Better to tell Lisa everything.

Serena reached over and patted his hand. "Don't look so horrified, Roy. I'm not some kind of monster. It's only something to keep in mind for the future. For our child. I'm sure you'd help *me* if I needed help. This is a family, isn't it?"

He looked at his watch. "I have to go. I have a patient in fifteen minutes."

"You look ashy. Really, you have the wrong idea." She smiled up at him.

"I sure hope so. Incidentally, I'd cut out the Rollerblading if I were you."

"I haven't done that in two months. It's much too cold."

"Good. So long, May."

"This whole meeting wasn't my idea," May said. "I want you to know that."

An unusually mild February afternoon: it felt like her lucky day. How long since it had been warm enough for a walk? Once she sealed and addressed the letter, she'd run a nice bath, then go out on her search.

It had not been an easy letter to write. Though Anna was more than willing to go public, via television, about her singular experience with the boiler man, she found herself reluctant, illogically, to commit it to paper, the more tangible medium. But perhaps this wasn't so illogical after all. Better to rouse their curiosity than reveal everything right off. Lure them with a hint, so they had a reason to get in touch. The prospect of hearing from a TV network elated her. How soon could she expect a reply? A couple of weeks, probably, maybe less. She must keep a close watch on the mail and instruct Ernesto to bring it up promptly. Secrecy was of the essence; Bea would squelch her project immediately if she knew. If she was chosen for the show, she would need to do something about her hair. What to wear? Simplicity was best for TV, no loud prints or stripes. The navy blue? No, that was an old-lady dress. Oprah went in for red. Well, there was plenty of time to decide, and to shop if necessary.

As the tub filled, it occurred to her that she might have had a bath in the morning—she couldn't recall. It didn't matter. There was no such thing as too clean, as she used to tell her children, and if today's search were successful, she should look her best.

She studied her body before she stepped into the tub. Not bad, considering. Funny, how when you first notice certain sags and wrinkles, you feel cast down, you can't believe you'll have to live with them forever, but after a while you're used to them and grateful they're not worse. Her breasts were tolerable: small was better than big at this point—there was less to droop. Her arms were still strong from all the lifting and hauling she'd done in her time. The flesh on her thighs was loose and flabby, but who ever really looked there? Too bad the hair down there was so sparse, and what remained was gray: pathetic. She could dye it with the stuff she used on her head, but it might sting, and the notion of sitting for half an hour with that smelly stuff on her was unappealing. It might linger, and a woman should always smell good there. You never know.

She was in the tub only five minutes when she heard the phone. When she got to it, dashing and dripping wet, no one was there. It must have been the Katrovas' phone across the courtyard, which sounded exactly the same. She'd soaked long enough anyway. She dressed quickly in jeans, a sweater, and sneakers and grabbed her coat and keys.

At the door she stopped. There was a low humming noise like some kind of machine. A vacuum next door, most likely.

Downstairs, Ernesto lounged on his chair. "Going out for a walk, Mrs. Anna? You got the right idea. Catch the sun while it lasts."

Exactly the way he spoke to the little children. He was barely more than a boy himself, and his hair was too short, like Nazis, the new kind, skinheads. No, Ernesto, with his small smirking eyes, did not please her any more than Carlos did. Not that he didn't do his job: how hard is it to be a doorman? You carry packages and hail taxis and watch out for hoodlums, and above all, you talk nice—to the tenants and especially to the boss. But he thought she was a crazy old lady, she could tell; his good manners seemed phony, as if the minute she was out of sight his smile might twist into a sneer. Five years ago she would have told him off good and proper, but she was losing her spirit; she couldn't work herself up to it. She gave him a nod and stepped outside. Maybe Sara was right—they should have found a woman doorman. A nice middle-aged woman who spoke English. Or Russian. But would that kind of person want to be a doorman?

Despite the rancid smell of dust and plaster from the construction site on the corner, the air was crisp and invigorating. Herb Brownstein could keep his Florida; there was nothing to beat a bright blue New York sky. She clutched the letter so she wouldn't forget to mail it. Three months ago she forgot to mail the phone bill, and when they called to say they were turning off the phone, she gave them an argument. Then after two days of no service, she discovered the envelope in her purse, dusty and flaking, caught in the teeth of her comb. With satisfaction, she dropped the letter in the corner box, the jangle of the lid like a harbinger of excitement, and proceeded to walk south, stopping at each building to scan the doormen. "You have an Oscar working here?" No luck. After a while she felt a little tired. And thirsty. She would get a soda at the hot dog stand at the park entrance. Maybe Oscar would walk by and she could explain how it had all been a misunderstanding, whatever it was—she hoped he had forgotten too. At their age, long friendship was not something you tossed aside lightly.

She could tell him about the insolent Ernesto and he would listen kindly and patiently as always. At the hot dog stand she discovered she had forgotten her purse.

"Listen, you know me, I own the building on the corner. Be a nice fellow and give me a Coke. I'll come back later and pay you."

"The building on the corner?" the man said, and Anna realized he was not their hot dog man at all but a stranger. The building on the corner was a church.

"The corner a few blocks up. Come on, I'm a neighbor. I'm good for the money. I left my pocketbook home."

The man shrugged and handed her a diet Coke.

"Not the diet. The regular."

He gave her a keen look, exchanged the soda, then snapped open the can and inserted the straw.

"Thank you. You're a gentleman and a scholar."

It might have been spring. In the park, toddlers played in the sandbox while their nannies chatted on the benches and homeless beggars took their ease, Bea's friend Maxwell among them. He waved, but Anna ignored him. Take a bath and get a job, was all she had to say, and she knew from experience that he didn't like hearing that. She strolled east and settled down on a bench in the sun to watch a group of girls in green uniforms play soccer. It was wonderful how the girls did everything nowadays, same as the boys. She would have liked a chance to kick a ball around too. If she weren't so tired she might just get up and try it. She took a deep breath and closed her eyes.

She awoke to chill darkness and pulled her coat closer around her. An empty soda can lay beside her on the bench. How long had she been in the park, and what for? It got dark so early these days, and it was hard to orient yourself in the park even in daylight. She wandered, turning down one path then another, passing a young black woman pushing an old white woman in a wheelchair; thank God that wasn't her yet. Oscar! Of course. She'd been looking for Oscar. Those tall buildings in the distance must be Central Park West. This time she knew exactly where she lived and where she was headed. Onward she strode.

"Mom? Al and I are in the neighborhood—well, not too far, up in Harlem. We thought we might drop over. Is that okay?"

In her haste to get to the phone—what new disaster could Anna have caused?—Bea still gripped the wet mop. Relieved, she leaned on it like a pilgrim's staff. "Oh, Janie. What time is it?"

"Almost eleven. Did I wake you? I'm sorry. We're hardly ever up here, so I thought . . ."

"You didn't wake me. I wish you had, I mean, given what's been going on the last few hours. Sure, come on over. There's not a thing here to eat, though, and I look a mess."

"Don't sweat it, Mom. You can tell me when we get there. We're at this club where Al's sister was singing. You'll finally get to meet her."

Moving at top speed, Bea finished mopping the bathroom floor and turned on the fan to hasten the drying of the ceiling. Dmitri, who was mopping in the apartments below and who would have to deal, yet again, with the sullen painters who spoke little English and less Russian, would no doubt stop in when he was done. An impromptu little party. She made a pot of coffee and changed her clothes just in time to answer the door.

"What is that smell?" said Jane.

"Can you smell it all the way out here? It's plaster, from the bathroom. You're looking much too thin, Jane. Al, let me look at you too. I haven't seen either of you in ages."

Al wrapped her in his bear hug and then presented Coral. "My Parisian sister."

"Not quite. I've been back for months. But it's true I'm still not assimilated." Coral stretched out an elegant hand. "Hi, Bea. I've heard a lot about you."

How beautiful, Bea thought. Coral had amber skin, a wide mouth, and enormous velvety eyes. Her hair was pulled straight back and fas-

217

tened in a bun, a style suited only to the finest of cheekbones. While Al and Jane wore their usual nondescript thrift shop black and cowboy boots, Coral was in a clingy red velour shift.

"Come on in. Careful, don't trip over the skates."

"Who's the blader?" asked Al. "Shimmer?"

"No, me. I started last year with Serena and May. It's Serena's way of getting us to exercise. Although she probably won't be skating for a while. She's—" She stopped in horror at her indiscretion; she had never before divulged delicate information without just cause. For all she knew, Anna's malady was contagious.

"She's what?" Jane pursued.

"She sprained her ankle. Nothing serious. So, what were you doing in Paris, Coral? Not that anyone needs a reason to be in Paris. Here, sit down. Have some coffee."

"This and that. A little singing. Working on my French, giving English lessons on the side."

"Coral's very modest," said Al. "She had plenty of work in Paris—she's a great cabaret singer—but she missed the family, right?"

Her smile was warm but reserved. "It was time to come home. I think I was avoiding trying to make it here, but now I'm ready. Except I've got to get my life together first. Job, apartment, all that. I've been staying with my parents, but, well, it's hard to live with parents after I've been on my own for two years."

"I can imagine. Around here everybody moves out as fast as they can even though we have these wonderful apartments. I don't understand it. Well, no, I do understand it, but I think it's something that can be overcome with goodwill. Anyhow, I'll come hear you sometime. I always like to hear Al. And what are you two up to?" Not getting married, that was for sure. Bea had nearly given up hope of that. Not because Al suffered from fear of commitment (FOC, the younger generation called it) or fear of intimacy (FOI, with a French accent). Rather it was Jane. She refused to be pressured into marriage, Al had sadly confided to Bea on several occasions. Nor did her life plans include children.

"My group is working on a new performance piece," Jane began. "We're using old tailors' mannequins and lip-synching—"

Bea was trying to look eagerly receptive when Dmitri burst in, haggard, in grimy jeans, bearing a mop and bucket.

"Ah, we have company!" he declared. "The downtowners! Don't hug me, I'm filthy," he warned Jane. He pressed her hand, then Al's. "I would kiss your hand," he told Coral, "but one cannot preserve old-world manners while carrying a mop. Did Bea tell you what occurred?"

"Not yet. Put that down and join us, darling. He's not really a derelict, Coral—we've just had a little domestic disaster. Is everything done now?"

"For tonight. Tomorrow will begin the serious work. The Harrises on seven were not very amiable about this incident, alas. No coffee, thank you. A little vodka for the help?" He sat down with the bottle in front of him.

"I told you they were like this," Jane said to Coral. "What was it this time, Mom?"

"Your grandmother took advantage of the thaw to go on one of her walks and left the bathtub running. She fell asleep in Central Park, and when she woke up she was lost. We called the police, but it was Dmitri who finally found her."

"I understand her habits," he murmured in between sips. "I too am a wanderer."

"She was somewhere near the obelisk, in the dark. She didn't know where she was, but at least she knew who she was. The water from her tub ruined the bathrooms in four apartments, including this one. It's going to cost a fortune. You should see what ours looks like. The tenants were calling all evening— Where are you going?"

Jane drifted, wraithlike, across the room. "You said we should see. I want to see." An instant later she was back. "It's terrible, you're right. It smells like old vomit."

"Thank you, Jane. You always had a way with words."

"What are you going to do about her?" Al asked. Jane sometimes

219

joked that it was Al's curiosity about her family—so unlike his highly decorous one—that kept him loyal. Perhaps she had a point, Bea thought.

"That is the question. It's really not safe anymore. Last month, did I tell you, Jane, she could have gassed herself to death, but thank God the windows were open. She knocks on people's doors, she throws their wet laundry on the floor in the basement when she needs the machine. I suppose"—Bea sighed—"I'll have to do something. I can't put it off anymore. But who could put up with her?"

"Maybe it's time, Mom. I mean, maybe you should look into, uh . . ."

"No. Not while I draw breath. No member of my family is going to live in an institution. She may be impossible, but she's my mother and I'll find a way."

"Even if you go nuts in the process?"

"I won't go nuts," said Bea. "I'm not the type. Sometimes I wish I were."

"How impossible is she, exactly?" asked Coral.

"Ha!" Dmitri roared.

"Sort of a cross between Bela Lugosi and Madonna?" Al suggested.

"You could hire me to look after her." Coral crossed her legs primly, as if at a job interview.

Again Dmitri roared.

"Why are you laughing? Don't you think I could manage?"

He smiled faintly and poured more vodka.

"That's very sweet of you, Coral," said Bea, "but I'm thinking more along the lines of professional help."

"She's not really sick, is she? It sounds like what you need is a kind of companion."

"Please. If you knew her, you'd realize it's out of the question."

"She's right, Coral," said Al. "Forget it. You're still in culture shock. You'd be better off working for Uncle Gerard."

"Oh, Uncle Gerard. He'd try to talk me into going to nursing school—he's been pushing that ever since I learned to read. And can you see *me,* a receptionist in a urologist's office? Dealing with all those old guys with prostate trouble?'' She grimaced in disgust. ''This way I'd have a place to live. I assume you'd want someone to live in? And I could have time to audition and rehearse, right? I wouldn't mind walking in the park with her or playing cards or whatever she likes. I worked for a while as companion to an old woman in Paris. I cooked and ran errands, and she gave me French conversation.''

''No French conversation here,'' said Jane. ''But you could learn Russian. Remember you were teaching me, Dmitri? I should've kept it up.''

''Why don't we drop the subject?'' said Bea. ''It's absurd. There are a million better opportunities for you. What did you study in college?''

''Anthropology.''

''Well, she is primitive,'' Jane said. ''You might be able to get an article out of it, if you ever returned to grad school.''

''Maybe I'll scramble some eggs. How does that sound?''

''We ate at the club. Look,'' Coral insisted, ''it would be useful for me. The main thing I need is time for my singing. As long as she doesn't mind that, and I can have flexible hours—''

''My dear child, I could never hire an educated person like you for this. It would be all wrong.''

''Because I'm black.''

''Not at all.'' They were plunged into an awkward silence; only Coral managed to smile and keep her gaze steady. ''Well, maybe a little,'' Bea admitted. ''It just doesn't feel right. It's all those old stereo-types.''

''It's reverse racism,'' said Coral.

''It's inappropriate. There are women who train for jobs like these. I'll find one.''

''They're black too, I bet.''

''Some are, some aren't. It's immaterial.''

''So you're not against having a black person, just an educated black person? Is that it?'' Coral asked.

''Whoa,'' said Al. ''Save that for someone who deserves it. You've got Bea all wrong.''

"Have I? Suppose I was a white singer who needed a job while I was getting myself set up? Would it be out of the question then?"

Shimmer appeared in the doorway, tying her terry-cloth robe. "I didn't know you were all coming over." She rubbed her eyes. "I was so tired after we picked up the plaster, I fell asleep."

A fortunate arrival, Bea thought, as Jane and Al hugged Shimmer and introduced Coral. Now they could talk of something else. Ships or shoes or sealing wax. Anything. But Coral, who was proving resolute, immediately explained the dilemma to Shimmer. "What do *you* think?" she concluded.

"You haven't met her," said Shimmer.

"I know, but what do you think, just in the abstract?"

"In the abstract, it would be great. For Grandma, I mean. For everyone. We wouldn't have to think about her all the time. Whenever we leave her alone, something happens. We have to take turns, like baby-sitting. Except what would she do when you were out auditioning?"

"I have plenty of friends in the same situation who could fill in. I could supply a constant chorus line. A rainbow coalition," she added, looking over at Bea.

"You don't exactly understand," said Bea. "There are things you wouldn't want to do. Cleaning, cooking. Menial work. I can't hire a whole staff."

"I do hate to clean, that's true. But for money . . ." Coral said cheerfully. "I've heard you cook for a living."

"That's different. It's my business."

"Bea's cooking is an art," said Dmitri.

"I'm an artist too. You'd be helping the arts. I bet you give money to the arts, don't you? And the NAACP, the ACLU, all of that stuff?"

She might be just the sort of person to manage Anna, Bea thought. But a piece of her mind kept its fretful resistance. "Doesn't anyone understand? Am I so wrong?"

"Yes," said Shimmer. "It's the same as when you didn't want a woman doorman. It's just prejudice."

"Oh, that woman doorman again! It's not the same at all. Prejudice!

You're another generation. You're lucky you don't know how it used to be.''

"That's the point, Mom. It isn't how it used to be."

Bea appealed to Dmitri.

"On the complexities of race in America, my dear Bea, on the legacy of slavery, I cannot be a good judge. I am still too much the outsider. But if the young lady wants the job . . ." He shrugged.

"The legacy of slavery, since you bring it up," said Coral, "is that black people should feel free to use white people when they need to. I only want to use you," she told Bea with a winning smile. "With your attitudes, you should jump at the chance."

"Cool it, Coral," said Al. "I don't see it that way. I'm not using anybody."

"You better not be." Jane gave him a mock punch in the jaw. "Oh, I forgot. I'm not really white people."

"This conversation is very distressing," said Bea. "Isn't there something else we can talk about?"

"Mom, she wants the job, so let her have it," said Jane. "She'll probably quit after a week anyway, so you won't suffer liberal guilt for too long."

"Don't be so sure. That I'd quit, I mean."

"You were always my supportive girl, Jane," said Bea wistfully. "Maybe I leaned on you too hard."

"Doesn't anyone care what I think?"

"Okay, brother, what do you think?"

"I think it sucks. Pop didn't send you to Brown to end up cleaning house for a nutty old lady—sorry, Bea. Mama's parents sent *her* to college so she wouldn't have to either. You want to regress three generations? The plantation's next, girl."

"No one, but no one, hears what *I* want. I want to come and go as I please. I don't want to be living in the room I grew up in. I want my mind free for my real work. Sure, I could sit at a computer at some slick corporation and let them show off their good politics, but why should I? And quite frankly I wouldn't mind living on Central Park West. I won't find too many jobs that would pay that rent."

"It's not even Central Park West," Al muttered. "It's a side street."

"I thought you, of all people, would be supportive."

"Supportive? Shit, Coral. How're you going to explain this to Mama and Pop?"

"The same way I explained going to Paris. They didn't like that, they won't like this, they're so out of it they won't like anything I do unless I become Lena Horne or the black Margaret Mead. I'll handle them."

"Oh, God," groaned Bea. "Look what we've gotten into now."

"It's late," said Coral. "Why don't I call you in the morning and we can discuss the details?"

"Are you going to be mad at me if I do this, Al?" said Bea.

"No. I'm going to be mad at her."

"Good night, Mom," said Jane. "Aren't you glad we came? Your problem is solved."

"*Voilà*," said Dmitri when they were out the door. "She'll be perfect for Anna. Don't you see?"

"He's right," agreed Shimmer. "Oh, I forgot to mention. Magenta's staying over again tomorrow night. Is that okay?"

"I guess so. Doesn't her mother ever wonder why she's here so much? Sometimes it feels like she's moving in."

"Her house is too quiet. She likes the atmosphere here. You should be flattered." She flopped down on the couch. "I don't feel like going back to sleep. Or do you two need your privacy or something?"

"No, sit with us awhile. We all need to recover from our mopping. Do you want a glass of milk?"

"Can I have some of the vodka?"

"Certainly not. Have a cup of coffee if you're feeling rebellious."

"No, that's my brother Sid you're thinking of. He was the prizefighter, not Lenny," Anna explained to Shimmer. "Lenny owned the delicatessen. But after Sid stopped fighting he went and worked for Lenny. They wanted me to work there too, but I didn't want any part of it.''

"So what did you do after high school?'' asked Coral. "Would you like a little more soup?''

"No, sweetheart, that was fine.'' Anna pushed her bowl away. "You make a very nice soup. A nice lunch. What did I do? I worked in an office, import-export. I learned typing and shorthand. But whenever I wasn't working, I was with the Young Socialists. That was my real passion. That's how I met your grandfather,'' she told Shimmer.

"I know. You were at a demonstration.'' Shimmer peeled an orange and handed sections around; Coral had bought two dozen oranges and arranged them in a pyramid in Anna's crystal bowl.

"It was on a picket line, some dress factory down on Ludlow Street, yes, Ludlow and Grand. Funny how I remember things from back then better than now. Our signs bumped into each other. He was a handsome fellow. Very dashing. I was particular in those days. I had what today they call self-esteem. They fussed over me because I was the baby of the family. Like you, Sara.''

"Shimmer. But I don't have self-esteem.''

"So get some. Who's stopping you? What about you?'' She turned to Coral. "You have self-esteem, I can tell. Are you also the baby?''

"Yes, there are only two of us, Al and me.''

"We were four, all dead now except me. The two boys, and my sister, Sonia. She got ground down, my poor sister.''

"Why? What happened to her?'' asked Coral.

"It's a sad story. You don't want to know from it.''

"No, tell us. Really, I love to hear stories.''

"You're sure? Not just because they're paying you? Okay.'' Anna settled back in the chair with pleasure. "I was the one with spirit and Sonia was the good-looking one. Tall, held herself straight like a queen, with her chin tilted up so people thought she was proud but she wasn't, just shy, and with very good posture. Posture was important in those days, like now you have fitness. But for all her good looks she didn't know how to talk to people. No confidence. So anyway, this fellow

225

starts to come around—for her, not me, I was just a kid. A doctor. We were very impressed, because in those days a doctor, well—to marry a doctor was the ultimate. The security, the status.''

''I wouldn't want to marry a doctor,'' said Shimmer. ''They're boring.''

''Neither would I,'' said Coral. ''My Uncle Gerard is so arrogant. He thinks he's better than the rest of us because he went to medical school. I don't know how many times I've heard him say he was the only black in his class.''

''I don't want to marry anyone, I don't think.''

''I'm not sure I do either. I might be persuaded. But never a doctor.''

''You'll both be persuaded fast enough, believe me. That doesn't change. But in those days, a doctor, what can I tell you? That's how it was. So my parents were ready to overlook a lot. And believe me, there was a lot to overlook. One reason he liked her was that she was so tall. He was little and puny. He wanted big children and he got them. You remember those cousins from Washington, Shimmer? How tall they are? So he married her and got what he wanted. What she wanted I don't know. She wasn't in the habit of saying, even to me, her kid sister. I suppose she was flattered that he liked her, being a doctor and all. He lived with his old parents and a sister. That was how they did in those days, the whole family together.''

''That's how we do here too,'' said Shimmer.

''No, it was different. Here it's all the divorces and shenanigans. Such goings-on we didn't have. Maybe among the rich, but not among us. For a single person to move out and get an apartment was unheard of. Like you, for instance,'' she said to Coral. ''A young girl like you out on her own would be a disgrace. They'd imagine she's doing all kinds of things. How old are you?''

''Twenty-four.''

''A disgrace. Now, no one thinks anything of it. Not even me. So anyway, the doctor's mother, she was a piece of work. They think I'm bad? They don't know what bad is.''

''You're not so bad, Grandma.''

"Thank you, Sara, I mean Shimmer, but let's not kid ourselves. I know what I am. This woman, though, could put me to shame. She made my poor sister's life miserable, ordering her around like some kind of servant girl and not her son's wife. My sister wasn't used to that kind of treatment. She wasn't prepared. She was a young girl like you, Coral, not even as old as you, and suddenly in a strange house with this witch, and her husband the doctor didn't stick up for her. I guess he expected her to take it, or else he was so busy doctoring he didn't notice. Like Eleanor Roosevelt, her life was. Except my sister didn't have such strength of character."

"What do you mean, Eleanor Roosevelt?" asked Shimmer.

"Don't they teach you anything in school? She too had a mother-in-law from hell, like you would say. And her husband, big deal that he was, he could hold his own with Churchill and de Gaulle but he didn't have the nerve to answer back his own mother. Well, after six months of this she ran away and came home. My sister, I mean, not Eleanor. It was unheard of but she did it. She came in the house sobbing—I remember, I was there, a quiet Saturday afternoon like today. This is Saturday, right?"

"Right," Coral assured her.

"Of course, otherwise Sara would be in school. You're back in school, aren't you? It's not still vacation?"

"No, it's February, Grandma. And I'm Shimmer."

"All right, Shimmer. So she came home and said she couldn't stand it anymore, the way the old lady treated her. She wasn't strong. Tall and regal, yes, but no backbone. She stayed home for a month, living like a girl again. It was nice having her back. I was lonesome without her. Maybe she was pregnant, I don't remember the timing—I was the baby so they never told me anything—but anyway, after a month they sent her back to him."

"No!" Coral gasped.

"You're a married woman now, they said, that's where you belong. They sent her right back even though she didn't want to go. And she went."

"That's terrible," said Shimmer.

"That couldn't happen today," said Coral. "She could get an abortion. The whole thing would never happen."

"So times are different, so what? That wouldn't happen, maybe, but other things happen. Look at the TV, you'll find plenty of stories. Or look at my Bea, for instance. She was very talented on the viola. Maybe she could have been as successful as her sister. And what happened? She became a cook. Did you know that?" she asked Shimmer.

"I knew she played, but I didn't know she was ever serious about it."

"She wasn't serious. If she was serious she would do it. Anyhow, with my sister, what could they do? He was her husband, after all."

"She was their daughter," said Coral. "Didn't they care what her life was like? What she was going through?"

"They cared. But you didn't give up a doctor so fast. And what would become of her, a married woman back in her parents' house? I guess they figured the old lady wouldn't live forever. As it turned out, she lived a good twelve years or more, and by that time my sister got used to it. Is there any more coffee, dear?"

"I'll heat it up. This is one of the most depressing stories I've ever heard."

"I warned you. And what did she get out of it, I ask you? That house with the long dark halls you had to grope your way through because he was too cheap to turn on the lights, and the bathroom stinking of urine so you would gag when you walked in, because the old man, the doctor's father, by then could barely see what he was doing. Okay, maybe you can't blame him, but why no one cleaned up after him . . . I guess after a while she didn't care or she didn't notice anymore, and as far as the doctor, forget it. Patients he could treat, but not clean up after his father. We used to think, look, it's a life—she had the house, the husband, the children. Without those things where is your life? Now they think differently."

"I would run away. Or kill myself," said Shimmer.

"I would never kill myself," said Coral. "I'd tell her off. I'd never let myself be treated that way."

"It was different. You girls can't understand."

"Damn right we can't. But you were in the Young Socialists. Didn't you know there were other options?"

"Sure, we talked a lot about how things were set up. Free love, we talked. Free this, free that. But in the family these ideas . . . They were just ideas. No one paid attention. I was just glad they let me go to the meetings—well, they knew they couldn't stop me. I talked to her but she didn't understand. I didn't understand myself. Her life and my ideas were two separate worlds. We were going to change the world, but meanwhile . . . It's a life, everyone thought. I thought so too." She drained her coffee with a slurping sound. "And it *is* a life. What did the Young Socialists accomplish? We didn't change the world. We didn't change much, except maybe for the unions, and look at them now, gone to hell, in bed with the bosses. I met my Mickey. That was the best thing it accomplished for me. And we bought the building with what my parents left after they sold the store. The doctor helped us and we paid him back."

"You used his money after all that?" Shimmer was aghast.

Anna nodded. "We used to hate the landlords, but that's what we became. You're on one side or the other, and whichever side you're on, that's who you become. Self-interest, we used to call it." She paused, chuckling. "They think I'm senile. But you see my mind still works a little bit. So, Coral, what about my hair? I want to have it nice for the party next month. You promised."

"Oh, the hair. I got so caught up, I almost forgot. Okay, I'll just clear these things away."

"Clear up later. I want the hair now."

"Hey, I have to make room, don't I? Shimmer, could you bring in the bottles?"

Coral spread newspaper on the kitchen table and placed a towel over Anna's shoulders. After studying the directions, she put on plastic gloves and poured a viscous green liquid into a bottle of clear fluid, shook it, then poured the mixture into a bowl. "Wet the hair first, it says. Come over to the sink, Anna. How about some music?"

Shimmer flicked on the radio and found a rock station. "How's that?"

"Cool! This is going to be fun."

"It's nice music," said Anna. "We could dance to that."

"Not now. You have to sit still while I do this. And keep your eyes closed. It could burn. There. Turn a little to the left. Now the right."

"If it comes out good," said Shimmer, "could you do mine?"

"No! Your mother would kill me and I'd lose my job."

"An old lady can do what she likes," said Anna. "You have to look normal awhile yet."

"I'll do it myself then."

"That's up to you, but I can't be responsible. Okay, this seems about right. That's the basic coloring. Now, Anna, did you decide where you want the green?"

"What did those girls we saw downtown have?"

"Some had streaks; some had tips; some did just the top. A friend of mine made two stripes. If you want tips, I have to cut some holes in a plastic bag."

"This is fantastic." Shimmer danced around the kitchen. "Wait till my mother sees." She began doing the dishes, dancing in place at the sink.

"Maybe a nice plain streak down the middle. Some other time I'd like to have what you have. Can you do that for me?"

"This?" Coral said, shaking her new African braids. "I'd have to take you to this place in Harlem where they did mine. They'd see if your hair is thick enough. Let's do one thing at a time. Okay, here goes." She applied the green dye down the center of Anna's head.

"Ugh! The smell is terrible."

"Sit still. It's no worse than what you've been using. What do you think, Shimmer? Turn around. Is this okay for a streak or should it be wider?"

"No, that's cool the way it is. You'll look real punk, Grandma."

"I will?"

"Now you have to wait half an hour, then we'll rinse it out. You can watch us dance meanwhile."

"I think I'll read the paper." She reached across the table for her glasses.

"No." Coral grabbed them away. "They'll get covered with dye. You have to sit. Sorry, that's the way it is."

"I forgot how hard it is to be beautiful."

At last Anna had a bright green streak down the center of her head. "The color is excellent," said Coral. "Now we'll style it."

"Let me. I'm good with hair." Shimmer combed Anna's hair in various ways, letting the streak fall to the right and then the left, while Coral held up the mirror.

"That! That's what I like, with the part in the middle and a little green on each side."

"You're a new woman." Coral switched off the radio. "I'll blow you dry."

"I think that's the door," Shimmer shouted over the noise of the dryer. She went to check and returned with Danny.

"Grandma, I was— Ohmygod." He stood transfixed, gazing at the hair, holding an open can of Coke.

"Turn that thing off!" Anna ordered. "What's the matter? You don't like it? I thought for a change."

Danny remained rooted to the spot, his gaze shifting to Coral. Beneath his open down coat he wore his "Go Ape" sweatshirt, advertising Ape Copiers, his place of employment.

"Hi," said Coral. "Remember me?"

"Uh, sure. What are you doing here? I feel like I'm in a dream."

"Is it a nightmare?" asked Shimmer. "Coral's living here. What do you think of Grandma's hair? You think it would look good on me?"

"I . . . I'm surprised. I almost didn't recognize you with the . . . those . . ."

"Is it that bad?" asked Anna. "Tell the truth."

"He means her braids," Shimmer explained.

"I thought I'd try it out. Do you like it?" Coral turned slowly, tossing the braids to and fro.

"Yes. You look so different, though."

"What about me?" Anna demanded.

"It's very unusual, Grandma. I mean, it's green."

"Of course it's green. That's the idea."

"Why didn't anyone tell me? Nobody tells me things."

"I have to tell you when I change my hair?"

"No, Grandma. He means tell him Coral is taking care of you. Because you were away. She's only been here a week or so. Weren't you at that Buddhist place?"

"Yeah, I just got back. I was going to say hi to Mom but she was out so I came up here."

"She's Rollerblading with Aunt May. Any day over forty degrees. They made a self-improvement pact."

"I didn't know she was a blader."

"Come around more often, you'll learn a lot," said Shimmer.

He finally stirred, going to kiss Anna on the cheek. "It's an interesting change, Grandma."

"What's that in your hand?"

"This? Coke. You want some?"

"No. Coke." She stared as if in a trance, then blinked herself out of it. "So now it's Buddhists. Did they make a Buddhist out of you?"

"No, we just meditated. I'm out of the habit of talking. It was a silent retreat."

"You're no big talker anyway. A silent retreat and you could stop altogether. Listen, children, I'm worn out after my beauty treatment. I have to take a nap. Throw this stuff down the toilet, Coral. It's stinking up the house."

"I will. All in good time."

At the door, Anna glanced again at the can Danny had set down on the table. "Coke," she muttered.

"Aren't you a singer anymore?" Danny sat down gingerly.

She laughed. "Sure. I'll always be a singer."

"So why do you want to do this?"

"Don't shoot. I can explain everything." And she did. "She's not as bad as they say. You just have to handle her right."

"Does my mother know about the hair?"

"Not yet. I wanted to check out a new club in SoHo yesterday, so I took Anna along. She loved it. She hadn't been downtown since it was all factories. You know how everyone down there's got this weird hair, and she liked it, so I thought, why not? Hair therapy, sort of."

Shimmer stood up. "I've got to go now."

"Don't go!" said Danny. "I mean, I've hardly seen you."

"I have to. Magenta's coming over. You can call me later. See you, Coral."

Danny wanted to flee but could not; his terror would be transparent, and he could not bear the thought of Coral's scorn. He imagined Tony or, even worse, Melissa asking again about the mysterious woman he had alluded to. Could he tell a craven lie? Or confess that he had run like a coward? No, he must stay, although his throat felt so constricted he could hardly swallow the coffee and cookies she set before him. Twenty minutes, he commanded himself. He must manage twenty minutes, then leave politely, like a man.

By then they had moved into the living room and Coral had asked about the retreat. She seemed genuinely interested; he found himself describing how difficult it was to empty his mind. The mind was like the sky, the Zen master said, and thoughts were like the clouds that passed across it and vanished. But he seemed unwilling to let the clouds pass. The master had even struck him, not very gently, on the shoulder with his staff. It had been embarrassing as well as painful at the time, but now it became an amusing anecdote. At least she was laughing along with him. She told him about auditioning; next week she'd be trying out for the chorus of the second-longest-running musical on Broadway. A long shot, but the assistant director had heard her at a club and stayed to meet her afterward. You never could tell.

"Hey, why don't you come hear me tonight? I'm singing at the Red Carpet. Down in the East Village? Ten-thirty."

"I didn't get an invitation." Suddenly Anna was in the doorway. "Why don't you ever invite me?"

"I will, another time. Tonight wouldn't work out. It'll be over too late. So, will you? But maybe you're busy."

"Well, I might . . ." Could she really be asking for his company? He glanced at his watch and was stunned to find that thirty-five minutes had passed. He had forgotten to feel tormented. The flickering anxiety that remained was almost pleasant. "I have a job till eight-thirty but I guess I could—"

"What kind of job?" asked Anna.

"Nothing much. I'm counting cars at a shopping mall in Queens."

"Counting cars? What kind of work is that?"

"Kind of, market research. I have a clicker, see?" He removed it from his pocket to show his grandmother, but she spurned it.

"A college-educated boy. Don't tell me any more, I don't want to get aggravated." She turned to Coral. "So what about me? Am I going to be here all alone?"

"No, Luz is coming to stay with you. Remember, she came last week?"

"The Spanish dancer? She was a nice girl. She taught me flamenco."

"Good. Maybe she'll do that again. So, I hope I'll see you there," she said to Danny.

"Go. What's your problem? You're too busy counting?"

"Okay. Sure," he agreed, before Anna could embarrass him further.

"Danny," she added as he turned to go, "tell Ernesto to bring up the mail. And another thing, I have a little errand for you. Here." She handed him a dollar.

"Grandma, please! I'm not that broke."

"Take it and listen to me. Walk down four or five blocks along the park. There's a hot dog man opposite the church. Give him the dollar and tell him it's from me. I owe him."

"What for?"

"A soda. What do you think, I'm buying drugs? And if you see your big brother, tell him to give me a call once in a while. I'm not dead yet."

As he made his way out, Danny's feet sank into cushions of cloud with each step, exactly as the Zen master had described the elusive experience of enlightenment.

"Why are you always so eager to get the mail? Are you expecting something important?" Coral asked teasingly.

"Don't you get sassy with me, young lady. That's my business."

"Okay! So, tell me a little about Danny."

X

You're sure this won't be too awkward, Roy? I mean, I could understand, in her position, if she felt some resentment—"

"Darling, you don't understand at all. Bea doesn't have a position, not in that sense." At the mirror, Roy cast a wistful glance at his chest before buttoning his shirt. A pity the honeymoon suntan was nearly faded; he had enjoyed viewing his bronzed body. There were tanning salons. . . . No! What was he thinking? Today the tanning salon, tomorrow touch up his graying temples . . . a slippery slope.

"And even if she did," he went on, "why would she resent *you*? I left her for Serena, and that was years ago. They're even friends now. We're all good friends, I told you. This'll be a simple little dinner with her and Shimmer. Bea just wants to be nice." His own words spurred Roy's eager anticipation. He had hardly seen Bea since they returned from Barbados; the honeymoon itself was the longest stretch he had ever been out of touch. But one doesn't phone a first wife while honeymooning with a third. Inappropriate, he would have said had a patient expressed such a wish.

Lisa took his place at the full-length mirror and studied her body in profile; the bottom half was encased in tight black leggings, her almost six-month pregnancy high and firm, volleyball size. "Good friends?" she repeated, slipping a loose embroidered shirt over her head. It reached halfway down her thighs.

"For the sake of the family. She has strong feelings about family."

"Well, it's just one evening. I guess I'll manage. At least the food'll be good, from what you tell me. And she seemed nice, that one time I met her at school. God, I feel so fat. Do I look very big?"

"You look fine, Lisa." In truth her face was a bit drawn, even wan, despite the remnants of the tan. She was not one of those women who bloom with pregnancy. She looked apprehensive and younger, so young that at times he felt he was escorting a careless teenager. On the plane home from Barbados, while Lisa was on one of her trips to the bathroom, the stewardess had asked what his daughter might like to drink.

"It's so dark in here." She was at her dresser, leaning forward to put on makeup. "I can hardly see what I'm doing. Maybe we could get a floor lamp."

"Sure, no problem." Roy looked around; he had never found the bedroom dark. It was certainly more cluttered than it used to be; besides Lisa's cosmetics and other personal effects, a small mound of stuffed animals occupied the window seat. He had drawn the line at the bubble wrap, insisting that she stow it in a drawer.

"You look hurt. It's a great apartment, really. It's just these old buildings, you know. I'll get used to it, maybe once I get some of my stuff up on the walls. Roy, when we get there, you will be . . . supportive, won't you? I mean, I'm a little tense about it."

"It'll go fine. There's nothing to worry about. Come."

"Roy! Welcome back!" Bea, resplendent in royal blue silk and festooned with beads, threw her arms around him. "You look wonderful. So rested. And Lisa! How good to see you. Roy's practically kept you under wraps." As she led them into the living room, there came a chorused shout of "Surprise!"

Amid her shock, Lisa was dazzled by the festivity of the scene, the room so much lighter and more colorful than Roy's apartment. "Did you know?" she managed to whisper to him.

"No, I had no idea," he whispered back, then repeated it loudly and exuberantly to the throng. He went about greeting people, tugging Lisa along. The weight of her stomach was dragging her down, and the baby chose this moment for a commotion of kicks. She let go of Roy's hand and fell behind. So many people! She knew his children, but who were all the others? The old woman in the corner must be Bea's mother, the landlady. Roy had said she was witchlike, but he never mentioned the green hair. And the bearded man in the Hawaiian shirt, busily slicing a baguette—wasn't he the super?

"So you're Roy's new wife. Well, he's certainly not one of those men who keep marrying the same woman all over again, is he? I'm Serena. You've heard of me?"

"Yes, some. So you too . . ." Bewildered yet pleased, Lisa gave a smile that acknowledged their shared condition. "When are you expecting?"

"Three, three and a half months."

"Same as me. Isn't that a coincidence? Roy didn't tell me you were, uh . . . And Melissa too, it looks like."

"We're a fertile bunch." Serena turned to the large woman beside her who was biting into a stuffed mushroom. "May, say hello to Lisa." May nodded and mumbled something. To Lisa's relief, Jane and Al suddenly appeared, wrapping her in hugs.

"Jane! You're almost the only one who's not pregnant. Or are you?"

"No. Horrors."

Al frowned. "I would be if I could."

The next minute it was Shimmer, stepping forward shyly.

"Shimmer, what a relief to see you. Who are all these people?"

"Well, the tall guy over there holding the bottle of champagne with all the facial hair is Dmitri, the super, but he's also my mother's boyfriend. You know Tony and Melissa. And see Timmy? He walks and talks now, thank God. We thought he never would. Every word he utters, you can see the relief on my mother's face. You know Magenta from school, right? She's here a lot. The resident alien, my mother calls her. That's my grandma, and next to her is Coral—she's Al's sister. She takes care of her but only for the apartment. She's really a singer. We did Grandma's hair and my mother didn't even make a peep, she's so glad to have her off her hands. And there's Danny, and—"

"Let me get a look at her. Bring her over," came Anna's crackling voice from across the room. She wore black jeans and a black sweatshirt studded with rhinestones that spelled "New York, New York," purchased on an excursion to Times Square with Coral. "So you're the new wife? The teacher?"

"Yes. You must be Shimmer's grandmother, Mrs., uh . . . Nice to meet you. I really like the building. It's very . . . solid-looking," said Lisa with a timid laugh. The old woman seemed impermeable, like plaster of Paris.

"You think it's nice now, you should've seen it forty years ago. The doormen had beautiful uniforms and spoke perfect English, the floors were waxed twice a week, even the chandeliers in the lobby were cleaned every month. And none of this racket of jackhammers all the time. But everything goes downhill. This is my roommate, Coral. Any day now you'll be paying to see her on Broadway, right, Coral?"

"Right. Hi, Lisa. Are you and Roy going to be living here?"

"Yes. Roy convinced me that—"

"Where else would you find a bargain like this? Plus all the free baby-sitting my daughter does," said Anna. "Look at all these big bellies. Especially that one." She gestured toward Serena. "She's going to make my other daughter a daddy. That's a new trick."

They all turned to Serena, sleek and glamorous even in pregnancy. She and Danny stood close together, apparently enjoying some private joke. Danny wore a white collarless shirt and baggy black pants; his newly grown hair was in a ponytail. The haze of meekness that had so long surrounded him had evaporated, replaced by the confident sheen of a man admired by women.

"I didn't realize she'd remarried," said Lisa. "Roy doesn't talk a lot about—"

"Remarried!" cried Anna. "So that's what they call it now? Go ask her how she got—"

"Lisa." Coral took her by the arm and glared at Anna. "You must try Bea's incredible spinach quiche." Shimmer frowned and followed along.

"What did she mean by that?" asked Lisa.

"Nothing. Serena and May live together, upstairs in the penthouse. You don't have a problem with that, do you?"

"No, but—"

"She just started showing one day," said Shimmer, "and we have no idea who—"

"Shimmer," said Coral, "could you take some food to your grandmother, please? I think she's hungry. She likes the veal wrapped in bacon."

"Did she go to a fertility clinic or something?" Lisa asked. "I always wondered how lesbians did it. Not *do* it, I know *that*. I mean, get babies. It must feel a little odd, not knowing where the other half of the genes comes from? But I guess it doesn't matter. People adopt all the time. I had this former boyfriend, just before Roy—his parents were killed in a car crash and he was brought up by an aunt and uncle, then years later he found out they weren't his aunt and uncle at all but friends of the family."

"Really? Well, every culture handles kinship structures differently. Some are very flexible. In Hawaii, for instance, people take in friends' and relatives' kids all the time. It's considered totally natural, no big deal."

"Hawaii? Have you been there?"

"No, I was an anthropology major so I have this storehouse of facts. Lifestyles of the poor and obscure. Let's move over here. It's too crowded at the table."

"Tony," came Melissa's sharp voice from the sofa where she nestled, cradling her stomach like a parcel, "will you *please* get that child out of the plants. Ever since he started walking he's in— Oh, thanks, Danny."

Danny had scooped up his nephew just in time to save the avocado tree from toppling. "Here we go, Timmy." He sat down beside Melissa, trapping Timmy between his legs. "Let's see you make a muscle. Fantastic! You want to show me what you learn in gymnastics class?"

"Oh, don't get him started tumbling, it's too crowded. Have some celery, sweetie. No, you don't want that, it's no good for you. Bea is the only person in town who still uses bacon. Tony, what does he have all over his hands? Is that dirt from the plants or what?"

"How the hell should I know? I can't watch him every single minute."

"You can't even watch him for five minutes. What're you going to do when there's another? Danny, how's it going with Coral?"

"Jesus! Can't a person have a private life in this family?"

"No. Haven't you learned that yet?" Tony said. "You're a lucky guy. From batting zero to five hundred. She's great. Grandma's green hair alone is a stroke of genius."

"I think Coral's lucky too. I'm glad she appreciates Danny. I would."

"Come on, both of you, you're embarrassing me."

"You embarrass easily. Unlike your brother. He expects to be appreciated no matter what. Aren't you both going to say hello to your new stepmother?"

"She looks kind of stunned," said Tony. "Maybe a surprise party wasn't the best idea."

"The best idea? I would say it ranks down there with your mother's hiring the local beggar to deliver her goodies. Poor thing. Lisa, I mean. She has no idea what she's gotten into. You don't think she knows, do you?"

"Knows what?" asked Danny.

"About the baby."

"The baby? All she has to do is look at you, Melissa. It's no secret anymore."

"Not ours, silly. I mean Serena's. Danny! Don't tell me you haven't figured it out."

"Figured what out?"

"I can't believe you. What did you think? An immaculate conception? Even Shimmer worked it out in her teenaged brain. You don't realize your father did his ex-wife the great favor of—"

"You've got to be kidding!"

"She's not kidding." Tony shook his head slowly, then gave a quick, harsh laugh as Danny gaped at Serena, across the room with Al and Jane.

"Judging from the looks of things," Melissa said, "he had a busy week. Oh, Lisa, hi. I didn't see you. How's it going? How was Jamaica?"

"Barbados. It was fine."

"Timmy, come here, say hello to your new . . . What would he call you? Stepgrandma doesn't seem appropriate. Especially when you're not even a mother yet. Oops, he got away again." The baby, scrambling from Danny's grip, darted over to Dmitri, who tossed him in the air. A moment later he approached with a flourish, balancing the stemware between his fingers, and carefully handed the baby to his mother.

"Glasses for everyone. This is Lisa, no? Dmitri Panov. We have nodded anonymously in the basement, but now we meet formally." He bowed and handed her an empty glass. "Congratulations. We're about to drink to your health. And for you, and for you." He handed glasses all around. "For Timmy? No, I presume not."

"Thanks, but no champagne for me, Dmitri. Lisa, you know it's very bad for you? Fetal alcohol syndrome. Can we have ginger ale?"

"Not even a sip to celebrate Roy's marriage?" He shook his head and moved on, Timmy trailing behind him. Lisa twirled the glass between her fingers.

"Sit down, Lisa," said Tony. "Here. You look a little . . ."

"Thanks. I'm . . . It's just all these people. I thought this was going to be a quiet little dinner."

"My mother likes to do things in a big way."

"What was that you were saying before?" she asked Melissa.

"Before what?"

"Now for the toast," called Dmitri from the table. "Who will offer the toast? Bea? The mother of us all." He opened the champagne with a loud pop and the cork went flying behind him toward the kitchen.

"Not me," said Bea. "Tony, will you make a toast?"

"I'm no good at toasts. How about Danny? Go on, Danny." He gave his brother a friendly shove toward the table.

"Just now, about Roy," Lisa said. "You were laughing about his being busy. You meant busy with Serena, didn't you?"

Dmitri began pouring the champagne, starting with Al and Jane, who stood holding hands near the window. "For the lovely daughter of the groom, very quiet today."

"Will you please tell me? I want to know."

"I'm not sure what you're talking about. We were laughing at Roy's being so busy getting the apartment ready before you went to Jamaica. I mean Barbados."

"Dad, Lisa, everyone here wishes you all the best." Danny began loudly. "I wasn't around for the first of these happy occasions but I'm glad to be . . ."

Lisa gripped the arms of her chair as if to leap up, but thought better of it and sank back down. "You don't all have to treat me like I'm some kind of idiot. I heard what you were saying. He got her pregnant, didn't he? They've still got a thing for each other, so why—" Her voice rose to a wail; tears spilled down her cheeks. "Why did he want to marry me then? That's what I don't understand."

"No, no, you've got it all wrong." Melissa soothed her. "That was over long ago. Serena's with May, it's practically a marriage, and Roy's crazy about you. That's obvious."

"Oh, is it? What's obvious is that—that—" She gestured wildly at Serena. "It's staring me in the face. *That's* what's obvious."

As Lisa's voice rose above the toast, the room went still. Everyone turned, drinks in hand, to stare. Timmy, again at large, tugged at Bea's skirt. "Lady crying," he said, and burst into tears himself.

"Go over to her, for God's sake," Bea whispered. Roy was not precisely tugging her skirt but half hiding behind her. With studied calm, he made his way through the room.

"Lisa, sweetheart, what's the trouble? Aren't you feeling well?"

"You! You stud! Don't come near me! How can you even speak to me after what you've done! How could you lie to me all these months? How could you!" she sobbed.

"What'd he do?" Al murmured to Jane.

"He knocked up Serena. Didn't I tell you?"

"No!" He set his drink down slowly, took off his red checked head-band, and wiped his face. "No."

"Yeah, man," Coral muttered. "Yeah. To keep it all in the family. What'sa matter, you some homeboy who never done heard of family values?"

"Lisa, you don't understand." Roy reached out to touch her but she flicked him off like a bug. "Okay, I won't deny it. I was going to tell you but— I can explain."

"Tony! Will you *please* go get Timmy from your mother and make him stop crying?"

"Explain!" Lisa sent a furious glance around the room, like an air-raid searchlight, beginning with Serena, who stood pale and erect, clutching May's arm. May's face was dark, as inscrutable as one of her masks. Bea yielded the crying baby to Tony and put her arm around Shimmer as if to protect her. Nearby stood Magenta, enrapt as if watching MTV. Anna sipped champagne and smirked.

"How are you going to explain *that*?" Lisa pointed at the evidence. "You were . . . *with* her at the same time as me. *I* didn't go after you. *I* didn't need any of this. I could've stayed with Billy Moran but you made him seem so immature. So irresponsible. Talk about irresponsible! If you wanted her, why didn't you just— Oh, this is so humiliating. Just let me get out of here." She rose to flee but Roy grabbed her arm.

"It's not like that. I only did it as a favor. Lisa, please stop making a scene in front of the whole— I can clear it all up if you'd only—"

"Clear it up!" She gave a bitter laugh, as if she had suddenly aged twenty years. "How the fuck can you—" She stopped abruptly and regarded the roomful of spectators. "I have to go now," she said quietly. "Sorry to spoil your party, Bea."

Without a word, Bea led her to the door. Roy slunk behind, glancing briefly over at Serena, who did not meet his eyes. But May cast him a look of smug contempt. Those dykes, he thought.

"Welcome to the family," cackled Anna.

"Oh, hush," Coral told her.

*

Lisa tried curling up in bed but that was too uncomfortable, so she rolled the quilt around her mummy style and lay flat on her back, staring at the ceiling, from which several large flakes of plaster appeared ready to drop. They ought to have that fixed . . . but what was she thinking? It wasn't her problem. She wasn't going to stay here. The baby was squirming around. Only this morning she was amused, watching her stomach change shape like a mound of dough kneaded by invisible fingers, but now she wished it would stop. She wished it would get out of her, had never gotten in. It was like an occupying force, a small platoon billeted in her private quarters, which she was powerless to evict. At once she felt guilty for such thoughts. It was hers, or half hers. More than half, since it was feeding on her body. Here to stay. She must find another apartment, far from these mad people. If only she hadn't given up her old place. She could have sublet it. "No one gives up a New York apartment," Adrienne told her, but how could she have foreseen anything like this? Once it was born she could work part-time, hire help, she would figure something out.

Roy entered and perched on the edge of the bed. "I know this must be a shock but remember, there's more than one way of looking at everything. You're putting the worst possible construction on it." He paused for encouragement, but his sweet Lisa, usually so open and talkative, lay mute.

"I was going to tell you, but we were so happy and . . . well, I kept putting it off. That was a mistake, I see now. It was all her idea. She came to me." He sought a truthful, sensible way of presenting the situation; it wasn't totally senseless, in the larger scheme of things. But how to explain the larger scheme of things? "I was taken by surprise. I guess I didn't think it through. It wasn't that I wanted to . . . To tell the truth, I didn't even particularly . . ." But that was not truthful. He did particularly. He always had.

"Just shut up. I'm not interested in the details. I want a divorce."

"Oh, now, Lisa. Now, sweetheart, that is truly senseless. We love each other, we're just starting out, the baby . . . Take it from someone who's been there, you don't get divorced so easily, over nothing. I mean, over something you can come to terms with. Lisa, I do love you."

"How could you?" She reached for her bubble wrap, great big bubbles from a new set of wineglasses; they made satisfying, irate pops.

"How could I what, love you?"

"Do that."

Roy began to feel slightly irritated by her naïveté. It was easy, he wanted to say. "I don't know. I did it. I wish I could undo it, but I can't. Look, I see how this could be hard to deal with. I could send you to Jonah Bradley, he's one of the best therapists around. But maybe you'd prefer a woman. There are plenty. To help you deal with this."

She laughed dully but her eyes flashed. "You think I need professional help because I married a scumbag? Why should I deal with your mess? The nerve. Deal with it! You deal with it."

"I'm trying to. Okay, maybe that wasn't such a good idea at this point. Will you please stop making that awful noise? Look, I want this marriage to work. I need it to work. And I don't have a problem with this. You're the one who—"

"I sure do have a problem. You expect me to watch that baby grow up and play with ours and everything? You must be joking. Leave me alone. Go sleep somewhere else, with one of your other wives. Do you sleep with Bea too? I wouldn't be surprised. A regular harem you've got here. No wonder you're so attached to it."

He crept into his study, shut the door tight, and reached for the phone. "Bea," he said, "you've got to talk to her. I can't do a thing with her. She won't listen to reason."

"Not now, Roy. I'm serving poached salmon to a dozen people. I can't blame her for getting hysterical but still, people have to eat."

Indeed they did. Roy thought ruefully of Bea's poached salmon, which was divine. Could he possibly dash upstairs for a little while? No. "I didn't mean this minute. Later. Tomorrow. But please, don't wait too long. You know how people's positions harden."

"A favor," echoed Lisa. "Some favor." She was calmer now. She had changed out of the sweaty clothes she spent the night in and taken an early morning shower. To her surprise she was even hungry, and helped herself to one of Bea's homemade croissants. The coffee was strong. Winter light filtered into Bea's warm kitchen, sharpening every angle, glazing every surface, and the smell of baking hung in the air. Her life was falling apart, it was true, but she might as well enjoy her breakfast.

"It was exactly the way I'm telling you. Serena and May were so eager for a child—you can imagine how that feels. And to Serena it seemed the simplest way, seeing that they'd once been close. Better than some stranger. Please believe me, Roy did it only to oblige. He was thoughtless, yes. They were all thoughtless, but there was nothing personal in it whatsoever."

"Nothing personal," Lisa said musingly. "I can't believe I'm sitting here listening to these words and not jumping up and down screaming. Not that I could jump anyway. You know, the odd thing is, Roy always seemed so sincere with me. That's what first attracted me."

"He is sincere." Bea poured more coffee for both of them. "You're absolutely right. He's sincere, and he loves you, and he tries to do the right thing by everyone. I'm sure he feels that even though he and Serena are divorced and in love with other people, they can still help each other out. They shared a life, after all. We all did. We still do. It's about human connection. Emotional ties aren't erased by a legal document, a scrap of paper, or because the sexual feelings are no longer—"

"That's just it, though, the sexual feelings. We're talking about a pregnancy, aren't we? While he was engaged to me!"

"But really you can't call that, what they did together, sexual. All right, technically they used sexual means, but in essence it wasn't much more sexual than having it done with a syringe. Roy's sexual feelings are focused on you. It wasn't deceiving you in the ordinary sense, like seeing another woman. This was done for the sake of family."

"Well, I sort of see what you mean, but still . . . It's not the way most people would see it, that's for sure. It's hard."

"I know. But most people . . . Think of the state of most families today. Just because two people can't stay married anymore, for what-ever reason, they think they have to destroy entire families, make chil-

246

dren and grandparents unhappy. If we lived that way, we'd all be much worse off. Shimmer wouldn't have her father nearby. Sure, when we separated, I could've chosen to be bitter and furious for the rest of my life. We could've had custody battles and alimony and a life of constant resentment. By the same token, if Roy and Serena couldn't be at least neighborly, May would have to find a new studio. If we'd cut off all emotional ties, Jane and Tony would have grown up in some awful orphanage in Vietnam, if they managed to grow up at all. And then we wouldn't have Melissa and Al and Coral. When I think of what Coral's done for Danny—he's a new man, but that's another story. No, keeping the family together is more important than sexual jealousy. Believe me, that passes.'' With help, she thought, it passes. With determination. With the long view.

Lisa sat pensive, munching on her croissant. "So you all, you all think that way? You live that way?"

"Yes."

"Roy too?"

"Roy too. Of course. Roy is what links us. Roy is very important to us."

"But he never told me. I mean, he never explained it the way you have."

"I guess we take it for granted. I'm only explaining it to you, Lisa dear"—Bea reached out to cover Lisa's hand with her own ample one—"because you had this very unfortunate shock. Roy should've told you about it—I can't argue with you there. He certainly should have. He must have tried a dozen times and not quite known how to go about it. I could almost feel sorry for him. My hunch is that he loves you so much, he was afraid of losing you."

"You really think that's why?"

Bea nodded judiciously and allowed herself to relax a bit. The hardest part was accomplished. Orientation, as it were. It had been easier with Serena, who was more sophisticated to begin with. Taking a deep breath, she reached for a croissant. She had gotten up early to have them ready. Luckily this wasn't a busy day, only a smallish birthday cake for an octogenarian. February was always a quiet time, party-wise, a relief after the Thanksgiving to New Year's rush. She had barely taken a bite when the phone rang.

"Excuse me a moment. Yes? . . . It's not shoveled? . . . I'm sorry. He must have had an early class. I'll make sure Ernesto does it . . . or Maxwell . . . You're right, Mrs. Melnikoff, it is dangerous and it should be done promptly. Absolutely . . . I'm sorry, Lisa, where were we?"

"Do you think he was thinking of me," Lisa asked shyly, "even when, you know, with Serena?"

Bea proffered a sly smile. "Who knows what a man thinks of at those moments? But I wouldn't be surprised."

"Still . . . Is that one chocolate? Oh, good, I love chocolate. When that baby is born, I mean Serena's, I can't imagine how I'll feel, knowing . . ."

"You might find you love it like part of the family. For Roy's sake, even. Your own baby will have a little, well, let's say cousin. When Tony and Jane arrived, I remember it so well, those children became my own the minute I laid eyes on them. Even before."

"But that was different. They were born before he knew you."

"But he had them with a stranger, not even an ex-wife like Serena. At least you can see who she is, and you'll know her better in time. God"—Bea sighed—"when I think of all the red tape, the letters to the army, our senators, everyone. The war was ending and those boat people kept coming. I lay awake nights imagining Roy's children, which made them mine, really, maybe starving or suffering somewhere. I know they weren't the only ones—I would have taken more if I could—but I had to get those two. Well, that's past. All I'm saying is, children are children. They belong to all of us. It doesn't really matter who . . ."

"Didn't you ever think about their mother? Maybe their mother wanted—"

"Of course I thought of their mother. I wouldn't have tried to take them from her. But when it turned out she was in the hospital, dying, then . . ."

Lisa felt suddenly older, a canniness springing in her, rampant as a weed. "Did Roy want them too," she asked, "or was it just you?" Yes, she felt she was seeing more clearly than ever before. It was very like the way she'd felt in college, at the end of a really good course, astonished at how her view of the world had shifted. Except that had taken months, and this was barely overnight. Bea was extraordinary. Perhaps, she thought in her new wisdom, Roy should never have left her.

"Yes, he wanted them." Bea paused. She wanted to be honest with this guileless girl. She could honestly say he wanted them—only he hadn't known how much until she impressed it on him. "But it's his nature to let things slide. In a way that helped. It made a good balance. When I got frantic at the delays, he'd calm me down. Also, we had Danny—he was a toddler while this was going on—and Roy was so wild over him that it made him feel less urgent about the twins. For me it worked the other way. Having the one, seeing what a child really meant, made me want the others even more."

"But after all that, then when he left you, I can't see how you weren't enraged, or devastated?"

"Devastated? No. Enraged? Well, you always have a choice about being enraged. I chose not to be. Besides, I didn't see it as Roy leaving me. Roy will never really leave. We simply weren't husband and wife anymore, technically. We wouldn't sleep in the same bed, and frankly, that didn't seem so important. More important was that our lives, all our lives, not be shattered. And I managed that. They're not."

"I don't know," said Lisa. "What you're telling me is either very smart or else deeply weird. I can't decide."

"Well, you can take your time figuring that out." Bea laughed. "I'm no intellectual. I'm just a cook. Though you know I did think about being a musician. I played the viola. But it just didn't happen. There wasn't time. So." She rubbed her hands together as after a done deal. "I hope you feel a little better now."

"I didn't ever grasp the way it was going to be." Lisa stood up. She understood from Bea, as one does with a doctor or an interviewer, that the conversation was over.

"No one ever grasps how it's going to be. Welcome to the family. We'll have our quiet little dinner soon, okay?" As Lisa was turning to go, Bea added, "Oh, and after the baby is born, maybe you'd like to go skating with us sometime? Join our little group." She reached for the phone. "Can you see yourself out? I've got to make sure that sidewalk gets shoveled."

XI

So will you do it?'' Magenta implored.

"All right, I mean, if it's the only way. I never did anything like that, with her money. She only gave me the secret code for an emergency.'' Shimmer moved the phone to her other ear, as if that might change the drift of the conversation. "It doesn't feel right.''

"This *is* an emergency. I've got to bring it all with me and my mom's balance is very low. I'll pay you back, Shimmer, I swear. You can deposit it and she'll never know the difference. People don't check their accounts so carefully. If she finds out I'll take the blame. Okay?''

"Okay,'' she murmured reluctantly.

"And you'll go with me?''

"All right, I guess.''

"What do you mean, you guess? Will you or not?''

"I will, but it's, like, scary. I mean, how do you know who he is and all?''

"I told you, this friend of someone from camp went to him, and it was okay. I know it's scary, but you don't have to do anything. I'm the one who has to—''

"But why do you have to go to Queens? It's not illegal or anything. You could go to one of those clinics that advertise in the subways. At least you know what you're getting.''

"They'll tell my mother. I'm sure they will. I think there's some law or something. And she'll kill me. She'll make my life hell.''

"Does he know?''

"No! That's the last thing I want, to get him involved in this. I'd have to call him at Oberlin. What can he do from there anyway?''

"Didn't he use, you know?"

"I don't know, sometimes. I don't remember. They keep coming off, or it's not in time. Whatever. The damage is done. Meet me tomorrow after history. We can cut gym. My appointment is at four and the subway takes forever."

"How'll we get back? You might not feel so great."

"A taxi? Can you get some extra?"

"I'll try. I'll see how much is there. But she's going to find out. You don't know. She seems ditsy but she's not really. I see her balancing those statements very carefully."

"Please, are you my friend or not?"

"Okay, okay. I'll get it."

"Can I sleep over after?"

"Yeah."

"Yes," Coral replied. "May I tell her who's calling, please?"

"Never mind who's calling." Anna's hoarse voice at her shoulder made Coral nearly jump out of her skin. She padded around in bare feet so you never knew where she might turn up.

She grabbed the phone from Coral's hand. "Hello, would you hold on a minute?" She covered the mouthpiece with her hand. "I'll take it in the bedroom. Make sure you hang up."

Anna amused her. As if she would deign to eavesdrop on an old woman's conversation. Coral settled on the couch again. From this angle she could look up from her book and see the park—its trees just beginning to show bright leaves—and the reservoir, the dogged joggers, even a few people riding horses along the bridle path. It was a dream apartment, airy, high-ceilinged, with fine old woodwork and pillowy furniture, and she was vastly pleased with herself for having negotiated her way into it. Even minding Anna was less onerous than she'd been led to expect. They understood each other. It might even be said that they were two of a kind. Only she wouldn't end up cranky, like Anna.

She would see to that. In Coral's view, Anna's generation of women, even privileged white women, had been frustrated at every turn. Small wonder that a woman of intelligence and energy devolved into a petty tyrant. Even Bea, who seemed to wield so much power, was bound hand and foot by domestic obligations. In power relationships, the masters were as locked into their roles as the slaves; Coral hadn't required those dozen social science courses to figure that out. She had no intention of letting anyone make constricting demands on her. She was prepared to sacrifice a great deal for success, but never her autonomy. The book on her lap was *For Colored Girls Who Have Considered Suicide, When the Rainbow Is Enuf.* A revival at an off-Broadway theater was planned for late spring, and the auditions were next week. Although the part in the second-longest-running musical might be better: steady work for as long as she wished. The callback, if it came, would be any day now, and she was jumpy. Several times she and Anna had raced for the phone and naturally, to Anna's chagrin, Coral won.

Anna poked her head into the living room. "I just wanted to make sure you hung up."

Coral rolled her eyes. Nonetheless her curiosity was piqued. Wasn't it part of her job to see that Anna didn't get into trouble? Those were precisely Bea's words. She removed her shoes and went down the hall to the linen closet, where she made a pretense of straightening the shelves, in case she should be discovered.

"An interview?" Anna was saying. "What kind of interview? What do I have to do? . . . Uh-huh . . . All right, give me the address again, slowly this time. . . . Will I get to meet the hostess?"

At the click of the phone Coral darted away and was back on the couch when Anna reappeared and sat down.

"What are you always rushing to the phone for?"

"I auditioned for a musical last week and I'm hoping they'll call me back. What about you?"

"I don't have to tell you."

"Of course you don't. But I told you. It's only fair, isn't it?"

"Mine's a secret. Yours isn't."

"Okay, if that's the way you want it." She returned to her reading.

She knew Anna well enough by now; an appeal to her sense of justice usually brought results. That was precisely what her family did not understand.

"I would tell you if I could."

Coral kept reading.

"Tomorrow we're going downtown for an appointment at three. Then you'll find out."

"Okay."

"You'll go with me?"

"I'll go with you."

"I'll tell you something, if you want. Something else, I mean."

"Yes?" Coral looked up.

"You won't laugh at me?"

"Have I ever laughed at you? Did I laugh when you wanted to dye your hair?"

"You sometimes laugh at other things. Not ha-ha but sarcasm."

"Well, if I do then I'm sorry. Come on, spill it."

"You think an old lady like me could have an interest in a man?"

"Why not? My Great-aunt Abigail got married when she was seventy-five. To a man three years younger. They're still together."

"You don't say! Well, I'm not interested in marriage anymore. Not even hanky-panky. I think I'm finally past it. Plus, I look in the mirror, I have to admit, this is not a body a man would chase after. But there's still companionship. You see what I'm getting at?"

"I think you've made yourself clear."

"You said you wouldn't be sarcastic. You remind me sometimes of my daughter May. It's not enough that she's gay but she's mean too. That's worse, if you ask me."

"Okay, no more sarcasm. Never again. Carry on."

There followed a melancholy tale of lost love. It seemed Anna had been romantically involved some eight or nine years ago with a former doorman who left in a huff after a lovers' quarrel.

"I know I have a sharp tongue, but he should have understood, don't you think? Some people are oversensitive."

"Mmm," Coral murmured.

Anna had been despondent ever since. They were so well suited; men like that, she noted, don't grow on trees. She explained her reluctance to telephone and, with some embarrassment, her protracted search in the places he was most likely to be found—the lobbies of local buildings. Those mysterious walks Bea mentioned, thought Coral. Aloud, she sympathized in earnest. The difficulty, as she perceived it, was that Anna was not venturing far enough afield.

"Going up and down Central Park West isn't going to work because you've already established that he's not there. How about West End Avenue or Riverside Drive?"

"It's so far to walk, all the way to the river."

"No big deal. We'll take the crosstown bus." Coral found herself engaged by a sense of mission. They would have a joint project, their time together acquiring a purpose beyond games of gin rummy and blackjack or worse, the sleazy daytime TV shows Anna insisted on watching. It would be an adventure, and Coral loved romantic adventure. She also loved strolling along the river. The stately old buildings and undulating path reminded her of walks along the Seine.

"Why didn't I think of that? I must be an old fool, just like they all think."

"Not at all. It's easy to overlook the obvious."

"You're a smart girl. So when do we go?"

"How about tomorrow morning, before we go downtown? We can have lunch out, make a day of it."

"This morning she said she'd be staying at a friend's house again, and when I said no, she didn't even answer. What can I do? She goes straight from school while I'm still at work."

"Do you know where she is?" asked Roy. It was Rhonda again, and apparently nothing had changed. Nevertheless he must be as patient and attentive as if he had not heard these words before.

"She calls to say she's okay but she doesn't always say where she is. It's like she's checking in at an office. I know I should be able to control her, but . . . No matter what I say, she gives me that look, as if I'm too stupid to bother with. I could deal with that. But this time I'm really scared. I have this feeling." Her tears overflowed and she reached for a tissue from the handy box on the table. "I can't explain it. I just know something's wrong."

"What feeling? What are you scared of?"

"I don't know."

"Do you think she's taking any drugs?"

"No, it's not that. She doesn't seem sleepy or manic or anything. So what do you think I should do?"

Sooner or later they all asked that. Someday, in a weak moment, he might just tell them. "Have you tried telling her how *you* feel? The things you tell me. That you care about her, you're concerned, you can't find a way to reach her?"

"Sure, it sounds easy, the way you put it, but I know she'd just glare at me. What would you do if she were your daughter?"

"If she were my daughter?"

"Yes. But how would you know, Dr. Power?" She laughed amid her tears, with a hint of mockery. "Maybe you don't have a daughter. Maybe you don't even know what I'm talking about, that feeling in your gut that something's wrong with your kid. Do you have a daughter?"

"Yes. As a matter of fact, I have two daughters." He paused. "And two sons." He hadn't meant to go so far, but it felt unjust, disloyal, even a trifle risky—tempting the gods—to omit Tony and Danny when he had acknowledged Jane and Sara.

"Really? Four children? So how do you handle this kind of thing? Or maybe you leave it to your wife. There must be a wife in the picture, with all those children, right?"

"Rhonda, this is about you, not me. Naturally we've all had difficulties with adolescent children. It's the name of the game. But the issue here is specifically you and Maggie."

"Oh, that's another thing, I don't know if I mentioned. I can't call her Maggie anymore. Some kind of nonsense she cooked up with her friends. Magenta. That's her new name. She only answers to Magenta.''

"Magenta." Something fluttered in Roy's chest, making him switch from automatic pilot. "Magenta, did you say?"

She made a wry face. "Yes. Why do you suppose they want to change their names?"

"Because they want to be someone else," he said absently.

"What's the matter? Did I say something wrong?"

"No. You can't say anything wrong here. You can say anything you like, you know that. Go on."

Even though Lisa had set up her small spindly desk in the spare room, with her paper clips, stapler, jar of pens, Scotch tape, and rubber cement equidistantly arrayed, Roy noted that she preferred to work, evenings, at the dining-room table like a child doing her homework. Like Jane, he recalled with a pang of nostalgia. Lisa sat with her legs tucked under her, in her gray sweatpants and an old sweater, biting her lips as she pored over student exams. Roy observed her from the kitchen, drawn there by a longing for a piece of pie, lemon chiffon pie, though he well knew that he would find none; still, he prowled about, in case it or something like it might have materialized.

Lisa looked up, feeling his stare. "Hi, sweetie. What is it?"

"Nothing. How's your work coming?"

"These tests are amazing. You explain something for weeks, but it doesn't seem to penetrate. You look like something's on your mind, Roy."

"I think I may run up to Bea's for a few minutes. I want to ask her something."

Lisa removed her reading glasses and uncurled her body. "Do you realize how often you drop in on Bea? I mean, you're married to me now, remember?"

"Lisa, darling, you can't possibly be jealous? I mean, Bea . . ."

She smiled. "No, I'm not. It would be practically, oh, I don't know, incestuous, wouldn't it?"

Incestuous? Roy's eyes widened. How she had changed lately. It was hardly a word, far less a notion, she would have come up with two months ago.

"It's just that you seem so dependent. Maybe you ought to give Bea a rest." She came over and wrapped her arms around him. "If you want company, I could do these later." She stroked his back. "Is that it? Is my big baby feeling neglected? Does he need special attention?"

"There was just something. About Shimmer. With kids, there're always things coming up." He could say this in all honesty, even though he was hoping Bea might have some pie around. Bea would know just how troubled this girl Magenta was. She might even suggest a way to handle the awkward professional situation with Rhonda.

"What about Shimmer? I know her pretty well. You want to sit down and talk about it? Or, I know, we could lie down and talk. How's that? Lying down, you never know what might happen. Come." She took his hand and led him to the bedroom. "Now, lie back and tell me what it is. Let me be the doctor. Where does it hurt? Here?"

"How can I concentrate when you do that?"

"Oh." She gave a mock pout. "You mean you don't like it?"

"I like it, of course I like it."

"But you really do want to talk? Okay." She sat up opposite him, keeping her hand on his leg. "What about Shimmer?"

"It's not Shimmer exactly. It's this friend of hers, Magenta. She mentions her a lot. Do you know her?"

"Maggie. Sure, I know her from school. She was at that disastrous party Bea made, remember?"

Roy had tried to erase all memory of that occasion, but when he reluctantly summoned it up—Lisa's accusations, Timmy's howls, the pained faces of his children—he could indeed locate an image of the girl, quite a good-looking girl in fact, a baby-faced blonde with wayward hair falling in her eyes. "Oh, yes. I was wondering if it's a good idea for Shimmer to be spending so much time with her. She sounds almost too grown up. Maybe troubled. What's she like?''

''I wouldn't worry on that score. She's a perfectly nice girl, does okay in school. I haven't had her in my classes, but I never heard of any trouble. I think her father died last year, so she may still be kind of down, but . . .''

''That's all you know?'' Any analysis of Bea's would have been far more incisive.

''Let's see. She does sports. Track, I think. I can't imagine she'd be a bad influence, if that's what you mean.'' She reached for his belt. ''Roy, do you remember the other night? What we did? And what you said about it?''

''Remind me.''

He watched her remove the sweatpants, then tug down the red bikini panties, stretched out of shape. It intrigued him that she removed her bottom clothes first, then the top. His former women had undressed from the top down. Did Lisa do this on purpose, knowing the piquant appeal of a woman naked from the waist down, and revert to the more conventional way when she was alone? In any case the Magenta business could wait a day; he wouldn't be seeing Rhonda until next week. Lisa was right; he should give Bea a rest.

''Roy, you're so quiet,'' she said a while later as she clambered off him. For the time being he couldn't get on top of her; she said the weight pressed on her stomach. ''Is anything wrong? Are you still thinking about Shimmer and that girl?''

''No, nothing's wrong.'' He was in fact supremely content, and in that unguarded moment he chuckled and said, ''Pie.''

''Pie?''

''Yes, I was thinking how nice that would be right now. Lemon chiffon, to be precise.''

''Pie. Well, I guess the honeymoon's over. It didn't last long, did it?''

''Oh, Lisa, don't take it so seriously. It was just a joke.''

''Roy, I'm not from the same generation as Bea. I'm out all day working. I don't bake. I thought I could manage to make you happy even without pie as a finale.''

"I am happy. And I didn't suggest that you bake. You wondered what I was thinking and I was foolish enough to tell you.''

"There're very nice pies in the supermarket. If you want pie so badly why don't you get dressed and go buy one? Or get Maxwell to go. He's always glad to earn a few dollars.''

"Lisa . . .''

"Did Serena bake pies too?''

"No.''

"Poor guy. Then you've been craving your home-baked pie for how long? Years now. But what am I saying? They're right upstairs, only a few steps away.''

"Oh, for chrissakes. A person can't even make a joke.''

Bea went to bed early. It had been a wearing day: shepherding the painters through the apartments damaged by Anna's recent bathtub mishap, choosing new rugs for the lobby, an engagement party to prepare. Dmitri had the flu, and with no one else around, she had been forced to enlist Maxwell, luckily at his usual post with a Styrofoam cup, to help get the food downtown. He waited on the street, since she could not risk having him appear. Shimmer and Magenta came home late and bedraggled and were listless at dinner; Magenta, so frequent a guest, generally helped with the dishes, but tonight she'd barely eaten, then gone straight to Shimmer's room without so much as a thank-you. Now the girls were parading back and forth to the bathroom; she hoped they weren't dyeing their hair again. Just as she was dropping off to sleep there came a hesitant knock on the bedroom door.

"Mom?'' Shimmer appeared, in her flower-sprigged granny nightgown.

"Yes, dear?''

She shuffled her way to the bed. "Mom?''

"Yes, it's me, Shimmer. What is it?"

"It's Maggie. I mean, Magenta. She's not feeling so well."

"What's the matter?" Bea sighed. It was late in the season for a flu epidemic. Well, Shimmer would have to go down to Dmitri's and fetch the Contac. She looked pale herself; she might be next. Better keep Lisa and Serena away.

"She's throwing up and . . ."

"And what?"

"Well, sort of bleeding."

Bea sat up straighter. "Sort of bleeding from where?"

"From—from . . . you know."

"A bad period?"

"Oh, no. It couldn't be that."

She leaped out of bed. "Tell me this minute what is going on."

"We—I mean, she—she said she had to do it."

Bea grabbed a robe. "I don't believe this. She didn't do it herself, did she? Not some coat hanger business?"

Shimmer, struck dumb, shook her head.

"Then where? For chrissakes, it's legal. You don't have to go to Puerto Rico anymore. Don't they teach you anything in school?"

"Mom, stop yelling." Shimmer cowered and stepped out of her way. "We didn't go to Puerto Rico. Just Queens."

"Queens! Idiots. Maggie," she called, rushing from the room. "Magenta, whatever your name is, where are you?"

Magenta was sitting doubled over on the toilet, retching and weeping, a bloody towel crumpled on her lap.

"Get up and let me see." Bea peered in the toilet. "Oh my God. Get her dressed," she said to Shimmer, "and get dressed yourself. We'll go to the emergency room. I'll call and have the doctor meet us there. Take it easy, Maggie, you'll be fine. Keep the towel there." In the bedroom she leafed through the address book. "With this whole extended family, why couldn't someone have married a doctor? It would be so convenient."

"Your Aunt Sonia married a doctor. Grandma told me all about it."

"God, is she still harping on that? He's long dead," she said as she dialed. "He left her a fortune and she spent it all on the horses at Hialeah. Hello? Yes, this is an emergency. Don't just stand there," she told Shimmer. "Go help her get ready."

Moments later Bea was dressed and in the hall. "Sara, where are you? Run downstairs and get the keys to the van from Dmitri. No, go upstairs and get Serena's. And find out where it is. I think Maxwell parked it for her."

"It's Shimmer, Mom, remember?" she said as she pulled on her jacket. Then she was out the door.

"Am I going to die?" Magenta wailed.

"What? No, of course you won't die. Here, sit with your feet up till she gets back."

"I want my mother. If I'm going to die I want my mother."

"I'll call her as soon as we get to the hospital."

"I want her to meet us there. She'll feel terrible if I died and she wasn't there."

"Stop this talk about dying. Okay, give me the number and I'll call."

There was no answer, only a machine.

"Didn't you leave a message?" cried Magenta.

"I guess I didn't." A wave of torpor was engulfing Bea. "I should have. I didn't know what to say."

Shimmer ran back in, waving a set of car keys. "It's right in front of the house."

"I want my mother," Magenta whined. "Where's my mother?"

"Let's go," said Bea, but she didn't move. She too wanted her mother. Then she remembered her mother was Anna.

"Mom, come on."

"Yes. Yes, all right." She roused herself. "I'll call again from the hospital, Maggie. I'll leave a message. You'll be fine. Come, lean on me. Sara, lock the door. Sorry, I mean Shimmer."

Forever after, Anna would think of Coral as her guardian angel. The girl had something, there was no doubt about it. She brought luck. All these years of searching, and now the very first building they walked into on Riverside Drive, half a mile away. There he stood (and had stood for eight years, it turned out, so near and yet so far!), bending over a desk as he had in her lobby, surrounded by packages and piles of mail. Except the lobby, in Anna's opinion, was nowhere near as nice as her own: the carpets worn, the flowers artificial. The uniform, too, was less becoming, a navy blue that didn't suit him as well as the maroon one he had worn while in her service.

"Oscar!" she cried, her hand on her heart.

"Mrs. Anna!" he responded, no less astonished.

Coral beamed.

After the breathless greetings, Coral discreetly proposed that she take a short walk while they became reacquainted. Would fifteen or twenty minutes be about right? Oscar didn't take his eyes off her as she sashayed out the door, Anna noticed. Well, who could blame him, with a figure like that? She wasn't jealous. It proved he was still a man.

He was fine, she was fine. The families, likewise. Anna was eager to get past the preliminaries but Oscar dwelt, somewhat dejectedly, on the crowded conditions in his sister's apartment: yet another grandniece. Oh, the noise, especially at his age.

At last there came a lull. Here was the moment for the apology she had so carefully rehearsed. I was hasty. Forgive me. You were the best doorman we ever had. We all miss you. Would you by any chance consider . . . ? But since Oscar didn't seem to bear a grudge, and it was all so long ago, and apologies were clumsy in any case, the planned phrases stuck on her tongue and instead she found herself saying brusquely, "So tell me, how much are they paying you here?"

Once the arrangements were made—and she had shown as subtly as her nature allowed that her interest in him was no longer predatory, or less predatory than before—she felt guilty about Coral. It was no way to treat a guardian angel. Sooner or later she would have to break the news, but for the moment, when Coral returned from her stroll, Anna greeted her with a broad smile and eyes aglow. She even hugged her and offered a fifty-dollar bonus. Coral stepped back from the hug and refused. She had done nothing out of the ordinary, she said coolly. She certainly hadn't done it for money. She felt rewarded enough by having engineered Anna's success.

At lunch she remained cool, and once they reached their next destination and Coral grasped the nature of the enterprise, she was horrified.

"You're not really going to do this, Anna?"

"And why not?" She had expected that a young person, especially one with theatrical connections herself, would applaud her initiative.

"You can't. You just can't. It's awful. Think of your family."

"Why? Do they think of me?" Anna was firm. She tried to swear Coral to silence, but Coral refused to be sworn. In the end she had to resort to desperate measures. "You like your job?"

"Sure."

"And you like the apartment. I know that."

"Yes, but—"

"Okay then."

While Coral was fixing dinner she got a phone call and took it in her room. Danny, it must be. Thank God the boy had found someone he cared about. Maybe soon he'd even go back to school and get a real job—all he needed was a little push. When they sat down to eat, Coral's earlier moodiness had passed. Oscar seemed very nice, she said kindly. Would Anna be seeing him again soon? Anna mumbled something vague, her pleasure alloyed by the acrid taste of betrayal in her throat.

"Maybe that's my mom," said Magenta at the sound of the doorbell. She was lying on the couch under a comforter.

"Maybe." Unlikely. Bea said it only to placate her. Had it been the elusive mother of Magenta, Ernesto would have rung from the lobby.

Rhonda had been unreachable throughout the long night and returned Bea's call only this afternoon, while Magenta slept. No need to rush from work, Bea assured her; the crisis was over. She herself would have taken wing, but not every mother was the same. This visitor, she thought as she made her unhurried way down the hall, was one of her own.

"Bea? I hope I'm not disturbing you." Lisa stepped in and shut the door against the draft. "This is going to sound silly, I know, but I wanted a recipe. Roy's got this bug in his head about pie—"

"Lisa, maybe I could call you later? I'm, uh, involved with Shimmer and Magenta. Some little problem came up." She waved airily.

"Magenta? Funny, Roy mentioned her just last night. I'll say hello." Lisa sailed past her to the living room.

"Roy mentioned her? Why? What about her?" No. Impossible. Not Roy. She shoved the thought back to the hell whence it came.

"Hi, you girls," said Lisa in her cheery teacher's voice. "How're you doing?"

"Hi," said Shimmer glumly.

"Oh, God," moaned Magenta. "Look at her!" She burst into tears.

"What's the matter?"

"Just look! Her stomach."

"What?" Lisa looked down in fright, as if the baby might have sprung forth undetected.

"She's pregnant!"

"You knew that," said Shimmer in the same dull voice. "You saw it at that party. Everyone in this family is pregnant."

"She's having a baby, and I lost mine!" she sobbed. "Mine is in some—some Dumpster somewhere."

"For heaven's sake, Magenta," Bea said sharply. "You didn't even want it. You're fifteen years old. You should be glad you're all right after last night."

"What happened? Oh, you poor thing," Lisa said after Bea explained. She sat down near Magenta and attempted to stroke her head.

"Stop! Go away!"

"There's the bell. Shimmer, could you get the intercom, please? Magenta, cut it out. Control yourself."

"It's her," Shimmer announced. "She's on her way up."

"Where is she? Is she okay?" Rhonda stood chalk-faced in the doorway. The same wispy blond hair as Magenta's, Bea saw, but unlike Magenta she appeared frail.

"She's fine. Everything's fine. Come on in."

Rhonda raced to the couch and threw her arms around Magenta. "My baby!"

"Oh, Mom, I thought I would die." Magenta sobbed. "It was so gross. Ask Shimmer. She came with me both times."

"Hi," said Shimmer.

"Why didn't you tell me?"

"I thought you'd kill me. Where were you? I was so worried."

Rhonda sat up, her face flushed pink. "I was out. I didn't pick up the message till this afternoon."

"Out where?"

"Just out, okay?"

"I'll make some coffee," said Bea.

"I'll do it." Shimmer repaired to the kitchen.

"Hi, I don't think we've met. I'm Lisa. I teach at Maggie's school."

"A teacher? You mean everyone knows about this except me? The whole school knows?"

"Nobody knows. I just happen to live here. In the building, I mean. I'm married to Shimmer's father."

"I thought—" Rhonda looked queryingly at Bea.

"Never mind. We're all family. She's really okay, Rhonda. The doctor said she should rest for a day or two but there's no serious damage done."

"Well, I know I should thank you. I do thank you. I appreciate all you've done. I mean, if she hadn't had your help, I hate to think . . . But really, you could have told me something was wrong. She's been staying here a lot. Didn't you notice anything—"

"Please, please calm down. I didn't notice. She came in and out with

Shimmer, and frankly . . . well, I just didn't notice anything wrong. There are so many people coming in and out.''

Rhonda turned to her daughter. ''Who was the boy? Well? You're not going to tell me?''

''Is it really so important?'' said Bea with a shrug. ''After all . . . Excuse me, is that someone at the door?''

In the hall she encountered Roy. ''Sorry, Bea, I rang but I guess you didn't hear.''

''I didn't hear because everyone is crying.''

''Who's crying? What's wrong?''

''Come in and see for yourself.''

''Roy!'' Lisa exclaimed. ''I didn't expect you till later.''

''Dr. Power? What are you doing here?''

''I might ask you the same thing, Rhonda.''

''I'm here because my daughter . . . You know. I keep telling you.'' She began weeping again. ''I'm sorry, I'm just so confused. Dr. Power, could you please tell me why you're—''

''He's not a doctor,'' Bea murmured.

''She knows that, Bea, but she insists. Hi, sweetheart.'' He kissed Lisa. ''I had a cancellation so I came home. Hello, Magenta. Where's Shimmer?''

''Right here, Dad,'' she said wearily, carrying in a tray with cups and saucers.

''Let me help you with that.'' Roy took the tray and set it on the coffee table.

''Dad? She's your daughter?'' Rhonda looked from Lisa to Bea. ''But you're the mother, right?''

''Right. I am definitely the mother. And you are . . . I see. Oh, Roy. Roy, really.''

''Wait a second. Do you mean that all along . . . ? You let me go on talking about her all these weeks?''

''I didn't know. How would I know? It's a small world.''

''Oh, now I get it. She's your patient?'' said Lisa.

''You figured it out.''

267

She flushed. "Don't talk to me that way!"

"I'm sorry, sweetheart. I'm just a little— Why are we all gathered here?"

"Magenta had a problem." In the midst of Bea's explanation, the wild clanging of an alarm began.

"What's that?" Rhonda cried. "A fire? Should we run? Why are you all just standing there?"

"It's only the elevator," said Bea, "or someone fooling with the roof door."

"Shouldn't you go check?"

"It'll stop."

"There's safety in numbers. That's what we always say," said Shimmer.

"If it's a fire I can't even run. I'll burn to a crisp," said Magenta. "And I don't even care."

"Listen to her. You see, I was right yesterday when I said I knew something was wrong."

"You were absolutely right. I should never doubt maternal instinct. I never will again."

"Oh, you are so totally unprofessional. It's outrageous. I could report you. I could sue."

"Please, there's no need to shout," he replied.

"There is a need, with that thing going off. It's maddening. How do you stand it?"

"We just do."

"And she won't tell me who the boy was. You must know, Shimmer, don't you?"

Shimmer turned and walked back to the kitchen.

"Look, Rhonda," Roy said, "I had no idea Magenta was your Maggie. I just realized yesterday, when you called her Magenta. In fact I came here now to ask Bea about her. I guess I should've asked as soon as I realized, but . . ." He glanced over at Lisa and had a visual flash of her tugging down the red bikini panties, the protruding belly, the wealth of dark hair. At that moment the alarm stopped. "I was, uh, tied up last night. How come you're here, by the way?"

"Me? I came to get the recipe for that pie."

"What pie?"

"That pie you wanted after we—"

"Oh, the lemon chiffon."

"Why are you talking about pie? My daughter almost bled to death and you're discussing pie? I want to know who the boy was. And I want to know why you both"—she glared at Roy and then Bea—"concealed information from me."

Shimmer returned with the coffeepot. "Who wants some?"

"No one concealed anything. Have some coffee. I could just as easily ask why you left me responsible for this child in an emergency and waited sixteen hours to return my call."

"Yeah, Mom. I had to worry about you while I was almost bleeding to death. Where were you?"

"I said I was out. Why are you looking at me like that? Don't you stay out lots of nights? Why can't I?" Yet again, tears streamed from her eyes. "There's this guy at the spa, I had dinner with him a few times and he asked if he could stay over, but I wasn't sure I should start bringing men home. Like, it might set a bad example. Ha."

"But Mom, that's great. Why didn't you tell me?"

"Because you never talk to me anymore, that's why. So last night he asked me to go home with him, and since you weren't coming home, I thought, Why not? I need a life too. I went straight to work from his place and I didn't have a chance to check my messages until lunch. I can't believe, the one time in a year I do that, and look what happens. So now I'm a bad mother."

"It's okay, really, Mom. Stop crying."

"You never mentioned you were seeing someone," said Roy.

Rhonda turned on him. "What business is it of yours? You're not a confessor. Just a therapist. And some therapist. Isn't there some professional code, I don't know, conflict of interest or something? All the time I talked about her she was right in your house."

"I keep telling you, I didn't know. You called her Maggie. And this isn't my house."

"But I am your daughter. You'll admit to that, right?"

"Of course, Shimmer. What do you mean? Anyway, I've hardly ever seen, uh, Magenta."

"I did see you a few times," said Magenta, "but you didn't pay much attention."

"This isn't your house?" asked Rhonda. "You walked in like it was your house."

"Well, it isn't. Not anymore. I live downstairs. The point is, she's your daughter. It's your job to know where she sleeps. When you said she was staying with a friend, I assumed you knew where."

"Roy," Lisa put in, "I thought you weren't supposed to be judgmental. She was doing her—"

"Lisa, please, I'm not in my office, and you really don't know—"

"At school we tell the parents those things, but a therapist . . . Aren't you supposed to be on her side?"

"It's not a question of sides."

"Oh, would you all just shut up!" Shimmer burst into tears.

Bea went to put her arms around her. "That's an excellent idea. Magenta should really rest. And Shimmer's worn out too."

"I feel fine now. I want to go home."

"Wait." Shimmer sniffled as she moved out of Bea's embrace. "Maybe we should tell. As long as everything's coming out?"

"What?" said Magenta.

"You know. You said you'd take the blame."

"What is it now?" asked Bea.

Both girls were silent. Then, "You promised," said Shimmer.

"I meant later on. I'm so tired."

"You promised."

Magenta fell into her mother's arms and wept.

"The money," Shimmer insisted.

"What about the money?" Rhonda asked. "Tell me. I won't get mad."

"I took it from your checking account," Shimmer told Bea. "Five hundred dollars."

"Oh, shit," groaned Roy. "Shimmer, don't you know better than that? It's wrong to take money."

"Roy, let it be. Can't you see she's upset? Of course she knows it's wrong. It's good that you told me, dear. That's a good girl."

"Mom, can't you even get mad at anything?" Shimmer seemed disappointed. Then, abruptly, she had a fit of giggles.

"I'm so sorry," said Rhonda, chastened. "I'll send you a check tomorrow. I may have to send it in installments, but I'll pay you back. I'm sorry there's been all this trouble. Maggie, get your things."

"We should be going too, Lisa."

Lisa was sprawled in the armchair, her legs stretched in front of her, her hands clasped around her belly. "I wanted that recipe. Lemon chiffon pie?"

Bea seemed not to have heard. She sat on the couch with her arm around Shimmer, comforting her, or perhaps clutching her for support.

"I guess the recipe can wait." Lisa lumbered to her feet and reached for Roy's hand.

"I don't know about next week, Dr. Power. I think maybe . . ."

"I can understand your hesitation. Let's talk on the phone, okay?"

At last they were gone. Bea still sat holding Shimmer. There was no need to speak; together they savored the tranquillity of the room. Bea was beyond relief, in the numbness that drapes the overwrought mind like a velvet shield. From the day's events, the only thought that rose clearly to consciousness was, Thank goodness it wasn't Shimmer.

How soothing it was to sit like this with her daughter. How long since they had sat quietly together? Too long. The warmth and smoothness of Shimmer's body nestled against hers were a reminder of the time, long ago, when she had carried her from room to room, before the advent of Snuglis; she had known this would be her last baby. How much had changed since then! She could hardly bear to think of all the changes. Better simply to relish the moment of peace, the closeness of her child, who was growing up too fast.

The phone rang and automatically Bea stirred, but her body refused to do more.

"Let it go, Mom," Shimmer said drowsily.

"I can't."

Shimmer implored her with a squeeze. "We'll listen to the machine."

"Bea," came Anna's voice, sharp and peremptory, "give me a call right away. I have something—"

"Oh, all right." Shimmer got up. At the sudden absence of her touch, it felt as though a layer of skin had been ripped away. "Hi, Grandma. Everything okay?" She answered Bea's questioning look with a hand patting the air. "Uh-huh . . . Really? That's great. . . . I can't, she's in the shower. I'll tell her as soon as she comes out. . . . Sure . . . Bye."

She returned to the couch but not to the shelter of Bea's arm. The moment was destroyed.

"What?" Bea asked.

"She found Oscar."

*

Hours later Bea was enjoying a different warmth and a deeper silence, the construction next door over for the day, and the street noises having ebbed to the occasional car alarm or siren. She lay with her head on Dmitri's chest, drained by love. Love unexpected. He had come up to report that his flu was over. Exhaustion claimed her every cell, and the memory of Magenta's blood swirling in the toilet bowl like an enigmatic hologram still made her slightly dizzy; she wanted only to lie in his arms. But after she told him all about it he had slowly roused her.

"You are becoming Russian," he said. "In Russia the women weep for love."

"They do? All the time?" Was it culturally learned behavior?

"Not all the time. Only when they are very, very pleased." He smiled with satisfaction.

Perhaps the women in his past life had been in the habit of weeping for pleasure, but Bea hadn't the heart to tell him she was weeping from weariness, and something else she could not name. Regret, apprehension, bewilderment. Well, she needn't tell him anything; she need only smile. Besides, the phone intruded. She reached for it, over Dmitri's objections, with a tantalizing mélange of curiosity and dread, her very private S&M.

"Bea, I'm sorry to call at this hour, but Anna just went to bed." Coral was whispering. "I need to talk to you."

"I heard already. Oscar. She must think you're an angel."

"Oh, that. That was nothing. No, it's something else. Could I possibly come down? I can't talk here. She sometimes listens in."

Coral apologized anew when she found Bea and Dmitri in bathrobes. It was only eleven; she didn't think they'd be sleeping.

"This happened right after we found Oscar. She wouldn't say where we were going till we got there. I'm not even sure I should be telling you—I don't like to police anybody—but I had a feeling you wouldn't be too happy about it, Bea."

"Well?"

"Okay. It's this TV program. Afternoon sleaze? You know, people go on and tell these awful things they've done? Drugs, incest, you name it. Don't you know about it?"

Bea was unfamiliar with the genre but Dmitri, to her surprise, was not. "Sometimes while I'm puttering around," he confessed. "To understand the culture."

"I wouldn't call it culture. It's garbage. She had this appointment, sort of like an interview. She wouldn't let me go in with her. She must have written to them. There've been a couple of mysterious phone calls, but I didn't ask. I mean, everyone has a private life. The thing is, she wants to tell her story on TV."

"What story? The Young Socialists?"

Dmitri exploded with laughter. "It is not a political program, Bea. Not social history."

"Something about a boiler man?" Coral suggested.

"What boiler man?"

Coral's lips were twitching, trying to suppress a smile. "I think she had a little fling once. Like maybe a hundred years ago? They're having a show on one-night stands. I guess she was auditioning." She smiled openly. "Like I do. I didn't know we had so much in common." Then she drew herself up lest she had been misunderstood. "I don't mean one-night stands, of course."

Bea felt the erotic glow of fifteen minutes ago fade like the coils of

273

her electric broiler. "I was hoping it might be something easy, like a fuse box or another flood. Okay, I'll call in the morning and head them off. Leave me the number. And thanks for telling me."

"I actually feel sort of bad about that. She made me promise I wouldn't tell. I don't know if I did the right thing."

"Of course you did the right thing. There's no moral dilemma. She's flipping out. Besides, your relationship—it's not like the sanctity of the confessional, you know." Or of the therapeutic couch. How often, in bed, had Roy violated professional secrecy, seeking her advice? Had she not colluded with him, there might be no Serena in her life, or in May's, for that matter. No Lisa, perhaps. No pregnancies. There might be the calm and order she longed for.

"You won't tell her I told you, will you? We've established some trust between us. And I like her, I really do. She'd never trust me again."

"I'm not happy with all this secrecy."

"Be sensible, Bea," said Dmitri. "Openness is overrated in this country."

"All right. I'll tell them she's not responsible for her actions. They'll have to give some excuse so she doesn't figure it out." Better still, she would get May to call. Not only should May do her fair share, but her manner was ideally suited for this mission.

She was barely settled back in bed when the phone rang again. "You never called me back," came the accusing voice.

"I'm sorry, Mom. It was a long day. I forgot."

Dmitri groaned.

"You got the message about Oscar?"

"Yes. Congratulations. I'm happy for you. I didn't realize you were searching. But now your search has been rewarded."

"It was that Coral who really did it. She's a smart one. Now listen, Bea, let me tell you what I arranged. I'm talking low so she doesn't hear."

Bea listened as commanded, her eyes closed in the dark. At last she mumbled a good-bye and laid her head on Dmitri's chest.

"So?" he queried. "A new fold?"

"Wrinkle," she corrected.

Coral knocked on Bea's door again the next morning, quite puzzled at why she had been summoned. To make matters worse, she felt guilty of bad faith, an unfamiliar sensation. She had always been up front about her actions, but in this family one was somehow drawn into duplicity. By rights she should have mentioned her plans last night, but she had needed to bask in her happy secret just a little longer. As well as mull over her options. Hadn't Dmitri said openness was overrated? But Bea was sure to be distressed, to say the least.

"Thanks for coming down. I didn't think we'd be meeting again so soon." Bea gave a nervous laugh, very unlike her.

"I told Anna I had some errands. A little white lie. It feels like you and I are sort of conspirators, you know what I mean?"

"I do. I appreciate your discretion. In fact I appreciate everything you've done. May and I both."

"Oh"—Coral waved nonchalantly—"it hasn't been hard at all."

"Do you want some coffee? A muffin?"

"Thanks, I've had breakfast." Get to the point, she thought. Like everyone, Coral hated awkward scenes. But unlike everyone, she preferred to plunge in and dispatch them as fast as possible. Whatever it was Bea wished to discuss could not be more delicate than her own news.

"This isn't easy for me to say, Coral, particularly after you've done such a good job. It's worked out even better than I'd hoped, which is why I hate to have to . . ."

"Have to what?"

"I hope you're not going to misinterpret this."

"It sounds like you're trying to tell me I'm fired. Is that it? Why?" She was surprised at her own response: her pride was assaulted. Awkward as quitting would have been, especially after having pressed so hard for the job, it was better to quit than to be fired. Fired! She'd never been fired from anything. She was the one who quit. Madame Régnier in Paris cried when she left, so devastated that she refused to utter a word of her hard-won English; all through college her summer employers had been sorry to see her go. Few people were as efficient and capable. Anna could have no earthly cause for complaint.

"Not fired. At least I hope that's not the way you'll see it. We've all grown so fond of you."

"Oh, come on, you're not going to tell me you consider me a member of the family?"

"Why not? Since you mention it, we do. Is that politically incorrect? Well, my notions of family are old-fashioned. They have nothing to do with today's wretched politics. Anyhow, what's happened is not about you. It's Oscar. You do know about Oscar?"

"Of course I know Oscar. I met him yesterday. I'm not the one who's senile, Bea."

"Nor am I. I meant I'm not sure you know the history." She paused to bite thoughtfully into a muffin. "Funny, I never knew those long walks had any purpose. I don't know if it makes her less crazy, or more."

"He was an old friend. She was trying to find him, the best way she knew how. What's so crazy about that?"

"Well, with your help she succeeded. And they made a little arrangement." Bea began speaking in haste, as if eager to rid herself of the words. "She offered him a room in the apartment, that is, to stay with her and do what you're doing. A few years ago he wouldn't have wanted this, but his situation is more crowded now. To make a long story short, he accepted."

Coral leaned back, her muscles loosening in relief. She must not relax too thoroughly, though. This was a moment to summon her strategies. "So that's it."

"Yes. I'm very sorry."

"And she never said a word. That crafty old thing. Well, this is ironic, Bea, but I have something to tell you too. I was afraid of how you'd take it. I really was."

She revealed the news of yesterday's coveted callback from the second-longest-running musical on Broadway. "I was hoping, but I didn't believe something like this could turn up so soon. It's a great piece of luck. I'll be working almost every night, and daytime rehearsals at the beginning.''

Bea looked so pleased that Coral feared she might leap up and smother her in an embrace. "That's wonderful! Congratulations! I want to see you in it. Let me know as soon as you start."

"That's what Danny said," Coral exclaimed in an unguarded impulse. "Only he demanded front-row tickets."

"Oh, so Danny knows?"

"He's the only one so far. I called him late last night. You do know," she said shyly, "that Danny and I have been seeing each other?"

"My dear, how could I not know? Everyone is delighted about it. But I'd never bring it up. I don't interfere in my children's lives. Especially Danny, he's so private. Well! That's a relief, about the job, I mean. I felt so rotten, having to tell you. And for no reason except my mother's whim. Who knows how it'll work out with Oscar, but it's what she wants. We can only hope for the best."

"I got a good feeling about him. Of course I only met him for a minute." At this juncture she must proceed with care. Bea was shrewd, not your standard do-gooder white-lady earth-mother by a long shot. Always a step ahead. It would not do to forget that. "Still, he can't do everything, can he?"

"What do you mean, everything?"

"I mean, there are some, well, female-type things. Like the hair." She gave a tentative smile. Unlike May, who shrieked in horror, Bea had made no comment about the green hair. "Personal things."

"Well, luckily she doesn't need a lot of physical care. Yet. Does she? Isn't she still bathing and dressing and all of that?"

Bea seemed a bit alarmed; Coral struggled with the benign desire to reassure her and the practical urge to alarm her further. "Sure. But she sometimes likes a little help. Things a woman could do better. And Oscar will need some time off. He's close to his family, isn't he?"

Bea walked to the window, gazed out for a moment—those joggers: oh, to have their endurance!—then returned and gave Coral a level glance. "You like the apartment, don't you?" It was Coral who had to lower her eyes first. "And Anna likes you."

"I like her too, I told you. And I did think it would be for a bit longer than this. You know, while I got my life together. And then there's Danny."

"How does Danny figure in this?"

"If I left he'd ask me to move in with him, I'm pretty sure. And I'm not ready for that. It wouldn't be fair. I don't want to give him the wrong idea."

This time it was Bea who turned away. It had been a relief, lately, to see Danny happy, or at least not wretched. No way would she risk spoiling that. "All right," she said. "I don't see why not. It's big enough. Do you think you and Oscar can work things out between you?"

"Oh, yes. That won't be a problem."

"But the money." Bea faced her squarely again. "You understand, if you're working full-time, it can't be the same. Not with both of you."

"Forget the money." Coral rose to leave. "I'll start getting paid by the show next week anyway. The apartment is more than enough."

On the phone moments later, May was amused at the television contretemps, as well as tickled at the opportunity, thrust upon her by Bea, to thwart her mother.

"Will you call right away, May? Don't forget."

"Have no fear."

"There's another development. A new fold, as Dmitri would say." Bea recounted her talk with Coral, which had left her a trifle shaken; May was often a steadying influence.

"So you let her wangle you into staying in the apartment."

"I wouldn't exactly say wangle. At least I was wangled in full consciousness. What's the harm? One more or less living there. I must say I had to admire the way she did it."

"Maybe you have met your match," observed May.

"Maybe."

"You might start delegating some more responsibility to her. The building, the family."

"Lay off, okay? How's Serena?"

"Blooming. It's amazing how she takes to pregnancy. I wouldn't be surprised if she wanted another."

"Oh, God. She'll have to get it a different way. Twice would never do."

"I suppose not," May agreed. "I still can't get over it—Oscar, I mean. Who would have thought it? You do know, Bea, that if and when things get really bad—I mean, if she really starts coming apart—they'll be out of there like a shot, Oscar and Coral both."

"I know," said Bea. "I know. I've got it in the back of my mind."

Part Four

•

Family Values

XII

Because of his cigar, a recent habit, Roy was alone at the far end of Bea's living room. "Smoke it if you must," she told him merrily—always more tolerant of weaknesses of the flesh than of the spirit—"but blow it out the window." He sat in his favorite armchair, with his favorite view of the park, content in his exile. The family party in progress was absorbing, and satisfying to watch, like a well-choreographed scene in a movie. Smoking engenders detachment, sharpening the senses as it clouds the air: Roy studied the kaleidoscopic patterns, the shifting group dynamics, as his loved ones drifted about. It was early April; the sky was balmy. Warming sunlight streamed in, deepening the colors of the women's dresses, gleaming off the wood surfaces, and adding a sheen to the newly dusted leaves of the avocado plant. It had grown to a small tree since he and Bea planted it, or rather Bea, while he watched. He remembered she broke a fingernail as she peeled the pit; then she inserted toothpicks and suspended it in a glass of water. He might have fetched the glass. So long ago, even before Shimmer was born. In their salad days. Salad indeed—they had eaten the avocado at dinner, then talked about Danny and some minor problem at school.

The mild hum of conversation was enlivened now and then by trilling laughter or the clink of plates. Across the room, standing at the table—more like huddling—were his three wives in animated conversation. Lisa seemed to be holding the floor, entertaining the others, and every so often they would laugh in unison. More like tittering. Could they by any chance be discussing him, comparing notes in the way men dread, and with good reason? No, that was pure projection. More likely it was the intimate details of pregnancy that women found so engrossing. In any case he would never know, which was just as well. Women shielded men from certain aspects of the intimate life, and fairly enough, just as men walked on the street side, historically, to shield women from the spatterings of horse-drawn carriages. That was no longer a danger, of course, but no new technology could banish the perils of the intimate life.

These were the moments that made it all worthwhile, he thought, when the abrasions of family life dwindled to insignificance and its glories stood in relief. He sensed the fabled pleasures of a patriarch, even though he felt neither powerful enough nor old enough to merit the term. Still, his family was united and happy. They had had their rough times, but now all was well. He must be having one of those rare moments of stasis, when the present reflects all the past and beams into the future. Wispy notions of Eastern philosophy, Danny's kind of thing, strayed across his mind.

The party marked his fifty-first birthday, three weeks away, and Bea's fiftieth, appropriately today, a Sunday. More Bea's party than his, fifty being the milestone, but Lisa and Serena, coproducers of the event, had been kind enough to include him in the honors.

Kind? Or was it indulgent? He puffed and blew the smoke obediently toward the open window. "We want to do something for Bea's birthday," Lisa had said in bed, rather shyly, a few weeks ago. "Serena and I, I mean." "That sounds nice, sweetie. What do you have in mind?" Only later did she remember his birthday was around the same time. He might have hinted a bit. A forgivable oversight, since at his last birthday they had just been getting acquainted. Serena or Bea would have been less apt to forget. "Oh, then sure," said Lisa, hardly missing a beat, "it'll be your party too." Bea was a fine mentor. Under her guidance Lisa was learning all sorts of graces and subtle shades of accommodation.

With a bland gaze Roy studied the remains of the enormous cake and its once finely sculpted lavender and mocha floral trim. In size and whiteness it had suggested a wedding cake, the kind that comes in tiers topped with wee plastic statues of a tuxedoed groom and a bride wrapped in tulle. Or it might have been an anniversary cake, only he and Bea had married in November, and it would be in poor taste to celebrate that. "Happy Birthday Bea and Roy" had been written in elegant chocolate script, with a candle for each of their decades. Now largely devoured, the cake was a ragged crumby shambles, its golden insides nakedly revealed, striations laid bare, flora smeared and wilted.

In contrast with the last gathering, this party was the opposite of a surprise. The honorees had been kept thoroughly abreast of the preparations—"Linen napkins are so much nicer than paper," Lisa would murmur in the dead of night, "and I hate paper plates"—so much so that Bea had finally intervened, offering to help. Soon she was setting aside bowls and platters from her daily labors, and Roy's freezer was commandeered for storage; there were evenings, after takeout dinners or Lisa's healthful, fat-free efforts, when only with enormous self-restraint had he kept his hands off the party food. Naturally Serena and Lisa had demurred—"It's your party, Bea; you shouldn't have to do the work"—but Bea said it made no sense to hire a rival of lesser talents, and they weren't about to do it themselves! In the end Bea had prepared her own party in her own apartment, with her hallmark dishes: the veal wrapped in bacon, the tortellini in pesto, the tiny quiches, the pirogi, the opulent salads—beets and arugula and fava beans and huge glistening olives. She took full advantage of nature's bounty; Roy hoped she would not be cleaning up too.

He watched Bea in profile, leaning against the arch that gave onto the hall. Her head was tilted back and her hair was lush, just loose enough to suggest sex, not enough to suggest sloppiness. She wore black silk slacks and a long flowered jacket, something that might have been picked up in a street market on exotic travels, except Roy knew she hadn't been anywhere exotic for some time. He really might have brought her something from the Barbados honeymoon. Lisa had come home with half a dozen brightly colored dresses. But pity for Bea was clearly misplaced; there was Dmitri leaning toward her with a broody, desirous look. As Roy watched, Dmitri smoothed down her hair and whispered something in her ear, at which she smiled slowly and know-ingly. Roy was glad. Yes, he assured himself, he was truly glad she had someone. Dmitri might talk vaguely about going away to study or work or seek adventure, but he would never go. Fortunately—for there could be no more of those infrequent and immensely gratifying hours spent together. Not now, when he must be true to Lisa and raise their child. Incestuous, Lisa had quipped. Not quite right, but not quite wrong either. On the other hand, things were so unpredictable, life so fluid, one could never say for sure. Never say never, as he often told his despairing patients.

His gaze flitted over Anna, seated across the room, dressed in a T-shirt and a long flimsy dress that looked like one of Shimmer's cast-offs, the absurd green hair complemented by blood-red lipstick. Stand-ing beside her like a bodyguard was the faithful Oscar. A happy pair, thought Roy. Stable. She had gotten what she wanted at last.

Not far from Anna sat May, like himself apart, near an open win-dow. But not alone. On her lap she held Timmy, who was lolling, maybe even napping. Roy couldn't remember May paying much atten-tion to Timmy before, or to any of the children, for that matter. Per-haps she was rehearsing for motherhood. Was it motherhood? It sure as hell wasn't fatherhood. Stop, he chided himself. Such prejudices were unworthy and out of date. He knew very well it would be called parenthood, and what they did with the child would be called parent-ing. Or perhaps May was merely studying the shape of Timmy's skull, in preparation for another of those hideous heads made of found objects.

She seemed content to sit apart and silent, absently stroking Timmy's hair. Well, taciturn May was not at her best at parties. When she was at her best he could not say. He tried to recall his relations with her before she lured Serena away. Had they ever really spoken? Strange that people could be in the same family for years and never exchange any significant words. Had May always regarded him with aloofness and faint contempt? Was she only reflecting his own atti-tude? If he had made some effort with her, taken some interest in her work and her tempestuous loves, maybe all the rest would never have happened. It was irrelevant by now, though. He did not crave Serena in her present state, engorged with his child. Over the last month her fine features had thickened and her golden hair lost its luster, while May had improved. He could even detect a slight resemblance to Bea, except she was larger than Bea, approaching the monumental, with a kind of stony beauty. With the child on her lap she suggested a Madonna, not an etherealized Raphael Madonna but one of the Picasso Madonnas he had seen last week at the Museum of Modern Art. Or something by Puvis de Chavannes. Bea would appreciate such an allusion; on Lisa, alas, it would be wasted. He had asked Lisa to come to the museum, but she said it was too hard to walk around with her eight-month burden.

Amid his reveries Shimmer approached, in bare feet and a flower-sprigged dress, as fresh and eager as if she were about to prance around a maypole. She was leading a hefty ponytailed boy by the hand. A boyfriend? Why had no one thought to tell him of this development?

"This is my father," she announced.

And why, moreover, had no one taught her to present the younger person to the older? There had been so many oversights. So many lapses. At least this one was minor and remediable. Roy half rose and held out his hand.

"Dad, this is Chuck."

"Hi, Chuck, glad to meet you."

"Hi, Dr. Power."

"I'm not actually a—" Roy began automatically, but Shimmer waved him silent.

"Dad, let it go, okay? So, are you enjoying your party?"

"Very much. It's a great party. So, uh, how long have you two known each other?"

"Since second grade." Chuck had an engaging space between his front teeth and a cleft in his chin. "We just never noticed each other till now."

"I noticed you, but girls always have to wait. Can I get you anything, Dad? You look kind of lonely here, all by yourself."

"No, I'm fine. It's because of the cigar. I like to watch."

"Like Chauncy Gardner," said Chuck with a grin, leaving Roy puzzled.

"So okay, Dad, just passing through. We're going to say hello to Grandma."

"That's nice, Shimmer. Have fun, you two."

"It's Sara."

"Sara?"

She nodded.

"I didn't know. Since when?"

She shrugged. "A week or so. Shimmer's a little silly, isn't it? At this point?"

Roy had to laugh. "What about Maggie?"

"She's still Magenta. I have a feeling she'll always be Magenta. Come on, Chuck." She took his hand and led him away.

Alone again, Roy scanned the room for Lisa. The group of wives had dispersed, and now she sat in a corner on a straight-backed chair, the only kind of chair she found bearable these days. The sight of her was reassuring. The sight of a wife in a crowd was always deeply reassuring. He wondered if women felt the same about husbands. On either side of her, on similarly austere chairs, were the two other expectant mothers, all three chattering earnestly. Such lovely women, each in her own way; they could be the three Graces, apart from the huge bellies. Two of them would be his children, a fact that never failed to send an icy twinge through his entrails. At least it was no secret now, and was, perforce, accepted. Melissa's would be his grandchild. In the three women rested his future, his immortality.

He studied Lisa. She seemed totally comfortable, as vivacious as when they first met. More comfortable, perhaps, than she was with him. It was remarkable, given the initial shock and its aftermath, that Lisa had so easily been assimilated into the family. Assimilated, yes, as if the family were a culture of its own and Lisa a foreigner he had introduced. She was so well assimilated that he sometimes felt he had no special claim on her. And yet he had wanted her for his very own. No one was his own, not quite. Not Bea, who belonged equally to everyone and no one; never Serena; not even the children. And now even Lisa was theirs. No, he thought. Don't let bitter thoughts spoil the moment. Count your blessings. Not theirs. Ours. He drew deeply on the cigar as if it could grant him heart's ease. Then he set it down and let his eyes close.

Melissa found herself unexpectedly happy at the party. It truly felt like a family. Her family. Ancient knots of suspicion were giving way; at long last, overcoming a lifetime of distrust, she could think of them as hers. Bea was right about family ties: they gave you a firm grounding, a sense of your place in the scheme of things, despite the transient conflicts. Jane and Al, whom Melissa generally regarded as airheads— though Al, at least, had some talent—today seemed witty and urbane, verging on glamorous. Even sweet, clumsy Danny was smiling and joking around, verging on charming. The reason for that was obvious: Coral. Coral might even become a friend and ally. She knew how to talk and how to dress; she brought a crisp breeze wherever she went. To an onlooker, Melissa imagined their little group might be labeled the three young couples, and the label didn't displease her. In an access of warmth, she announced, "We're taking the same house out in Amagansett for July, and hopefully the baby will be settled down by then, so why don't you all come out for a week or so?"

"Great idea," said Jane. "You were just talking about taking some time off, Al."

"Sure. Yeah, thanks very much. I'll have to check my schedule, though. I have some gigs coming up on the Jersey shore. But thanks, really."

"Maybe we should wait and see how the house works out," said Tony. "And the new baby. With Timmy and the nanny, you know, it could get a little hairy."

"I don't see why. There's plenty of room."

"I'll come," Danny said. "It'll be my only chance to get away all summer. I'm sort of broke for a change. What about you, Coral?"

"I'd love to, really I would. But with this new job I'm not sure I can manage it."

"Well, whatever. I thought it might be fun. Let me know if you change your minds." Melissa stalked off, back to Serena and Lisa. Better to talk about symptoms. Better not to give in to sentimental impulses. The hell with family. You were on your own. She had always known it.

"Everything okay, Mrs. Anna? Can I get you anything?" Oscar leaned down to his charge.

"No, not this minute. What time is it?"

"Almost five."

"Am I going to miss *Jeopardy!*?"

"No, that is the weekdays. This is Sunday."

"I forgot. Did we go out today?"

"We walked in the park this morning, remember?"

"That's right. How's my hair? You think it's becoming?"

"It's beautiful, like I tell you. My sister-in-law, she's a good stylist, always work in the best places."

"Remind me, who's that blond one over there with the big belly?"

"Your previous son-in-law's wife of before. Ms. Serena. Now the good friend of your daughter."

"Bea? Don't be silly. She has the Russian."

"Your other daughter. Ms. May."

"Oh. Oscar?"

"Yes, Mrs. Anna?"

"You're not going to leave, are you?"

"No, I don't want no other job. This place is fine for me."

"Tell me the truth." Lisa looked earnestly at Melissa. "Is it really so painful?"

"Not at all. Not if you like feeling you're being turned inside out through your asshole."

"Oh. Thanks a whole lot. I mean, like you couldn't be a little more graphic, could you?"

"Have them put you out. Then you won't feel a thing."

"No, I want to be aware the whole time. Roy and I have been doing very well at Lamaze. We practice the breathing and everything at home. A lot of it is in the mind, our teacher says. If you call it pain it feels more like pain than if you call it contractions."

"I wish he'd go to Lamaze classes with me," Serena said. "May has to be dragged each week."

"I tried natural childbirth with Timmy. But after eighteen hours you're glad they invented anesthesia. You can call that by a lot of different names too—Demerol, Stadol, Phenergan . . . Just look at my ankles." Melissa extended her legs with distaste. "They used to be so nice. Now they're all puffy. It happened last time too."

Serena and Lisa both examined their ankles, which were unchanged. "Tough," said Serena. "Lisa, do you realize that even though our babies will be half sisters, there's no special name for what we'll be to each of them? I mean, me to yours and you to mine? I think there ought to be a name, in this day and age."

"We'll all feel related in some way or other, I suppose. Cousins, sort of? The name doesn't matter."

"If it matters whether you call pain pain or contractions, maybe this matters too," Melissa remarked.

"I really don't think we have to dwell on it," Lisa replied, studying her fingernails.

"Why not? It passes the time. I haven't been sleeping well and May sleeps like a log, so I lie awake and figure it all out. Melissa's baby is the one with the most formal relationships. For one thing, she'll be your stepgranddaughter."

"Why do you keep calling them all she? Some of them might be boys. Although I would like a girl, to balance out Timmy."

"Well, whatever it is, Lisa will be the stepgrandmother."

"Grandmother?" Lisa was horrified. "Must we keep talking about this? It's all very silly."

"So what? Our daughters will also be Melissa's baby's aunts, because they're Tony's half sisters. And of course Bea will be the grandmother. But our children won't be anything to Bea, technically. That seems very unfair. I think there ought to be some official name for what Bea is to our children."

"In societies where there's polygamy," Melissa said, "I bet there's a name for that. We could ask Coral. She knows all about those things."

"You're teasing me," Lisa protested. "You two are mean."

"We're trying to make you laugh. Break down and laugh. Our babies will also be Melissa's sisters-in-law."

"Okay, are you satisfied? I'm laughing."

"Thank God. I didn't know how long it would take."

"So will you stop now? It makes me uncomfortable."

"Discomfort is no excuse. Where did you learn that?" Serena asked. "In therapy?"

"In a way, Lisa, you're my mother-in-law. Imagine that," said Melissa. "Funny, I've never resented you."

"Why, do you resent Bea?"

"No, actually. Bea's a very good mother-in-law."

"Yes. I sometimes feel like she's my mother-in-law too," said Lisa.

"Now she's getting into the spirit," said Serena. "I knew she had possibilities. Good material. That's what Bea says."

"Bea says that about me?"

"In all sincerity. Have no fear."

"My parents are coming in from Portland when the baby is born," Lisa said. "How are we going to explain all this to them? That's what I lie awake wondering when I can't sleep."

"We won't explain anything," said Serena. "We can be very discreet if we try."

"What's with the gigs on the Jersey shore? You never mentioned that. I thought summer was a slow time."

"You never know what might come up. I heard some of the guys talking. . . ."

"You're a terrible liar, Al. Don't even try. I know you're not crazy about Melissa, but if Danny and Coral come, we could have a good time. You love the beach. And it's a freebie."

"I can pay for my own vacations." Al began carefully spreading pâté on a cracker. "Want some?"

She waved the food away. "What's wrong? You're acting weird. Talk to me."

"This isn't a good time to talk about it."

"About what?" Jane's voice rose to a squeak. "What are we talking about? And why do you keep eating? Eating's not going to help."

"Listen, sugar," Al said between bites, "how about we talk later? When we have some privacy?"

"We can have privacy right here." She took his arm and dragged him into the hall, stepping on Dmitri's foot in passing. "Sorry," she mumbled. "Now, what's going on?"

"Janie. Oh, man." He turned to the wall and pounded it with his fist. "I just don't know how to say this."

"You met someone else?"

"No," he said hastily. "There's no one else. I don't want anyone else. It's just that . . ."

"Shit, Al, will you spit it out?"

"Okay. I'm thirty-five years old. I want—I want to get married. Have kids. With you. I've told you, but you won't take it seriously. When I look at those three women in there, I feel . . . like my life is going by. I'm sorry, Janie. That's what I feel."

"I can't believe this. You really want that life? You want to see me changing diapers and pushing a stroller? Cooking your dinner every night? Giving up my—my . . . everything. You don't know me at all," she said, weeping. "You don't have the slightest idea who I am or what I'm all about. Oh, go away. Leave me alone."

Al turned and started for the living room.

"Come back," she cried. "I didn't mean it literally. God, you take everything so literally. You just want to get off easy. Well, this isn't so easy. Tell me, what did you expect when we started?"

"I don't know. It just started. I loved you. I still love you. I thought

293

maybe you'd change your mind. But you know what happens. If I mention kids you act like I asked you to chop off your legs or something."

"To me it would be like chopping off my legs. Can you see me onstage with a kid strapped to my back? You know what *I* think when I look at the three of them? I think, Thank God that's not me. I'm not going to end up like my mother, taking care of everyone, with no life of her own."

"I guess that's it then. It won't work. I'm sorry, babe. You're a great person, but—"

"Oh, don't give me that shit. A great person! If you really thought that you wouldn't care about—"

"I do care, though. That's the point."

"You are so conventional. Just look at you." She looked him up and down with scorn. "You're even wearing a suit."

"It was a big party, I thought . . . What's wrong with a suit once in a while? When I put it on, you said it looked cool. Janie, you don't mean these things. You're just angry."

"You're damn right I'm angry. And look how you choose to tell me. Right in the middle of a birthday party. Mr. Sensitive. You think that's sensitive?"

"I didn't want to tell you now. You made me tell you."

"When were you planning to tell me? Oh, let's stop. Go away. Leave." She slumped down the wall till she reached the floor, hugged her knees to her chest, and cried.

"I don't want to leave in the middle of the party. It's no way to treat your family."

"Fine. Go back in there and have a great time. Then you can go home and pack. Oh, shit, it's your apartment. I forgot. So you're throwing me out. What the fuck am I supposed to do now?"

He joined her on the floor and put his arm around her. "Jane, sugar, I'd never throw you out. Stay as long as you want. But I need you to know where it's at for me."

"Are you deaf too? I said go away."

"You can't just sit here on the floor crying. I can't leave you here like this."

"Why not? This is my mother's house. I can do whatever I want here."

Danny and Coral stood side by side gazing out the window. "You didn't seem too thrilled," he said, "about going to Tony and Melissa's this summer."

"Well, I do love the beach, but with the new job, how can I?"

"On your day off. The jitney's only two hours. You can stay over and get back in time for the eight o'clock curtain."

"I'll see. Can we maybe discuss this later? Summer's a ways off."

"Is it something that needs discussion? That doesn't sound so good. What is it? You don't like my family?"

"No," she said quickly. "Your family's fine."

"It's me you don't like, then?"

"Of course I like you—"

"Then—"

"Danny, not here. Please?"

"Why not here? It's as good a place as any. I guess I didn't read the signals right. I thought everything was going great. Am I wrong?"

"It was. I mean, it is. Danny, we've only been going out a few weeks and you're acting as if, you know."

"It's two months."

"Okay, two months. I'm just not ready to—"

"I get it. Now that you're in the show, there're a lot of new people around. You want to keep your options open."

"Oh, this is so awkward. And you're such a nice guy. I mean really, you're a great guy."

"That's it. A great guy. The kiss of death."

"I didn't say I never want to see you again. You're making a big deal out of . . . I just wasn't ready to make summer plans, that's all."

"Sure. Next thing you'll want to be friends."

"I didn't say that. But if it happened, isn't that better than—"

"I don't want a friend, Coral. Friendship is not what I thought we were doing. Tell me, the other night, back at my place? Were you faking it?"

Her skin darkened. "Faking it? What do you mean?"

"You know what I mean. Was all that just a performance? I mean, I know you're an actress. If it was, you were very convincing."

"I don't think I deserve that. That's not a very nice thing to say. For your information, no, I was not faking it. Look, it's been fine. It's terrific. I don't know why you're doing this. . . ."

"Is it because of the race thing? Is that it? It's not an issue for me. I wasn't brought up that way, you can see for yourself. If it's an issue for you, we can talk about it, work it out." He covered his face in frustration. "Oh, God, this is so awful to bring up."

"It's not that. I mean, it's always an issue, nothing can change that, but that wouldn't stop me. Look, I could easily say that was the problem, but it wouldn't be true."

"So what is the problem?"

"I don't know! Problem was the wrong word. There's no problem. I don't know how we got to this point. You're making me feel pressured, that's all."

"Fuck it! And I thought this time— I really thought . . ."

Roy must have dozed, for he gave a start as the loud shout of "Toast, toast!" resounded in his stomach. He opened his eyes to a scene of déjà vu. Dmitri was poised to open a bottle of champagne. The cork popped, foam spewed from the bottle like a genie, and he went around the room pouring. When the three pregnant women refused, Sara was sent to fetch ginger ale.

Not déjà vu, Roy realized. The feeling was not mysterious or inexplicable, nor had the scene occurred in another life or a time warp; he remembered clearly, if unwillingly, the merciless surprise party for him and Lisa. And yet it had all turned out all right.

"This time Tony will give the toast. Come on."

Tony, looking gray-faced, stepped forward from behind Al and demurred, but the others insisted. He had looked poorly for some time,

Roy mused. Perhaps things were not going well at work. When was the last time they'd really spoken? He would call tomorrow and arrange a lunch; an old-fashioned father and son talk was in order.

"To my parents," Tony began, without enthusiasm.

Should he go and stand next to Bea? Roy wondered. No, not while Dmitri held her in his fierce grip.

"To my parents, who have done so much for all of us. They've created a wonderful, uh, sense of family, and they've been through a lot without losing their sense of . . ." He paused, and the silence went on too long. "They've always . . ." Again he stopped, and seemed to be choking back a sob. Finish up, thought Roy. Just finish up. "They're an example to us all, of—of . . ." Tears spurted out of Tony's eyes and he brushed them away boyishly, with a fist.

"Enough toasting," Bea cried gaily, and went to give Tony a hug. "Let's have our champagne."

"Speech, speech," someone shouted. Others took up the cry.

"That's you, Roy," Bea called from across the room. "I'm no speechmaker."

"Me?" He had been quiet in his corner for so long that the demand was an assault.

"It's your party, Dad," Sara sang out.

Must he rise? Yes. He stubbed out the smoldering butt. His brief sleep had put him at an even greater distance. There was a film between himself and his loved ones, who had become a roomful of well-dressed strangers. Waiting.

"I want to thank my dear wife, Lisa, as well as Serena for this wonderful occasion, and I thank you all for coming. It makes me and Bea—I think I can speak for Bea, can't I?"

"Sure, go ahead and speak for me. Why not?"

"It makes me and Bea tremendously happy to have you here, and to know that the family is going to be larger very soon." He gave a gracious nod to the three women on their hard chairs. Had they been doing needlework, as in a Victorian novel, they might have resembled the three fates. One spun, one cut—he couldn't remember the precise details. "Seeing you all gathered together makes me feel . . ." What did it make him feel? Nothing he could say simply or in public. With dismay, he heard himself run on like some right-wing politician exalting family values. It was a relief to round out a cliché and stop.

The applause was polite, though not fervent. Perhaps under the circumstances he shouldn't have mentioned the impending births. But surely it was better to acknowledge the situation than deny it. Not that denial was possible.

"Tony? Are you okay?"

Melissa found him standing with his back to the crowd, fingering the leaves of the avocado plant.

"Fine."

"You were upset when you made the toast. What is it?"

"Nothing. I'm not in a party mood."

"I know I didn't check with you first when I invited them all out. I said it on impulse, but I thought you'd like it. Having Jane, and all."

"I don't like making plans so far ahead."

"We're taking the house, though, aren't we? You said you'd send in the deposit."

"Where's Timmy? Maybe I'll take him for a walk."

"He's napping in the bedroom. Tony," she said plaintively, touching his shoulder. "What's the trouble? I thought things were going better."

"Nothing, I told you." He started to move away.

"Hold on a minute. You're making me mad, you know? Why won't you talk to me? I have a right to know what's going on."

"I can't talk now. Just cool it, will you?" He turned and fled, leaving her gaping after him. In the hall he nearly stumbled on Jane, who was sitting on the floor. She looked up but he didn't speak, just made for the door.

"Your family's great," said Chuck, sitting close to Sara on the couch and munching a sandwich. "My family's so uptight, like, I can't imagine them having a party like this. And your mother . . . They're all fantastic."

"You really think so?" she said wryly.

"Yeah. Why, you mean they're not so great? Are there awful secrets or something?"

"No," she responded. "That's the thing. There are no secrets at all."

Timmy had just gotten to sleep, Melissa said as she opened the door the next evening. Crying, wanting his father. Her posture, usually so erect, was slumped as she led Jane and Danny into the living room.

She was not hysterical, as Jane had expected from her phone call. Dry-eyed, deflated, Melissa lowered herself onto the couch, resting her hands on her stomach. It was the first time Jane had seen her downright shabby, in old sweatpants and a T-shirt, her hair frizzy, her face haggard, yellowish circles under her eyes.

"A fax," she said in a weak voice. "A fucking fax. Can you believe it? From the airport. I picked Timmy up at his play group and found it in the machine. He didn't even have the decency to call."

A message on the machine would have been no better, maybe worse, Jane thought, but held her tongue. She was almost too overwhelmed to speak anyway. Never, never had Tony made any major move without telling her first. Melissa was astonished too.

"You really didn't know?"

"No, I swear. I'm as shocked as you are."

"It's not a total surprise," said Danny. "He's been talking about going to Vietnam ever since high school. To find his roots. Remember, Jane?"

"He said a lot of crazy things. But who ever thought he'd do it?"

"Fuck his roots," said Melissa. "His roots are right here. He'll have another kid in a month and he didn't even want to see it. I could die in childbirth and he wouldn't even know. Or care, probably."

"You won't die. Anyway, he might be back by then," said Danny. "Did he say anything about when he'd come back?"

"No. Go read it for yourself. It's over there on the table. Maybe he'll never be back. It could take a long time, digging up roots. I don't know if I'd want him back, after this."

Danny rose and walked to the table. The fax had evidently been crumpled up and then spread out flat, perhaps many times, so that already it looked like old news. Melissa was right; the tone was officious. The words might have been addressed to a secretary, even an office temp with no stake in daily affairs. It gave no details, stated only that he was flying to Saigon that afternoon and would E-mail his whereabouts soon, that his trip was urgent and its duration unknown. The brief personal note at the end was even more cruel, in context: "Sorry. I have to figure out my life."

Danny brought three beers from the kitchen. He and Jane drank, but Melissa didn't move.

"Do you realize all three of us have been abandoned?" she said.

"That's an awful word," said Jane. "I don't see it exactly that way."

"Dumped, then? Is that better?"

The silence took on such weight that Jane had to get up and look out the window. The street below was empty. The streetlight was garish, and the neon sign of the café on the corner blinked on and off maddeningly, its merry icon of two clinking martini glasses a sorry mockery. "There's no sense sitting here. I'll go uptown and tell Mom and Dad. It's better than telling them over the phone."

"I'll stay here tonight, so you won't be alone," Danny told Melissa.

"Okay, if you want," she said with indifference. "I've got the bassinet and all the baby things piled in the extra bedroom, but I think you can still open the couch. What am I supposed to do tomorrow? Go to work? What do you do when your husband disappears? What do I tell Timmy?" She leaned back on the couch and closed her eyes.

"We'll figure it all out later. Janie, maybe you should go stay with Al tonight. I'm sure it would be okay with him."

"No," she said firmly, putting on her jacket. "What's over is over. I've got to get used to it."

"I'll never get used to it," Melissa groaned, her eyes still closed. "Now I know how my mother felt."

She would, thought Danny. People get used to anything. Melissa's situation was worse than his—being left after years of marriage, with Timmy, and the new baby coming. Or so it would seem to an impartial observer. Yet he could not resist the seductive feeling that no misery surpassed his own, simply because it was his own; no one else's loneliness could be quite so tragic. Even objectively, one could make the case that being left after a long history was not as bad as being left before anything had truly begun. At least she had something tangible, he thought, while he had almost nothing, only a tantalizing glimpse of something he would never possess.

The air hung heavy and funereal in Bea's living room. Jane watched her parents, so vocal in good times or bad, turn mute. Over and over she had to repeat the meager contents of Tony's fax, as if by repetition the words might procreate and yield motives, a narrative, a hint of resolution. But they remained barren, and soon the questions too were exhausted.

"Where's Shimmer?" Jane asked, only to hear a human voice.

"Out with Chuck. She's back to Sara now, remember?"

"Oh, right. I forgot. I thought Shimmer was kind of nice."

"I got used to it myself," Bea agreed.

"No, it's a good sign that she's back to Sara," Roy put in, but his contribution was ignored.

"Years ago Tony was angry because we didn't keep his Vietnamese name," said Bea after a while. "But I thought it passed. He never actually said to call him Thao. I would have. I mean, what does it matter?" She looked at Jane with apprehension. "You don't feel that way, do you? You won't suddenly do anything crazy? Or make us call you Xuan?"

"No."

"Why don't you stay here tonight? So you're not all alone."

"Everyone's worried about my being alone. You think I'm some kind of waif. I can manage fine on my own."

"I should have paid more attention," said Roy, "when he talked about going back there. Maybe we should have sent him when he was a teenager. Gotten it out of his system."

301

"How? It wasn't exactly a tourist Mecca, as I recall," said Bea. "By the way, Janie, did I mention there's going to be an empty apartment next month? You know the D line—didn't you have a friend in 5D? It's not so big that you'd feel lost in it. The kitchen was remodeled last year—"

"Mom, I told you before I don't want to move back."

"I know, but I think you've set your mind against it without thinking it through. I don't mean forever, just until you get things sorted out. So you feel you have a home."

"But it's not my home anymore. My life is downtown, my friends, my work, everything. I know you mean well, but no. I'm fine staying at Danny's place for now."

"I always thought you and Al would manage to stay together," Bea said wistfully. "I never dreamed he'd throw you out like this."

"Bea," said Roy, "let her alone."

"He didn't throw me out, Mom. I could've stayed till I found another place, but I didn't want to. It was his place all along. I moved into his life and now I've moved out. I didn't deliver what he wanted. It's like a transaction."

"That's why people get married."

"To have an apartment?"

"To have stability, not be moving in and out of each other's lives. Making and breaking transactions."

"Mom, come on. Marriage is a transaction too. It's the ultimate transaction."

"Well, maybe ultimate is good. I'll miss him."

"*You'll* miss him!" Jane exclaimed. "Look, I'm going now." They didn't stir. "You won't sit here like this all night, will you?" As she bent to kiss them good-bye, she envisioned them aging, their bodies dense, rooted to their seats, maybe in some institution. Lost, clinging together like brother and sister. Hansel and Gretel. "Hansel and Gretel" had been Tony's favorite fairy tale when they first learned to read English. He used to make her act it out with him, but after a time she said they were too old and refused to play.

"What could he possibly do there?" said Bea, when they were alone.

302

"Make money," Roy replied morosely. "There are hordes of young people there getting the capitalist machine started. The result of the war."

"He was making money here. Maybe he'll go back to the land. The rice paddies."

"He'll be back soon enough, Bea."

"Aren't you worried?"

"Of course I'm worried. But it's beyond our control. We have to let go. Do you want a drink?"

"No."

"Neither do I."

"Let go," she mused. But letting go—whatever that really meant—did not seem a question of will, a simple matter of opening the hand. She thought of scenes from movies where desperate bodies clung to the ledges of buildings, their tensed fingers gradually losing their grip. The next scene—the body in free fall—was usually not shown. Free fall: the words had a nice sound, but the end was inevitable. Anyway, the image did not apply; she felt more like the solid but helpless ledge than the slipping body.

"It's the two of them working so hard, and the baby," she said. "The pregnancy. It's too much stress. They think they can manage it all, but it's impossible."

"It's more than that. Tony was always discontent."

"They're all discontent."

"Don't make yourself feel worse, Bea. It's not as if he's dead. We did the best we could."

"Did we really?"

Roy took her hand. It lay limp in his. "We can't let ourselves sink like this. We have to be strong. For . . ."

"For what?"

"For everything that's coming."

"Yes. It's far from over, isn't it?"

"Bea, I've never heard you this way. Even when we got divorced."

"This is worse. This is our child. We've lost him."

"It's just a trip."

"Maybe Melissa could take that apartment in the D line. Then when the lease next door is up we could break down the wall if she wants more space."

"Bea, really, isn't that a little extreme? She has a good apartment."

"But that way we could all help with the new baby. She'll need help." She cocked her head to give him a look of raw irony. "We'll have enough for our own play group."

Roy moved closer. "Bea, hold my hand."

"I am."

"No you're not. Not really."

"I feel like he's escaped," she said with a little laugh. "Isn't that strange? I want to go after him and protect him."

Roy put his arm around her. "Bea. I want to feel better. I want you to feel better."

"No."

"No?"

"How can you even think of it?"

"I don't know. It's easy," he said sadly.

"Go home to your wife."

"It's not the same thing. He's not her child. Anyway, she's too far along. Please."

"You're outrageous."

"Can't we at least lie down?"

"No, Roy. There are limits."

XIII

"Careful of the puddle," said May. "Do you think you can walk?"

"I'm fine. It's only during the contractions." Serena climbed out of the taxi, one hand grasping May's arm, the other supporting her belly.

The driver sped off the instant Bea slammed the door, no doubt in relief, she thought. Serena's moans could frighten the most heroic. A thunderstorm had left the air chilly and damp, more like fall than spring, and at one in the morning the street was deserted except for the whoosh of sparse traffic, headlights haloed by mist; it was so quiet that the clicking of the traffic light on the corner was audible. Then a siren broke the silence with a distant aria that rose to an excruciating pitch as it neared; the ambulance careened around the corner and swooped into the driveway.

They stood contemplating the hospital's glass doors, tinted a forbidding green. "I wish I didn't have to go in. I always associate hospitals with death," Serena said, still clutching her belly. "Bea? Do you think Roy will come?"

"I left a message. They must have turned the phone off. Where would they be at this hour?"

"What do you need Roy for?" May held the door open. "We're both here. I'll stay with you the whole time."

"He did come! Look!" Serena waved exultantly. "Roy? Over here, Roy."

Indeed, at the far end of the gleaming, sterile lobby, its floor polished to a slippery sheen, its mustard-colored armchairs arranged in austere rectangles, stood Roy, hunched in his Windbreaker, deep in discussion with a clerk at the admissions desk. He turned, his shoulders rising in surprise. The woman in the wheelchair beside him turned as well. Even forty feet away, Bea could hear her panting.

"I knew he'd come." Serena set off across the room.

"He came with Lisa, don't you see? And don't walk so fast. You could fall." May gripped her arm firmly as Bea strode ahead.

"I see why you weren't home when I called. How's it going?" She patted Lisa's shoulder.

"Awful," she moaned. "Why didn't anyone tell me? Roy, what's taking so long?"

"Just another minute, darling." He greeted Serena and May. On second thought, he bent down and kissed Serena. "This is a coincidence."

"Oh, there's another one. Oh, God! I have to sit down." May shoved the nearest chair beneath Serena.

"If you'll give me your insurance card, sir, we can get you upstairs."

"Yes, yes, I'm looking for it." He rummaged through his wallet and a heap of cards fell to the floor. A few people planted on the mustard chairs eyed their group with the torpid, fishy glance of strangers waiting out their private crises. "Here we go." He handed the card to the clerk.

"What would you do if he couldn't find it?" said Lisa, recovered from her contraction. "Let me give birth down here?"

"I can't help it, ma'am. We can't admit anyone without an insurance card. Has your doctor been called?"

"She's been called, for chrissakes. What more do you need, our birth certificates?" Lisa removed a small square of bubble wrap from her pocket and produced a tattoo of sharp crackles.

"Take it easy, darling. I'm sure this lady is doing her best."

"Bea said I should speak up. Remember, Bea? You said I had to figure out what I wanted, my own best interests, and all that?"

"Yes, sure, but you have to choose your moments. Stay calm now and let Roy handle it."

May, squatting beside Serena, massaged her stomach while she groaned.

"Can't I do anything?" said Bea.

"Find the card," said May, tossing her Serena's tote bag.

306

Lisa was wheeled off with Roy following after, attempting a jaunty wave. Eventually Serena too was placed in a wheelchair.

"The labor room is this way," said the attendant, holding the elevator door. "You ladies can wait in the waiting room."

"Number one, I'm no lady," May replied, "and number two, I'm staying with her."

"Are you the next of kin?"

"Yes. We took the course. You want to see my diploma? Now mind your manners, Vikram"—she peered at the badge on his shirt—"and drive."

Bea found the upstairs waiting room deserted except for a bearded young man in a long black coat and skullcap, reading a thick book with rough-cut pages. He glanced up at her and promptly glanced away in seeming aversion. How different was this dull, stony ambience from the excitement of the emergency room, where she had taken Magenta scarcely more than a month ago, though it seemed like years; so much had happened since. How different, too, was the flavor of her apprehension: no sour panic this time, but something more rich and fierce. She sat for a moment, then headed for the bank of phones on the far wall, which was adorned by pastel paintings of flowers, as if an aspiring orderly had been charmed by Georgia O'Keeffe.

"It's lonely here," she told Dmitri when he finally picked up. "People shouldn't have to wait in hospitals by themselves. Your thoughts go haywire."

He had never refused her anything—not that she had demanded much. Now she waited out his silence, remembering his mysterious grief. If indeed there was any such grief—she was beginning to have her doubts. And dammit, she had done plenty for him. She looked over at the man in the corner, but if he felt her gaze, he refused to look up. A maternity waiting room should be a convivial place—the approach of new life, the family of man—but he was an emissary from a dark realm, ominously stroking his beard.

"I'll come. Of course," Dmitri said at last. "Can I bring you anything?"

"Thank you. A slice of pizza, maybe?"

"If I find a place open."

Bea leafed through a copy of *People* magazine. A woman whose husband had beaten her for twenty years described how, after a course of therapy, he had reformed. Now, when he felt the urge to beat her, he went out to the barn and chopped wood. His wife was heartened by the change and looked forward to a peaceful old age, but Bea felt her optimism was misplaced. As she considered mortal folly, she sensed footsteps approaching. Too soon for Dmitri. Please, let it be a stranger; for just a little while, she wanted nothing to happen. She craved two empty hours to prepare her soul for the new family configuration. Danny stood before her.

"So you got my message," he said.

"What message?"

"The message I left a half hour ago? I'm here with Melissa."

"Melissa?" A stab of hunger sliced through her. Pizza! Dmitri! "Melissa's having the baby?"

"Yes! I told it all to your machine. The contractions woke her and she called me at the copy shop. I thought maybe you could stay with Timmy, but you didn't answer so she got a neighbor to come in." He paused, out of breath. "So what are you doing here?" As he sat down beside her, the bearded man across the room peeked at them surreptitiously, then turned back to his book.

Bea explained in a whisper; she had the frivolous desire to keep the bearded man in confusion. She pictured herself, hours from now, playing back the urgent messages. By then, with luck, the new generation would safely have arrived. How odd it would be, listening and knowing the results of the dramas they foretold. She was sinking into a metaphysical stupor—was it Einstein who introduced the notion of bending time?—but struggled to rouse herself. "We should get in touch with Tony."

"Oh, Tony," Danny said with scorn. "We can E-mail him when it's all over. If he cared he'd be back by now."

"I had a letter the other day. He has an apartment and he's looking up relatives. He's learning the language. Relearning."

"I know. He E-mails Melissa every few days. It's disgusting. There's a whole colony of slick types there making their first million. He'll fit right in."

"That's not what he's there for. Does she write back?"

"Yeah, not that he deserves it. I wanted to go into the labor room with her but they wouldn't let me. All these regulations, it's like the army."

"The labor room? Oh, Danny, I don't think that would be appropriate."

"I don't care. I'll try again in a while. Maybe there'll be a different nurse. May got past them, didn't she?"

"Yes, but that's different. She's a parent. And she took the course." Certain people—May, for one—could talk their way into any place, but Danny, she thought, was not one of them. Fortunately, in this case.

"Mom, there's something you ought to know. Two things, actually."

"Are you sure? Lately words like that strike terror in me."

He grinned. "You might like this. The first, anyway."

"Jane's not pregnant, is she?"

He shook his head. "I'm thinking of going back to film school in the fall. In fact I'm pretty sure."

"Danny!" Bea almost levitated from her chair. "That's wonderful! I'm so glad."

"I started this ESL course so I can teach over the summer, to help pay for it. I don't want to borrow more money from you and Dad."

"How did this come about?"

"That has to do with the second thing. I've had a lot of encouragement."

"God knows we encouraged you. But you called it nagging."

"Mom, I—I think I'm in love. I mean I know it."

Bea's heart thudded. Would this boy never stop courting misery? "Danny, sweetheart, she tried to tell you weeks ago. She just isn't—" Her voice faded into a dull wake, her tongue having lagged behind her brain. "Not—not Coral?"

"Not Coral. Melissa."

"No." It came out louder than she intended. She glanced at the bearded man, but his eyes were steadfastly lowered.

"Yes. I never really knew her before, but now, staying with her . . . This is the real thing. It's the first time I ever felt like this."

"But you can't! She's married to Tony. You can't be in love with your brother's wife." There must be vending machines nearby, she thought wildly. Something salty, to raise the blood pressure. Fritos were nice. Or those little cracker and peanut butter sandwiches.

Danny drew back. "Why can't I?"

"I don't have to explain. It's obvious. You just can't."

"I don't see why not. My father's in love with my sister's teacher, my ex-stepmother is in love with my aunt, you're in love with the super, and Grandma's in love with the doorman, so why the hell can't I be in love with my brother's wife?"

This time the bearded man let the book drop to his knees and stared openly. Bea suppressed the savage urge to give him a grin, as she might to a stranger who had overheard her child utter something devilishly clever.

It was a shock, hours later, to open her eyes to the hospital waiting room. She had dreamed she was safe in her kitchen. She'd just had another baby, easily and painlessly—it slid out while she chatted with the doctor, who resembled Dmitri. He picked up the baby, exclaimed something in Russian, and kissed Bea as she lay on the table. The baby, when he placed it on her chest, looked like Tony, with dark almond-shaped eyes, sallow skin, and silky black hair. She insisted on getting right back to work—a batch of miniature spinach quiches for the local abortion clinic's annual benefit lunch. But just as she was wringing out the spinach, May came barging in and threatened to take the baby away, claiming it was hers. May had green hair. Bea wondered why, but was too busy fighting over the baby to ask. May grabbed it from its cradle and they tugged the small bundle back and forth, while the baby's head turned into one of May's sculpted heads made of found objects, its mouth a set of gears fixed in a grimace. Then Danny appeared and snatched it from both of them, threatening to throw it out the window. This should have been terrifying but somehow it wasn't. Instead they laughed and laughed.

But it was just a dream, already slipping away. The pink tinge of dawn seeped in, softening the stern glare of the waiting room. Through slitted eyes, Bea saw Jane and Dmitri bent over a crossword puzzle book. The bearded man was gone, perhaps a new father, perhaps frightened off by the danger of contamination.

"Coward," said Dmitri. "Four letters. I should have brought my thesaurus."

"Noel," said Jane.

"Noel! You're so smart. Ah, Bea is arisen. Hello, my love."

"Hi, Mom. You look stunned. I'm not psychic. When I got home from rehearsal I found a message from Danny. It's like a race, isn't it? Who'll pop first."

On the Formica coffee table was the remaining half of a large pizza. How sage of Dmitri to have brought a whole pie. Bea reached for a slice.

"Secretary. Ten letters."

"Where's Danny?" Bea asked.

"Amanuensis." Jane spelled it for him. "He saw Melissa's doctor go by and chased her down the hall."

She had eaten no more than a couple of bites when Danny raced in. "It's a girl! She had a girl! It's all over! Less than four hours!"

They shrieked and embraced as required at such moments, until a nurse came in and demanded silence. "This is a hospital," she said, as if they had failed to notice.

"Twice a grandmother, Bea," Dmitri said.

"It's true. One was a lark but two is serious. It's a chastening thought."

"Chastening! That's the word, Jane," he cried. "Subduing the pride of, ten letters. Is it ten letters?"

"Yes," said Jane. "Can we see her?"

"Not yet. They had to put her out."

"Someone should call her parents," Bea said, gnawing on a crust. "Could you, Danny?"

"Me?"

"Well, since you . . ."

"Her father and his latest wife are in Rio. And her mother, well."

"Alcoholics are still mothers. Oh, never mind. I'll do it myself later."

"I'll call, Mom," said Jane. "Then I'll go home. This place gives me the creeps. You don't need me, do you? Let me know when something happens."

"I'll go see if I can get a look at the baby through the window," said Danny. "I can't sit still."

Remember it's not your baby, Bea wanted to warn him. But did it really matter? All the children are ours, she had told Lisa in her moment of crisis. Maybe it would do Danny good to feel some responsibility.

With her head on Dmitri's shoulder, Bea had almost drifted off to sleep again when Danny returned, flanked by Coral and Sara.

"Look who I ran into in the hall!"

To her amazement, Coral and Danny were laughing and bumping shoulders like old friends. How volatile was erotic love, how easily transferred, as if not intrinsically connected to any object but existing in a free-floating state. Like anxiety.

"I woke up and saw all these messages blinking," said Sara, "so I listened and figured you were here. So I called Coral and we decided to come too."

"This is so exciting," said Coral. "We saw Melissa's baby in the nursery. She's so pretty. She looks a little Vietnamese. You can tell."

"I should have brought more pizza," said Dmitri. "I could go out and fetch some."

"I'm an aunt again," said Sara. "What's happening with the others?"

"Nothing yet. Soon I'll go and ask at the desk. Does my mother know what's going on?"

Coral opened her mouth to speak, then hesitated.

"What? Is she all right?"

"Sure. It's just . . . She heard me go out so I told her where I was going. And she said . . ."

"Well, what?"

"She said she hoped everyone would be back from the hospital in time to see her on TV tomorrow. I'm sorry, Bea."

"But how could she? May called them. I thought that was all over."

"Whatever May said, they still seem to like her story. I think she got Oscar to take her there again."

"Oscar! That snake!"

"He does whatever she wants."

"She's actually going on the show?" cried Sara. "You didn't even tell me, Coral."

"Didn't you know? How could you let them? I mean, this is impossible. She can't do it."

"I can't be there all the time, Bea. We discussed that. Oscar's the one responsible now, and I'm certainly not supervising him. I just thought I'd sort of prepare you, so you wouldn't be totally shocked."

"Would someone tell me what this is all about?" When Danny heard Sara's giggling account, he roared with laughter. "One-night stands? When was her last? Maybe the hot dog man. She asked me to give him some money."

"It's not funny," said Bea. "It won't be funny when she gets on and talks about it, and God knows what else thrown in."

"I don't see what you're so worried about. You don't have one-night stands. It's just the opposite. You all stay together forever. You can't separate."

It was too much to expect the children to understand. If Anna were asked the right questions—if the right thread were pulled—the family history would unravel like a half-finished sweater. She must be stopped. "She must be stopped."

"You can't do anything at five in the morning," said Danny. "Unless you want me to go over and tie her up. Gag her."

"Perhaps your fears are exaggerated, Bea," said Dmitri. "No one you know watches that trash."

"Oh, no? You do. I bet half the people in the building do too. All the retirees. That's not even the point. The point is, what ever happened to privacy?" From the alarm on her children's faces she realized she was shouting. They had rarely heard her shout. "To discretion?"

313

"What ever happened," asked Coral quietly, "to letting people do what they want?"

Alone and in pairs, they had ambled through the corridors, peering at the names of patients on the doors, or pausing before larger, locked portals bearing plaques with the awesome titles of diseases. They had been to the coffee shop. They had viewed Melissa's new baby. Now their talk was sporadic, their spirits listless. On and off they dozed on the unyielding chairs, in contrast with the bustle around them. For with morning the waiting room had grown lively. Phones rang, nurses and orderlies scurried past, and clumps of people, anxious and jovial in turn, sat chatting in English, Spanish, and Chinese. Bea wondered if a study—would it be a flow chart?—had ever been undertaken about the hours at which babies were born. Danny and Sara had made their entrance, in civilized fashion, in the late morning. She recalled how, shortly before Sara's birth, Roy had been shaving, a meticulous procedure; when she urged him to hurry, he cut himself on the throat in two places and arrived at the hospital looking like a candidate for treatment, perhaps someone caught in a vicious drug war over turf.

Sara slept on the couch, while beside her, Danny studied his ESL book.

"Tell me something," Bea murmured. "You're in love, okay. What about her?"

He blushed deeply. "Really, Mom. I mean, she was nine months pregnant. What could she *do*?"

"Danny! I'm not asking you what she *did*. I'm asking you how she *feels*."

He stared at her, wordless, then got up and joined Coral and Dmitri, working on another puzzle. "Dmitri, you would like this. My ESL teacher was explaining how hard it is to teach English vowel sounds because they keep changing for no apparent reason. You can't make a rule. I mean, we take it for granted, but foreigners . . . For example, let's see: wand, ward, land."

"Word, ford, cold," said Dmitri.

Bea regarded them with irritation. How could they be playing word games? If they weren't sleeping, she thought unreasonably, they should be worrying.

"Mind and mint," said Sara, unexpectedly awake.

"There is a rule there," Dmitri said. "When the final letter is—"

"It's a girl! She had a girl!" Roy, all disheveled, bounded into the room. Amid the exultation, he gave Danny and Dmitri cigars, though it would have been unthinkable to smoke them right then and there. Dmitri sniffed expertly while Danny held his gingerly, as if the mere contact might cause terminal illness.

"Can't I have a cigar too?" said Coral. "I'd like to try one."

"Sure, take two. Give one to Al. I miss Al. He should be here. Lisa was great, a real trouper. She stayed awake the whole time," he said proudly, as though it were a moral feat. "Just like you, Bea. You were great too. A gorgeous baby. It looks a little like Sara."

"What are you going to name her, Dad?"

"It was going to be Matthew if it was a boy. But I'm glad it's a girl. Girls are easier." He rumpled Sara's hair. "Prettier too."

"Danny was a beautiful baby," said Bea.

"Sure he was." Roy slapped his son's shoulder. "Lisa likes Joanna but I think that's too close to Jane. What do you think of Phyllis or Felice?"

"Oh, not Phyllis," groaned Sara. "No one is named Phyllis anymore."

"Wait a minute," he said. "What about the others?"

Bea told him about Melissa. "But we haven't heard a thing about Serena. It's been over eight hours."

"That's not so long. Remember how long it took you with Danny? The doctor had to reach in and pull you out, kiddo."

Danny winced. Coral chuckled and poked him in the ribs.

As if on cue, May appeared in the doorway, her face pale and her shirt rumpled, as if she had been clutching it with a damp hand. One boot was unlaced. Definitely not the moment, Bea decided, to mention Anna's impending performance.

"This is a ghastly process. I had no idea." She slumped into a chair.

"Well, what's going on?"

"That's just it—it goes on and on. It seems it's sort of stuck. She keeps pushing, but nothing happens. She's worn out. Breathing and counting, it's all a crock if you ask me. A couple of good screams might help a lot, but she's being a stoic. Her Lutheran upbringing. The doctor says if it doesn't start moving soon, she'll have to do a caesarean. I just came out to take a breather, no pun intended. So what's happening? You all look happy, or you did until just now."

Out of the gloom, Dmitri informed her of the other births.

"Good." May nodded soberly. "Let's hope it's contagious. I'd better go back."

"I'll go with you." Bea started to get up.

"That's okay. You take it easy, Bea. I'll go." Roy took May's arm and they trudged toward the hall.

"I think I'll go see Melissa again," said Danny. Coral followed him. The best of friends.

When Roy returned, Bea was waiting in the hall. She took his arm and led him on a stroll past the nurses' station. Arm in arm, they must appear the most sedate of youngish grandparents, she thought, as she spoke with deliberate calm.

"One-night stands?" He looked baffled. "When was this?"

"I don't know. Maybe forty years ago? A man who came to fix the boiler. He's probably dead. Please don't laugh."

"But it's so funny."

"It won't be so funny when your patients see it. Like Rhonda, for instance?"

"Rhonda's gone. And who can blame her, after that . . . No, I don't think my patients are the type . . . Oh, I see. You think she'll . . ."

"Of course she will, if she gets the slightest chance. And if I call and ask her not to, it would only make her more eager. Also, if she realizes Coral told me her secret a few weeks ago and we tried to stop her, she'll throw her out of the apartment." They stopped walking simultaneously and shared a look of perfect understanding, their thoughts progressing in unison as if through a maze. "Coral thinks she's within her rights."

"Sure," Roy said. "The universal right to make a fool of yourself.

316

Well, there's nothing really to do. It'll pass like everything else. Anyhow, we're not so unusual. You should hear the stories I hear. We're pretty run-of-the-mill.''

''Maybe she'll have some kind of accident on the way. Nothing serious, a broken bone or two.''

''I was thinking exactly that, but I didn't like to say. Although Oscar is so diligent, he'd never let that happen.''

''Unless I can get home in time to stop her. But I can't leave May like this. Have you called Lisa's parents, by the way?''

''Oh, Lord, I totally forgot.'' He pawed through his pockets. ''I have their number here somewhere. They'll probably fly out and stay a week or so.''

''You mustn't let them find out, you know. About Serena. Assuming everything's all right.''

''Of course not. They're a bit dense anyhow. They'll never think to ask.''

''I'm worried about her. Did you get to see her just now?''

''No, I couldn't get past the nurse. She was like a gorgon.''

''Do you think it could be retribution?''

''Bea, really.''

''I mean for the way it was conceived.''

''I *know* what you mean. No. Stop thinking that way.'' Their stroll had brought them to a picture window, facing east. ''Now you've got me thinking.'' They watched the sun emerge from a bank of clouds, blazing, still low in its patient climb.

''I know what you're thinking now, Roy.''

''No. I did not think that.''

''Yes you did.''

''Maybe for half a second, but I rejected it.''

''This is May's child too. I want it to be all right. Never mind the inconvenience. Please don't think anything bad, Roy.''

''I'm not, I swear. You're the one thinking about it longer than I did. You're projecting.''

''Don't talk to me in jargon. I saw it on your face first.''

''Bea, will you stop? You're giving me the chills. We're not God,

317

you know, deciding things with our thoughts. We can't do a thing except wait."

"Do you believe in prayer?"

"No. But go ahead and pray if you want. I won't laugh at you. The sun is out. It's a good moment."

"They say prayer itself is effective even if you're not a believer."

"Fine. So pray."

"I prayed when the twins were coming over. I was afraid the plane might crash, after all those months looking for them. Every night for a week."

"You never told me."

"And they arrived safely."

"So maybe it works."

"All right. Go away, though. I'm self-conscious."

"You're not going to go down on your knees?" he asked, glancing quickly around the corridor. An orderly was pushing a mop in slow motion, while down the hall another wheeled a stretcher with a body covered by a sheet. As it passed, they were relieved to see the face uncovered—eyes open and lips stirring.

"No, I'll do it standing here. Go on. I'm glad Lisa and the baby are all right."

"Thank you, Bea."

"Don't tell anyone what we just talked about."

"I won't. I love you, Bea. I love you more than ever. Oh, God, now I've made you cry. Please don't cry. I'm sorry. I'm so sorry."

Please, let that not happen to May, she prayed. It would be too cruel. That was her entire prayer; in this unfamiliar genre she didn't know how to proceed. Then an idea struck her: she would do nothing to stop Anna. Yes, let her go on that grotesque show and say whatever she pleased, as long as Serena and the baby were all right. She hoped she had been properly understood, if indeed there existed any force in the universe capable of receiving her proposal. Who ever said the gods were intelligent? It would be better to put it in writing, like the notes people leave at shrines. Anxiety has driven me round the bend, she thought. Still, she felt better after offering her bargain. Someone came up beside her. Dmitri? No, that was too much to hope for. It was Sara.

"Is a caesarean very bad, Mom?"

"No. Lots of people have them."

"So why are you crying?"

She turned to Sara and stroked her hair. "I'm fine. It's been a long night, that's all. You know, dear, all these babies make me think . . . You are using birth control, aren't you?"

Sara pulled away. "You already asked me that twice."

"I know. But it's on my mind. Especially after Magenta."

"Magenta! I'm not like her."

"No, but still. I made so many mistakes. Sometimes I think there were things I should have told the others. Maybe it would have helped. That's why I'm telling you."

"But I know all about it. Anyway, it's my private life."

"If you got pregnant or—or sick, it would be my private life too."

"AIDS, you mean. I'm not going to get AIDS. We're in high school. It's not like we have a long history."

"You can't be too careful."

"But we're not even *doing* it yet," she squealed. "Just because the rest of you are always jumping into bed, it doesn't mean I have to be the same way. Get off my case, okay?" She wheeled around and stomped down the hall.

An hour later, Roy locked himself in a stall in the men's room to weep tears of relief. What he had told Bea was true: he had thought it for only an instant—how simple, how alluring, if the whole business would just go away—but he could not forgive himself that instant, and had been plagued ever since by the dread of a cruel retribution. Even if he hadn't truly meant it, had squashed it at once as he would a bug un-derfoot, that the wicked thought had arisen in him was undeniable. His own child! He could never forget it. He could only be grateful that it had passed unnoticed by the gods of childbirth, whoever they might be. His spotty knowledge of mythologies turned up no gods dedicated to childbirth, a rather significant omission. He knew he was being wildly irrational, but he couldn't help it. No one could be rational all the time. He could only weep, and be grateful that Bea did not have access to the men's room.

It was a boy, May had reported, teary with relief and exhaustion. The caesarean had proved unnecessary; at the last minute, the stuck baby came unstuck and emerged a fine, strapping fair-haired boy. Everyone trooped jubilantly to the nursery window for the first viewing. The thought of May raising his son, of his own son calling May Mom, or Mommy, was more disquieting than ever with the child a physical reality. But he wouldn't dwell on that now. There would be ample time for that.

At last he washed his face and prepared to come out of hiding. He felt refreshed and his step was lighter, now that his night's labors were done. Had any man ever awaited three births at once, excluding triplets? Seen in a certain light, his situation might make history; he rewarded his wit with a sly grin at the mirror. He wouldn't linger too long with Serena: his place was with Lisa.

At Serena's door a nurse stopped him. "This patient is very tired. You'd better wait awhile."

What a stunning woman. Not so young, late thirties or more, with black hair drawn back tight and satiny skin the color of weak tea. Filipina? Maybe Middle Eastern. Willful and firm. A face with character and bone structure; age made fewer inroads on a face like that.

He smoothed down his damp hair. "I'm the father. I'll just stay a moment."

"The father?" She was perplexed; the dark eyes narrowed.

"Yes. I know she had a rough time." He wished to prolong the conversation, at least find out where she was from. "How's she doing?"

"All right, only she's tired. I had to turn a whole bunch away. There are two people in there now. This is really against regulations."

"I'll send one of them out, I promise. Were you with her the whole time?"

"No, I'm a floor nurse. But I know this patient needs rest." She hugged the clipboard to her chest.

Forget it, Roy thought. At a time like this! Her rigor was quickly effacing her appeal. "One minute. Word of honor." He flashed a smile and slipped past, grazing her cool arm. Still, what a face.

It was a double room, but the other bed was empty, sheets stretched tight in the forbidding hospital style. Bea appeared to be dozing in a chair, and May gave a feeble wave. Serena, chalky and drawn, was propped up on pillows. Roy kissed her and took her hand. Again he was choked with tears.

"I'm so relieved. So glad. I'm sorry you had such a hard time."

She smiled weakly. "It's a boy."

"I know."

"I had it all planned, I mean, the way we did it. It was supposed to be a girl."

"Sorry," he said with a laugh. Why did men find themselves so often apologizing? "I did my best. I followed instructions, remember?" He hoped Bea was sleeping.

"You did."

"What does it matter?" May put in testily. "It's a baby. It's got all its parts. That's what counts." She kicked off her boots and climbed onto the empty bed, pulling the curtain around her. Roy took the empty chair beside Bea.

"He's a pretty boy," said Serena.

"I saw him. He looks like you."

"That's what they say. I heard about the others. Congratulations. Not too many men accomplish what you did, all in one night."

"Thanks. But I had nothing to do with Melissa's."

Bea moaned softly.

"Roy, would you do me a favor?" Serena asked in a faint voice. "Call my folks? I'm not up to it."

"Sure. How are they, anyway? It's been ages."

"Fine. Getting on. My father's close to eighty."

"Well, this will make them happy."

"I guess. There's only one thing."

"Yes?"

"I haven't told them how . . . you know, how the baby came about."

He smiled. "I should hope not. Not at their age."

"No, I mean I haven't even told them about May. That I'm living with May."

"You haven't?"

"No. Roy, would you mind pouring me some water? I don't feel like moving. The pitcher's right there. Thanks. And let me have that mirror, would you? God, I look like something that rose from the dead."

He did not contradict her. "So?"

"I thought, at their age, why should they have to cope with that. There aren't a whole lot of gay women in rural Minnesota. I know them. They couldn't deal with it. It was hard enough for me to deal with."

For you! thought Roy with a twinge of the old bitterness. "What have you told them, then?"

"Well, not much, sort of."

"But they know we're divorced." He felt light-headed and confused after the long night, and could not even recall when he'd eaten last. "They must. I spoke to them myself." He couldn't be imagining it— he remembered clearly Serena standing beside him when he insisted on calling her parents. It was only decent, he felt, to say a few words on his own. She had begged him not to mention May. He had assumed the chill in their voices was inevitable; now it dawned on him that she must have cast him as the defector.

"That was bad enough. I never even told them when Donald was killed. I mean, look, they haven't got that much longer. They don't have to know everything."

"I don't get it. Where do they think this baby is coming from?"

"I . . . You're not going to like this, Roy, but I . . ."

He sat mute, determined not to assist further.

"I told them . . . I didn't want to confuse them or totally lie to them, so I told them you and I got back together."

Bea's eyes flicked open. "You told them that?"

"It didn't seem a complete lie, just a little bending of the truth. I mean, for a little while we did. Technically. I thought about it a lot, and it seemed the easiest way. I had to tell them *something*."

"Serena." No words came. He didn't recall her possessing such layers of deviousness—she who had been too merciful to leave Donald—but perhaps he had never understood her. Or else she had evolved under Bea's guidance. Though, to be quite fair, Bea seemed as astonished as he was.

"Does May know about this?" she asked.

Serena nodded. She was looking out the window, though there was nothing to see except a large brick building, another section of the hospital. Roy followed her gaze into a honeycomb of offices. People in white coats sat at computers; others talked on the phone; all was tranquil and orderly.

"What does she think?"

"She's not thrilled." She sipped slowly from her glass of water. Her color was returning. "But what can she do? The baby was her idea. She has to accept some compromises."

"They might want to visit," said Roy. "You might want to go out there sometime with the baby. Have you thought of that? I—I don't know what to say."

"I thought if any of that happens, maybe you could just cooperate. It wouldn't be for long. Maybe it won't ever happen—you know how my mother hates to fly. If I go out there I'll say you were busy or something."

Bea and Roy exchanged another ancient look, a look they had used when one of the teenagers did something bafflingly perverse.

"Cooperate," he echoed.

"Yes. Why are you both staring at me like that? It's not as if I committed a crime. It doesn't hurt anyone. It makes things easier all around. Why is it so wrong?"

"Because," Bea said, "it's not the truth. Because this baby and who it belongs to is part of your parents' lives, and you're concealing the truth about their lives from them. It's not . . . ." She trailed off, feeling a trickle of bad faith that might gather into a surge if unchecked. No, this line of reasoning was perilous. "It's one thing not to tell them that Roy . . . Oh, don't you see, it's just not fair to anyone." Of course, she thought, if they watched afternoon sleaze, the injustice done Serena's parents in regard to truth might soon be rectified.

"I don't see it that way at all," she said petulantly. "They're old people. Why upset them for no good reason? People don't have to know everything."

"Not everything," said Bea. "But certain things."

"Let it go, Bea," mumbled Roy. "It's done. It's too late."

"I'm so tired. I must sleep awhile. So, you'll call them? Tell them I'll call myself a little later. I'll give you the number. And, Roy?"

"What?"

"Act like, you know?"

He peeked in at May on his way out, sprawled on the bed, fast asleep. He felt a faint tenderness for her. Almost pity. In the hall he and Bea faced each other.

"She has attended your school for wives."

"You give me too much credit. She's gone far beyond me."

Dmitri was sleeping over his crossword book. The others were dispersed, visiting the new mothers, the coffee shop, the gift shop, blithely availing themselves of the facilities as if it were a hotel. No use keeping track. They were beyond her. Let them go their ways. Bea stood alone gazing at the pink and tan babies behind the glass. They all looked alike. New babies had always looked alike to her, had never especially charmed her, their helplessness superseding any distinctions of feature. There was something absurd, even ignoble, about their helplessness. If the nurses didn't come in to feed them, they would perish right there in their cribs. Perhaps if they knew what was in store for them, some of them would choose to perish. Off in a corner a tiny one fluttered in an incubator, its bare chest laced with labyrinthine wires and heaving with each breath. There was a time when she would have felt strenuous hope for that child like a band tugging at her own chest. Now she felt nothing. Maybe she had finally attained the vaunted detachment Roy and his colleagues preached.

She leaned closer to read the labels on the cribs. Serena's and Lisa's babies lay peacefully asleep, Lisa's with a finger in her mouth, while Melissa's kicked and fretted. It was not her own superstitious prayer that had delivered them safe. It was not even fate; she did not believe in fate. It was merely how things had turned out, good luck as unmerited as bad would have been.

Bea did not mind her lack of sentiment. What she could not endure was her lack of purpose. This was no time to feel empty and detached. She would need renewed zeal. There was so much to be done for them. They would have to be taught everything. Curiosity. Loyalty. Adventure. Accommodation. They had mothers, but she didn't trust them. This, she knew, was an inadmissible thought. Heresy. Foolish people had been raising children from time immemorial. Yes, but just look. Everything was falling apart. She could not hold back entropy single-handed, but she must at least make an effort. What else was there to do? Beyond her effort waited a great chaos ready to engulf. A great void. She steeled herself against it. By force of will she roused her energies until she felt life moving through her, a quickening of life, as if the very lives of the new children were pulsing in her chest.